*But at the end of the day, I know that it doesn't matter. I don't trust anyone, and no one here trusts me either, for good reason. I'd been the worst of the worst, and a part of me is still that person. I was programmed to be emotionless, to obey orders, to kill without question. And because of the nanoplasm, I'm faster and fiercer than anyone else. I'm death in a girl's body.*

*It stands to reason that people will hate me.*

# THE RIVEN CHRONICLES

# THE
# ALMOST
# GIRL

## AMALIE HOWARD

**Sky Pony Press**

NEW YORK

First published by Strange Chemistry, an Angry Robot imprint, a member of the Osprey Group, 2014

This paperback edition published by Sky Pony Press, 2016

Sky Pony Press books may be purchased in bulk at special discounts for sales promotion, corporate gifts, fund-raising, or educational purposes. Special editions can also be created to specifications. For details, contact the Special Sales Department, Sky Pony Press, 307 West 36th Street, 11th Floor, New York, NY 10018 or info@skyhorsepublishing.com.

Sky Pony® is a registered trademark of Skyhorse Publishing, Inc.®, a Delaware corporation.

Visit our website at www.skyponypress.com.

10 9 8 7 6 5 4 3 2 1

Library of Congress Cataloging-in-Publication Data is available on file.

Cover illustration by Steven Wood
Cover design by Sarah Brody

Print ISBN: 978-1-5107-0171-7
Ebook ISBN: 978-1-5107-0174-8

Printed in the United States of America

# CONTENTS

# PROLOGUE

# THREE YEARS EARLIER

THE SLIGHT FIGURE is lithe and quick, a shadow of a shadow in the darkness. It runs along the edgy gloom of the halogen-lit streets, flying over electric fences and scaling walls with the practiced ease of a skilled athlete. One would never suspect that it was being chased by an entire army of soldiers, but it was, several hundred of them.

In a fluid twist to gauge the remaining distance from its pursuers, the runner's profile is visible for a brief second. It is the face of young girl, barely fourteen, as she glides into a narrow alley. Blood drips from a self-inflicted gash in her arm, the silver implant she'd dug from the wound slipping from her fingers to the oily ground before it is crushed beneath her boot.

Glancing at the gauge on her wrist, she sees a red flash that tells her that she's nearly at the eversion checkpoint. Her timing and positioning must be exact for the universe transition. She ducks into a crouch as the first soldier of the small army reaches the dark alleyway; he is faster than the others.

They're always fast.

"Surrender yourself," a voice says. The soldier stands, weapon at the ready. He knows that she is there. The girl steps out from behind a crate. There is no fear on her face, just a silent calmness, an acceptance of the situation. The soldiers are programmed to obey and to subdue hostiles, but she tries to divert them anyway. She knows that nothing she says will deter the soldier—after all, she's been their leader for the better part of a year.

And now, she is the traitor . . . the fugitive.

"Stand down, Lieutenant," she says firmly in a husky voice far too mature for her years. The soldier doesn't even acknowledge her words. "That is an order."

"Surrender," he repeats, raising the electro-rod slightly. "General."

His pre-programmed voice is dead, just like the rest of him, but he understands exactly who she is. He's half-alive but still far from a mindless drone. She sees a glimmer of blue sparks at the rod's three-pronged tip. He'd have it set to stun, she knew, but she wasn't going back alive. She couldn't go back.

"Okay. Have it your way," she says.

The girl lunges at him, barely half his size, to slide on her knees beneath the blunt edge of the metal rod swinging toward her head. Her hand snakes out, a fist thumping into the hard, cold flesh beneath his ribs lightning-fast, and the soldier grunts, doubling over at the dull crack. In a reverse motion, her fist slices past his Achilles tendon, the blade between her fingers a blur, and he crumples to the floor.

They may be immune to pain, but they're still made of flesh and bone.

Not losing momentum, she jabs him in the back of the neck just above the top of his spine with the point of her knife. The strike is snake-like and true. A spark and the sharp smell of singed flesh, and in a matter of seconds, the soldier is lying prostrate on the ground, twitching slightly, disabled for the moment.

Glancing around, the girl listens for sounds of the others before quickly emptying the soldier's pockets. As well as the rod, she sticks a communication earpiece, a long-handled knife, six packets of dried food dust, and two pen-like instruments into her own black knapsack.

It is more than she could have hoped for.

The soldier stirs with a whining noise, and the girl grasps his face between her hands, pulling open his eyelids with her thumbs and forefingers. His skin is cold and clammy but he's not dead; far from it. Her blow to his cortex chip would only have caused it to reboot, but the nanocells in his retina would still be relaying real time to her pursuers. She wants the message to be clear and stares directly into his eyes, straddling his chest with her knees.

"Don't try to find me," she growls. "Don't send anyone. If you do, they will end up like this one; that I can promise you."

Her hands twist, tugging the soldier's chin upward and jamming his knife into the back of his neck. It is such a smooth motion of her hands that the soldier's body barely twitches as she severs his spinal cord, the critical connector between the brain and the body. Her face will be the last thing her pursuers see. The light in his eyes fades but it's only a trick of the shadowed gloom around them. There's no life in these creatures . . . only death.

The sensor on her wrist flashes to blue. Without a backward glance, she is away in an instant, swallowed up by the inky darkness, punching in a sequence on a flat computer-like device connected to the sensor. After a moment, all that's left in her wake is a brief shimmer in the fabric of space and air. She's gone.

# PART ONE

# THE OTHERWORLD

# 1

# PRESENT DAY
## COLORADO

MY THOUGHTS RAIN like spatters of blood against the colorless landscape of drab walls and wooden faces. A bell rings, and it is a mad rush as chairs are pushed back loudly. A tall woman with a no-nonsense face calls for silence.

"The class roster for the end-of-year projects has been posted in the hallway. You have been paired in groups of four with a different assignment based on what we have covered this semester. If you don't know your partners, I suggest you meet them quickly, as these projects will count for half of your final grade."

A collective groan rolls its way across the classroom.

"But Mrs. Taylor," a girl three rows across stands and complains loudly, "why can't we pick our own groups? Wouldn't that be better for everyone?"

"Miss Hall, in the future, if you'd like to say something, please refrain from yelling it across the classroom. The groups have been allocated according to last year's class standings."

"But—"

"The groups are final, Miss Hall." Mrs. Taylor's voice brooks no argument, and the girl falls silent although her face remains puckered with frustration as she exits the classroom.

I sit huddled at the back, waiting until the classroom is almost empty before gathering my things and walking noiselessly to the front.

"Mrs. Taylor?" I ask. My voice is slightly roughened from a lack of sleep, and the teacher jumps, looking up questioningly. I paste a suitably contrite look on my face. "Sorry to startle you, I'm . . . er . . . Riven. I transferred in last week. About the groups . . ."

"Ah, yes, Riven, I do have a note about you, as a matter of fact," Mrs. Taylor says, shuffling through a pile of papers on the desk. "You have already been assigned. It's on the board along with the others. If you run into any trouble, let me know." Mrs. Taylor pushes her wire-rimmed glasses up her nose, her dark eyes sharp. "Anything else?"

"No, that's it," I mumble, unable to hold back the yawn that overtakes my facial muscles.

"Are you alright? You look quite pale."

"I'm fine, just tired. Jet lag." I smile and hoist my backpack over my arm. "Thanks, Mrs. Taylor."

"Riven?" I freeze at the door and turn my head in her direction. Her black eyes are still piercing, unsettling as if they can see right through me. I feel an odd, unwelcome shiver take hold at the base of my spine. "Welcome to Horrow."

"Thanks," I mumble and shift away from her impaling gaze. She's looking at me as if she knows who I am . . . an imposter, a stranger.

A killer.

I sneak a glance into the classroom once I'm in the hallway, and Mrs. Taylor is back to studying the papers on her desk. I must have been wrong. I yawn again as exhaustion consumes me. In my tired delirium, I'm starting to imagine things. I've been pushing myself way too hard without enough rest intervals between jumps. It's foolish and reckless.

Black dots fill my vision. I'm disoriented as if the ground is tilting beneath my soles. I glance down, only to see the checkered tile floor undulating like a breaking wave. Gasping for breath, I haul open the first door I see.

A janitor's closet.

Leaning against the cool plastic of a recycling bin, I breathe in huge gulps of stale closet air. The fatigue is becoming worse, ever since the last jump. My fingers begin to shake uncontrollably as I smooth open the crumpled paper with my new class schedule.

Thirty class schedules in as many months, with time slowly running out. Trying to locate the boy here has been like looking for a drop in a bucket of water—nearly impossible. But I can't give up. I won't. Because in my gut, I can sense that there are already others here . . . others looking for him.

And I *have* to find him first.

Swallowing, I blink back the grit from my burning eyes and squint in the dim light at my schedule. I have gym and then lunch. I won't make it to lunch, it's an absolute certainty. My body slides down the side of the bin and I sit in the muted shadows as light filters in from the cracks underneath the door. Maybe I'll just sit here for a second to catch my breath.

My eyelids droop heavily, and then there is only sweet, aching darkness.

When I open my eyes again, there is no longer any light seeping through the door and there is only silence beyond it. I must have slept through the entire day on the floor of this tiny closet. I inch my way up, hearing my joints creak painfully, and crack open the door. The hallway is deserted, the clock on the wall showing four o'clock in the morning. A chill sweeps along my skin as the fluorescent light flickers eerily. School hallways just aren't the same without kids in them. Suppressing a shudder, I exit through a side entrance onto one of the practice football fields as the door locks behind me with a soft click.

Early fall, and the night is dark and cold. I tug my black sweater down along my arms. It's only when I reach the empty parking lot where the Ducati is parked that I feel the first painful rumble in my stomach. I haven't eaten anything today. Swearing at my own carelessness, I unwrap a snack bar from my backpack with clammy hands and shove it into my mouth.

It's one of my few rules of survival—always eat. In my condition, hunger can bring on far worse things, things that you can't come back from, not in this world anyway, and my body is unstable enough already. The food slides down like hard cardboard along the soft sides of my throat and I gag, but force myself to swallow. There's a bottle of water in my backpack and I drink it so quickly that half of it spills down my sweater. I'm hoping that it isn't already too late. I throw on my helmet and take a deep breath. I have to make it back to the motel. It's only a few miles.

Tires squealing in protest against the cold asphalt, I pull out onto the main road and ride as fast as I dare over the speed limit. The last thing I need is to get pulled over. It happened once before when the sickness started. The cop ended up in the hospital that night, and I had to leave town quickly, trusting that what I'd been looking for hadn't been there. I couldn't risk anything similar happening, not again and not here.

I stop at a red light, concentrating on taking slow mechanical breaths. But the pain in my belly only deepens as if in silent mockery of my efforts.

*You can make it,* I tell myself firmly, accelerating across the intersection.

The panic recedes but then returns in a wave so violent that I am gasping as my back arches like a bow. There's no way I can make it. How could I have been so foolish to think that I could beat the odds . . . beat time?

*Too late, too late, too late.*

A brutal wave of nausea drives me to jerk roughly on the Ducati's handlebars, the motorcycle's wheels protesting angrily on the asphalt, just as a lance-like pain stabs through me. My fingers jam reflexively against the throttle, twisting it. The bike lurches forward and careens across the two opposite lanes, my thighs burning from gripping the sides of the tank to steady it.

That's when the shakes start. Within seconds, I can feel my hands curl into hardened claws, my body spasming uncontrollably. My eyes roll back and I barely see the oncoming lights, as the bike swings precariously once more to the left, grinding off the road and spinning into gravel. My body is flung like a sack of rocks as the Ducati skids to a shattered halt on its side.

The sky above me is dark and wide with nothing in it. No stars, no moon, nothing. Just blackness. I suck in a shallow breath, keeping my jaw tightly closed, knowing how easily I can bite my own tongue off if I'm not careful. My chest aches with the strained intake of air, but I already know from years of training that it's mostly bruises, and nothing's broken. Hot white dots cloud my vision and I focus myself, searching for my backpack. It was flung from me upon impact with the ground, but it's just a foot away.

*Reach out slowly, the bag is right there*, I tell myself, but my body refuses to cooperate. Inside I know that it is too late, I can feel myself shutting down. I should have rested today, stayed in bed and given myself a chance to recuperate from the jump, but I'd been stupid, arrogant. I hadn't wanted to lose any time, and now I'm going to pay the price. My eyes slip shut.

As if from afar, I hear a rustling and then a loud banging. Someone yelling. Shadows flit across my closed eyelids. "Help," I whisper. "Help."

"Oh God! She came off a bike. Don't move her; she could have a concussion."

"Hey! Hey, you okay?"

The voices are dull as if coming from far away. My thoughts won't even turn toward them. Noises followed by a dull thud as someone stoops beside me. Gentle fingers slip across my arm, moving upward to open my visor.

*Backpack.* I try to say my single thought but my tongue is thick against my teeth. I can only open and close sticky lips that taste like metal.

"She's alive! Help me get this helmet off. Careful with her."

My head lolls backward as the helmet slips off, but I'm caught by strong hands and cradled gently. A bottle is placed against my lips and I feel cool water trickle into my mouth, washing away the coppery taste. It hurts to swallow, but I ignore the pain. The water moistens my gums and loosens my tongue.

"Injector . . . backpack . . ." It won't be long before I go into shock. "Have to . . . stick . . ."

"Don't worry, I got it. I'm allergic, too," one of the voices says. I hear a rustle and feel the rough jab of the needle piercing into my skin through my jeans, and then soft fingers are brushing against my forehead. "Hang on, it's going to be okay."

"Should we call 911?" the other voice asks. "What's with the needle?"

"No hospital, please. Be okay . . ." I direct my plea to the one who'd administered the auto-injector. "Please, can't afford . . ."

"Rest," the voice says. "It's okay, Jake, looks like an allergic reaction. Could be peanuts, bees, anything, don't know." I hear the rustling of a wrapper. "My aunt's off tonight. I'll take her home with me and see what she says. If she says to go to the hospital, I'll take her."

"What about her bike? We shouldn't just leave it, right? We can probably get it in the back of my truck," the voice belonging to Jake says. "I can take a better look at it tomorrow."

"Okay. Help me get her inside first. Careful, she may be hurt from when it went off the road."

"Thank you," I murmur as they lift me gently into the backseat of the truck. They are the only words I can manage before my brain shuts down. I can feel the serum making its way through my body, stopping my cells from going into anaphylactic shock.

The boy's right—I am having an allergic reaction, just not to any food.

In some dark corner of my mind, I know that I should be worried or be afraid that I have fallen into the wrong hands, but somehow I know . . . I *trust* that I am safe. The thing is, I can't remember the last time I felt safe. Oblivion sweeps my remaining consciousness away.

When I open my eyes again, I'm lying in a bed in an airy room. It's quiet and peaceful. A fan on the ceiling wafts cool air into my face, and for a second it feels as if I'm in some kind of dream. Then I see the boy slumped in the armchair in front of the window and instantly know that this is reality. He seems asleep, although I can't really tell from the way his hair is curling into his face. I search for my backpack. It's sitting next to him on the floor. Sitting up gingerly, I swing my left leg over the side of the bed and wince at the pain now radiating up my back and around my ribs.

"You shouldn't really move, you know." The boy is awake now and I can feel him watching me carefully. I ignore him and shift my other leg to the floor. The pain is excruciating, echoing along every nerve ending like fire.

"My aunt says you need to keep that leg up," he says and moves to stand next to me, his hand pressing onto my shoulder. With his free hand, he carelessly shoves the hair out of his face and sits beside me on the edge of the bed. "You're pretty banged up."

Our eyes collide and it is like I am being sucked into a vortex that I can't control.

It's *him*.

The boy I'm supposed to find.

His hair is lighter, almost golden brown, and swept to the side around his face, but his nose and chin are the spitting image of the one I know. And his eyes . . . those impossibly green eyes, filled with vibrant life. I'd prepared myself that he would look like him but they're *so* alike that it leaves me speechless.

And he found me. He *saved* me.

I shake myself hard. What are the odds? Searching for someone for nearly three years only to find them via an accident of fate? The questions make my head pound, and I blink, disoriented.

"Where am I. . . . What happened?" I croak. My voice is unfamiliar. Weak.

"Don't you remember? You crashed your bike and had some kind of crazy allergic reaction. You're at my house now. You didn't want me to take you to the hospital because you said something about money, so I brought you here," he says in a rush and then clarifies, "My aunt's a doctor."

"How long have I been here?" I try to stand, gasping at the soreness of my ribs.

His nearness is overwhelming, confusing me as thoughts of Cale race through my clouded brain. My throat is raw, and the effort to swallow makes my head pound. A wave of dizziness overcomes me and I fall back to the bed. A knife-like pain slices through my leg.

The boy leans forward to grasp my shoulder gently. "Look, you really should—"

"Don't touch me," I snap, flinching away from the warmth in his fingers. My body may be beaten, but it's still poised to attack. The boy's offended expression throws me, and my anger fades as my brain struggles to keep up. "Sorry, I'm still a little freaked out, and I don't like people touching me," I say by way of apology. He still looks miffed so I force a tiny smile to my lips. "You go to Horrow, right?"

"Yes, we're in the same physics class," he says, the hurt look draining away slowly, "and in the same project group. I only knew who you were because Mrs. Taylor asked me to help you out if you needed a hand since you're new. You started last week, right?"

"Yes," I say, remembering the profile of a boy I'd barely given a second glance to. I grind my teeth together—that had been sheer carelessness on my part. Or maybe all those jumps are finally catching up to me; otherwise, why else would I be lying here in this bed, weak as a newborn kitten?

"I'm Caden, by the way," he says, sticking his hand out. Staring at his fingers as if they're snakes, I raise my hand in an awkward half wave. My smile feels forced. His hand falls away, and the weird look returns to his face. "You're not too friendly, are you?"

I breathe out the pent-up air in my lungs and feel the rush of adrenaline recede. I stare at the boy through the corner of my eye who could be Cale. No, not Cale. They may look the same, but they're entirely different people underneath their doppelganger skins.

"Sorry. I mean, I know who you are," I whisper under my breath.

*It's not Cale*, I remind myself for good measure.

My head still feels wobbly like some kind of horrible hangover. Only, I wouldn't know what that would be like—the only time I'd tasted spirits had been with Cale, celebrating the Winter Solstice when I was ten. It was an experience I never want to repeat. But I'd seen other people drunk enough to guess what a hangover would feel like.

A tremor runs through my hands and I flex them automatically. My veins are blue against my skin, the tendons still corded and raised along the backs of my hands. Black and blue bruises mottle the length of both arms. My torso probably looks worse. A hollow feeling fills my stomach as I realize just how close the shakes had brought me to an irreversible outcome last night. Now that I'd found the boy, I needed to have all my wits functioning. Others would be close, too. The ones who would also come for him.

"I like your tattoo," Caden says, interrupting the turn of my thoughts. Instinctively, my fingers touch the gold circular seal and the three black lines—two whole and one broken—beneath it on my neck. "Does it mean anything?"

I almost want to laugh. A filial brand and a line for each traitor I'd killed? He'd be running away as fast as he could or calling the police if he even guessed what it meant.

"No."

"So, what's your name?" Caden asks, shoving his hands in his pockets. I had to give him credit for trying. In that, he was just like Cale—neither of them took "no" for an answer.

"Riven."

"I thought that was your last name?"

"Riven is my last name," I say, and bite back a grin at his immediate frown. "I only have one name. Where I come from we don't have two names, just one." I see his frown deepen, and kick myself for my telling choice of words.

"Where you come from," he repeats slowly. "Everyone has two names here, unless you're like Usher or Madonna." At my blank stare, he clarifies, "You know, the singers?"

I nod quickly. I've seen them on the television. "Just Riven," I say.

"Just Riven." He draws my name out slowly like he's trying to taste it or something. "That's a weird name. I mean, unique," he says hastily. "Does it mean anything?"

"It means ripped apart."

"Oh." I can see that he's at a loss for words. I don't blame him. Back home, my name strikes fear into anyone who hears it—but that's more a factor of the reputation that precedes me than anything else.

From his expression, I can see him wondering why someone would name a child such an odd, violent name. I feel my lips curling in a smile—as far as names go, I like the fierceness of it, the simplicity. In a weird way, it fits me.

After a couple minutes, Caden speaks. "No idea what mine means. So, is that from Asia or Africa, then? You know, where people have one last name? Is that where you grew up?"

I can only manage a terse nod. At Caden's questions, I wish I could pull out the notebook in my backpack and leaf through it. Even after three years of blending in—appearance, accent, and behavior-wise—I'm still not familiar with the exact geographical topography of this world. His questions are making my head spin, and I can't afford to make any more mistakes, not when I am almost home . . . now that I've finally found him.

I shake myself mentally once more. If my body were stronger, I'd grab him and go, but in my weakened condition, that would be certain suicide for us both. I'd die, and he'd never make it without me. Not there.

My eyes fall to the glass of water sitting on the bedside table next to an alarm clock, and I take a slow sip. It's almost eleven on Saturday morning. I need to make some kind of exit and compose myself for travel. And the travel I'm talking about is not as simple as buying an airplane ticket and showing up at a mass-transit airport; it's way more complicated. Any number of things could go wrong, especially when there is more than one traveler—one of them a fugitive, the other a target.

"You don't look Asian," Caden continues his monologue, considering I'm barely participating in the conversation. "I mean, you look like me, well, except the hair. Yours has green and blue in it," he points out. I touch the strands and remember that I'd dyed it four schools before, after the incident with the police. It was haphazardly chopped around my face except for a single braid that wound down one side.

"It's cool, your hair," Caden adds and then reddens. "For a punk look, I mean."

I'd butchered it myself when I'd been short on time, leaving only the slim blue and gold braid. I hadn't been able to let it go—the only reminder of my position, my *rank*. But overall, it was an edgy, fierce look that tended to make people stay away, which I'd liked.

It wasn't doing much to shut Caden up, though. "You definitely stand out, especially at Horrow," he remarks. "The girls are all pretty much vanilla. You meet any of them yet?"

"No. I keep to myself."

A wry smile. "I get it. You don't like being touched, you want to be alone, and you're not looking for any friends."

Caden moves to stand near the window and moves my backpack from the floor to the chair. He doesn't open it but just stares at it thoughtfully. It's a brief respite from the conversation, so I use the silence to figure out how to tactfully say thank you and leave.

He eyes me. "What exactly happened to you last night?"

But I'm saved from having to respond to Caden or tell him rudely to shut up when a neatly dressed woman enters the room. She is no taller than I am but sturdily built; she looks like a strong woman. Her dark hair is pulled off of her face into a tidy bun at the base of her neck. She has kind eyes with lines at the corners, but there's something else in them, too . . . warning that her kindness shouldn't be mistaken for weakness.

"How's our patient doing this morning?"

She glances at Caden, who is still flushed, and then back to me where I'm sitting on the edge of the bed with a frown on my face. A strange expression curls the corners of her lips upward, and I can feel my brows snapping together even more tightly. I don't recognize or like the amused look on her face, as if she thinks there's something going on between the two of us.

"I'm Caden's aunt," she says to me. "He's been in here constantly. I've never seen him so solicitous of anyone."

"What? I wasn't." Caden flushes and stares at the ground.

"I hope you haven't been keeping her from resting, Caden. She needs to keep that foot elevated."

"It's fine," I say, and then more clearly, "My foot?" For the first time, I notice that I am wearing some sort of cotton pants, and I wonder whether Caden's aunt had removed my own clothes. Curiously, I don't feel any embarrassment because I'm more worried about whether the injury will slow me down.

"Lay back," she tells me gently and places a hand against my forehead. "That's good."

"What happened?" I repeat, trying to pull the pajama material up to see. She stalls my hand.

"Try not to move, you have some badly bruised ribs, too. It's your ankle, nothing too serious. You must have torn a ligament from the convulsions or from when you fell, but you do need to keep pressure off of it for now. I iced it and wrapped it last night. Let's have a look."

Carefully unwrapping the bandage, I see that my ankle is a blotchy greenish purple and twice the size of my other foot. I am sure that it looks far worse than it is. I wiggle my toes slowly and I know from experience it's a good sign. It means nothing's broken.

"A lot of the swelling has gone down, which is good," Caden's aunt says. I can't imagine my ankle being any fatter, but it must have been because even Caden is nodding.

"It matches your hair," Caden remarks. I ignore him, more concerned with trying to calculate how much this injury will set me back.

"How long?" I ask.

"A few weeks."

"A few weeks!" I gasp. "Can't you do anything to speed it up?"

She gives me a gentle smile while deftly rewrapping the bandage across my ankle. "No, honey. Best you can do to recover quickly is rest, ice, compression, and elevation. R.I.C.E. Simple enough to remember, right? If the pain gets any worse or it doesn't get better, you'll need to get it checked out. For now, I can give you some ibuprofen to help with the pain and the swelling."

"No meds. I can manage the pain," I say. "I'm allergic to most medications," I add at her curious look. The truth is that anything that inhibits the functions of the brain is a risk, especially during eversion. I need to be clear.

"I guess that explains why you had such a high-tech injector in your bag," Caden chimes in, pulling the pen-like instrument from the front pocket of the backpack where he'd replaced it the night before. "I've never seen anything like it. My emergency one is like a plastic piece of crap compared to yours. Bees are my nemesis," he reminds me, twisting the silver cylinder between his fingers.

I smile, a cheap attempt at reassurance and normalcy even though my heart is pounding. I've never wanted to lurch forward and grab anything more than at that moment. Like the teacher earlier, I feel that Caden's aunt can see right through me. Her blue eyes are as sharp as Mrs. Taylor's had been, and although there's no mistrust in them, I feel uncomfortable just the same.

It's one of the reasons that I don't like getting close to people. Too many questions. And too many that can't be answered. But I know that I owe them both some kind of explanation for my bizarre behavior . . . and for the injector that looks like it comes from some kind of super advanced robotics lab.

"Mine is a little more complicated," I say. "I'm not allergic to bees or food. It's a . . . a genetic brain thing. If I don't take my medication regularly, like yesterday, things can go south pretty quickly, especially with the seizures. Sometimes something as simple as hunger can set it off." I glance up to test the waters. They are both watching me, but with more concern than any kind of disbelief on their faces. My lies are getting more convincing. "The injector is custom-made for my condition. You couldn't use it," I say in Caden's direction. "And it's really expensive, so . . ."

I don't have to finish my sentence before Caden carefully replaces the injector in the backpack.

"Sorry," he says stuffing his hands in his pockets. "So, are you okay now?"

I nod slowly. I haven't had to use the injector before but it has definitely come in handy to say the least. I am alive. Each cylinder has six doses, so I have five remaining. I hope fervently that I don't have to use them. Even thinking about the pain makes my head spin. Caden's aunt pulls the sheet up and pats my forehead.

"You can stay here as long as you need to, Riven. Can I call someone for you? Your parents? They must be worried."

"No thanks," I say quickly. "My father is out of town on business. He usually calls me to check in. You can talk to him then."

She frowns for a second but nods. "You're welcome to stay as long as you like."

"I will. Thanks for taking care of me, Mrs. . . . ?" I trail off realizing that I don't even know their family name.

"Just call me June."

"Thank you, June," I say.

I'm overwhelmed at her generosity, letting some stranger into her home. I could have easily been one of the others looking for the boy. How easy would it be to kill him? One swipe of a knife, a pillow over the face, a twist of a finger? They're so trusting, these people. Back home, getting within an arm's length of another person is virtually impossible, much less getting into someone else's home. It's astonishing that the boy has survived for so long.

The odds weren't in his favor, yet here he was, unhurt and obviously thriving . . . hidden in plain sight. And I'd found him quite by accident—this town hadn't been on my list. I'd just stopped here on my way to Wyoming and randomly decided to stay for a few days to recuperate after the last eversion. It had been a spur of the moment decision.

I glance at Caden, chewing on his thumb and staring at me out of the corner of his eye. He seems to be just like all the other kids of this world, so oblivious to everything but their immediate sphere of existence. Watching him, I know that he has been well protected, but he is clearly unprepared.

He thinks he's just a normal boy. But I know better.

He has no idea about anything—no idea of who is after him or what's coming for him. I frown. So how *has* he survived? How has he been able to stay here undetected and in the dark about who he really is for this long?

There is only one answer that I can think of. It is one that chills me to my bones.

Someone has to be helping him.

Someone who knows that I would be coming.

# 2

# BLACKOUT

CADEN AND HIS aunt insisted I stay with them until late Sunday afternoon. In spite of June's protests, I took a taxi back to the cash-only cheap motel on the outskirts of town as soon as I could. Due to her expert care, my injury is healing well, albeit slowly. In my world, muscle and tissue would be repaired in minutes in a laser lab. Still, I'm surprised that after just two days, I can bear weight on it. I sigh, frustrated. It couldn't have come at a worse time. Despite racking my brain for alternatives, I am a sitting duck. Attempting to evert with any kind of physical weakness is a death sentence. Eversion doesn't just cause physical stress—any kind of strain that sends mixed messages to the brain could upset the timing and the result. And no one wants to end up inside out with a jump gone wrong.

Hauling myself out of bed, I clear my mind and perform a series of meditational exercises that send energy flowing through my body. Despite the hollow ache in my ribs, it feels good. I stretch each muscle carefully until my movements are fluid and limber, taking care with my ankle, then move into a series of simple calisthenics that has a fine sheen of sweat coating my skin when I'm finished. It's a process that I repeat every morning without fail, with the exception of last Saturday. I frown, redoing the exercises once more, a compensation of sorts for the missed interval. Even impaired, I can take on a couple of Vectors, but probably no more than three. I have to be prepared for the worst.

I unfold the leather case lying tucked inside the back of my bag. Shiny silver knives and an array of weapons greet me, and I finger one of their edges carefully. They've never failed me. Without glancing behind me, I flick two toward the back of the motel door and they lodge with thick precision into the wood of the narrow doorjamb. Not much of a target, but I shrug and retrieve the blades. I repeat the knife throws, managing to get both in the same entry points as before. Better.

Grabbing the crutches I'd borrowed from June, I hobble to the door, swearing under my breath. Having to move this slowly is worse than the pain. I hitch a ride to school in the back of a pickup truck, and before I can lose my nerve, I grit my teeth and awkwardly shuffle my way up the stairs to the doors. I'd like nothing more than to not have to attend another day of high school now that I've found Caden, but I also don't want anything to happen to him, either. I still have that feeling of things not being quite right, and vigilance and caution are two things that have kept me alive all these years.

So another day of Horrow High it is.

Trudging to my class, I realize that I don't know anything about Caden. The little I do know tells me that he is nothing like Cale. It confuses me. Still, what did I expect? They're not exactly the same people—made even more dissimilar by the whole nature-versus-nurture thing. But the truth is, I don't need to know anything about him. Why should I care? He's a target, and one that I need to get back as quickly as possible.

"Hey, Riven! How's the leg?"

"Thanks for the general announcement," I growl sourly just as Caden walks alongside me with two of his football friends in tow. "It's fine."

"Guys, this is Riven. New girl," Caden says to his friends with a wide grin. "But be warned—"

"Hey, I'm Jake," a redheaded boy interrupts with a smile. "I was there the other night with Cade when you trashed your bike. . . ." Jake trails off at the dark scowl on my face.

Caden laughs. "As I was saying, just don't mention her riding skills or ask her about anything personal; she gets a little touchy about that. And she's not interested in making friends, so forget I introduced her and move along."

I shoot him a withering glare just in time to see a willowy blonde swing her arms around Caden from the back. Her demeanor is not friendly, nor is the acid warning look she launches in my direction. My body tenses immediately, and already my brain is calculating the distance to exits and casualty ratios of the dozens of kids swirling around me. I force myself to relax.

She's a kid, not a threat.

The adrenaline seeps from my system as the girl tosses an icy smile in my direction, her designer white pants like a second skin and a pink shirt unbuttoned enough to show a lacy pink bra, leaving little to the imagination.

"Who's your friend?" the blonde says to Caden, her tone dripping venom. My hand hovers over the blade wedged into my belt. No metal detectors in this school makes it a hell of a lot easier to deal with threats, unlike the public schools in New York, which had been an eye-opening experience. I'd received detention for a week because of a concealed knife in my boot. Forcing my hand to my side, I try to act normal.

"Hey Sadie, this is Riven. She's new." Caden says and turns to embrace Sadie, who jumps up to wrap her very long cheer-leader legs around his waist. I want to laugh at her overtly terri-torial display, but something inside tells me that this will prob-ably not be the best thing to do. Still, I can't quite help myself, and the side of my lips twitches into a smirk. Sadie's eyes nar-row and I bend my head, biting my lip to stifle my amusement.

"Nice name," she drawls after a minute, her tone indicating that my name is anything but nice. A cutting response rises to my lips, but provoking this girl won't accomplish much, other than to serve my own ego. And I need to keep a low profile.

"Thanks," I say instead and quicken my step. "Catch you later, Caden."

"It's just Cade, remember?"

I shoot a hand in the air and keep walking. Cade, Caden, it makes no difference to me.

"Where'd that one get dragged in from, juvie rehab?"

Sadie's scornful words reach me as I walk into the class-room, but I don't hear Caden's response. It wouldn't surprise me one bit if he said that I was a foreign transfer. This time, I can't hold back my laugh, and it comes until I feel tears run-ning down my cheeks and the sides of my stomach ache from it. They couldn't imagine just how foreign I actually am. I am still snorting even when class begins and Mrs. Taylor's eyes laser me with a quelling look.

"Class, please sit in your designated project groups. We will be working on them during the second half of class today."

Groans mix in with the noisy screech of chairs as students move around, shuffling to other tables, and for the first time I look around the classroom, staring at faces with interest instead of my usual detached assessment of potential danger. I see them as people instead of targets or threats, and I am surprised by how young they all are. Not that I am much older, but the truth is, I feel older.

*Harder.*

Half of these kids haven't felt the sharp edge of hunger or had to fight for anything in their lives. They are plump, satisfied, and ignorant. Where I'm from, our training begins the minute we are born, and we face survival tests far worse than a quiz on Shakespeare before the age of five. Education is mandatory, but so are other things—physical education, weapons education, *life* education.

I realize that I'm judging once more and give myself a shake. *Be fair*, I think. It's not their fault that they are the way they are, and have evolved in a different world under a different set of rules and circumstances. They are people, the same flesh and blood as I am.

*Well, maybe not Sadie*, I think with a grin, *she's pure venomous angst.*

The ones in my group seem likable enough: a girl, Charisma, who is quiet but friendly; Caden, of course; and another jumpy thin boy, Philip, with an overbite and fingernails bitten to the quick. His head is already buried in his physics textbook. Leafing mentally through my slang file, he is what most in this world would call a nerd or a geek, but where I'm from, Philip would be a coveted asset. Someone with his skills would be selected in a heartbeat. My father would have loved him.

Caden opens his books on the table and leans back in his chair, grinning at me. "Hey, Crutches, let me know if you need any help." He's joking, of course, knowing what my response will be. I shoot him a look communicating exactly what I will do with my crutches if he offers to help me again. His grin widens and I can't help smiling back at him, the acidic thought of my father melting away.

I feel eyes lasering into my back, but I refuse to give their owner the satisfaction of a response. Sadie is a nuisance, nothing more, and truth be told, I'd rather pass the next few weeks in anonymity instead of some full-on teenage feud with a hormonally-challenged seventeen-year-old who thinks I'm after her boyfriend.

At seventeen, in Neospes, you're a full-grown contributor, responsible for a heck of a lot more than picking out a prom dress or fighting over a boy. If you have disagreements with another, you duel it out. It's that simple. If you need intervention for bigger disputes or feuds, you get it in front of the Royal Tribunal. Here, in the capricious world of high school, it's an entirely different story. I sigh. Needless to say, I've had enough of this version of high school to last me a lifetime.

"So what's the verdict?" a low voice says. Caden is staring at me with a raised eyebrow and a half smile.

"What?"

"Your analysis of us? Of me? Come on, be honest, what do you really think?"

It is one of my few unguarded moments, and for a second, I see a flash of Cale's perceptiveness in him. My face composes itself into its normal emotionless mask, but Caden's knowing expression is so hauntingly familiar that it throws me. I feel an uncomfortable warmth seeping up into my neck and across my ear lobes. I don't like this feeling. It makes my response far sharper than it should be.

"You like being the center of attention, you're smart but lazy, you want to get out of this town as soon as you graduate, and your girlfriend is a bitch. How's that?" The words snap like rubber bands from my lips, but as soon as I say them, I find myself wanting to take them back. My anger is directed at myself, not anyone else.

Charisma is staring at me slack-jawed, and geek-boy has even raised his head from his book, looking nervously from Caden to me and back again as if expecting a full-on brawl right there in the middle of physics. But Caden's expression is measured, and he holds my challenging stare easily.

A slow smile. "Three out of four, so not bad."

Again, spoken so much like Cale. I know I shouldn't be surprised at the similarities, but nonetheless, I am. My teeth are ground together so tightly that my jaw aches. I don't want to feel anything for Caden other than as a means to an end. He isn't Cale.

"Your girlfriend isn't a bitch?"

A laugh. "No, she is, but Sadie's harmless. Remind me to tell you about it later," Caden says just as Mrs. Taylor raps on her desk. There won't be a "later" if I have anything to say about it. If our brief exchange is any indication of what the next few days will bring, I'll watch over him from a distance. I can't risk any rapport with him—my loyalty is to Cale, and this boy is nothing more than a target. I look away, pretending to listen to Mrs. Taylor.

Newton's laws of motion are a familiar subject, and while it's something that I learned long ago, that doesn't mean that I don't have to pay attention. I learned that lesson the hard way in Boston when I carelessly answered a question with an analysis worthy of a doctorate-level dissertation. They treated me like some kind of second-coming prodigy. Needless to say, I didn't stay at that school too much longer. Drawing attention tended to draw other bad things . . . way worse things.

Like Vectors.

I suppress an automatic shudder, and not even the workbook equations of motion can distract me. The Vectors are one of the most-feared and worst creations of my world. They are engineered creatures, made from human corpses . . . reanimated dead beings with one purpose: to hunt and to kill.

Our technology is advanced, but we learned a hard lesson with artificial intelligence centuries before. While this world was embroiled in the French Revolution, my world was facing its worst crisis in history—the Tech War—a war that had devastated us to the point that topographical boundaries had been unrecognizable and continents reshaped. Whole oceans were destroyed. What had once been lush forests were now dusty plains of gray acidic ash. Parts of my world are still black and oozing with toxic matter. But people survived, eventually reclaiming and rebuilding what they could.

The Vectors were a new kind of soldier, created after the laws were put in place against any kind of self-evolving robotic intelligence. Nanogen technology became the perfect combination of programmable robotics and human genetics, and the Vectors were bred to supplement human loss, to protect and defend those who survived. They had been the brilliantly sick creation of a madman.

My father.

"You okay?" Caden whispers, distracting me. "You look ill."

"I'm fine."

But I'm not fine. Everything inside of me feels like it's on fire. My ribs are splintering with alternating bands of hot and cold surging like rotating tides. There's a strange buzzing sensation in my head, and I can feel myself becoming light-headed and fuzzy with each passing second. What the hell is happening to me?

"Riven, can you hear me? Riven!"

Caden's face swims blurrily into my vision. And then it's Cale's. I reach toward him but he fades away, and I am left alone, terrified. There is nothing but darkness and the faces of the Vectors, inexorably closing in.

When I awaken this time, I am lying in a sterile room with metal leads stuck to my chest and plastic tubing stretching across my face. White light stabs into my eyes and I lurch upright. Panicked, I pull against the tubes and wiring only to cause a frantic beeping. Someone in a white coat rushes into the room, and I shrink back, hands protectively curled in front of my chest.

"It's okay, Riven, it's okay. Calm down, you're safe. It's me, June." Caden's aunt is standing next to me, a soft smile on her face. "We really need to stop meeting like this," she says as she checks the monitor and replaces the oxygen tubing under my nose.

"Where am I? What happened?"

"You went into circulatory shock and you fainted." I eye the wires and she smiles again. "They're just monitoring your heart rate. I took a look at your foot, and it's healing quickly, faster than I expected."

"I can't be here," I choke out as June uncaps a syringe and deftly injects it into my arm. "What's that? I don't want any drugs!"

"It's just a sedative. Riven—"

"No! You don't understand. I need to leave. They'll find me. They'll find all of you." My heart rate escalates with every breath, and concern crosses June's face.

"Calm down. You're not making any sense. Who'll find you? Your parents? Well, that's good. I meant to ask you. For some reason, none of the numbers listed on your file at school seem to work. We need to get in contact with them and let them know you've been admitted to the clinic."

"My dad is out of town." It's a programmed response.

"Cell phone?"

"No. He calls me, remember?" My mind is racing trying to assess the situation. Somehow, my body is failing. I know that something isn't right—I can feel it inside of me, the holes, and I clutch my chest. I need to get out of there. "June, hospitals . . . I can't be here." I'm gasping for air with each word. "Please. My mother . . . she died in a room just like this one . . . please!"

I am not even pretending at this point. White spots are exploding like clouds of mist behind my eyelids. All I can see are the memories I do have of my mother tied down in a white room with tubes embedded in every part of her, screaming her head off.

Waiting to die.

It's all I can do not to rip out the tubes attached to me, and then tears are running down my face, and I can't stop them, there's so much pain—like everything is dying inside of me. Where did it all come from? What's happening? What is wrong with me?

And then I am screaming, staring at the red dot on my arm. "What did you do? What did you do to me? What kind of *poison* did you put in me? Get it out, get it out!"

"Help me restrain her arms," I hear June say. "Gentle with her."

I fight like I have never fought before, as if I am fighting to keep my very last breath, scratching and scraping, kicking and punching. The full weight of a body collapses against me, and my arms thud, pinned to my sides against the bed. I am drowning in a sea of my tears, the salt of them covering my cheeks and my lips. My body stills and the world grows unnaturally quiet. Now I'm the one waiting to die.

In my mind, I see the Vectors. They're coming.

"Please," I whisper. "Please, June. Don't let me die here."

"Don't worry, darling. You're safe now."

Something cool swirls around my veins, and then the world goes dark once more.

Voices and colors fade in and out.

"Is she going to be okay?" That one I recognize. It's Caden's. I want to tell him that I'm fine, but my lips won't cooperate. My bones feel like syrup, like there's nothing inside of the skin that's holding my body together. Darkness takes me again.

". . . no consent for testing . . . can't draw blood . . ."

". . . levels stabilized . . ."

". . . take her home . . . haven't been able to locate her father. . . ." That last one is June's lilting voice.

I sleep again.

Images move along in an endless collage, bits of white and gray intermingling. Later on, there are bits of sky and swatches of green. The sound disappears. There's only the quiet of gentle voices murmuring around me, like the sound of rain.

My mind is quieter now, no longer so manic, allowing me to think and feel and process. A soft voice tells me that everything is going to be okay. Is it June or is it Caden? But I listen, and once more feel that sense of safety, of trust. And again, I know that I am breaking one of my own hard and fast rules.

*Never trust anyone. Especially the Otherworlders.*

But do I really have a choice? Other than Caden and June, I've thought of them as nothing but a means to an end. Did I think of them as people? They aren't *real* to me. They're a parallel species that has nothing to do with me. But if trusting them means that maybe I can stay alive, then I'll have a sliver of a chance to get back home. A full-body internal scan will detect anything that is wrong with me in seconds.

*If* I can make it back.

Strong arms are carrying me. My eyelids hurt but they open and close like heavy drapes. Within moments, I am back in a familiar room . . . the airy one with the fan and gauzy white curtains.

"Caden, don't stay too long. She needs to get some rest," June says as she props the pillows behind my head. I manage a weak smile. I can't even begin to express my gratitude, but something in her eyes tells me that she knows more than she's saying. Or is it just my constant sense of paranoia?

Caden brushes the hair out of my face. His green eyes are soft and comforting.

"You're awake. How are you feeling?" he asks.

"I've been better." My voice feels like I haven't used it in years and rubs against the inside of my throat like gritty sandpaper. Caden pours me a glass of water from the pitcher, and I sip gratefully.

"Has this ever happened to you before?"

"No." Nothing like this has ever happened to me before. I've never been sick or fainted a day in my life. I wonder if it has to do with the pills or the injector or being here this long. I stare at Caden and then say the words that are playing on the tip of my tongue. "Thanks, by the way. That's twice now you've saved me. I don't know if I like it."

"Why?"

"I don't like owing people."

"You don't owe me anything, Riven. You needed help and I was in the right place at the right time, that's all."

We are quiet for a moment. The edge of the bed dips under Caden's weight as he sits next to me and rests his head on his hands propped on his knees. A silky lock of hair curls into his face.

"I like your hair long," I murmur. "I mean, I like it short, too."

"You've never seen me with short hair." Caden's voice is quiet, but I can see his eyes narrow. I want to kick myself. In the next moment, I decide that I am done with conversation. All it will lead to is confusion and questions and doubt when the time comes. Caden is staring at me, waiting for an explanation. I shrug and take a big gulp of water.

"You look like someone I know. He has short hair."

"You mean Cale?"

I choke and almost spit water all over the room as a wave of shocked coughing overcomes me. "*What* did you say?" I whisper after several painful seconds.

"Cale. You said his name while you were unconscious in the hospital. I think you thought I was him." He pauses, watching me carefully. "Now it all makes sense."

I am overwhelmed by my own stupid carelessness. What else did I say? Did I talk about what I was doing here? About who Caden really was? I can't process the questions fast enough as ten more pop up in their place. What have I done? I should have just risked it and everted the minute I'd found Caden, and dealt with the consequences later. He was the important one, and *he* was healthy enough. That was all that mattered.

*You're thinking crazy, Riven,* I tell myself. *If you everted from here, without you Caden wouldn't have half a chance in the Outers before he got to the city. The Outers would have swallowed him whole.*

Caden's voice interrupts the ominous chaos of my thoughts. "So, who is he?"

"A friend," I say.

Cale is far more than that—he's my best friend, my brother, my liege—but I know that explaining any of it won't make much difference. Caden won't understand our politics, or any of the intricacies of who I am to Cale. I'm bound to Cale in a way that these people could never fathom . . . one bred of steel and blood and undying loyalty.

"In the hospital, it sounded like he was a lot more than that, more like a boyfriend."

"Not that it's any of your business, but no, he's my best friend." I cough and take another sip of water. "Did I talk about anything else? You know, while I was in there?"

"Only about your mother and how she died. I'm sorry."

I frown but I do have a vague recollection of begging June to let me leave. "It was a long time ago. She had a brain tumor." I pause, hesitating. "Did I say anything else? About . . . Cale?"

Caden shakes his head, and my relief is so great I can feel my entire body relax in my next breath. But it is too soon. He is struggling with the lie. I can see it in his eyes. The dread fills me again.

"Tell me," I say. "I won't get mad, I promise."

"You said, 'I'm sorry I failed you. Sorry I didn't come back right away.' Or something like that." A pause, and then Caden's green eyes meet and hold mine. "Is he okay?"

"No."

My voice is so quiet that Caden strains forward to hear it. Unthinkingly, I tuck the lock of hair back over his ear. Something in his eyes flares at my touch. I hardly notice what I've done, but it doesn't matter. Suddenly everything is so clear that it feels like I can see for days . . . the clarity that comes after a fever breaks. I take a deep breath and things become even clearer.

Caden isn't Cale.

*I know what I have to do.*

My sense of conviction is so strong that Caden shies away instinctively, a far cry from the warmth I'd felt from him just before. My mask is back, my chilling words matching the icy hardness he must see on my face. It is a reflex action almost, the sudden shape of my purpose here. I don't question the calmness that settles into me; in fact, it feels like old, comfortable clothing. It's as if everything inside of me has somehow been magically reset . . . who I am, my duty, my mission.

And my mission is to secure the target.

I shake my head slowly. "I was wrong before. I haven't failed him. I've found what he needs, and I will get it to him." The words are hopping on my tongue, burning to get out. "There is nothing, dead or alive, that will stop me."

# 3

# SECRETS

"RIVEN, YOU LOOK wonderful. I can't believe that brace is off your ankle already!"

June's face is welcoming and warm at the door, but I steel myself against it. I am not here to make friends or have any further doubts as to *why* I'm here. Still, I don't want to be rude when she opens the door wide and invites me inside.

"Good genes," I acknowledge with a small smile, hovering near the entrance. "I can't stay, but wanted to come by to say thank you, and also to get my bike. I'm okay to ride now," I assure her hurriedly as her brows begin to knit together. "I'm really alright. I can walk, run, everything's back to normal."

"I'm not comfortable with you getting on a motorcycle this soon. Especially one that was in an accident barely a week ago. Not to mention what else happened—the shock and fainting."

"June, I'm fine. It was only stress, and I've been taking better care of myself. Plus, Cade told me that Jake checked out the bike already," I interject hastily. "Really, I've been riding that thing forever, and I'm safer on that than in anything on four wheels. And my ankle's fine, I swear."

June shoots me a skeptical look. "Just let me have a quick look to be sure. It will make me feel better." Knowing that getting out of there will be a lot easier if I just let her look for herself, I nod and sit on the chair closest to me. Her fingers are warm against my skin as she gently feels along the bones and then twists my ankle to the left and right. "Any pain?"

I shake my head. "It's been fine for a few days now."

"Good genes," she says repeating my earlier words and then frowns. "Maybe I was wrong about the torn ligament; could have been just a mild sprain that looked worse than it was." She checks my eyes, heart rate, and blood pressure. "All good, too."

I can see June second-guessing her own diagnosis. She's too good of a doctor to have been wrong, and she knows it. Quickly, I say, "I'm just glad I'm better now. Crutches are a pain. Being the local fainting gimp is even worse."

The truth is, I feel better than I have in years. Ever. I can't explain it, but it's as if a switch has been turned on inside of me—my body feels limber, my brain crystal clear. Maybe I'm finally getting used to this place.

A smile. "I still want you to take it easy for a couple more days. There's no swelling, but with this kind of recovery, I wouldn't want you to overdo it just because it looks and feels okay."

"Got it."

She's silent for a while, then says quietly, "Amazing," her fingers still resting against my foot.

"June? Caden said that my keys were in the kitchen," I suggest helpfully.

As if in a trance, June blinks and stands, but I can see that her brain is still furiously ticking. "Oh, yes, of course. Caden isn't here; he's at a fencing meet at the school, I think," she says while she's looking for the keys in the kitchen. "But I think he would have put them in one of these drawers."

"Fencing?"

June shrugs. "Don't look at me. I like chess myself, but he has a natural affinity for it, and while I'm not a fan of any com-bat-weapon sport, he does seem to enjoy it. I've only been to a few of his meets, but he's pretty good. Or so I see." She grins. "Have you *seen* the trophy shelves in his room?"

I shake my head. No. "Fencing," I repeat softly to myself.

The sport itself is beautiful to watch, as elaborate as danc-ing, with elongated parries and delicate thrusts. I know it well because we are all trained in the art of most hand-to-hand combat techniques by the tender age of five, and all manner of weaponry by seven. Swords, bows, knives, spears, axes, and guns . . . everything you could conceivably use to dispatch an enemy. The sword has always been my favorite. Cale always favored the crossbow. For a second, the memory of one of our first training sessions together flashes through my brain, and June fidgeting through the drawers in the kitchen fades into the background.

We had been assigned to one another for formal training, and had to face a mock obstacle course with various threats. I'd just turned eight. Though I was small for my age, I was lightning-fast and held the advantage of having held a sword before the age of two. Already, I was at the top of my age group in any kind of martial arts training.

When we were paired up for the test before the final assignments on specialized-weapon training, we automatically sized the other up. His shock of glossy brown hair made him look impish, but the expression on his face was boldly confident.

"You're small," he said, his voice matching the arrogant expression. "Looks like I'll have to pick up the slack."

"How come you're not paired with someone at your own level?" I blurted out.

"Guess they think you need babysitting."

I'd felt like slapping him. My scowl was fierce, but he'd just laughed in my face as if I were nothing more than a kitten defending its toy. I found this boy's arrogance to be so grating and his overconfidence so irritating that I vowed then and there to teach him a lesson.

"Try to keep up," I snarled, and took off just as the whistle blew, jumping over fences and scaling walls. I didn't even look behind me to see if he was keeping up, even though part of the test was to protect your partner at all times. I was too angry. Irrationally, I wanted to show this rude boy exactly what I *could* do.

Two hologen targets jumped up in front of me, one a wild jaguar and the other some kind of bird. I shot them with the rifle slung across my back, both easy hits. It was then that I heard the shout of pain, and in that brief second, the red clouding my brain cleared. The boy was hurt.

I could go back and get him, or I could leave him.

Just as I was deciding to press forward—let him tough it out on his own—something niggled at the base of my neck.

I *couldn't* leave him, it wouldn't be right. Resigned, I turned around and backtracked, only to find him leaning against a tree calmly chewing on an apple.

I frowned. "I heard someone cry out."

"Yeah, it was a new kind of hologen. It made human noises. I killed it." His nonchalant words were almost enough to make me miss the blood dripping from his sleeve. Almost.

"You're hurt?"

"That's mostly the thing's blood. But it did break my leg. I can't walk." He finished the apple, tossing the core near the body of the dead creature. "You should go on; I'll tell the trainers that I tripped. You should finish."

I could feel the guilt at leaving him earlier ripping through me like acid. "No, it's my fault. I shouldn't have left. I broke the rules and you got hurt."

"We could default."

"No!" I shouted. Defaulting meant quitting, and a strike that would go on your training record, even if something happened that was no fault of your own. Failure was not an option, not for any of us. If you couldn't defend yourself in the field, you were as good as dead. It was as simple as that. "We'll figure something else out," I said confidently despite the hole of anxiety in my stomach.

"I guess I shouldn't have teased you." It was the smallest offer of truce and barely an apology, but I took it anyway. He had been hurt because of me . . . because I deserted him.

"I'm Riven," I said, sealing the fragile truce. "Can you walk if you hold on to me?"

"You're half my size; we'll never make it. Just leave me."

"Shut up," I told him. "I'm stronger than I look."

And so, with me half dragging, half pushing him along, we inched through the rest of the course. When we ran out of bullets in my rifle, we stood back-to-back, sword and crossbow in hand to take out our enemies. I admired the boy's skill with his weapons, switching fluidly from longbow to crossbow and back before I could blink. Anything that got too close, I fought off capably with my sword and, occasionally, a short knife.

In the end, it wasn't the most graceful completion of the course, but we came out together panting, winded, and utterly exhausted. The medical team rushed out of nowhere so quickly that I didn't have a chance to say anything more to the boy before he was hover-ported away, surrounded by a team of elite guards. It was surprising but I didn't think too much more about it.

It was only afterwards that I learned that my partner was the son of the Monarch of Neospes. A prince. Mortified, I kept waiting for the soldiers who would surely come to arrest me for my heedless words and thoughtless actions in the holo dome, but I needn't have worried. From that point on, the boy who I would come to know as Cale always asked for me, and only me, to partner with him.

One day, when I asked him why he'd always chosen me, he responded flippantly, "Someone needs to protect the little people."

But later in a rare moment of unguarded honesty, Cale told me that it was because I'd come back for him without knowing who he was, even after his intentionally provoking words. He'd liked that I had never even considered giving up or leaving him behind. I remember telling him that quitting would never be an option for me. It wasn't then, and it would never be now.

And just like back then, Cale knows that he can count on me. And that can't change, not now, not ever.

"Riven?"

I jerk out of my thoughts so quickly that my fingers are on the hilt of a knife tucked into a side pocket of my pants before I can exhale the breath hitched in my lungs. I relax, my brain belatedly recognizing June's voice and release my hot fingers.

"Sorry," I breathe. "Homework on the brain."

"The hospital just paged me and I need to go," June says pulling on her jacket. Her face is apologetic. "Your keys aren't in here; they must be on Caden's desk somewhere. Can you have a look and lock the door on your way out? Take the stairs just past the room you were in. Second door on the left. You take care of yourself, okay?"

She's out the door before I can even nod. But I am too grateful to speak—she's just given me the opportunity I've been looking for. An engine turns over, and I wait until I see her car pulling out of the driveway before I make my way upstairs.

Pictures line the hallway walls in a variety of colors and shapes with faces and landscapes filling their matte frames. They weave a story of vibrant life as I climb the staircase. Some of the frames are new and some antique, with some photos in black and white, while others are in color. Despite the hodge-podge, there's a beautiful artistry and a love beneath it all connecting it together. It's breathtaking.

It's only seconds later that I realize that Caden isn't in a single one.

Pushing open the door to the first room, I tell myself that I'm not snooping, merely familiarizing myself with the layout, but I still feel uncomfortable. This room is obviously June's room, with cherry furniture and a large four-poster bed covered with a hand-quilted floral bedspread. The room is airy and overlooks the street. A thickly bound book and a pair of glasses are resting on the bedside table. The room is feminine yet strong, just as she is.

Crossing the few feet to the right side of the room, I perform a cursory search. I don't know what I'm looking for . . . clues, weapons, anything that will tell me who June really is, because I know without a doubt that she isn't Caden's aunt, if only because of the photos in the hallway.

Why is she helping him?

A fluttery feeling tingles along the back of my neck, and I spin around in attack mode. But nothing is there. I can't shake the feeling that has now sunk into my bones, that feeling of being watched. I wonder if half of it is my own imagination combined with the events of the last few days.

I give myself a mental shake. The house is empty; I would know instantly if it weren't. Turning my attention back to the job at hand, I make my way to June's dresser, sliding my hands along the walls and along its backside. The drawers are filled with clothes, nothing exceptional. Something snatches my attention on the bedside table. The heavy gold letters on the book are like a neon warning.

*Quantum Mechanics: Intuition or Theory?*

This time, I can't control the realization that rushes through me. June knows a lot more than she's letting on. How much *does* she know? Did she know about me?

No. I've been careful. Haven't I? The self-doubt crawls in, cold and relentless. I haven't really been myself lately, getting injured, fainting, and ending up in a hospital. Being all too careless. I could have let something unintentional slip over the past few weeks.

*No,* my inner voice argues. *You are meticulous. She doesn't know anything other than what she knew anyway. Otherwise, why would she have left you here alone if she thought you were dangerous? There's no way.*

Mollified somewhat, I run my finger along the edge of the book. Quantum mechanics isn't exactly bedtime reading material. Hefting it up, I flip open the cover, skimming through the first quarter, and almost drop it to the floor. Instead, I sink to the bed and hold the book carefully on my lap. In a cutout hidden in its pages, in a bed of soft chamois, lies an innocuous-looking gun, barely palm-sized. I know instantly that it is loaded and it is lethal.

There's a magazine of bullets in a slim brown box next to the gun in the book. I examine them carefully. Custom hollow-points, meant to shred the inside of a target. The blue markings on the side of the box indicate that there's some kind of modified burst mechanism within the bullet. These have been specifically designed to annihilate whatever or whomever they come into contact with. I place the bullets back into the case and replace the book.

Before closing the cover, I stare for a long second. The gun is new. From the minimal residue and shiny oiled insides, it's probably only been fired a few times. If June, who for all intents and purposes is a civilian, is anticipating this level of danger, then I've been miscalculating things all along.

She's expecting someone. Or something.

After I've smoothed the bed and verified that everything is back in its place, I exit the room. Across the hall is another bedroom. This room, unlike the others I've been in, is completely sparse, with a single bed with a metal frame and a slim desk sitting under the window. It appears to be unused, but still, instinct propels my feet to cross over to the nearest closet door. Empty. I release the breath I've unconsciously been holding. Maybe it's a spare room that June hasn't gotten to yet. Still, something about its sparse efficiency strikes a familiar chord inside of me. The clock on the wall is five minutes fast, which is curious because it matches the time on my own watch. Time can be your own worst enemy. I, too, prefer to always be ahead of it. Retracing my footsteps, I close the door behind me and make my way to the next door. A decent-sized bathroom.

The third door is Caden's room.

I know it instantly but something holds me back, my fingers hovering on the doorknob. Why am I so afraid to open it? Caden means nothing to me. A shiver sweeps through me, tingling along the undersides of my arms and up my neck, and a forgotten sense of anxiety hits me full force. Instinctively, my fingers draw back.

Drawing a shaky breath, I check the other doors down the hallway. One leads to another bathroom, the next to a linen closet, and the third to a stairway to a shadowy attic that's filled with old furniture. On the attic steps, I sit staring at Caden's door as if the devil himself is on the other side. Why is my imagination suddenly running wild? Why am I afraid? There's nothing there, nothing that can harm me.

"Get it together, Riv!" I tell myself harshly. "He's just a kid like everyone else here, nothing more than that. Now find your keys and let's go." I catch a glimpse of myself in the long mirror at the end of the hallway, and I have to laugh.

"Keep talking to yourself and you know where you'll end up," I say to the fierce-looking girl, and watch her pitiful attempt to stare me down. I step closer. "The loony bin," I inform her threateningly and then roll my eyes as she shakes her head and grins at me.

I wonder briefly if losing your mind is a part of the eversion sickness that afflicts about fifty percent of the people who attempt it, because not only am I talking to no one in particular, but my hair is sticking out like a prickly bush, and my light-gray eyes have a slightly desperate quality to their shadowy dark-circled edges. I look like a homeless runaway.

I tug on the second-hand Grateful Dead T-shirt, some obscure musical band that I'd never heard of, and hike my jeans out of the beat-up black combat boots. Not much I can do about the hair, but I try anyway, fingering the choppy locks lying on either side of the blue-and-silver braid hanging to my shoulder. Better, but not much. I may feel like a million bucks inside, but I definitely don't look it. I shrug. Once I get back, I can work on my appearance. Right now, I have a job to do.

Find my stupid keys.

With a hiss of exasperation, I stride to Caden's door and shove it open. The room is painted in rich intertwining hues of blue creating the illusion of being submerged underwater. A large bed occupies most of the space, leaving room for little else, but I expect that's the point. It's an undersea sanctuary of sorts, and one that is only truly appreciated lying down. Complete immersion. It's beautiful and serene, not at all what I'd expected.

As I am crossing over to Caden's desk, my brain registers other details, like the shelves above the window alcove, covered in trophies. The majority of them are for fencing, but some, again not surprisingly, are for archery. A small sound escapes my lips, half gasp, half cry of some sort, and a knot immediately forms in my belly. With the bow, Cale had been an expert marksman. It shouldn't be so strange that they have so much in common, given what they are, but the similarities are still overwhelming.

A tiny amateurish landscape painting above the bed catches my eye, and I lean against the mattress for a closer look. It is all I can do not to fall backwards as my weight dips into the bed in a very unnatural way, as if I am on some kind of strange floating device. Instead, I spring backward to compensate and bang my still-healing ankle into the desk chair next to the bed.

"Mother of . . ." I mutter, launching the offending chair across the room, as a cloud of pain threatens to suffocate me. "Ouch!"

"I'd hate to know what that poor chair did to deserve such treatment."

I blink the stars in my vision away. Caden is leaning nonchalantly against the door, his mouth twisted in a grin, and shaking his head in mock consternation.

"Hey," I blurt out. "Sorry, June told me to look for my keys up here. She couldn't find them where you said in the kitchen. I hope you don't mind." The words blend together in a rush, and

I'm not entirely sure why they sound a trifle defensive. I can't believe I hadn't heard him come in. "She told me to come up."

"Yeah, I forgot that I'd moved them. They're in my desk drawer. In the back."

"What?" Why would he have put my keys in there? I know I'm frowning.

He shrugs as he walks toward me. "I thought you were going to do something stupid like try to ride right after the accident, so I hid them."

"I wasn't—"

"Sure," Caden says, his grin widening, and reaches around me. I feel my entire body freeze as his arms graze against mine, and suddenly I am holding my breath. Every second feels elongated as the smell of the sweat on his skin from his fencing meet seeps into my nostrils. He smells so much like Cale that my knees buckle . . . but that's impossible. There's no conceivable way that they should even smell alike. Is there? My confusion must be apparent because Cale—I mean Caden—grasps my arms.

"Riven? What's wrong? You're staring at me like I'm a ghost."

"I need to sit," I rasp, ignoring the keychain he's holding in one hand. "Not on your bed," I say hastily. "Something's wrong with it. It's . . . broken or something. Soggy."

Caden's laugh rings through the room. "It's just a waterbed. They're supposed to be soggy."

"A *water* what?" The thought is inconceivable to me . . . a bed with *water* in it. When I think of the scarcity and the high cost of water where I come from, the thought of the overindulgence of Caden's bed makes me physically sick. I shake my head to cover my discomfort. "I don't get it. Why don't you have a real bed?"

"It is a real bed. Don't you know what a waterbed is?" I shake my head, still mute. "They're pretty common. I like the feel of it, and it's good for my back. Something about it is calming, and when I lie on it, in the silence, I really feel like I'm in the middle of the ocean. Come on, try it."

"No."

But I have to admit that I am intrigued. The whole notion of the sea and the ocean is as foreign to me as my entire existence probably is to Caden. He reads my hesitation—and my curiosity—easily.

"Here," he says, and turns my shoulders so that my back is facing the bed. "Don't jerk down; just sit gently. Good. Now lie back."

I comply until the top of the bed is literally cupping my entire body. "It feels so weird," I say.

"One sec, check this out."

I barely notice when Caden pulls the shades over his windows and presses a switch on a light in one corner of the room, so taken I am with the gently sloshing motion of the waterbed. But in the next moment, I'm transported to another world as white bands of light radiate against the blue mosaic of the walls, and the deep sound of marine life thrums into my ears from a box on the bedside table. I can't even speak, far less breathe, when I feel Caden lie on his back next to me, the movement from his weight sending a slow, rolling wave into my right side.

"This is . . ."

But I can't find the right words for the magnitude of the feelings inside of me. I have never ever seen a real ocean other

than in pictures, and this is as close to that as I have ever gotten, even if it is just an illusion of light and sense.

"Incredible, right?"

"Amazing," I whisper in a childlike voice. "Does the ocean
really look like this?"

"In the right spot, if the sun is shining down through the
water, this comes pretty close. I think I've loved the ocean
ever since I can remember," Caden says in a quiet voice. "I
don't remember much about when I was really little, but I do
remember my mom taking me to this seaside village when I
was seven years old, and she couldn't get me out of the water,
even when it was so dark that I couldn't see two feet in front
of me. Back then, I had to have my bedroom painted blue,
too." Caden laughs, a sound halfway between humor and
pain.

"Your mom? Is she here?"

Caden turns to face me, a shadow crossing his features, and
shakes his head slowly. "No. She died."

"How?"

"When I was eight. Seizure, they said." His mouth twists.
"Some kind of brain or nervous system infection, but the doctors weren't really sure."

"I'm sorry."

"Thanks. It's okay. I miss her but it was a long time ago."

I turn back to stare at the ceiling, the light and sound
doing nothing to dissipate the sudden weight in my chest, but
I remain silent. There's nothing I can say—death is a natural
part of life for me, but knowing that Caden's mother had died
from eversion sickness leaves me cold. I couldn't imagine how

painful it would have been, or how hard it would have been for Caden to watch his mother die.

*Cale's* mother.

A shiver runs through me, and warm fingers slide against my wrist. The shiver deepens. The water bed shifts, rolling me upward as Caden turns on his side to face me. I can feel him staring at me, but I keep my eyes glued to the ceiling. His fingers skim downward to cover my closed fist in his hand.

I can't move. My entire body is rigid at the light touch.

"Who are you really, Riven?" he whispers, his right hand shadowing the blue swirls for a second before lifting to move the braid out of my face. He holds it for a second, studying it before releasing it. My breath catches. The sheer force of him imprisons me, as his fingers trail down my face, turning my chin toward his. "You seem so tough on the outside, but you're not. Not really."

My eyes meet his. They are warm but unreadable. His thumb stirs against my temple.

"You don't know anything about me." The words are sticky on my tongue, clumsy. For some reason, I feel inexplicably awkward.

"I know you're not like other girls, but I know you aren't as hard as you pretend to be," Caden says, propping himself up on one shoulder and cupping the right side of my face in his palm. Caden's eyes are liquid like the imaginary water wonderland surrounding us, his irises mirroring shades of hazy blue. They are mesmerizing. His head bends toward mine, and all the breath steals out of me.

"I can't stop thinking about you," he murmurs. "You're so different." His words slice through me like ice shards as I pull away. What the hell am I doing? I *am* different . . . more different than he knows. I jerk sideways and upwards, causing the bed to undulate violently, and wrench my hand out of his.

He's a mark, for heaven's sake. A *mark!*

"What's wrong? You okay?" Caden asks quickly. An embarrassed look flits across his face for a second, but it's gone as quickly as it came. He hasn't done anything wrong, and I hadn't done anything to dissuade him. I'd been idiotic to ignore the obvious signals—the bed, the lights, his gentle touch—but my senses had been muddled by the magic of the ambient lights and sounds.

For the hundredth time since I've been here, I curse myself, but the truth is, I'm far better at fighting than I am at flirting . . . or clearly, even recognizing it. I glare at him.

"I'm fine," I say, snapping the words through my teeth, struggling to compose myself as self-disgust rages through me—I'd been stupid to let myself go like that. But my self-loathing still boils over. It's poisoning my throat, the inside of my eyes, and I want to scream. My fingers curl into fists, but my voice, when I speak, is calm. It is inflectionless, emotionless.

"You are right about one thing. I'm not like other girls." I meet his gaze and hold it ruthlessly until his drops away. I grab my keys off his desk and walk to the door, glancing once more over my shoulder. "I'm worse. Don't for a second delude yourself otherwise."

# 4

# PREPARATION

IT IS A tide of moving bodies, all flowing toward the door. Friday afternoon, and they all can't escape the confines of the classroom fast enough. I don't know why I even bother to continue going to Horrow anymore. I've already set the plan in motion—we're heading for Denver this weekend to see some play that June had gotten Caden tickets for. The timing will be perfect, and I need him to be willing, at least until we evert. There's really no reason to be at school, but I tell myself that it is for Caden's own safety.

The truth is that I'm enjoying high school for the first time in months, and in particular, this physics class. Something about Mrs. Taylor's no-nonsense confidence reminds me of my teachers back home. Not surprisingly, given who my father is, physics has always been one of my strong suits. I like this class even if it is rudimentary.

"Riven, can you stay a minute, please?" Mrs. Taylor asks just as I walk past her desk.

I nod to Caden who's walking ahead of me. "I'll meet you in the quad."

Since the other day in his room, neither of us has spoken about what happened. But sometimes, I see an odd look in his eyes whenever he thinks I'm not looking, and he is quick to conceal it when I do. I don't know what to make of it, but it's not like it has any bearing on the job I'm here to do.

One thing I've learned about high school here is that it is a roiling mass of boys, girls, frenemies, and insta-crushes . . . in love one day and at loggerheads the next. I didn't expect Caden to be exempt—this was his world, after all—but for my part, what had happened was already forgotten. I rule my emotions. They do not rule me.

"Make that the gym," Caden tells me, hefting a large bag with his fencing gear. "I have a meet, remember?"

"Okay, I'll come by when I'm done." I nod again and walk over to Mrs. Taylor with a sense of foreboding born of following years of pure gut instinct. Did I repeat the mistake I'd made in Boston? Said something that is way beyond my supposed educational level? Written about some theory that doesn't already exist in this universe?

"Yes, Mrs. Taylor?"

She glances up, her eyes as dark and piercing as ever over her wire-rimmed glasses. "Sit down, please. I want to discuss the last quiz."

"I had help," I blurt out before she can say anything else, but she stares at me with those obsidian eyes until I sit down. Stupidly, I realize that insinuating that I'd had help for a quiz meant that I'd been cheating. Still, Mrs. Taylor doesn't say anything, and even with all my training I find that I can't read her at all, and my palms are clammy with sweat. She shuffles through the pile of papers and moves mine to the top. Even from where I am sitting, the huge circled letter *D* is glaring. *D?* That couldn't possibly be right. But still, I couldn't have done better if I'd planned it. I can't help the smile that sweeps across my face.

Mrs. Taylor glares at me over her glasses. "Obviously, you didn't have help," she remarks, her sarcasm stinging like a wet slap. "And this is no laughing matter, young lady. May I remind you that if you fail my class, you will have to take it again in summer school?"

I almost laugh out loud. I definitely won't be around by summer. I compose myself. "I'm sorry, Mrs. Taylor. I will try to do better." I'm about to rise when I realize that Mrs. Taylor hasn't quite finished with me.

"The thing that confuses me, Riven, is that your transcripts from previous schools are more than satisfactory, and you also seem to have an excellent grasp of the material during class-time and in discussion group, both of which suggest to me that you either weren't prepared for the quiz or, more likely, that you deliberately answered incorrectly."

I'm at a loss for words. "I wasn't prepared," I begin but the look on her face freezes any more lies from leaving my lips. My ploy, it seems, has drawn more attention than if I'd aced the test. Squirming inside at my gauche stupidity, I wait for her to continue.

"I also see from your transcripts from your last five schools that you have moved around quite a bit, more than usual for a girl your age."

"My father's job requires him to travel."

"Seems excessive. What field, if I may ask?" Mrs. Taylor's mild expression suggests that she is merely curious, but I take nothing for granted, especially if it is something that can compromise my safety. Or Caden's.

*Trust no one.* They were the last words that Cale said to me.

I shrug and smile. "Sales. He doesn't really talk about it." My smile turns calculating. "Kind of like the mob." But Mrs. Taylor doesn't take the bait, and instead regards me with an unreadable smile of her own. Something uncomfortable slides along my spine; apart from June, she's the first person to make me uneasy the whole time I've been looking for Caden, and I don't like the feeling at all. "Can I go now?" I say, more testily than I'd intended.

"In a minute. I want to ask you about one more thing. Your discussion group's project is the law of universal gravitation, correct?"

"Yes." The uncomfortable feeling digging into my spine spreads its fingers along my ribs and across my chest. It's Boston all over again. I can see it in Mrs. Taylor's slightly fixated expression.

"Mr. Perkins . . . Philip," she amends at my blank face, "your group partner, mentioned the other day that you had an interesting contention regarding the laws of gravity."

My mind is racing now, trying to recall every bit of the offhand discussion I'd had with Philip. Bored out of my mind during one of the group sessions, I'd wanted to have a little fun, poking holes into Philip's vast amount of book knowledge and his theories. What's to say that this scenario couldn't exist? Or what about this principle? Have you ever thought about if this could happen? And the killer, what about *sub-quantum gravitational distortion*? Little did I know that he would have gone back to Mrs. Taylor. I grit my teeth to keep from kicking myself.

*Stupid, stupid, stupid!*

I paste a vacuous look on my face and twirl a strand of hair around my finger just as I'd seen Sadie doing earlier. It makes me sick to my stomach to be imitating someone that vapid, but I grit my teeth and twirl as if my life depends on it.

"Philip," I repeat in what I hope is a dreamy voice. "I think he really likes me. I was only trying to impress him, Mrs. Taylor. The thing is, I don't know the first thing about gravity except what they say on that television show, *Star Trek*. That's where I got the ideas. Did he say something bad about me?"

By the end of my mini-tirade, my voice has degenerated into an irritating whine. I am sickened at the empty-headed sound of it, but know that I have no choice. Hopefully, Mrs. Taylor will believe me, but the truth is I have no idea about *Star Trek* other than a couple reruns I'd seen at a motel in Philadelphia, which I'd thought hilarious. I can only hope that my impersonation of a vacuous valley girl will work.

"Which episode?" she asks without batting an eye.

"I think it was called 'Gravity,' it was about some kind of gravitational distortion." Mrs. Taylor's eyes are relentless but I force myself to look as clueless as possible. My relief is palpable when I sense rather than see her shoulders relax and her body tilts away from me.

"Sometimes the writers of those television shows deserve more credit than they're given," she says after a long moment.

"I wouldn't know," I say. "Most of the time I have help . . . even at the other schools. People tend to feel sorry for me. Boys, in particular." Something tells me I'm pushing it, but I can't seem to stop the excessive overcompensation for my slip with Philip, even though I'm obviously in the clear.

The thoughtfulness in Mrs. Taylor's eyes wanes to actual distaste, and I squirm in my seat. In a different world, I'm sure she and I could have had a scintillating conversation about sub-quantum theory and gravitational distortion.

It is the reason I am even able to come here, after all.

I stare at the floor chewing on my lip until Mrs. Taylor says briskly, "Well, thanks for clearing that up. *Star Trek* aside, I will expect you to perform better on the next quiz. And try to take on your share of the work, will you, Riven?"

I'm almost home free, but for some reason, I stop at the door. Even though it shouldn't matter, it bothers me that she thinks I'm some sort of vapid idiot who would use others to get ahead. Failing is just not a part of who I am.

"I'm sorry. I'll do better next time. I just want you to know that this isn't who I am. I pull my own weight and I don't cheat."

Aware that I'm babbling for no reason, I'm already out the door, so I nearly miss the speculative glance she sends in my direction, but I've had enough interrogation for one day. Mrs. Taylor will be no more than a distant memory in a few days. Maybe as a good-bye present, I'll leave her a paper on sub-quantum string theory and its practical application to move between universes. Then again, altering the course of history is a big no-no, as in strictly—we're talking punishable by imprisonment—forbidden.

Outside, the day has waned to a cool, clear evening. I check my watch. Caden's meet will be in full swing . . . and full of more people. I have the biggest urge to race back to my motel room and lie on the bed in the dark for a while where it's quiet and I am alone, and where I can think. Instead, I sit on a nearby bench and close my eyes just for a moment.

All of this interaction is tiresome. Remembering what to say and what not to say takes a huge toll after a while, and I'm mentally exhausted, especially after the confrontation with Mrs. Taylor. Before, I'd shift in and out, looking for Caden and then move on. Now that I've found him, coupled with my hindrance of an injury, I've had more interaction with these people than I'd ever intended. And it's literally draining.

Plus, too much contact means bad things could happen. It means that my presence could unknowingly set something into motion . . . a disturbance in the natural course of events. It means that others—not just the Vectors—could find me, such as the Guardians, who monitor such disturbances.

I've never met a Guardian, but Cale's father told me that they were there to make sure that people on both sides stayed where they were supposed to be. For centuries, the Guardians have been an elite group bound to the same code on both sides, preventing people from shifting, under the Laws of Eversion after the Great Infection of 1927. They answer only to the Faction, a group of leaders supposedly older than the monarchy of my world.

You evert, you die. It's as simple as that. If the environmental differences don't get you, the Guardians will.

Only with Caden, the Guardians had failed. Until recently, everyone thought that Caden was dead. But obviously, he isn't dead . . . he is very much alive, a secret that Cale only revealed to me a few months ago when he mysteriously became sick. So, somehow, Caden has managed to outwit them and survive all this time. I can't quite shake the feeling that there's something more, something I am missing that's right in front of my face . . . something essential to his survival here.

He told me that his mother had died here, from a seizure. She probably had the pills that my father had given her, but they didn't help. My father warned that the pills with their brain stabilization agents wouldn't work for everyone, and everting would only put more pressure on the body's central nervous system. But the plain truth is that we don't belong here, and the universe has its own way of righting wrongs, of fixing inconsistencies. Her seizure was just that . . . nature's way of dealing with cheaters.

I take in a few deep breaths and complete a set of mental exercises to clear my head. A quick glance at my watch suggests that the meet should nearly be over, so I start to make my way across the quad. A part of me doesn't want to watch Caden fence—I don't want to see what a natural he is, just like Cale.

*Cale.*

For a second, I wonder how he's doing. Whether he's surviving in what has become a sea of snakes and traitors. They won't kill him, that I am sure of, because they need his name too much to control the people of Neospes; loyalty to the monarchy was too hard-won to be usurped by a single coup. We were too careful, too suspicious of sudden changes.

People trusted Cale's family. They trusted his father, and now he was dead . . . assassinated in cold blood by his half brother, a bloodthirsty man greedy for power. Without a doubt, I know that Cale is next. His life is collateral for the moment . . . collateral for support. His uncle will keep him alive for as long as it suits his purpose. I have to trust that he is somehow holding on; otherwise, everything I'm doing will be for nothing.

Fear for Cale's safety clouds my mind so much that I almost crash into a group of kids standing in a shadowy corner near the gym.

"Watch where you're going!" shouts a slurred voice. Foul breath blows into my face, and I almost gag.

"Sorry," I say, and then belatedly recognize one of the faces in the crowd: Charisma, the other girl from my physics discussion group. The slurred voice belongs to a dark-haired guy she's leaning against . . . the one with the foul breath. He's obviously drunk or high on something, and she looks dazed but doesn't say anything.

"Hey, Charisma," I say, but she won't even meet my eyes, as if she's staring right through me. Something about the way the guy's arm is wrapped around her shoulders rubs me the wrong way and I hesitate.

*It's not your problem*, my inner voice hisses. *None of these people, other than Caden, are. Keep walking.*

I listen, take two steps, and halt. Even though I've only had a few classes with Charisma, she's grown on me with her upbeat personality and her willingness to help others. She's one of those types of people I wish I could be more like—selfless and caring— but I am so far beyond that person, it's not even funny. Hardness and cynicism drive me. With so much loss in my world, allowing myself to care about anything other than my own survival is a death sentence. I guess a part of me feels drawn to Charisma for that reason. She seems untouched by anything ugly.

"Hey, you okay?" I ask her.

"She's fine," the boy says, pulling her away from me in the opposite direction.

"I wasn't talking to you," I say to him, and grab Charisma's shoulders so that she's facing me. Her eyes are dilated, and she's looking at me as if she's trying to focus but can't. "Charisma, are you okay?"

"I told you she was fine!" the boy snaps, pushing me backward with one hand. My brain registers two things in immediate succession. One, Charisma is drugged, and two, this boy is lucid enough to shove me backward. My body kicks into battle mode, and everything slows to the point where I can sense the movements of his friends behind me.

"She's not fine, and I am going to take her home. Back off; I don't want to hurt you," I say quietly. I figure I should prepare him for what's about to happen.

"You, and what army?" he jeers in a loud voice. Instantly, he has the attention of everyone within ten feet of us. "Look, guys, we have a late addition to the party. Get her a drink before she hurts herself."

He laughs, and his friends join in. Someone thrusts a cup in my face, and even without tasting it, I know that there's something wrong with it. I can smell it. My eyes narrow and I bat the cup away with the back of one hand.

"You guys don't go here, do you?" More slurred laughter. They must have come for the meet and then decided to take advantage of girls while they were at their drink fest. "Don't you know it's a crime to drug people's drinks?"

"Lookit, we got ourselves a deputy," one of the boys giggles. "You gonna arrest us?"

"Arrest me, arrest me, Ociffer. I'm underage!" another says.

I glare him into silence. Where I come from, there's no drinking age. Consuming spirits is a rite of passage, and considering it's cheaper and more accessible than water, people don't make that much of a big deal over it. It's mostly consumed in toasts and celebrations. And frankly, people are too busy to risk the effects on their day-to-day responsibilities.

"I don't want any trouble. I just want Charisma. Just pass her over, and you can go back to getting yourselves drunk."

"Charisma wants to stay," the dark-haired boy says and turns to her. "Don't you, baby?"

"Mmhmm . . ." Charisma murmurs incoherently. A line of drool has made its way down her chin, and she's starting to teeter on her feet. The boy glares at me with a vile expression in his eyes and then kisses her while I am watching, his tongue slithering over her mouth. I don't flinch, not even when he grabs the front of her chest. "You're my girl, aren't you baby?"

"Touch her again, and it will be the last thing you do."

"You mean like this—"

I break his fingers with a single flex of my own before he can even touch the front of her dress, and then I'm on the move, spinning backward and knocking two of the guys behind me off their feet. The fourth boy takes one look at me and flees in the opposite direction.

I turn back to where Charisma is still standing near the dark-haired boy, who is screaming on his knees and clutching his mauled fingers. With his uninjured hand, he removes a switchblade from his pocket and brandishes it, weaving unsteadily to his feet. Out of the corner of my eye, I notice that Charisma has teetered her way to a tree and has slumped down against its trunk. At least she's out of harm's way, but I know that I don't have a lot of time. She can't fall asleep before I can get her some help.

"You're going to be sorry," the boy snarls, pointing the knife at me.

This time, I can't stop from laughing. "Someone once told me that if you point a knife, you'd better be prepared to use it," I inform him. His answer is to swipe at my face, an attack that I dodge easily. "You should know that where I come from, I graduated the top of my class in hand-to-hand combat."

"What are you? Some kind of army grunt?"

"Something like that. Bet you're wishing that you'd just let her go when I'd asked you, right?" I know my lack of fear must be aggravating him, but honestly, it's like fighting an uncoordinated toddler. Given the odds, I could quite conceivably fight him blindfolded.

"Shut up. Who has the knife, anyway?" he taunts lunging blindly at me.

I spin again and clip the knife out of his hand with the heel of my boot so that it flies upward and lands in my own fist. "This knife?"

"Doesn't matter. I don't need it," he says with forced bravado. His eyes dart to the motionless forms of his friends. I can see the fear in his eyes and a dawning understanding of what he has gotten himself into, underscored by sheer disbelief that a *girl* is somehow getting the best of all of them. It is the same fear that makes him charge toward me in a football-type tackle.

I dance out of the way and laugh again. I'm exhilarated. It's the first real combat exercise I've had in weeks, this coming from someone who typically trains three hours a day in a rigorous simulation mode and then another hour in actual combat. I should be sluggish, but I'm wired. Ever since the clinic, it's as if I can feel the neurons firing inside of me, getting stronger. And now, my body feels wired, like it's plugged in to a giant electrical outlet, every move charged with lethal fire. I am invincible.

My last move has brought me near to where Charisma is sitting, and I notice that her head is slumping forward onto her knees. She's nearly unconscious. A surge of anger rips through me and I advance on the boy. His eyes widen because now I am no longer laughing. My face is dead, emotionless. It is a look that has been partially responsible for the rank I hold in my own world.

"You like to take advantage of defenseless girls?" His head snaps back as my fist makes contact with his right cheek. It's barely a touch, but he stumbles backward. "You put something in their drinks, and then what do you do? Pretend to care about them? Then you hurt them?"

Each word is a staccato of fury. Fury at what girls here had to put up with over and over again. I've seen it at almost every school I've been to, and until now, I'd always walked away, telling myself that there was nothing I could do.

Where I come from, girls—*women*—know how to defend themselves from everything and everyone: human, animal, or machine. Drugged or not, any girl from my world would have had this guy, or one three times his size, on his backside before he could even lay a finger on her.

In this world, in neighborhood high schools, others like this boy prey on innocent girls, and more often than not get away with it because the girls are too ashamed or humiliated or aren't able to remember to do anything about it. It sickens me. Drugging another person in my world for something as revolting as sexual gratification is an offense punishable by exile—a fate more feared than death. Let's just say it doesn't happen too often. Exile is *not* a gentle end.

Someone needs to teach this boy a lesson. For Charisma, I'd be that person.

I grab the boy by the front of his shirt and pull him close to me. He's a fair head taller than I am, but I am practically holding him off the ground. I press the butt of his knife against his crotch so deeply that I can see the water spring into his eyes. My voice is a low snarl. "I ever see you near her, I will end you. Got it?"

Without waiting for any acknowledgement, I spear my knee into his groin, feeling the immediate grunt radiating up through his entire body as he collapses against me, crying. I shove him away, a whimper from Charisma drawing my attention. The boy is curled into a fetal ball on the ground, but I still send his knife spinning behind me without a backward glance. I know without looking that it thumps right into the sliver of space on the ground between his stomach and his thighs. The sudden sour odor of urine permeates the night air.

I lift Charisma easily. "It's okay; you're safe now," I tell her. "But you need to stay awake for just a few more minutes, okay?"

"Mmm . . . okay."

After I file a report with school security with a condensed version of the events and accompany Charisma in the ambulance to the local hospital, where she will stay overnight—apparently, the boy had used some kind of hypnotic sedative in an excessive amount—I catch a cab back to Horrow. But the parking lot is empty, and it looks like I've missed the whole meet, and Caden, too.

A sense of exhaustion overcomes me, and I rest my head against the handlebars of my bike. I want to leave this place as fast as I can. Everything about it unnerves me. I want to go back to where I belong, where I feel whole. Here, I am starting to feel broken, the natural result of living in a broken world. Although they have more landmass, water, and people than we do, I have no doubt that this world is far more lost than mine.

Gritting my teeth, I rev the bike with one thing on my mind. Come hell or high water, we are leaving tomorrow. With a sense of rejuvenated intent, I ride to Caden's house. I don't let the fact that his car isn't in the driveway or that there aren't lights on in the house deter my new sense of purpose. I'll wait. Throwing a jacket across my shoulders, I make my way to the front porch, but there's already someone there.

My heart plummets to my stomach in a free fall that is magnified by the fact that time has slowed to abnormal proportions. My blood thunders in my ears like a solid force.

"Shae," I breathe.

My sister. My family. My enemy.

# 5

# CONFLICT ARISING

"I KNEW THEY'D send you sooner or later."

The breath that leaves my lips in response to the husky familiarity of her voice is deflating and harsh, taking with it every bone in my body.

"No one . . . sent me. I came alone," I manage in a shaky voice.

Shae looks more or less the same as when I saw her last, right before she caught me off guard armed with a double electro-rod, except that there's an oozing red gash across her face. Hair in blond dreadlocks, tanned face, if thinner, and eyes the color of a glacial sky. Those cold eyes were the last thing I'd seen before she'd everted.

Seeing her now is like being dunked in a bucket of ice until my entire body feels like it's going to peel out of my skin. I want to run to her so badly it hurts, but underneath it all her betrayal is as fresh as it was thirteen years before, and the pain just as sharp. She left me with no regrets and no explanations. The monarchy had branded her a traitor, and I had to live with her shame until I built myself into something large and powerful enough to eclipse it.

I hate her. That isn't going to change. Not now, not ever.

"So you're the one helping Caden," I say. "I should have guessed. I learned everything I know about covering up the marks of eversion from you."

"And yet you found me."

I laugh, a hollow sound made harsh with a coil of emotions I can't begin to unravel. "It wasn't easy to track you, trust me. You were careful, I'll give you that . . . everting and then traveling by their transportation. Smart. But my coming here was just pure luck."

"Luck," Shae repeats, a small frown creasing her brow. I notice that there are more bruises and cuts along her arms, all of them fresh.

"Maybe I sensed you in my subconscious?" I offer snidely. I can't keep the sarcasm from my voice. "So who's June, really? Does she know who you are?"

"No." Shae shrugs her shoulders, not giving up much. I raise a skeptical eyebrow, and Shae continues. "She's part of an organization here that helps with supervised independent living until Caden turns eighteen."

I return her shrug, thinking of the gun I found. It makes no difference to me whether Shae's lying about June or not. She's not my target. "Is Caden here?" I ask abruptly.

Shae's face is expressionless but her body is poised, anticipating an attack. "I know why you're here, and I can't let you take him back," she says.

"You don't know anything," I snap, bristling. "And I'm not a little girl anymore. You don't get to make decisions for me or tell me what I can and can't do."

"You don't understand—"

"That's what you said when you left. I'm older now. Try me," I say, folding my arms across my stomach and tapping a booted foot against the flagstone path. My fingers close comfortingly around the handle of a blade that's tucked into the waistband of my second-hand black fatigues. I don't trust anyone, far less Shae, who's deceived more than her share of people.

She stands, both hands in the air, and I back away a couple steps in instinctive response. "If you take him back, they're going to kill him. The Vectors looking for him have drawn the attention of the Guardians on this side. We don't have a lot of time. I have to take him somewhere safe. All I'm asking is for you to trust me."

"Trust you?" I sputter and laugh at the same time. "Like that's going to happen."

"You think you can stop the Vectors? There's a dozen of them within hours, less even, of finding us. Where do you think I was? I was fighting them, trying to lead them *away* from Caden. They're coming here, Riven. For him. And for you."

"I can take care of myself."

"And Caden? Can you take care of him?" Shae says staring at me as if she's trying to anticipate what I'm going to say. "He's a prince, unless you've forgotten."

I stare back. My voice is cold. "No, he isn't. He's more than that, Shae. You know that. He has a purpose. And you must know why I have to take him back. Cale is dying."

"Then they will both die. What you're doing is suicide."

"Don't you even care that your home is about to be at the mercy of a madman if Caden *doesn't* go back? What's the alternative? That he stays here and lives out a life he wasn't meant for, while everyone we know, everyone we love, dies or is enslaved by Murek? You know how unstable the king's brother is."

Shae sighs, the movement rippling wearily through her whole body, and interrupts my tirade. "Riven, he doesn't know."

"What?"

"Caden doesn't know anything about who he is or where he came from, none of it. He had very little memory of his life in Neospes and what little he did remember, Leila erased. She never meant for him to go back, you know. They were going to kill him."

"It doesn't matter," I snap. "He's needed there now."

Shae sits on the step again, her entire body slumping forward. Pain spasms across her face from the movement.

"Not that I care, but what happened?" I ask, nodding at the gashes on her arms.

"Two Vectors. I took care of it." She sighs and leans against the railing. "Did our father send them?"

I spit on the ground and nod. "Yes. He's with them, but you knew that already, didn't you?" I see the flare of pity in her eyes—meant for me—but I ignore it. "Look, you haven't been back to the city in years. Neospes is on the brink of war, and more people will die if we allow Murek to take control of the monarchy. He has an army of Vectors at his back and he means to control our world, and this one, too, I expect. It's why I have to help Cale. He's got no one he can trust, and he *has* to live, or we all die."

"I know more than you think," Shae says. "But sacrificing Caden isn't the answer, Riven. I took an oath to protect him. What makes his life worth any less than Cale's? Or yours? Or mine? This is the only place he's safe."

I take a deep breath, trying to calm the sudden rush of anger swirling inside of me at her blindness. "Safe for what, Shae?" I growl. "Caden has a purpose, one which he is bound to fulfill. I took an oath, too, to protect our *king*. You and I both know that this is what he was born for."

"You're wrong. Leila left because she loved her son too much to let him die."

"Cale's her son!"

"Caden is, too."

"He's not her son," I mutter doggedly.

We're at an impasse, staring at each other with stubborn fury. I'm not above using force to get my way, but Shae's just taken out two Vectors. Alone. I'm not about to make any rash and stupid decisions about her combat skills or apparent exhaustion. The silence hangs between us like an impenetrable wall as we stare at each other across the five feet that may as well be an abyss between us. After a few tense minutes, Shae clears her throat.

"Do you remember that day? When I left?" she asks, and I give the barest of nods. It's a day etched into my memory so deeply that I couldn't forget it if I tried. "I wanted to take you with me, but you wouldn't go," she says. Her laugh is empty. "You remember what you called me?"

*Defector.*

She doesn't have to say it; we both know what I said.

"That was the day I realized that you were your father's daughter. He robbed you of anything close to love," Shae says. "You chose to stay with him out of fear of him rather than out of love for me. He owned you then, and he owns you now."

"I am nothing like him," I grit out. "*No one* owns me."

"He used to say that I could never be a killer, because I was too emotional. Said I *loved* too much. How can someone love too much? He said I was too much like Mom. Soft. I proved him wrong, even though I died a little bit inside every time I took a life." At Shae's words, my eyes feel like there's sand behind them, and a boulder settles in the pit of my stomach. "But he was right about you, wasn't he? The stone-cold sister? The one who wouldn't be torn by emotion, the one who kills without feeling a thing? Servant to the monarchy . . . obeying orders without question. He's made you into their killing machine. So what? You're going to kill me now, *Riven*?"

Her words are like daggers, hardening every bit of resolve I'd lost over the last few weeks. Living in this world has softened me, made me forget who I am. But Shae's right. I am a killer. And I obey. It's what I do.

She wanted stone-cold? I step forward and pull a bone-handled sword from the underside of my backpack so that it lies flush down the length of my thigh. Her eyes narrow at my blatant challenge.

"If I have to," I say. "I'm taking him whether you like it or not, Shae. He is nothing more than a target to me; you said it yourself." I stare at her with cold eyes, feeling nothing but icy purpose. "You chose your path and I chose mine. And you are nothing but an obstacle that I am more than willing to remove."

Shae pulls herself to her feet, a slender double-edged sword materializing in her left hand. "So be it," she agrees. "But you know I can't let you do that."

"Can't let her do what?" a familiar voice calls out. Caden is striding up the driveway with his bag of gear slung over one shoulder and carrying a trophy. I turn around, twisting my hand in a backwards motion so that my blade slides under my backpack into its sheath. His timing couldn't have been worse. Or maybe it's a blessing in disguise.

"Nice trophy," Shae says, discreetly pocketing her own blade. "You win again?"

Caden dumps his bag on the grass and tosses the trophy on top of it with a grin and a thumbs-up. "You're back," he says to Shae with raised eyebrows. "Visiting?"

"Checking in."

"My warden," Caden says to me still grinning. The cocky side-ways smile reminds me so much of Cale that my breath hitches in my throat. I am beginning to hate these moments when I'm caught off guard, when the two of them start to merge into one, or worse, when Caden starts to become someone real on his own.

"Hey," I say tightly.

"Thought you were going to the meet?" he asks, his shoulder brushing mine.

"I know, but I got caught up, something with Charisma. I'll fill you in later," I say, flicking an eye over to Shae, who seems to be watching us both with more than a little curiosity. Without thinking, I step away, and the immediate quirk of Shae's eyebrow irritates me. I know exactly what it's meant to say, mocking my earlier words.

*Just a target?*

I return her look evenly.

Caden's gaze pans slowly from Shae to me, and back again. There's very little family resemblance between us, considering we're only half sisters, but we've been trained by the same people, a fact that's evident in the similar set of our shoulders and the stance of our feet. It's an environmental similarity, and obviously one that Shae hasn't lost, despite all her years here.

Belatedly noticing Shae's appearance, Caden walks past me and sits next to her. "You look like hell. What happened to you?"

Shae smiles, and it is a smile that I haven't seen in a very long time. "You should see the other guy," she jokes, and then says, "It's no big deal. I tripped over my own two feet. You know how clumsy I can be." She says those last words with a fleeting look toward me.

But they have already drawn me into a near-forgotten memory.

When we were little, Shae used to be constantly teased about how clumsy she was, tripping over furniture or nothing in particular. But the minute she got on the combat field, it was as if she transformed into the most graceful fighter. In the arena, no one could match Shae's skill. Rising quickly into the ranks of the elite, Shae's name became known by many, something that made her fall to disgrace—and our family's shame—even more noticeable.

I had to bear the brunt of it after she left, but it had only made me stronger and compelled me to outperform every other kid in my training classes. By the time I was twelve, I was put into elite training—the youngest ever—and at fourteen, the coveted rank of general was mine. Of course, that made no difference now. At Cale's request, barely two months after my inauguration, I'd left to find Caden.

Three years later, I'd finally found him. And her.

"That cut on your face looks nasty," Caden says, interrupting my thoughts. "June has some antibiotic cream that you should put on it."

Going into the house with Shae is not part of my plan. It's confined and I'm not as familiar with the layout as she would be. In hindsight, I realize that the bare and spartan room would have been hers. I should have known . . . its austerity and the clock set ahead like mine should have been dead giveaways. Instead, I'd been blind.

*Careless.*

Caden pokes his head around the front door. "You coming or what?"

I hesitate. The truth is, I feel much safer outside, even with the deepening twilight shadows already dappling the front lawn. Night isn't too far behind, but at least it's out in the open. But I don't trust Shae either, and I don't know whether she'd try to escape with Caden. Making a decision, I nod and walk up the porch steps.

Inside, while Caden cleans the cut on Shae's face in the kitchen, I sit at a stool beside the granite island separating us.

"So, Shae," I say casually, picking up an apple from a bowl on the countertop and biting into it. "You don't live here?"

Shae's eyes laser onto mine, but I keep my expression blank. "No. I go to college a couple hours away."

"Funny that Caden never mentioned you."

Caden laughs, pouring antiseptic cleaner onto a gauze cloth. "What's to mention? She's sour, unfriendly, falls down all the time, and gets very pissed when I talk about her to anyone, like she's some kind of secret agent. So I just pretend she doesn't exist. Works for everyone."

"Shut up, Caden," Shae says grimacing. "Ouch, ease up on that stuff, will you?"

"Stop being a baby," he shoots back and winks at me. "Shae's my unofficial warden. I swear she's got spies everywhere telling her my every move like I'm in witness protection."

"Caden . . ." Shae growls in warning.

I know that voice, but I draw the fire in my direction. "Seems pretty safe here from what I can tell." I grin at Caden. "Something you're not telling me? Like you're some kind of *Princess Diaries* royalty?" If looks could kill, I'd be incinerated, but I deliberately don't look at Shae.

Caden snorts and rolls his eyes. "I wish. No, Shae's just Shae. Super protective ever since my mom died." Shae looks like she's going to explode and starts to get up, but Caden pushes her back down onto the stool. "Look, you can't move while I do this, or it'll get all messed up and won't heal properly." I take another bite of my apple and watch as he deftly places tiny strips of surgical tape across the cleaned and medicated wound.

"How long have you guys lived here? With June?"

"Ten years next February."

"You've been here this whole time?" He shoots me an odd look, and I rush to clarify. "I mean, I thought you'd lived on the East Coast and moved around."

"We moved here after my mom died. I told you, remember?"

Now I'm confused. I'd tracked them across fifteen states in the past three years. And then it hits me. I've tracked *Shae* . . . the decoy, not them. He's been here all along living a normal life while she's been everting back and forth to throw anyone looking for them off the scent. Our eyes meet and I know that my guess is right.

I frown. Everting so many times at what cost? Genetically, human bodies aren't built to jump back and forth. Our cells start to break down, even with the pills reinforcing them.

"Cade, do you know if June's got any more of those painkillers in her medicine cabinet? My leg's killing me," Shae asks, glancing at Caden and breaking our connection.

"The ones for your migraines?" he asks. I shoot Shae a sharp glance but she ignores me.

"Yeah."

"Think so. Be right back."

As Caden leaves the room, Shae and I stare at each other across the granite divider. The seconds stretch into silent agonized minutes. Migraines are the first sign of brain degeneration. Despite her betrayal, I wouldn't want anyone to suffer that kind of pain.

"Shae . . ." My voice almost fails me. "How long?"

"A few months ago. Don't worry. I'm not going anywhere just yet." She leans forward, pressing her palms on the counter and correctly interpreting my frown. "And I can still take you out if I have to," she warns.

"If you can't protect him, then at least give him a chance with me."

"I *can* protect him," Shae says. "It could be years before anything more happens."

"But it could be less."

The onset of migraines is the beginning of the end; the only unknown is exactly how long it takes before the appearance of brain tumors and the fatal seizures, like the one that had taken Leila, Caden's mother. Sometimes it could be years, other times weeks. It depends on physiology.

"He doesn't belong there, Riv," Shae says.

"Don't call me that," I snap, ignoring the stab of hollowness in my belly. "Once I get him to Cale, we will be safe."

"Safe?" she hisses. "You're taking him to his death."

"Shae, we've been through this; it's what he was born for. If you die, he's not going to survive much longer. Neither will Cale. At least let Caden fulfill his purpose." I move slowly around the granite island until I'm standing right in front of her. I grasp her shoulders gently. "I know what you promised Leila," I say. "But she made a promise, too, seventeen years ago. If you don't let me do this, they're both going to die. Caden here and Cale there. At least if I can get Caden back, one of them has a fighting chance to live. Can't you see that?"

Shae's eyes are wet with tears. "What if that chance belongs to Caden?" she whispers. "What gives us the right to choose who lives and who dies?"

"Shae, that choice was made years ago."

"But he's different. I know you've seen it, *felt* it. I saw the way you looked at each other today."

My fingers tighten of their own volition in denial, digging into the flesh of her arms. "No, he isn't. He's nothing but a ghost."

I can feel her body flinch under my hands at my biting words. She squares her shoulders. "You and I both know that he's more than that. Caden is strong. He'll be fine with or without me," she says stubbornly.

I step back, releasing her, and walk to the other side of the island. I pick up my half-eaten apple and study the browning parts of the white flesh. My voice is almost a whisper.

"And if you die, how are you going to tell him? That he's from another *universe*? That you've lied to him for his whole life? What's he going to do if he comes up against a Guardian? Or worse . . . *Vectors*? His blood *and* Cale's blood will be on your hands."

"He doesn't have to know about—"

A loud crash and a scream from upstairs have us both bolting like a gunshot for the staircase. The fear on Shae's face is mirrored by the fear on mine, but her fear is rooted in losing Caden. Mine is tied to losing Cale. I take the steps up two at a time with Shae hot on my heels, weapons already in hand and prepared for the worse.

But what awaits us is more deadly than either of us can ever imagine. The odor is unmistakable; it's the smell of death.

Blood, breath, and bones inside of me fall prey to an instant crippling fear.

The Vectors are here.

# 6

# DEAD MAN WALKING

"HOW MANY?" SHAE asks me.

We eye each other in silent truce for the moment, our only objective to see Caden safe despite our polar opposite endgames.

"At least two, I think," I say. Her eyes widen and I can see that she's thinking about running in there no matter the cost. "Wait," I whisper urgently. "Can you get around to the bathroom that connects your room to Caden's?" Shae nods. "Okay, on my mark, in three." She nods but hesitates. I place a hand on her fingers and squeeze. "Don't worry, Shae; they won't kill him. They have orders to take him back to Murek."

Shae shoots me a defeated smile, and I stare at the raw cuts on her hands for a second. Her fingers twist to squeeze mine, and a strange sensation chokes my chest. We both know that she's not at her fighting best, and if things take a turn for the worse, there's a very real chance that she'll die. The choking feeling spreads to my neck and paralyzes every muscle in my face. Time slows between us, and suddenly it's as if the years—

and the betrayal—separating us no longer exist. My numb fingers tighten around hers.

"Wind at your back, sister," Shae says. My eyes are burning so fiercely that they feel like they will catch fire at any moment.

"And at yours," I choke out.

But she's already gone in a whisper of movement. I suffocate the useless emotion inside of me, knowing it will only help my enemy, and eye the time carefully on my watch. I know that Shae's doing the same. The seconds count down, and with a final short breath, I shove open the door. My just-drawn breath hitches at the scene before me.

I was wrong.

There are four of them. One's holding Caden in a choke hold, the others are staring at us with merciless, dead eyes. I haven't faced a Vector in years, and I'd forgotten how *normal* they seem. They look human: extra-large military-type people, but still people. But if you look more carefully, you notice things like the unnatural pasty pallor of their skin and the bluish tinge of their eyes . . . their very dead eyes. The Vectors aren't human. Not anymore.

"Riven," Caden wheezes. "Look out!"

I duck and spin just as one of the Vectors slides in my direction, swinging an electro-rod to my head, and skewer him with one of my blades. For a dead creature, it's incredibly agile for its size. It barely twitches from the impact, lunging toward me again. I spin and scissor my blades across its waist, seeing fabric and skin split apart. But there's no blood, only a brackish gray-blue fluid.

Out of the corner of my eye, I see that Shae has been cornered by the other two, but she's wielding her double-edged saber like it's a lethal piece of ribbon, wheeling and ducking with mesmerizing speed. I turn back to the Vector lurching toward me, its gashes healing before my eyes, but I follow Shae's lead and keep slicing, opening new wounds as quickly as the old ones regenerate.

Despite how easily I'd fought the boys earlier, with this Vector it's only a matter of minutes before I'm out of breath and my newfound confidence wavers. The training exercises I've been doing are woefully inadequate, child's play compared to fighting these things. Three years is a long time to lose my edge.

I grit my teeth—this is what I've worked for, what I was born for. Sparing a glance toward Caden, his body held paralyzed by the well-placed pincer grip of the Vector beside him, there's no way I'm going to give up. Not now.

Pain ricochets through me as the Vector's electro-rod catches me on the thigh, and I slam backward into another of the Vectors behind me. Without thinking, I clip my elbow backward, slamming into its head, before diving toward the first aggressor. Though I am far from out of shape, they are faster and smarter than I remember.

The one facing me seems to anticipate my every move, forestalling every turn and bend as if it can read my mind. I need to trick it somehow, take back the advantage. I swing my swords as if I'm possessed, spinning under the Vector's outraised arms until I see my opening.

"Game over," I hiss, slamming my heel against the back of its leg. The creature crumples to its knees, and I waste no time in crossing my arms together as hard as I can, the swords in each hand meeting to cleave the Vector's head completely off its shoulders. I watch, huge gulps of searing breath filling my chest, as it keels over with a sick clump.

Caden is watching us with horrified eyes, his gaze swinging from Shae back to me in disbelief. But he's the least of my worries right now. The other Vector is now holding him immobile on the shoulder with one hand while tapping into a handheld computer with the other. The Vector isn't concerned with any of us, its mission different from the others. I gasp, recognizing the device in its hands. It sets the coordinates and parameters for eversion.

"Shae, he's going to eve—" I begin turning toward Shae and freeze. The two Vectors have Shae up against the wall, barely a hair's breadth from killing her. Her face is covered in blood, old wounds reopened and new ones oozing red. Her eyes lock with mine and I can see the regret in the curl of her lips. My head's already shaking before I dart forward, arms raised and weapons out.

"No!" I scream. "Cease! That is an order."

To my utter disbelief, both Vectors stop, turning in dumb submission toward me. Shae's shock reflects my own. My brain is spinning. These must have been sent here before I defected and are still somehow programmed to obey my orders.

"Release her," I say quickly, not wasting a second. Shae slumps to the floor but still manages to swing her saber into the Achilles tendons of the one closest to her. Taking no chances, even before its body collapses, her sword is already buried in the back of its neck severing its spinal column. She's hurt badly. I can hear it in her labored breathing and see it in her eyes.

"Riven."

The soft voice behind me is a whisper of a warning, but the tiny hairs on the back of my neck are already standing at stiff attention. I turn to meet the eyes of the Vector restraining Caden whose attention had been on the eversion device. That attention is now riveted on me like a laser. Its eyes are a lightless black with the familiar blue halo surrounding the pupils.

But the similarities end there.

There's something different about this one, I can feel it deep in my bones. Like the others, its uniform is black, but there's a jagged swatch of red cloth across his chest in the shape of a crescent moon. Every part of me knows that it means something terrible.

"Kill them," it says in a guttural growl. "*That* is an order, soldier."

I blink. It's some kind of leader, then, a commander. The command is directed at the remaining Vector, but its stare remains focused on me. It's impossible. Vectors don't have tone. Tone infers functioning emotional capability, and they're dead. A shiver of cold dread runs down my spine.

*Aren't they?*

"Now!" it growls again.

But the remaining Vector is motionless, staring from me to him as if confused. Its programming must not have been overridden to counter a direct order from me, its last leader, even with an order from its new one. The window of opportunity is no bigger than a sliver, but I grasp it without a second thought.

"Kill it," I shout, jerking my head in the big commander Vector's direction.

It's all I can do to get out of the way as the Vector launches its considerable bulk toward its commanding officer. But within the blink of an eye, its body is flung back in our direction and crashes into a bookcase. Splintered wood peppers the air like wooden darts, and I shield my eyes instinctively, covering Shae's body with mine.

The big Vector is motionless, still holding Caden. It flicked its attacker off like a bothersome gnat with one finger.

"Again!" I scream at the fallen Vector. "Get up. Don't stop until it's destroyed."

Even as the words drop from my lips and the creature launches itself once more in silent submission, I pull a silver instrument shaped like a four-leafed clover from my boot and fling it toward Caden. He's not the target; the fingers pinching into his shoulder are. My aim is true and the star clips off the Vector's fingers cleanly.

"Caden, get down!" I yell, but he doesn't move even though thick grayish blue fluid is spraying into his face from the Vector's severed fingers. I gnash my teeth.

"Go . . ." Shae wheezes as if sensing my hesitation to leave her unprotected, ". . . be fine for a minute."

There's no time to think as I take Caden down in a football tackle that would rival any in this world's Super Bowl, rolling underneath the desk just as the two Vectors smash into the floor beside us. Even though the commanding Vector is pummeling the one below it, its stare is still fixated on me as if I'm the one it's punishing. I rip my eyes away with effort and kick it in the side so that the one fighting for us gets some leverage to twist over and above it.

"You hurt?" I ask Caden urgently.

"No," he rasps. "But my legs feel funny. What did that thing to do me? What *is* that thing? Are they going to kill us?" His voice is rising with every second and I can see the terrified panic building in his eyes as they dart toward the two grappling on the other side of the desk.

"No. You're going to be fine," I say. "Can you get over to Shae?" He nods and I squeeze his hand. "Pull her into the bathroom if you can and close the door. Here, take this." I don't look at him. I don't want him to see the panic in my eyes. Instead, I shove one of the swords that had fallen to the ground into his hands and push him toward Shae. "Don't be afraid to use it."

I take a deep breath and turn to the two remaining Vectors. The one that obeyed me is not going to last much longer. It doesn't have much of a face and its ribs are concave in a way that suggests imminent fatality. It's only a matter of time before the nanobes inside of it stop communicating, and I need it alive for questioning. If it's loyal to me, there's no way I can let such a windfall go.

With all the strength I can summon, I kick the Vector commander in the face, hearing the crunch of bone as my blow dislocates its jaw. Blue liquid seeps down the side of its face as my boot tears away skin and tissue from its chin, exposing filed, jagged teeth. It turns toward me, a sick grin tugging the exposed tissue upward, and digs a heavily booted foot into the other Vector's chest until gray-blue fluid pools around his sole.

*Emotion*? Impossible.

But it *is* a grin . . . a horrible mockery of a grin. Vectors are inanimate, robot-cell controlled hosts. They don't think for themselves, and they certainly don't smile.

But this one does.

"What are you?" I whisper as it twists its head in both hands to realign its neck, staring at me with a knowing expression. I have never felt such fear, not even when I was running for my life to escape Murek's guard.

"A general," it answers. "Like you."

"I am no general," I snap.

"Yes, you were a colossal failure, weren't you?"

"You don't know what you're talking about. You're a machine. You're dead." I don't know why I feel the need to defend myself against the poisonous words of this thing, but something about it reminds me of my father . . . judging me, even now.

"That's where you're wrong," it says. "Come home, Riven. Bring the boy. All will be well." The Vector bends its head in a conciliatory way, which only makes it seem more macabre without half its face, but I am mesmerized by its last words. And terrified.

"You don't want to kill him?" The thing wavers as if reading something on my face and I deaden my expression, but it's too late.

"No," it says. The word is a lie. There's no way they'd keep Caden alive. Murek wants Cale dead. It made sense to reason that they wanted Caden dead, too. Unless . . . "Why do you think I wouldn't kill this boy?" the Vector says, distracting my ugly train of thought. It holds a black-gloved hand up that's easily twice the size of mine. "It would be so easy," it says squeezing his fist.

"So why didn't you?" I hide the fear sliding around inside of me with bravado, but I know without a doubt that I can't trust anything this creature says. But I need to buy time . . . time to think.

"Orders are orders. I don't ask questions."

"Why are you different from the others?" I say. "How can you talk?"

"That is the question," the Vector says taking a step toward me. It's not aggressive, but I step back anyway and feel the bed frame against the back of my knees. I'm nearly trapped. The only way around the creature will be over the bed to the bathroom door or the window. "Your father created me after you left."

"Are you alive?"

That gruesome smile again. "More than the others. Less than you." Its cryptic words irritate me. It's as if the thing is playing some kind of game, one that I'm sure has no rules.

"Why would they make you?" I say. The Vector smiles again, and I can feel the bottom of my stomach drop even before it says the words. The sick pleasure on its face makes me want to retch.

"Because the Lord King is dead."

"You're lying."

Everything inside of me feels like it's disappearing—bones, blood, air—until I'm nothing but a shell collapsing upon itself. I can't even breathe. In slow motion, I fall back against the side of the bed, legs buckling, but my senses haven't completely deserted me, and out of the corner of my eye, I see the Vector reach for a long-handled spiked weapon. On autopilot, I scramble across the bed and shove myself to the other side just as it lifts the entire bed frame with one hand and smashes it against the wall. Chunks of wood and steel explode into the exposed parts of my body.

Before I can move, the Vector's spike swings toward my head, and I dive forward, my swords cleaving into its calves before rolling to its left. It barely deters the creature, and I fend off another attack, sparks flying as our weapons meet in mid-air. The vibration echoes painfully down my arm, and I can see a detached metal spike protruding from the flesh of my upper arm. My shirt is sticky with blood. I don't want to bleed to death by trying to pull it out, so I grit my teeth and leave it, hefting my other arm high while protecting my body with my injured arm.

Scanning the room, I notice that the bed frame is blocking the bathroom door and the nearby window is locked, which means precious extra seconds lost trying to unlock it. The Vector's bulk shields the bedroom door. The window is the only choice I've got, and if worse comes to worse, I can go through it headfirst and hope for the best. Either way, it seems that I'm facing the possibility of broken bones. I need to distract the creature to buy some time.

I lower myself into a crouch and sweep my leg out, but the Vector moves out of the way, fast for something of such size. I switch to words, hoping beyond hope that making it think will help slow it down.

"You know how I know you're lying? About the king?" It watches me like a bird toying with a worm half-submerged in the dirt. "Because people, important people, know about Caden. Cale's alive; otherwise, Murek would just forget about Caden and rule Neospes as he's always wanted."

I pause again, snaking my uninjured arm out to catch it across his left flank. Blue liquid seeps through its clothing and drips to the floor. Now we're even.

"Did he teach you to lie?" I continue my one-sided conversation, gaining confidence with each breath. "My father? He's very good at lying. After all, he convinced me to lead your kind. But he had a hidden agenda, didn't he?"

I spin and jab at my opponent's body, but it anticipates my movements this time and dodges, only to return a blow that stuns me senseless. Something wet and warm plasters my hair to my scalp, but I can barely feel it beneath the hot welt flowering against the side of my face. I spit a mouthful of blood to the floor and lean against the wall. My vision begins to blur as the Vector morphs into three separate beings, each wavering like smoke.

"That all you got?" I grit out, holding my sword across my body and praying that my shaking legs don't give out. The Vector pauses with another grin, as if sensing impending victory. My only comforting thought is that Shae and Caden are safe. She'll get what she wanted—Caden will never return to Neospes.

And I would have failed . . . in my promise to Cale. But if the Vector is right, then it won't matter either way. I stare into its dead blue eyes, and smile. "We will never let you take him."

"You have no choice, General," the thing says finally, removing the pocket device from his vest. "The boy will go back, and so will you, dead or alive. Your father wants you alive, of course. But Lord Murek has no preference. Regardless, you cannot stop me."

"But I can," a voice says, just as the sound of a cannon tears through the room. The Vector pitches forward as gunfire rips through its bulk, June's hollow-points doing what they're designed to do. It's a volley of bullets as Caden holds June's semiautomatic gun with shaky calm.

"Aim for the head, Caden," I try to shout, but my voice is barely a whisper as I feel myself sliding downward against the wall. "It'll only regenerate anywhere else."

But my words are lost beneath the sound of the exploding shells as the acrid smell of gunpowder fills my nose. I can feel my cells desperately trying to re-engage, when the incongruity of the situation hits me. Caden's the one protecting me. I want to laugh, but only a choked gurgle takes shape in my mouth as Caden empties round after round into the monster.

After what seems like an eternity, Caden flings the spent gun to the floor and brandishes the sword I'd handed him earlier. My eyes are on fire, but I have to see if one of the bullets has miraculously hit the Vector in the head or in the spine. It's the only way to stop them. But instead, I watch in horrified slow motion as the Vector pushes off the wall, provoked to the point of rage, and hurls its bullet-ridden body toward Caden.

"Caden, run!" It's all I can manage as black stars cloud my vision, unconsciousness threatening to sweep me away. But Caden ignores my warning, darting to the left and sliding to his knees, before reaching upward and back to pierce the sword's tip into the Vector's exposed back. The thing stumbles forward toward me, gurgling, as the sword lodges in its spine. Game over.

For a second, our eyes meet, and before I can even blink, the air in the room shimmers for a second, and without warning, the Vector disappears. The only memory of it is the red-hot end of Caden's sword, neatly lasered to half its size, and a blackened patch on the carpet. I'd forgotten about the eversion device.

The monster is gone. For now.

But it knows where we are, and it's only a matter of time before it comes back with more. It's my last thought before I slip into an unwelcome oblivion.

# ٦

# TRUTH BE TOLD

MY VISION IS swimming when I awaken. The room is dark, lit only by a single flickering candle. It hurts to focus, and I am confused because Cale and Caden are both in the room, staring at me with wide frightened eyes.

"You okay?" they ask me simultaneously. I lift my hand toward their faces.

"How is this possible?" I rasp. "Where . . . am I?"

"You're safe, Riven," they both say. "Drink this."

A cold rim touches my lips and I sip the liquid gratefully. My throat feels like it is on fire when the liquid touches it, but I feel better and less woozy as it goes down. A small silver flask dances at the edge of my vision. "What is that?"

"Shae said to give it to you."

"Shae's here, too?" My head is ringing, and the feeling that something isn't quite right slips around inside of it. "Cale?"

"No. Riven, it's me. It's Caden. Here, drink some more."

I sip obediently, the liquid tearing a path again into my insides. It's bitter but warming. I sit up, pushing my elbows back against the pillows. Surprisingly, it takes very little effort to move, despite the pain in my head that would suggest otherwise. The room starts to take shape, and as I grow more and more awake, I realize that nothing else hurts.

"Where am I?" I ask again after a couple minutes. "What happened?"

"Don't you remember?" Caden says. "Those things that attacked us?"

And then it's like a tidal wave as the events from earlier come rushing back. My fingers curl into the scratchy blankets on the sides of my legs.

"How long have I been out?"

"Only a couple hours."

"Where are we?"

Caden comes closer, and the metal cot dips as he sits next to me. "We're in the basement. It used to be a tornado shelter back in the early fifties. It's why Shae picked this house out of all the others. She's a bit of a Miss Doomsday, but I guess she was right." He nods over to the far side of the room that's still shrouded in darkness. "She's pretty hurt, but I gave her some stuff that June uses for head injuries. It's a mild sedative, too, so she's sleeping now. She didn't want to call 911."

No, Shae wouldn't; too many questions. I hobble over to where she's lying on a cot similar to mine and stare at her bloodied face. Caden has cleaned off some of the blood, but her injuries are starting to blacken and swell. She looks far worse for wear than I. My fingers drift to her neck, and I can feel a faint but steady pulse. Her breathing is shallow and wheezy. Caden has cut off the legs of her pants to bandage some of her wounds, but his efforts are amateur at best. It won't be long before her cuts become infected. And the migraines. . . . Those are the beginning of the end. The injector in my bag would help, but unless she gets real help from our doctors, it would only provide temporary relief at best.

"She doesn't look so good," I say.

"I used what we had." Caden's voice is apologetic. "Riven, we need to get her to a hospital."

"No." I shake my head emphatically. "No hospitals; too many questions that we can't afford to answer. They wouldn't be able to help her, anyway. I need to get my backpack. Does June have a medical kit upstairs?"

"Yes, but I don't even know how to use half the stuff June has in there. It's hospital-grade stuff."

"Then we're going to need to figure it out," I say flatly, resting my hand against Shae's hot forehead. "And fast." Infection has already begun to set in. I walk back to my cot, where Caden is still sitting, and squat to retrieve my boots.

"Riven," Caden asks quietly, "what were those things?"

I stare at him, wondering how after all these years Shae could have single-handedly protected him from ever coming up against them. I don't even know what she's told him, if anything at all. My guess is nothing. She's tried to protect him the only way she knew how—by keeping him in the dark, letting him have as normal a life as possible here with some kind of chance to be happy. Glancing over my shoulder at her sleeping form, I am unsure of what to say, but Caden is far from stupid, and he certainly isn't blind. I settle for something near the truth.

"They're called Vectors, a government experiment. Reanimated corpses."

"Reanimated? Like zombies?"

I shake my head, a faint smile at his childlike response curling my lips. "Zombies are dead, period. And they aren't real. Vectors are very real dead bodies, controlled by nanobes. Tiny little microscopic robots that operate inside the hosts."

"Microscopic *robots*?" His expression is skeptical. "You're kidding, right?" I shoot him a look and raise an eyebrow. "Is that even possible?" he asks.

A dozen mocking responses slip to my lips, but I stifle them. I lace up my left boot and start on my right. "Not everything's impossible. Remember the blue fluid?" Caden nods. "That's nanoplasm . . . the robots."

"I don't get it; why dead bodies?"

"Easier to control than live ones, I expect," I say bluntly, and grab my weapons, walking over to the steel door. "How do you open this thing?"

Caden grabs my arm. "Where are you going? Those things, the Vectors, could be up there. What do they want, anyway?"

I try to keep the fear slinking around deep inside my belly out of my eyes.

*They want you.*

"I need to check the bodies to see if there's anything we can use. And Shae needs something I have in my backpack. I'll be back; just sit tight." I watch as he unbolts the heavy door. "Lock it behind me. When I come back, ask me who our physics teacher is, okay?"

"Okay," he says, squeezing his fingers, his hand still on my shoulder. "Be safe, Riven."

I climb the basement stairs carefully, hearing the heavy steel bolts fall into place behind me. The entire entrance has been reinforced with some kind of thick metal, and I trail my fingers across the shiny, cool surface. Shae has definitely made sure to be prepared for something. The door at the top leads into the kitchen. It's a narrow trapdoor-like entrance that I'd never noticed before, not any of the previous times I'd been in their kitchen. It, too, is heavily reinforced, with special seals and gaskets. There are no visible handles for re-entry, so I stick a nearby cookbook in the gap. I have no idea if it will hold or not, but it's the best I can come up with.

It's quiet, which isn't necessarily a good thing, so I'm cautious when I make my way back upstairs. The room is a shambles, furniture tossed and broken, blood and blue fluid spattered everywhere, with three dead creatures in various stages of decay gracing the floor. The smell is putrid, like a wall of rotting human compost curling against me, and I feel the responding bile rise in my throat. That's the thing with Vectors—when the nanoplasm dies, the bodies decompose rapidly. My father had once said that it was a disgusting but necessary element of control. As a society, we'd learned that the hard way.

Trying not to breathe and careful not to touch any of the fluid, I methodically check each of the Vectors for weapons and anything else of use. I pocket an electro-gun, some rods, a couple metal golf balls that I'm sure are some kind of high-tech explosive devices, as well as any wireless communications headgear I can find. I'm onto the third in less than five minutes when I hear a faint sound. My weapons are at the ready before I'm even in a standing position. I tiptoe to the bedroom door, ears straining, but everything is quiet. I must have imagined the sound.

The low whine behind me catches me off guard and I swing around to an empty room until I realize that the sound is coming from the third Vector. It's not dead! I pull what's left of its head to face me, wincing at the stench of its wounds. If it's not dead, it will be soon.

"Soldier," I say urgently. "Can you hear me?" No response. I tug on its jacket and its head lolls forward. "Answer me. That's a direct order."

Its uninjured eye cracks open and the entire pupil is covered in pale bluish ooze. I doubt it can even see me, but somehow it's registering my voice.

"Who sent you?"

The Vector's eyes roll back in its head. "Is Cale dead?" There's nothing, and I rephrase, desperate now. "Is the *Lord King* dead?"

The Vector's head moves slightly from left to right. It's a no! My relief is tangible, and I sink back onto my haunches. It's more than I could have hoped for. "What does my father want?"

A single outstretched finger points to me. The Vector's eye rolls back into its head, and its mouth opens and closes haphazardly, as if choking. The hand thumps to the floor. Within seconds, its head lolls to the side, and the pungent smell intensifies as its internal organs degrade and liquify. Swallowing past the sourness in my mouth, I release the jacket and finish my search of its body, pocketing a pair of infrared glasses and a silver pearl-like earpiece communications device.

I move to leave but pause at the door, thinking ahead. I don't have a plan in place, but if any of us are to make it back to Neospes, we will need clothing. The Vector's uniforms are designed to keep their bodies protected and are made from a rare type of engineered fabric-like armor, which also provides warmth and heat depending on weather conditions, both of which are unpredictable in Neospes. It would be stupid to leave them.

I frown at the task at hand but move quickly before I have time to think about what I'm doing. In no time at all, I have three sets of uniforms peeled off of the Vectors' bodies. They stink, but I can't help that. I put them along with the weapons in Caden's fencing bag and sling it over my back.

Now for the medical kit.

At the door, I glance back into the room. Looking at their naked, decaying flesh is far more repulsive than seeing them clothed. Curved ribs and sharp hip bones protrude against their milky, opaque skin with grotesque prominence: the stuff of nightmares. Blue veins traverse their near-transparent skin to route the nanoplasm from their artificial central nervous systems to the rest of their bodies, like a ghostly blue spider-web. They barely look human now. Instead, they look like rotting, dead wraiths. I shake my head, swallowing thickly—the Vectors are true abominations of my culture.

The sound of the front door jerks me out of my thoughts.

"Hello? Caden? Anyone home?" It's June's voice. She must have come home early. I glance down at my filthy shirt and grab one of Caden's clean T-shirts off the dresser, shrugging into it. "What is that horrific *smell*?"

"Hey, June," I call out, taking the steps down three at a time. "Sorry, we were doing an experiment for bio. Went bad. I wouldn't go up there if I were you for at least ten minutes." The last things I need her seeing are the three dead bodies in her house that look like something out of a science fiction movie. I fake an embarrassed grin and offer her an apologetic look.

"Why am I not surprised?" she says slowly, after glancing with narrowed eyes to the stairs before putting her keys and bag on the counter. I hesitate—I still need to get the medical supplies.

"June, we were looking for your . . . medical bag?" I ask in as casual a manner as I can manage.

"Why?" So much for putting anything past her as her eyes meet mine, immediately full of concern. "Are you hurt?"

"Nothing major," I say quickly. "I hurt my leg fooling around with Caden's foils earlier. I'm worried that it will get infected." It's not an outright lie, as one of the Vectors caught the back of my calf, but it's not like I've paid much attention to it with everything else going on.

"Well, let me just wash up and I'll take a quick look. My bag's in my office."

"I'll get it," I say, and all but sprint to June's office. I grab the bag and a couple of the blankets laying on her couch, and go back to the kitchen where she's still washing her hands. June stares quizzically at the blankets and the medical bag in my arms, and her eyes flick to mine. She dries her hands slowly, her gaze drifting between Caden's gear bag, the blankets, and me. Then her eyes flit to the staircase.

"What's going on, Riven?" Her voice is quiet, but there's something in it that raises the hairs on the back of my neck. It's an instinct that has kept me alive all these years. Her gaze settles on some fluid spattered on my collar peeking out over Caden's shirt. My stomach sinks. I can see something dawning in her eyes. Mistrust. Fear.

Gently placing the bag on the floor, I shift my balance from toe to heel and back again. There is no easy way to explain what I'm about to do, no lie that will make my actions any less terrible. She has to go down below, willing or not. And the fact is, I don't know June, which means I can't trust her. I edge closer and place my hands in the air in a nonthreatening motion.

Not missing a beat, June edges nearer to the kitchen island so that it stands between us. "Where is Caden?" she asks carefully.

"Caden's fine." My voice is inflectionless and slow. "You have to trust me, June. But I need your help. Shae's hurt."

"Shae?" A small furrow of worry shadows her brow, but she steels her expression almost immediately. "Shae's not home. She'd have called to let me know."

"She came back today," I say. "She had an accident."

A sharp glance. "And the dead Vectors upstairs?"

"What?" This time it's my eyes that rivet on hers. "What do *you* know about Vectors?"

She has taken me by surprise, and just as I'm considering leaping across the island and knocking her unconscious, a small voice has us both spinning around. Shae's leaning against the wall, her face a mottled collage of purples in the fluorescent lighting. Climbing the stairs from the secret room has her wheezing.

"June's a . . . Guardian, Riven," she gasps, besieged by a round of ugly sounding coughs. A trail of bloody spit runs down her chin as her body slumps down against the wall. I stare at June's impassive face, incredulous.

A Guardian! My hands grasp the hilts of the blades tucked into my waistband.

"*Was* a Guardian," June corrects, this time placing both her own hands in the air. She turns her head toward Shae, and I understand what she wants to do. I nod but don't release the handles of my weapons lying flat against my back. She cradles Shae's head against her. "Can you pass me the bag?" she asks me. Her eyes, so warm before, are now cold and expressionless.

Unconsciously, I steel my expression to equal hers. "You can't help her. She's everted too much. She needs more than the help you can give her."

"I can try."

With a glance at Shae, I push the bag across with the toe of my boot, ever cautious. I am the enemy here, the one who has come to take Caden back. I can't trust either of them, even after what happened with the Vectors.

"*Was* a Guardian?" I ask, after a couple minutes watching her take out several glass bottles from her bag. "I didn't think someone could stop being a Guardian."

"Well, I did."

"Why?"

"Look at you; you're just a kid," June says softly, not answering my question.

"I'm not a child," I snap back.

June's eyes are gentle. "But you are, Riven. Look around you, look at the *children* in your school: they're kids. The same age as you are. You're babies trained to kill." I can't stand the pity in her voice, and I bristle.

"They're useless and wouldn't last a minute in Neospes. Answer the question, June."

She gives me a long, searching look as if she's trying to see inside my head. "I didn't believe in executing innocent people . . . innocent kids." Now it's my turn to stare at her. "The Guardians honor a code to protect the fabric of the universe," June continues. "You know what would happen if people were to jump back and forth, don't you?" It's a rhetorical question, so I remain silent. "The threat of infection, of disease, is of course the worst, not to mention altering the course of a civilization's future. We honor an agreement between the worlds to protect each side from the other . . . more so to protect this world from the greed of yours. Eversion was never meant to be permanent. It was a mistake to let it go this far, to create an algorithm that allows abominations like the Vectors to come here."

"What do you mean, it was a mistake?"

June answers my question with an equally blunt one of her own. "Why do you think Murek wants Caden so badly?"

"I don't know." It's not a lie. I have many theories but none of them strike me as accurate. The truth is I have no idea why he wants Caden, especially if Murek wants to rule Neospes. Getting rid of him would be the easiest thing to do, after Cale is out of the way. It makes no sense that he would want him so badly. "So why does he?"

"Pass me the blankets," she tells me, and I comply automatically. She makes Shae, who keeps slipping in and out of consciousness, more comfortable on the floor. I glance at my watch, knowing that each second we remain here becomes more and more risky. June sends a sidelong glance in my direction and continues speaking while sticking a thermometer into Shae's mouth. "It is a secret that many would kill to protect." She pauses as if assessing whether to tell me or not, and I wait, silent. Nothing prepares me for the next words that come out of her mouth. "Caden, like Cale, is a hybrid. A product of both universes."

"That's impossible," I shoot back. "I may not know Murek's endgame, but I do know what happens to any progeny that comes out of any union between universes. They are abominations and are all to be disposed of . . . by you, the Guardians, and the Vectors." I can hardly keep the vitriol out of my voice. "It's the law. You track them, and the Vectors eliminate them."

June is calm. "It's true. Caden's mother was from this world. She never returned, because of her children. It was only when Caden was in danger that she came back, but she couldn't survive. Her immune system had become too weakened to protect her. And that is the sole reason I stopped being one of them. Caden was an innocent child. And Leila, too. . . ." She trails off.

"I don't get it. Why do you care about either of them?"

After another searching look, June sighs. "We grew up together. She was like my sister. My first mistake was to tell her what I was, and from then on, she couldn't let it go. We were barely your age, but it consumed her to the point of obsession. My second mistake was that she everted there because of me . . . all because I was careless and told her in the first place.

"She went so far as to major in quantum mechanics at school, and even though I wouldn't tell her anything I knew—I was terrified of the consequences—she was determined to find a way. And she did. That was the night she almost got herself killed trying to evert using some home-designed calculation that she must have stolen from my notes somehow. She almost succeeded, too, but in the end, her body couldn't take the force and started to collapse on itself, half stuck in this world, half of it in yours. I panicked, and instead of going to my father as I should have for help, I everted us both to Neospes." She glances at me, breaking off to place a cold compress on Shae's head after cleaning off the remaining blood on her face. I keep my face composed despite my racing thoughts.

"Your father saved her. Her injuries were too great for us to return, and by the time she was well enough to make the jump back, it was too late. The Lord King was fascinated by her, and then she got pregnant. That was the last time I saw her until she came to me ten years ago with Caden." June shrugs. "How could I say no to what she was asking? For help. For protection. It was my fault she went there in the first place. I broke the law, and she was the one who paid the price. I owed her."

"But she's from *here*," I say.

"The Lord King of Neospes doesn't answer to the law. He forbade her to return."

I frown to cover my sense of shock at what she is telling me about Cale, about Cale's father . . . about who his mother is. I can't get my mind around it.

"That's a large debt," I say for lack of anything else. June shrugs again, her lips twisting in a sad, wry smile.

"It is what it is."

Despite my shock, her story rings true as I think back to all of the times I'd seen Cale's mother. She always seemed so odd to me, as if her mind was always somewhere else, like she didn't quite fit in with everyone else in Neospes. She used to wear these long, flowing, brightly colored dresses—custom-tailored, Cale had once told me—instead of the standard black or gray tunic and leggings that most of us wore. I'd always thought the dresses fanciful and strange. And now I know—she had never belonged there at all.

"Did Shae tell you anything about me?" I ask June abruptly.

"No," she says, checking Shae's eyes with a thin instrument. "She didn't have to. I realized what you were after the clinic."

My eyes narrow. I voice the words pounding in my head. "What I was?"

"A soldier of Neospes."

"And yet you still trusted me with Caden?" I couldn't help the derision in my voice.

"Not at first—I wanted to keep you close—but then I saw something there . . . something about the way you were with him. And he with you. I thought you cared about him. But I was wrong, wasn't I?"

My teeth grind together, and what escapes my lips is little more than a snarl despite the unfamiliar tug in my chest her words provoke. "You *are* wrong. I don't give a damn about him. Caden is a target, nothing more."

"Riven?"

We both turn at the quiet voice behind us. The betrayal on Caden's face hits me like a slap. I meet his eyes and drop them just as quickly. I don't know how long he's been standing there, but I know it's been long enough for him to hear my last few words. I sling my backpack across my chest as if it's some kind of shield, a distraction maybe, and rifle through its contents until I find what I am looking for. I slide the silver case toward June. I won't need it anymore—when I return to Neospes, I won't be coming back.

"Give her this. It will help." I stand, slowly stretching my legs. I nod toward the stairs and grab the bags of gear I've piled together before leaning over the gas stove in the middle of the kitchen island to tuck one of the metal golf balls that I'd found on one of the dead Vectors in the middle of the grate. I'm business now, emotion tucked deep. "More of them will come, if they're not here already. We need to move and seal the door. Either you come down with me or you can stay here to greet them. One way or another, there's not going to be much left up here. It's your call."

I don't look at Caden as I push past him to the trapdoor above the basement stairs. Truth is, I can't even look at him. My curiously burning eyes won't allow it.

# UNDERGROUND

BY THE TIME I've carried Shae down the stairs along with a few extra supplies that June's thrown in, I've almost forgotten that Caden's even there. But I feel him staring at me, with heavy thoughtful glances that make me far more unsettled than if they were filled with anger. June has gone quiet as well, but I expected that. Knowing what she knows, I'd be the last person she would ever fully trust, but still, there's an uneasy understanding between us that at the moment we both need each other.

"Where does this lead?" I ask her, noticing another steel door that opens to a dark tunnel behind it.

She stares at me before answering and throws me a ratty map. "Couple miles underground. This tunnel forks to the hospital and to an abandoned building near Horrow." She jabs at the map I've opened. "See all the tunnels? There's an entire web of them down here, most of them collapsed and unusable. Used to be a safe house for an old underground military base back in the forties," June adds, noticing my expression as

I peruse the piece of paper. "It's why Shae chose it." She moves over to check on Shae. "She's looking better," she murmurs more to herself than to me.

"It won't last," I blurt out before I can stop myself. I tuck the map into my back pocket. "She's everted too much already. Her brain can't take the pressure."

"What pressure?" The low voice belongs to Caden. He's sitting on the cot I was lying on earlier, pretending to sort through the gear in his fencing bag. "What does *everted* mean?"

I pause for a beat before answering him. "Ever heard of the bends?"

"Decompression sickness? Like when you come up too fast from a deep depth and pressurized gases are released into the body too quickly?"

I have to fight the instant urge to eyeroll. Caden's so technical even with the little things. "Exactly. Well, it's like the bends, only it starts in the brain. Then it becomes physical because humans aren't built to evert"—I spare a glance at Shae's twitching form, knowing she can still hear me—"to jump between universes. Our bodies are too frail, and when they start to break down, they become susceptible to infection and disease." June's fists are clenched at her side, her eyes unreadable. "It's why the Guardians were put in place. To stop any contamination."

"That makes no sense. Guardians? Contamination?" Caden says, lurching to his feet, interrupting my quiet words. "Listen to yourself. People don't *jump* between universes!"

I shake my head and amend my earlier thought. He may be good with the little things, but when it comes to the big picture, he can be pretty obtuse. "Where did you think those things came from, Caden? From the zoo? They're from somewhere else, a world just like this one, only far, far worse."

"No," he says. "How is that even *possible*?"

"A lot of things are possible." I glare at June. "Didn't you tell him anything?"

"We didn't have to," June says. "Until you got here."

I stiffen at her tone, but Caden moves to stand in front of me. "What are you talking about? What haven't they told me, Riven?"

"Get out of my face, Caden. I mean it." I can hear the desperation in his voice even in the face of his bravado, but there's nothing I can say. Telling him anything at all means that I'd have to tell him why I'm there in the first place . . . that I'm as bad as the Vectors . . . that June is right about me. I push past him, pretending to study the crates of food along the wall. "I thought you were into all of this sci-fi stuff? All those DVDs in your room about stargates and whatnot? You're the genius; you figure it out."

"Those are movies." Caden's words are slow and deliberate. "They're made up, you know. Science fiction?"

"More like science fact."

The only sound in the room is the shallow hiss of Shae's breathing. Caden is staring at me, disbelief, confusion, and anger written all over his face. I'm not surprised. When Cale first told me about the existence of this world, I thought he was been playing me. But in the end, I understood that technology and physics theory had made it not only plausible, but also possible. And the universe was far wider than any of us really knew. Cale speculated that hundreds of other universes existed, but ours was one of the few to come into parallel contact with another.

I throw my palms into the air and raise an eyebrow. Caden faces my challenge with narrowed eyes, and I can see his mind ticking through the probabilities. "Even if it were possible," he says grudgingly, "are you saying that Shae—my *cousin*—is sick because she jumped from this world to another universe and back?"

"Yes. That's exactly what I'm saying." I gesture at myself. "She everted, just as I did. And just like June, once upon a time." Caden rocks back onto his heels, his face as white as a sheet, staring from June back to me as if we're ghosts. I know I'm being blunt, but I don't have time to sugarcoat secrets that Shae and June had concealed from him. "And she's not your cousin. She's your warden. Your word, not mine."

"Are you serious, right now? I was kidding when I said that."

"Well, I'm not. Look, I don't care if you believe me, or think we're on the *USS Enterprise*, or think you're dreaming. More of those things are going to come, and I need to think for a second without having to explain the nuts and bolts of quantum physics theory to you. Think about it for half a second and you'll see that it's not as improbable as it seems." I open the duffel bag and lay out all of the devices I took off the Vectors. I'm so rattled that I can't help myself when I pick up one of the golf balls and thrust it into Caden's face. "Does this look like any technology you've ever seen? No? It's not from here. None of us are, except for June." I stare him in the eyes, my words like bullets.

"What are you saying? That *I'm* not?"

I turn to June, who's staring at me with a clenched jaw. "Tell him."

June sighs but doesn't shy away from the task. "She's right, Caden. What she says is true."

"No. No, that's impossible."

"It's true, Caden," June says. "Shae would tell you the same."

"So you lied to me? All this time?" Caden hisses to her before spinning to walk away and then twisting back around in the same step. "Were you ever going to tell me?" June doesn't answer, but her expression clearly says that they hadn't planned to. "I don't believe this," Caden mutters. "This is insane."

"Believe it," I say flatly just as Shae turns heavily on the bed to face us, gasping. June was right. She's looking better after the injector, but she's clearly still in a lot of pain.

"I'm sorry, Cade," she wheezes, ". . . my fault."

Caden turns toward me, with a measured glance at Shae's tortured expression. His eyes are gentle. "Still, it doesn't make sense. Even if I believed you, then why would Shae endanger herself, knowing the risks of doing it over and over? That she'd . . . die?"

I can't help the twist of my lips nor the snarl that slips from them. "To protect you."

June is already on her feet at my tone, her body bridling and ready to defend Caden. I unclench my jaw and try to breathe the spiraling rage out of my body. June feels no such self-control and she's in my face before I take two breaths.

"It's not his fault! That was Shae's cho—"

The explosion takes us by surprise, even though I was the one who'd left the gas stove burning in the kitchen, and we're all slammed to the ground in different directions. Pain rockets through my head and along my sides as I thump against the steel door I've been standing next to. Despite the intense throbbing in my head, I jump to shaky feet. Years of training force me to do an automatic check of myself for injuries.

The Vectors are back.

They'd be the only things that could have triggered the gas. Everting generates minute pockets of electricity, but for some reason when the Vectors do it, the electrical fields are bigger . . . big enough to ignite a gas-filled room. The golf balls would have done the rest, and no doubt there won't be much left of the bodies, or anything else aboveground, for that matter.

A hazy memory drifts through my head—now I remember why the golf balls are called cleaners. Hot enough to incinerate bones and liquefy metal, such that anything in their path would be completely vaporized. The heat from the fire diffuses through the heavy trapdoor despite its thickness.

"What the hell was that?" Caden grunts, following my lead to stand on shaky legs.

"A cleaner. One of those silver balls." I dust the grit from my clothes and blink the soreness from my eyes. A glance in Shae's direction confirms that she's unhurt; I can hear her labored breathing over the ringing in my ears. "We need to move. It won't be long before they find that door. And they will. Murek won't stop now."

"Who's Murek?" Caden says.

"A dictator." I toss a pack toward him, hard. "Get this on. Take only what you need."

"Where are we going? We can't leave. What about school?" The inane question throws me for a second and I stare at him. He reddens and adds, "Shae said—"

"School's out, Caden. And I'm in charge, not Shae."

I know he's confused, but school is probably a comforting routine. I bring myself back to the task at hand, a part of my brain belatedly realizing that June hasn't gotten up.

"June, you okay?" In the seconds that it takes to turn around, the quiet sense of knowing is already like a shiver across my neck. Shae, for her part, is staring at June's inert body a few feet from where she's now sitting. The antidote injector has done its job—despite her bloody clothing and the unexpected force of the explosion, Shae looks nearly back to normal.

"June's dead," she says.

Her voice breaks the silence and my sudden inability to move. Within seconds, I am at June's side with Caden not far behind me, and I gently pull her body toward me. She's been thrown against something sharp and her death was instant. The gash on her head is bloody, her sightless eyes wide open and looking right through me—questioning . . . judging even in death. Hastily, I close them and turn to Shae with a deep breath.

"Are you okay? Okay to go?" I ask her, not hiding the urgency in my voice. We don't have a lot of time.

She nods, distracted, and I can see that her attention is on Caden. The broken look in his eyes reminds me of someone with little experience with death, but my words fade before I can speak them. In my world, death is an expected companion—whether in our brutal history or a foray gone wrong outside the city wall—and I've seen more than my fair share of it. Instead, my fingers find Caden's and I squeeze them, suddenly conscious of Shae's stare that is fluttering like a moth between our hands and my face. I wrench my hand away as if his fingers are on fire.

"We need to go," I growl, removing June's map from my pocket and opening it next to Shae on a small crate beside the bed. "Have you been down all of these?"

Shae ignores me with a glare and pulls the blanket off her bed and tucks it carefully over June. I watch as she and Caden lift the body up to place it gently on the bed. Apart from the blood, June looks like she could be sleeping. Caden stands next to the cot as if he's in some kind of trance, and doesn't move until Shae grasps his shoulders with both hands, turning him to face her and shaking him.

"Caden, remember what I taught you—we take them with us in our hearts. Let her go, okay? There's nothing you could have done; it was just her time." Her voice is thready but grows stronger by the second as she pulls him into a tight hug. "We will always carry her with us."

The pressure behind my nose and eyes is sudden, like a blow to the head, at the sound of Shae's words, so achingly familiar. She told me the same thing when our mother died. The emotion flooding my body is hot and eviscerating. I swallow past the solid lump in my throat and meet Caden's wet eyes. He's staring at me over Shae's shoulder, and the moment is unending, the mirrored empathy in them acting like a salve on my ridiculous emotions. It is all I can do to tear myself away, grateful for the moment when Shae moves to break the silent and unexpected raw connection stretching between us.

I compose myself, digging my nails into clammy palms so hard that it stings. "Moving on," I repeat stonily. "The tunnels?"

"Haven't changed a bit, have you, Riv? Still as cold as ice."

"Occupational hazard," I toss back, smoothing the map on the crate. I'm clenching my teeth so tightly it feels like they will shatter at any moment. I can't look at Caden even though I know he, unlike Shae, is looking at me and seeing right through my bluster. Thankfully, he says nothing.

Shae kneels beside me and jabs at a spot on the map. "We're here." She traces her finger along a faded brown line. "We need to get to here. It's a long way, about twenty miles."

"That's not too bad," I say. On foot and injured, that distance would take about six hours, give or take some rest time for Shae. On my own, it'd be a couple hours max, but I've trained hard, running large distances across unfriendly terrain for years. Shae's still hurt, despite her brave rallying, and Caden . . . well, there's no way he can maintain my speed without any training.

Shae disrupts my thought process. "That's just the exit point of the tunnel. We still need to get to the Denver airport, which is at least another forty miles away. That's the closest eversion point. Aboveground, I mean," she adds. "There's a bus station not too far from where we get out. It's straightforward." I stare at her with narrowed eyes. It's the closest she's come to admitting that she'll trust me with Caden. She shrugs, understanding my skeptical glance, and jerks her head down toward her body, still wrapped in bloodstained bandages.

She doesn't have much choice. Without her, Caden only has me. And without me, he would be a sure thing for the Vectors. I can see the question in her eyes—whether I'll protect him—and there's only one answer I can give. I nod.

"Why can't we . . . evert from here?" Caden asks, interrupting our wordless exchange. "I mean, those things, the Vectors did, like Riven said. . . ."

"They're dead, remember?" Shae answers. "They're designed to evert when and where as necessary. We're not. It doesn't hurt them because their cells are already dead. We have to find certain areas where there's a zero point gravitational field so we can pass through with the least amount of physical and mental aftereffects."

"But what about you? You're sick already. Won't that be bad? I won't leave you, Shae. I can't. Not after . . ." Caden trails off to stare at June's body.

"Let's cross that bridge when we come to it," Shae says gently. "Right now, we need to get out of here with everything we can carry, and fast. Can you get the food packs off that shelf and the gear from the trunks over in the corner?"

"Where are we going?"

"Somewhere safe. I promise I will tell you everything, but for now, we need to get our gear together and get out of here, or we're not going to have that chance. Remember what I told you back in New York? We have to be ready to leave at a second's notice. Nothing's changed. It's the same."

"But that's back when I thought we were minors not wanting to get separated," he argues. "This is different. Isn't it?"

"Yes, and I promise I will explain when I can. Right now, we need to move."

Shae's become the leader I used to know; the confidence in her voice has Caden in automatic reaction mode. She pulls June's medical bag toward her, tugging two dark turtlenecks and two pairs of black cargos from a nearby box, which she places on the bed, and begins to undress. I'm startled at the mottled colors of her skin, the bruises from her earlier fight fading into a shocking kaleidoscope of purple, yellow, and black, interspaced with bands of red, dirty bandages. Her body, despite its damages, is wiry with lean, corded muscle. I watch as she deftly changes the dressings, smearing antiseptic cream across any open wounds.

"I don't heal as quickly as you do, remember?" Shae says with a wry smile, noticing my look. We'd always used to joke about that, my ability to heal quickly, and we'd always put it down to different fathers and the luck of genetics. I used to feel like a freak, but Shae was the one to help me see it for what it was—a gift, and one that I'd used to my every advantage in battle. "Here, these are for you," she adds, throwing one each of the turtlenecks and pants in my direction. "We're still close to the same size."

I catch it one-handed, looking away as she tugs on her clothes, irritated by her thoughtfulness. Instead, I concentrate on cleaning the blood and pale blue gore from my twin ninjata blades with gun oil until they're as spotless as mirrored glass. Both deadly Artok weapons, they were a gift from Cale. Skilled assassins, the Artok are a tribe from the East, and what's left of them live in Sector Seven in Neospes, one of the few areas on the periphery of the core. My mother's grandfather had been Artok. Cale liked the symbolism of it, and I liked his unexpected kindness.

I put the ninjatas carefully to the side and line up all the other items from my backpack on the floor—sleeping bag, rope, tools, blanket, a collapsible tent, emergency food packets, a survival kit with various first-aid items including the silver case with the anti-eversion injector, which I open; only three left out of the five slots on the cylinder.

Designed to counter the physical effects of jumping between universes, they were yet another concoction invented by my father's medical team. I frown, staring at the syringes. They are effective, but they're only meant to be temporary fixes to combat cell degradation. The weekly pills are supposed to be taken during the jumps, and the injectors are meant for emergency purposes if anything goes wrong.

I fish deeper into my backpack and pull out a circular silver case. Diligent about taking the stabilization pills—well, at least until lately—I've only had to use one of the injectors since I've been here. I have several years' worth of pills left—I've been prepared to be in this world for as long as it took to find Caden.

But now, Shae would need both cases, at least until we get back to Neospes, where most of the damage to her nervous system could be reversed with our medical technology. I slide the cases over to her with one hand. If she makes it. . . .

"You keep these, in case we get separated or anything," I say gruffly.

"Won't you need them?"

"I don't plan on coming back here."

"Riv—" she begins.

"Don't," I say. "Just take them. You need them more than I do. And like you said, I heal quickly." I pause, and stare at the ground. "Plus, I haven't taken the pills in weeks, and I don't feel any different. No headaches, nothing. It's like I've adapted or something." I shrug. "After I crashed my bike, my body went supernova on me. Figure I nearly died and it wanted to live. Or something like that."

Shae's eyes narrow. "You always did recover fast. That's weird, though."

"Don't you think I know that?"

"Strong survival instinct." Her mouth opens and closes like she wants to say something more, but can't find the words. Her hesitation is grating.

"What?" I snap.

"You ever wonder why . . . your body can do those things?"

I stare at her. "No. Everyone's wired differently. I heal fast. You've known that for years. What's the big deal?"

"Nothing." Her lips twist, her eyes dropping away from mine as she puts the cases into her own pack. "Thanks."

The silence is like a web between us, sticky with so much left unsaid over all the years. It's suffocating, the way she's been watching me when she thinks I'm not looking, studying me like I'm some kind of pariah. I can't stand it.

"No problem," I grit out, and pull the gear bag I'd packed upstairs toward me, removing the Vectors' uniforms. Luckily, they don't stink as much anymore. They're designed with a special self-cleaning technology that eliminates body odors, meant for hours of prolonged use. I dab at some of the stains that look fresh with a rag and smooth them out in front of me just in case—who knows how long the Vectors had been wearing them?

They don't look like much, but are engineered for the rough terrain outside of the city wall, where the days are hot and the nights freezing cold. The solar panels on the back and shoulders store and diffuse heat through the suit as needed, and the ventilation pockets recycle sweat for cooling during hot weather. A multitude of pockets and utility latches hold anything from food to gear to weapons. I run my fingers from shoulder to cuff on one of the suits to skim lightly over the recessed keypad in the wristband indented with various symbols. The keypad controls the suit's special programming.

"What are those?" I jump in surprise when Caden squats down beside me. "Wait a sec! Are these the Vectors' uniforms? The dead things?" I almost laugh at the unbridled disgust on his face. I nod. "Nasty," he adds, and moves away to lug a couple more trunks over to Shae.

"Maybe, but you won't be saying that when your bones think they're shattering inside of you from the cold," I mutter under my breath, rolling up the suits into their reversible pouches sewn into the leg cuffs and tucking them into my backpack. I repack all of the other items, including the ones I also took off the Vectors, and refill the water pouches that fit along the sides of my pack with some of the jugs of drinking water lining the wall.

"Is there a bathroom down here?" I ask Shae, who nods toward a door on the left side of the room.

Inside the cramped space that's little more than a closet with a toilet and a tiny sink, I remove my filthy torn shirt and wipe the blood from my neck and chest. I don't even bother to smooth the mess that's my hair, but I wash my face with the trickle from the tap, dabbing the cool water under my arms and along my sides. I remove my torn pants and twist over the toilet to examine the wound on my leg where the Vector had caught me with the electro-rod, but I'm surprised to see that it's barely a thin, blackened welt under the crusty blood. I frown— I've never healed this fast before. Must have felt worse than it looked. I clean it off and pull on Shae's clean clothes before walking out. The pants are a little snug, but they're clean and not ripped.

In the outer room, Shae and Caden are leaning over a case lined with all manner of weapons—guns, knives, chains, maces, spears, bows, and swords.

"Guns won't kill Vectors," Shae is explaining to Caden. "They're programmed to dodge the trajectory of bullets. Something about the sound of the metal, I think." Brandishing a curved knife, she adds, "The only way to kill them, as you saw, is a sharp blow to the head or severing the spinal column."

"But people are much slower than bullets," Caden argues.

"But we're less noticeable," I interject, heading over to them. "That's our advantage over them. By the first bullet, they know where you are. If you miss, you're dead. It's a small window, but usable." I pull on the worn black leather harness over my shoulders and slip my short swords into their sheaths flat against my back. Choosing two short knives from the pile, I tuck those into my backpack along with a handful of four-pointed steel throwing stars. "It's all about speed, flexibility, and unpredictability. With a knife or a sword, you have to get in real close, but once you strike true, they go down."

Shae hefts a mini-crossbow in her hand. "This is my favorite."

"I don't get it. What's the difference between that and a gun?" Caden asks. "Plus, I got the one with bullets upstairs, remember?"

"Like I said, Vectors can hear bullets coming a mile away. Arrows are a lot quieter. Half the time, taking out a Vector quietly is the biggest challenge, because who knows what else you can attract, or how many of them?" Shae says. "And you didn't kill the one upstairs. They can withstand a lot of physical damage as long as you don't touch their vulnerable spots. It's a waste."

"Which weapon should I use, then?" Caden asks.

"The saber," I say quickly. "It's the perfect weapon for you. It'd be like fencing, only you're fighting for your life, not points."

"Super," Caden's droll response elicits a short laugh from Shae, and I, too, fight to keep the smile from my mouth, but the moment of levity is gone like a breath in the wind. They share a look that I ignore.

"We need to move," I tell them. "Shae, how're you feeling?"

"Good," she responds, hoisting her backpack on her shoulders. Her color is back, and she's standing in fighting stance. That's one thing about the anti-eversion injectors—they pack a combined punch of pain inhibitors, counteractive pressure meds, and a low dose of epinephrine to get the nervous system functional. Shae tosses a headlamp in my direction and looks at me expectantly.

"Okay, we follow you. Let's go," I say, pulling the lamp over my forehead. "Caden's in the middle, and I'll be behind him."

We make our way through the steel door, dropping the heavy bar across the back once it's shut. If the Vectors make it into the basement room, it won't be much of a deterrent to them, but it will still take considerable force to open it from the inside.

The tunnel smells musty, and it's dark, with the three beams from our lamps barely piercing the blackness. No one speaks as we make our way, walking as fast as possible. There's enough room for us to probably walk three abreast, but we remain in single file with Shae at the lead and me at the rear. After nearly forty minutes of hard walking, the tunnel forks. Shae takes the one on the left without missing a beat, and I have to force myself to not pull out the map in my pocket. I am flying blind and it's not a feeling I like. Nor do I like depending on a sister who lied to me in the first place, even if we are now working against a common enemy.

"Are you sure this is the right way?" I can't stop myself from asking.

"Yes. I've done this dozens of times before," Shae shouts back.

Her words do little to reassure. The tunnel walls are starting to close in, and all I want to do is sprint as fast as I can to the other end. I've never been good with being underground. Performing routine security checks in the belowground shelters back home used to have me breaking out in cold sweats. I practice my old trick, counting softly in my head backwards from one hundred and breathing in through my nose and out through my mouth. It helps a little.

Our pace is grueling, and the calming breaths I'm trying to take in are becoming more and more like shallow pants. I slow for a second to pull an ultrathin device from my pocket, one that I'd taken from one of the Vectors. It tells me how far we've already traveled—we're just past the halfway point of twenty miles. I pocket the electronic tablet and almost crash into Caden's back.

It's only at that moment that I realize a loud rushing noise is coming from a ragged-edged vent in the ceiling, and we're in a wider band of rock. The space is a roughly hewn cave, its walls dotted with smaller caves and darker tunnels. Both Shae and Caden are standing in front of a three-fork tunnel at the far end, their heads together, staring at a piece of paper. They both glance at me.

"What's the matter?" I ask. "We're almost there; why are we stopped?"

"The right tunnel may be faster, according to this map," Shae says. I nod impatiently. All I want to do is get out of here as fast as possible. It's only after I follow Caden's shadowy form into the tunnel that the thought occurs to me that Shae had said she'd done this trek dozens of times before.

Why would she suggest a new route? What had they been talking about in the seconds before I caught up with them in the noisy area? My brain jumps into overdrive as the pieces come together enough to make me freeze in my tracks.

But I'm a half second too late.

There's no one ahead of me. In that exact moment, the silence drums into my ears and it's so dead quiet that I don't even hear footsteps. The only sound is that of my breathing. I curse my stupidity.

My eyes strain forward into the darkness, the beam from my penlight offering little clarity. No one is there; they're gone.

But they have to be close. Shae knows these tunnels inside out—there has to be some kind of alcove nearby, somewhere they're hiding. I close my eyes and exhale silently, letting my other senses do the work. But Shae knows me too well. There's nothing, no movement at all. I could be alone, even though every instinct inside of me screams that I'm not.

Clenching my teeth, I delve into my pack, searching futilely for the pair of infrared glasses I'd taken off the dead Vector in Caden's house. I hear an indistinct noise like the sound of some tiny animal rustling around behind me, and my hands grasp the hilts of my blades as I swing around. Nothing. The darkness surrounds me, heavy and dry, as I inch back the way we'd come. I release my grip on the swords, leaving them in their sheaths for the moment—I can't risk hitting Caden. Shae, I don't really care about one way or another. She has proven that she is still my enemy. I resort to words instead of blades.

"Shae? What are you doing?" I whisper furiously into the dark. "We need to stay together. You're hurt and you need me. Shae! Where are you?"

I'm still inching along when I sense the shift in the air and I swing around into a crouched stance, protecting my body instinctively with my forearms. The cold tip of an electro-rod presses against the soft spot just beneath my ear, and my body freezes. I forgot how quiet Shae can be, catching me unaware for years during training when we were little. I gnash my teeth in frustration. Her voice in my ear is soft with bittersweet notes of regret.

"I'm sorry, Riv. I can't let you take him. Don't try to find us."

"Shae, don't—"

"And I'm sorry for this, too."

I feel a sharp zap against my skin, and then the darkness blinds me.

# 9

# THE PREY

LIGHTS BLINK IN and out. Warm sun flickers against my eyelids. I can hear someone laughing, and I turn toward the voice from where I'm lying, hefting myself onto my elbows. Lights flash again, this time like popping light bulbs exploding behind my eyelids, as a searing pain lances through my shoulder.

Coughing, I taste burnt blood.

It all comes back to me in a rush. Caden, the Vectors, the dark tunnel . . . Shae. There is no sunlight, no laughter. Instead, I'm breathing in the rank, dusty air of the tunnel where my sister has left me. Pulling myself to my knees, I'm still groggy from the electro-shock. Obviously, Shae had set it to stun, but it still hurts something fierce.

Gingerly, I touch the welt along the side of my neck and wince. She's been generous; this stun is more or less mild. I would have taken out an enemy—even if it were my sister— without a second thought. Those rods have a kill setting that could liquefy the insides of anything human, and melt the internal wiring of anything not human. But even so, one of the stun settings could knock a live person out for days at a time.

I look at my watch quickly, noting that I've only been out for a few hours. A quick check of my body, other than the welt on my neck and a cut on my lip from where I'd fallen, tells me that I'm otherwise unhurt. My pack lies off to the side, hanging drunkenly off one arm, and I hoist it onto my lap. They haven't touched it. My blades are still snug against my back under my jacket. At least Shae hasn't left me with nothing to protect myself, even though I wouldn't have done the same.

I haul myself up against the wall and stand, trying to get my bearings and ignoring the dizziness that threatens to make my knees buckle.

"Get a grip, Riven," I snarl to myself. "It's not like you've never been on the wrong end of an electro-rod before."

Grabbing my pack, I remove the first-aid kit and pour some cold liquid from a slim bottle onto a piece of gauze, careful not to let it touch my fingers. I dab it onto my neck, a shiver snaking through me as an icy sensation immediately dulls the raw ache of the welt. The liquid anesthetic hardens into a thin, flexible shell over the sore area, its inner-layer seeping into my skin to deaden raw nerve endings and rebuild cells. Within seconds, the pain is gone, and within an hour I know my neck will be as good as new.

Normally, I'd just leave my wounds to heal on their own, but now I have no time to lose. The cell-regeneration remedy is yet another of my father's inventions . . . and one that I'd steadfastly refused to use. Using anything of his makes me sick to my stomach, but now it's a necessity to find Caden quickly.

It's a brutal reminder of what is at stake—I can't let my hatred for my father affect my decisions and actions now.

Pocketing the bottle, I try to reorient myself. I shine my flashlight down one end of the tunnel, and it's soon swallowed up by the blackness. I do the same down the other end. Eyesight isn't going to help me, so I close my eyes, engaging my other senses and letting the flow of the stale air in the tunnel waft around me. The changes are subtle, but they're there—the ones that tell me which direction has more movement in the airflow.

Without hesitation, I sprint down the tunnel on confident feet. Recalling the treacherous, veiny patchwork of the tunnel map, I know I can get lost with a single wrong turn, so I'm careful not to veer off the pathway. If I can make my way back to the place where the tunnels fork into three, I'll be able to figure out which way they've gone and track them from there.

I run past several other tunnels and alcoves that I haven't noticed before, refusing to let any fear enter my mind. But it does, inexorably. And I know I've made the wrong choice.

*Just backtrack*, I tell myself silently. *Follow your feet, and trust your instincts.*

I can hardly help the next thought that follows that one—as my instincts had told me to trust Shae? But they hadn't; my emotions had. I grit my teeth and press on, clearing my mind of any thought but getting to the end of the tunnel. And within minutes, I do.

Only it's a dead end.

I punch my fist into the wall and a shower of pebbles scatters at my feet. How could I have missed a turn? I stayed straight, didn't I? Could I have missed it somewhere?

*Think!* I urge myself. I retrace the path in my head, then backtrack about half a mile before I see it—a barely discernable twist in the path. I had veered in the wrong direction into what was now clearly an offshoot from the main tunnel. I take a deep breath to calm my racing nerves. Things could be far worse. I could have ended up running in circles or gotten even more lost.

Back on the right track, it's no time at all before I am in the area with the four tunnels—the one that we'd come from, and the three we'd chosen among. Squatting down, I notice faint scuff marks in the dirt in front of the tunnel on the far left. A slight color change in the ground suggests that this tunnel has been used more than the others. I check my watch. Shae and Caden are probably near the other end, if not out already, but the window of opportunity isn't completely closed for me to track them. Still, I have to move, and fast.

I'm just about to enter the leftmost tunnel when something stops me dead in my tracks—the sound of something heavy moving, something coming from behind me . . . something big. The hairs on the back of my neck stand at stiff attention, because I know that it can't be Caden and Shae. They would never have gone back.

It has to be Vectors. They've found us. Or more precisely, found me.

I deliberate between making a beeline down the tunnel and facing them head-on. But I have no idea how many there are. For a second, my body feels like it is splitting down the middle with equal urges to fight and flee pulling me in opposite directions. It's not in my nature to run, but fighting an unknown number of Vectors in such an enclosed space will not be to my advantage, despite my skills.

I decide to wedge myself into one of the many alcoves lining the walls of the cave. I'll get some idea of their numbers and assess potential attack options. And, at the very least, their tracking technology is far better than mine, and we are looking for the same thing.

*The enemy of my enemy is my friend.*

Not that I'll ever align myself with Vectors, but I will use them however I need to, and then get rid of them when I don't. Hoisting myself up the cave wall, I find a recessed nook and crawl inside to wait, pressing my body back into the dark space until rocks are digging painfully into my flesh.

My eyes adjust slowly to the muted dark of the outer cave. I've covered my scuff marks in the dirt and sprinkled myself with anti-tracking dust from the bottom of my pack. They probably aren't even looking for me, but I have to play it safe on the off chance that they are. My father has his own reasons for wanting me back in Neospes.

It isn't long before they enter the big cave: three of them, with one a familiar face, the ruthless commander from before. My teeth clench. The smell of them hits me like a rolling wave, the pungent scent of formaldehyde. Even though I'm used to it, it's something that automatically raises the hairs on my whole body. In Neospes, we cremate our dead, except for the Vector soldiers, who are put through an unnatural rigorous embalming process. They carry the smell of death like armor.

Halogen lights on their uniforms illuminate the cave. I watch the commander carefully. It was a tough fight earlier,

and its ability to speak had been unnerving. I can't help noticing that its bullet-ridden body has been completely repaired in
a matter of hours. It's nothing for our reconstructive technology—the technological differences between my world and this
one are like night and day. But then my mind flashes back to
the abundance of water in this world and extravagances like
Caden's waterbed. Limitless water over advanced robotics is a
no-brainer. So is a world without creatures like these, without
the Vectors.

With inhuman stealth, the Vectors move purposefully,
examining the ground in front of the three tunnels. The big one
turns to study the rest of the cave, and I imagine his eyes slow-
ing and stopping at my alcove. I can hear the blood rushing in
my ears and the shakiness of my breath in the dead silence. I'm
barely breathing, and even though I know he can't possibly see
me, for a split second, it feels like our eyes connect. Adrenaline
rushes through my bloodstream, but then the moment is gone
as he turns back to his subordinates, pressing a series of buttons on the wrist-pad of his suit to initiate the tracking device.

"Two trails," he says. His voice is guttural, and as before, it
chills me to the bone.

A red light streams from his wrist as it scans the entrances to
both tunnels. Yellow markings spin through the red, more on
the right than the left: heat readings. The commander moves
over to that tunnel pressing another series of buttons, and the
light switches to a pale laser-like blue. A long noise bleeps on
his console, loud in the silence and almost making me jump. '

"The tracks return," he growls and studies the device before
stepping over to the far left tunnel to repeat the sequence. This

time there are three short beeps, and he nods, satisfied. "The boy went this way. Move out," he commands.

The other two nod and immediately obey, disappearing into the tunnel. For a moment, the Vector commander turns around and re-scans the room. His gaze doesn't stop at my hiding place this time, but I can feel his suspicion, and this, too, is unlike the traditional programming of the Vectors. They operate by computer rules and programming algorithms, not instinct. Can he somehow sense me? He punches another sequence of numbers into the wrist-pad, different from the ones he used before. Unconsciously, I press myself deeper against the wall and ignore the searing slice of stone against my skin.

My heart jumps into my throat as he flashes the same blue tracker in a slow clockwise circle. I can only hope that the anti-tracker dust will do its job. As the blue light filters into my cave, I can see the analysis data in the light discoloring its surface, and I hold my breath. These scanners are built to analyze individual scent—yet another advanced biometric profile weapon incorporated into the suits—almost like electronic sniffer dogs. Terrified, I wait for the beeps that will surely come if he's looking for me, but there's no sound.

The light moves past my cave, but I don't exhale until the Vector commander has completed his scan and followed the other two into the tunnel. My muscles remain clenched until enough time has passed by, when I scramble out of my cramped hiding space. It takes only a couple minutes for my blood to recirculate through my body, but I am already moving, digging through the bottom of my pack and locating the infrared glasses I couldn't find earlier. There's no way I can see in the dark or use the penlight—they'll see me coming from a mile away.

I head into the tunnel, walking as quickly as I dare. I am tracking on scent alone, the unique smell of their dead flesh wafting on the stale air in the tunnel. The sharp odor of it makes me remember the first time I saw one of them.

It'd been during a time when my whole family was still together—my father, my mother, Shae, and I—a time before betrayal and lies ripped us apart. At only six, and one of the youngest recruits, I'd been released from training early and called to my father's underground experimental lab. At the time, he was the head scientist in the advanced robotics and genetic testing facility, and already navigating the waters of reanimating the dead with cyborg technology.

Using my unrestricted passkey—being his daughter had its privileges—I found him on one of the lower levels in one of the test labs. Unnoticed in a corner of the outer office, I stared fascinated through the glass wall into the room beyond where my father had just finished decontaminating a corpse on a long silver table. Decontamination, my father once explained to me, meant getting rid of all internal bodily fluids and unnecessary organs, and preserving the remaining husk and heart with an electro-chemical solution.

"It's all biological," he said to me. "The body is a capable host, even though it's no longer alive. With the nanoplasm, we can use and program these shells to operate almost as well as a fully functioning *live* person would. And they would make even better soldiers, as there's no emotion, just programming." He paused and looked at me with dark, narrowed eyes. "And the beauty of them is that they're expendable. One command, and the nanoplasm shuts down. No loss, nothing compromised. Think of it as a type of recycling."

"How do they go to the bathroom?" my perfectly logical, then six-year-old self asked in all seriousness. My father smiled widely and lifted me onto his desk.

"Smart question," he answered. "The simple answer is that they don't. We remove all the parts that we don't need, like the kidneys or the liver or the stomach. We keep the heart because it moves the nanoplasm around the body, and we keep part of the brain and spinal cord to process the information we give it."

"What makes it go, then? Like how does it work? What do they eat?" I cocked my head and frowned. "It's not a *robot*, is it?" Even then I couldn't keep the trepidation out of my voice, having learned about our violent history in my civilization lessons. The Tech War had obliterated our world, leaving the sparse little we had now as a harsh lesson of the perils of artificial intelligence.

"No, princess. They're safe. This nanoplasm responds to programming only. It's not self-aware." He patted my head reassuringly, as only he could. "And they don't eat anything; they have a special lithia core that keeps the heart pumping and the brain ticking. Once you compromise the spinal cord or the brain, it's an automatic kill switch. Don't worry, sweet; it's all under control this time."

"What are they called?"

"Vectors."

The entire process disgusted and fascinated me at the same time. I couldn't imagine, even then, how a dead person could be used as a soldier, and watching my father at work was the first time I was able to see the process up close and personal. I remained crouched in my corner, thrilled and terrified of being caught, watching as my father and his team worked the corpse from top to bottom.

Machines around the body beeped constantly, with long tubes of various sizes connected to the table. They were filled with metallic-colored fluids. Slowly, in succession, two of the tubes were emptied, and then combined into a larger tube before being injected into the dead man's body. Two of my father's assistants exited to another adjoining secure room filled with flashing computer screens. My father followed them just as the third tube with the silvery blue fluid slowly started emptying like the others into the body beneath it.

He punched some numbers into the keypad on one of the desktops. Something was starting to happen in the room. The corpse on the table bucked and began convulsing against the metal shackles connecting it to the table. I could see the bunched muscles of its arms and legs cording as if it were in terrible pain, even though my father had said that they couldn't feel anything. And then suddenly, it stopped moving, and the only noise was the long sound of a flatline.

"Damn it!" I heard my father swear and punch the wall before stalking out of the room into his office, where I was hiding. He raked his hands through his hair as he studied some papers lining his desk, grinding his teeth in frustration. Not wanting to get caught in the crossfire of his anger—which could be nasty at times—I curled my body into as tight a ball as I could manage, pressing myself into the wall behind me, and prayed that he wouldn't notice me.

"We did the sequencing right. What did I miss? What did I miss?" he muttered to himself before punching a button on the intercom and hissing to his assistants, "Get me another prepped body. We go again in thirty minutes!" Without even looking in my corner, he left his office through the outer door, slamming it behind him. A shaky breath left my mouth but I stayed curled tightly for several seconds before standing very carefully.

The area was empty . . . except for me and the Vector lying on the table. I couldn't help myself, knowing that I only had a few minutes before my father or his assistants returned, and without hesitation, I punched in the code on the inner door. My birthday. In hindsight, I always wondered how my brilliant father could be so clueless or predictable as to use his daughter's birth date as a code on one of the most dangerous areas in the facility. But the thought of it made me feel warm inside—he may not be the most demonstrative of fathers, but this was a sign, a sign that I mattered. Ignoring the warning clench of my stomach muscles, I pushed open the door.

Inside the room, I approached the body with trepidation, even though I knew it was not operational. The test had failed. My nose wrinkled against the suffocating chemical smell that caused my eyes to sting. Still, I inched nearer. Up close, the thing was huge—a dead giant of a man. His skin was a dull gray color, bleached out by all the compounds preventing it from decaying, but the metallic fluids now inside of him still gave his body muscular definition. Clad only in a pair of medical undergarments, his bare chest and arms were sleek and hair-less, his head shaved. I moved closer to the table and placed my hand carefully alongside the hand caught by the metal shackle on the table. It was ten times the size of mine!

A long red scar on the giant's side caught my attention and I bent closer. This was where the lithia cell my father had told me about would have been inserted to connect to the lower spine. I ran my finger along the cold line of flesh and shivered. It felt like clammy linoleum. The man also had a tattoo running along the top of his thigh that read TEST SPECIMEN 74. Seventy-four of them they'd already burned through . . . no wonder my father had been so upset. It wasn't like we had dozens of dead people lying around; as a society, we valued life too much.

I was so intent on staring at the number and thinking about how few of us were left in our tiny pocket of the world, that I didn't feel the yank on my head until it was too late, and the tears were already springing to my eyes in agony as *something* hauled on my braid with brute, uncompromising force.

Panicked, I wondered whether my hair had gotten caught on the table somehow, and twisted despite the tearing sensation on my scalp to see what I was caught on. Instead, I found myself face-to-face with a milky-blue stare that was so devoid of any life that my terror made me freeze completely.

The giant was alive! But it wasn't possible. The experiment had failed.

At the exact moment that I realized that the experiment hadn't failed, the alarms in the room went off, and things gal-vanized into motion as the dead man broke through the steel shackle like it was butter—oblivious to the silvery-blue fluid that poured down its forearm from where the sharp steel edges had razored through flesh—and taking my head with it until I was half spread-eagled over its body. It was as if my head were on fire, my skin tearing off of my skull and my hair loosening in whole clumping handfuls.

Close up, its eyes were even more terrifying, sucking the life out of me with their blank deadness, completely devoid of any soul. The thing opened its mouth, and I started screaming. I didn't stop screaming, not until hands pulled me back, and I felt someone cutting away its grip on my hair. Voices fluttered in and out. I could see huge steel needles being jammed into the thing's side as people tried to hold the giant in place until it finally shut down. I glanced at its face once more, and even though it was completely lifeless, its colorless blue eyes still stared at me as if the creature wanted to swallow me whole.

For years afterward, I couldn't even look at them—their gray faces and milky-blue eyes, terrifying—a constant reminder of that moment when I'd been caught unaware. I'd never trusted them, not ever, not even when I'd led them. They were a means to an end, and Murek, the legion commander at the time, had loved them because of their absolute loyalty. Despite my own reservations, my father had been right. The Vectors had made excellent soldiers.

Finding myself in a new open cave area underground, I bring myself back to the present, clearing my head from my memories to focus on the task at hand. They are great soldiers, but their allegiance is and will always be to Murek and the crown—a loyalty that is programmed into the very fluid that runs in their dead veins. Even though the one in Caden's house somehow recognized me as its general, I know that it had been a glitch—and one that will be quickly rectified. Nothing will stand in the way of getting Caden . . . not even me.

There's only one exit out of the space at the far end, and I make my way there on silent, swift feet. I am so intent on getting into the tunnel that I don't sense the attack until it is too late, as something large and heavy tackles me to the ground. My night-vision glasses are jerked from my head in the collision, and I'm suddenly flying blind. Without losing a beat, I roll and kick upward with all the force I can muster, feeling my boots connect with a thick body and pushing it off of me. In a flash, I'm in a crouch, taking three steps back. I loosen my backpack and remove the swords from their sheaths against my back.

I can't see it, but I know it's one of the Vectors. It has a slight advantage because it can see me. I say slight because part of our training means fighting blindfolded. All of our senses are honed to the point of razor-sleek sharpness, and facing an opponent in darkness is par for the course. I take a deep breath and pull it into my center, letting it fill me. Closing my eyes, I exhale and wait.

The air shifts to my left and instead of spinning away, I move toward it, at the last minute grinding to my knees and slashing outward with my blades. They strike into something thick and heavy—a leg or upper thigh. The thing makes no sound, but now I can hear it moving as it drags one foot slightly. It lunges toward me once more, and this time I wait and take the hit on my left flank, moving out slightly so that I don't receive the full weight of the strike.

With Vectors, hesitation is the difference between life and death. Ignoring the pain, I whirl alongside the Vector's body until I am facing its back. My swords don't falter, swinging up and scissoring across the back of its neck in a smooth decisive motion born from years of honing the same move in training and in actual combat. I hear the thump of its head followed by the second thump of its body, and pull the thin penlight from my pocket, trying to filter the sharp light through my fingers. I'm still cautious. The creature had been waiting for me, but there's no other movement or noise.

I retrieve my glasses quickly—they aren't broken, thankfully—and find my pack. In the muted green glare of the glasses, the Vector's shape is a dull outline. I quickly divest him of any of his gear that I can carry, including a wireless communications headpiece, which I tuck into my ear, and an electro-coil, a flexible strand of wire attached to a thick short handle, which I slip into my boot. I haul his body to the side of the area and move toward the tunnel.

That's when the screaming starts.

# 10

# REVERSAL OF FORTUNE

I BOLT DOWN the narrow passageway without any thought for my own well-being. All I can hear is Shae's bloodcurdling scream, and it chills me to the bone. It sounds as if she's being gutted while still alive. I'm flat-out running because I know the Vectors have no use for her, and while I am still upset at her betrayal, there's no way I'd want my sister to suffer or die at the hands of those things . . . and especially not the big one.

But as I draw closer, I can see that he's not there. And neither is Caden.

I refuse to panic, or even imagine that somehow the big one has already taken Caden back. I take a deep breath—first, I have to help Shae. The infrared green vision of my goggles identifies thrashing movement down the tunnel in front of me, and I click a button on the side of the arm that magnifies the image—there are only two of them and I recognize Shae's wiry frame immediately.

The Vector lifts her body and slams it into the side of the wall like a sack of potatoes. I dart forward, ducking my head and full-on tackling him to the ground. There's a dull thud as our bodies crash to the dirt, and I'm rolling, sword in hand, before I can even take another breath.

The Vector is just as quick and already on his feet facing me. I spare a glance at Shae. I can smell the rusty odor of blood in the cramped space. Dread makes me dash forward, but I misjudge the Vector's movement, as his fist catches me in the solar plexus and knocks all the air out of me.

Gasping, my knees buckle and I swing my blade weakly across its side, but not before its elbow catches me in the back of the head. My face smashes against the rough rock of the tunnel, and I can feel the sharp sting of my skin peel off against the stone even as stars blind my vision. The Vector is on top of me before I can move, bashing my weapons out of my hands. I curl into a ball to protect myself, because I can't get a strike in edgewise.

Shae claws at its body from behind, and distracted, it slams a heel in her direction. I hear a vicious thump—presumably her body against the tunnel wall behind us—before it swings back to me, blows crunching into my ribs like a jackhammer. The pain is excruciating, but I force myself to stay focused.

Somehow, I have to get out of this, if only to find Caden. If I don't, we are all lost. The thought gives me a boost of strength as my hand slides down the side of my leg into my boot to grasp the handle of the electro-coil I took off the other Vector earlier. With a lurch, I flip my body around and jam my legs against the wall with all the force I can muster, wrapping one knee around the thing's head. In quick succession, I twist to the side and jerk my knee backward, but I'm not quick enough.

I'm thwarted as the Vector's knee smashes into my skull, disabling my glasses . . . and suddenly, I'm blinking as my eyes adjust from infrared vision to shadowy darkness. In that second, it's on top of me, crushing the breath from my chest with its weight. Fingers close around my windpipe and I can only kick wildly, my strength seeping out of me, clawing at its face and head in desperation. But it's too strong and I can't find the leverage to get out from under it.

Suddenly, the Vector crumples like a dead weight against me, its steel fingers loosening around my neck, and I'm wheezing long breaths of the stale tunnel air like it's the freshest I've ever breathed. A flashlight flicks on and Shae's there, a dripping electro-coil in her hand and the severed Vector's head a few feet away from where she's standing.

"Don't you think we're even, because we aren't," I rasp, squeezing out from beneath the creature. Shae smiles weakly and helps to kick the rest of the Vector's body off of me. "Where's Caden?" I ask her, and then say in the same breath, "How badly are you hurt?" Even in the dim light of the flashlight, I can see that her shirt is soaked with blood and she's holding her middle with one arm.

"Just a scratch," she says, but I know that she's lying—there's too much blood and a heavy, foul odor of charred flesh. "Don't worry; Caden's safe. He's outside. The big one shot me . . . he got too close, and I couldn't slow Caden down, so I told him to go, and then I backtracked."

"Outside where?"

"He's safe," Shae repeats resolutely, and I glare at her. Nothing but mistrust is left between us. My eyes narrow.

"Are you sure? What about the big one? Did you get it?"

Shae's eyes darken with frustration. "Just before you got here, it everted. I almost had it. One minute my blade was at its neck, and the next it was gone. It talked, too. About you."

I stare at her sharply. "What did it say?"

"That you were a fugitive, that you would betray Caden, and me, that you weren't to be trusted." I keep my eyes fixed on hers, and her voice continues softly. "But I knew that already. Then it said that it was sorry . . . sorry that it hadn't killed me when it had the chance." She pauses, and I know what she's going to say even before she finishes her story. "That's what got me, the knowing in its voice, like it somehow *knew* me. I hesitated with the kill strike and then it was gone."

"It's father's latest creation," I say flatly. "*Thinking* Vectors, as if they aren't terrible enough already. It's some new prototype, one with its own memories. Did you hear its voice? It's the same as his." Softly to myself, I say, "A tribute to his vanity." My eyes connect with Shae's, and for a second, it's like we're trainees again, but the moment is gone in a breath, suffocated by everything since between us. "We need to get out of here." I know that she isn't going to tell me where Caden is, but I can track him easily enough on my own once we get outside. "Which way is out?"

Shae nods back in the direction from where I'd come. "That way. Look, Riv, I'm sorry . . . for back there."

I don't look at her, and instead pocket the dead Vector's special terrain glasses, which are way more advanced than the night-vision ones I have. "Forget it. You did what you had to. I would have done the same. Or probably worse." I shrug. It's no secret between us what I am or what I'm capable of. "You're okay to walk at least until we get outside?"

Shae nods and falls into step with me. "It doesn't mean I'm not sorry. I just can't let anything happen to him."

"Well, you did a good job of that, didn't you?" As soon as the words are out of my mouth, I regret them. She did the only thing she could have, short of killing Caden herself. "I just mean he has no training and he's on his own."

"He has training," Shae says softly. "Haven't you seen him fence?"

"No." I'd missed his meet the one time I'd promised to go, helping to save Charisma from those predators. "Why?"

"I taught him. All the techniques I know. It's why he's so good; he's ranked number one in the state." Before Shae defected, she'd been a master swordswoman. Though her personal preference was the crossbow, she'd been chosen to instruct others, myself included, in the intricacies of sword martial arts. She'd been the best of the best, until she'd trained me.

"What did you fight against? Dummies filled with straw?" I snicker.

"He fought me. He's good, Riv."

"Good enough to fight a Vector?" I shoot back.

"Good enough to fight you." I remain silent, feeling the threat thick in the air. I pick up the pace a bit, knowing that it won't be easy for Shae, but she doesn't complain, despite her slightly labored breathing. We've both been trained to withstand near-fatal injuries, and I don't feel any sympathy despite her being my sister. She'd simply refuse any offer of my help, anyway. "The Vector also said there's a bounty on your head. They want you alive."

"I know. *He* wants me back."

"Why?" Shae asks.

I shrug. "To punish me, I suppose. I did torch their biggest genetic research lab before I left."

"You didn't!" I can hear the smile in Shae's voice, and I stifle the brief whisper of pride that flutters inside of me.

"That was years ago," I say flatly. "Who knows what he's planning now."

We make our way out from the underground after a few more miles, and we end up in a deserted warehouse on the far outskirts of a neighboring town. I pull a couple bales of hay over the trapdoor that we just exited. It won't stop anything from getting out, but we'll at least have some notice if the hay starts moving.

Shae fumbles in her pack and jams one of my injectors into her leg before collapsing to the ground and closing her eyes. Two in the space of a few hours is not exactly what they're designed for, but I can see that our pace has cost her. Despite my reticence, I move to her side. I owe her my life, not that I would ever tell her that. She doesn't protest when I unbuckle her vest, only to see a gaping hole on her left side with singed, blackened edges. A shard of something shiny glimmers on the inside of the wound.

"Part of the electro-rod," she rasps, wincing as my fingers gently touch the sides of it.

"Why didn't you say something before?" I grit out. My voice is angry, but it's directed at myself, not her. I can't think about how painful it would have been, and I feel even guiltier for not checking in the tunnel or at least offering some help.

"No time before. Just need to . . . get it out now."

I nod and spray my hands with an alcohol solution from my med-kit. I can only imagine what had happened before I got there, when I'd first heard her scream. The Vectors are known for operating their electro-rods in open wounds. Even on the stun setting, the agony is brutal, like a laser on skinless tissue. It's one of their well-used torture techniques. The Vector must have wedged it so hard into her that the silver tip of it had shattered.

My body cringes with a phantom pain that isn't mine. The agony would have been excruciating. I shiver and assess the damage carefully. The good thing is that the electric shock somewhat cauterized the gash, which means that at least Shae won't bleed to death. Waiting for the adrenaline from the injector to kick in, as gently as I can, I pull out the shard of silver and check carefully for any other stray pieces. By the time I'm certain there aren't any left, I've removed twelve shards.

I glance at Shae. Her eyes are closed and her breathing is shallow but even. I use the rest of my father's numbing repair liquid to patch up the gaping wound, deftly taping a square of thick padded gauze from the med-kit over it. Tearing a strip from around the base of my shirt, I wrap the material as tightly as I can around her waist. I'm not entirely sure that the liquid and the bandage will do the trick, but it's all I can do.

"Thank you," Shae whispers, staring at me as I buckle her vest closed. "Why are you even helping me? You should just leave me. You want me dead, remember?"

"I don't want you dead," I say dully. Despite my anger at what she's done, I don't want her to be hurt by my hands. She is my sister, after all. Me wanting to kill her and someone else doing it are two totally different things. "Shae, I don't want you dead," I repeat firmly, as if to convince her and myself at the same time, and slide down the wall to sit by her side. "Look, I can't promise you anything, but trust me, I don't want to hurt Caden. The Vectors do—they want to kill him. For all I know, Cale could already be dead and Caden is going to be the last hope in his line. Either way, I need him. We need him. Don't you get it?"

"He's a person, too. He's real. Surely you can see that?" she says, countering my question with one of her own, and for a second, I'm afraid to answer. Because the truth is, for some reason when I think about him, my chest tightens in jerky response. And I know that Caden isn't just a target anymore. I don't answer Shae, but she sees the reaction in my eyes. "I see you do," she says softly.

"What I feel doesn't matter."

"Yes, it does," she pauses, her voice quiet. "Because it means I can trust you with him. And trust that you'll do the right thing. I thought I saw it before, but you were so cold, I just didn't know. You've always been so good at keeping your feelings hidden. But now, I see it. You do care about him. Don't you, Riv?"

I hate the way her words are making my feelings about Caden even more real than they already are. And I'm not ready to deal with them yet. I'm not ready to open myself up to anyone, especially not Shae. I don't look at her.

"They're not going to stop until he's dead," I say softly. "Until we're all dead or taken."

"He's back at Horrow," Shae says after a while. She digs into her pack and takes out the circular case of stabilization pills. She pops a couple into her mouth. "That's where he went."

"Horrow?" I reply, ignoring the stab of immediate concern that twists through me at the sight of her taking more pills on top of the injector. The meds can turn toxic in the body with overuse. She must be more desperate than I thought, to risk dying. "But that's the first place they'll look."

Shae shakes her head and smiles. "That's the beauty of it. They won't. Vectors don't understand high school, or the concept of school in this world, because their programmers don't understand it."

"What?" I say, confused.

"The idea of high school for kids this age doesn't exist in Neospes. It's a foreign concept to us. So, unless the Vectors were ordered specifically to look there, they won't. Make sense?"

"Not really," I say. "Won't they still track him there?"

"Eventually, but we have a day or two at least. Caden won't lead them directly back there."

But the more I think about it, what she's saying makes an uncanny sort of sense. The Vectors follow orders— they don't have the intuitive sense to think for themselves. They *tracked* Shae back to their house. I think back to when I came here on my own years ago, and the concept of school was so utterly alien to me that it'd been a huge adjustment to even try to pretend to be a high school student. In fact, I still am not good at it, which is why more often than not I usually get the "most likely to be a sociopath" label.

"I don't get it. Why do we even have to go back there? Caden should meet us. We should stick to the plan and get to the eversion point. That's what we're—"

Shae's expression freezes the rest of my words on my lips. "That's not an option anymore. I got a text before. It's crawling with Vectors. The minute they knew where we were heading, they swarmed it. They're waiting for us. It's a trap, Riven."

"So what are you saying? We can't get out?"

"Not from there, not anymore. We need to regroup and rethink." I stare at her, my eyes narrowed. Her last betrayal is still an open wound, and despite her earlier words about trusting me, I can't trust her for a second where Caden is concerned. "What do you mean, you got a text? From who?"

"A Guardian." Shae doesn't offer any more explanation other than those two words, but I continue to press. It's not enough for me. I need to know what her plans are and who her friends are . . . and whether they, too, will toss me over to the Vectors the first chance they get. I have no doubt they would know exactly who I am. Plus, Guardians are solitary in nature and spread out in this world. More than one in any one area is an anomaly.

"*Another* Guardian? At Horrow?"

A glare in response to my doggedness. "Yes. Let's go."

Shae stands wearily. If she's in pain, she certainly doesn't show it, but I know that she's operating on pure will right now. The stabilization pills on top of the injector would have helped slow her heartbeat and numb most of the pain. People always used to say I was the tough one, "the ice queen," they'd called me. But Shae's got a core of solid steel—she could probably outlast me ten times over on sheer will alone. Only, I remember now that Shae isn't operating just on will; she's got a body packed full of an explosive cocktail of meds.

"Shae, the pills—"

"I know what I'm doing," she growls.

"Do you?" I ask gently, and follow as she moves to the back of the warehouse to throw open a door to a small wooden shed that I had noticed upon my first look around. She pulls out a grungy half-rusted dirt bike and then another. Then she stops to look at me.

"I'm dying, Riven. My body is dying. I can feel it. It's been through too much." Her words are no surprise, but I'm shaken all the same. They echo in the dead silence between us.

"We can go to a clinic, the one where June worked. They'll help you."

A strained laugh. "Are you kidding? And what will they do when they find strange fluids and medicine from the injector inside of me that don't even exist here? That's only going to draw more attention to us . . . to Caden. As far as I see, I've got about one more solid fight in me, and I'm not going to go down without it." Her eyes meet mine. "Actually, I don't intend to go down at all if I can help it, and if by some miracle, I make it back to Neospes, maybe . . . he . . . Father or someone else can help. . . ."

Perhaps it's the blunt admission that she's dying, but I have no idea what comes over me as I grab Shae so tightly that we both almost fall over. She stinks of blood and gore and Vector fluid, but all I can smell is the scent of lilacs and sunshine and horse-riding leather—the scent of our childhood—and it's

nearly my undoing. Shoving her away roughly without daring
to meet her eyes, I hoist myself onto one of the bikes and grunt
over my shoulder, "You okay to ride?"

"Yes," she says. I keep my eyes downcast. My thoughts are
heavy and spinning. Wanting to kill an enemy, even if the
enemy is my sister, is far different from knowing that I will lose
her regardless . . . knowing that she's going to die and there's
nothing I can do about it, even if I wanted to. Which I don't.

*Do I?*

A dull ache takes hold of my forehead and nose, and then
my eyes are stinging with an unfamiliar soreness. I thought I
had purged all emotion after the betrayal of my father, but the
hot sadness snaking through my veins right now screams otherwise. I gun the engine, letting the roar of it dull my thoughts
and the vibrations beneath me soothe my knife-edged anguish.

*Emotion is weakness,* my inner voice says. She's just a person,
nothing more.

*She's my sister.*

One who betrayed you.

*I would have done the same.*

She'll betray you again.

I don't have an answer. The argument bounces off the walls of
my brain . . . the logical side of me saying that the odds are Shae
will deceive me again. But this previously dormant side, this
quiet *feeling* side, argues otherwise. Still, despite my unexpected
compassion, deep down I know that it's too late for either of us.
She's dying and I'll have to let her go when the time comes.

Shae's bike growls past me and I follow her down the dirt
road that leads to a main road. It's deserted. I glance down at

my watch. It's early, just before six in the morning on a Wednesday. Shae doesn't stay on the main road, and soon we're off on another circuitous gravelly road that winds up into the base of the Rockies. Even though there are barely any other people around, she isn't taking any chances of being tracked.

The view is overwhelming, and my breath stops in my throat at the sight of a deep lake-filled gorge on my left. The water is like glass, so reflective with the barest tint of the rising sun dancing across its surface that it's like looking at heaven and earth wrapped up in each other's arms. I have never seen anything so incredibly beautiful in my life. I haven't even realized that I've come to a stop on my bike until Shae backtracks toward me.

"What are you doing?"

It takes me a minute to find my voice, and even when I do, it's raspy and hollow with longing. "I've never seen anything like this. Ever. Can you imagine having water like this back home?"

"It's called the Horsetooth Reservoir, and we used to," Shae says softly. "Before the war."

"It's so pure, so untouched . . . so beautiful." My voice trails off and I'm lost once more in a silent reverence that's so sweet, I am consumed by it. Watching the sun's rays dance across the surface as they shimmer over the tops of the mountains, it feels like I'm in another world, one so perfect that all I have to do is breathe and believe. There's no war or hate or pain, just beauty. Soothed by the water's glittering depths, somehow I feel restored.

After a few minutes, I gun the bike's engine and nod to Shae. We ride in silence until we reach the edges of Fort

Collins. Time seemed to go a lot more quickly to get back than when we had left, but in all fairness, we had been on foot in the underground tunnels. Things are starting to get a little busier. Ever careful, we stick to the lesser-known roads off the main street running through the town, but nothing seems different from the hustle and bustle of any other standard weekday morning. Still, I am diligent in assessing anything at all that looks out of place. We are very careful not to go anywhere near their old house, although by now it's probably razed to the ground. No doubt, someone will be watching.

After a while, Shae pulls off to the side and I follow suit. "What's up?" I ask her. On both sides of us are quiet horse farms, and the only living things are two ravens circling overhead and a few grazing animals that look like horses off in the distance on the left. At the top of a small hill on the right side of the road is a rambling farmhouse.

"Did you notice anything coming into town?"

I shake my head. "No."

"I didn't see anything either," she says. "Doesn't mean they aren't here, so we need to be extra cautious, just in case." Shae looks almost back to normal. The fresh air has put some color back into her cheeks, but I know that it's probably all still a façade. I can tell by the slight hitch of her left side and from the way she's holding herself.

"How's your wound?" I ask.

"I'll live," she says. "We should split up."

My eyes narrow immediately. "No way," I snap. "You can't make it on your own, and the truth is, I don't trust you."

"Riv, we don't have a choice. We have a better chance of getting to him separately." Her voice wavers. "And the *truth* is, do you really think I could outrun anyone—even you—in this condition? And you know that," she adds gently. "Go to Horrow. You're still a student there. I'll meet you afterward in the parking lot next to the gym."

A thought occurs to me, one that I hadn't followed up on earlier in the conversation, about the Horrow connection. A hazy recollection of Caden asking about school in the basement of his house flits through my brain. Maybe it'd been more than just a comfort. Is it some kind of safe house?

I frown at Shae. "We are running for our lives. Why is Caden in *school*, of all places?"

"Like I said, it's the safest place he can be right now. Gym. After school. Okay?"

I nod, my eyes burning into her face, daring her to betray me. But I know she's right—there's no way she could outrun me, not in her condition. "What then? What's your plan? What's to stop me from just taking Caden and leaving the minute I get there?"

"Because you need my help, and he won't go anywhere without me. We have allies, Riven. They will protect him." She moves over to stand near me, where I'm still straddling my bike. "There's a lot you don't know, Riv. I didn't know if I could trust you, but now"—Shae pauses, gesturing to her body—"it seems like I have no choice. I'll tell you everything. Three o'clock at the gym, I promise." I don't even notice as she slides her fingers along mine, hooking her little finger into the crook of mine. "Sister-swear," she whispers, and all I can feel is the hot imprint of her skin against my own with the force of a hundred memories behind it.

I may be a fool, but I trust her.

# 11

# REVELATIONS

I STARE DOWN at my filthy shirt and the dried blue remnants of dead Vector under my fingernails. Shae's already left, and I'm standing on the road facing the farmhouse that I saw before. I can't see my face, but I can feel the dirt from the tunnels caking my skin. There's no way I can go to Horrow looking like I've just been at the wrong end of a rodeo bullfight gone bad. What I would give for a long hot shower!

For a brief second, I toy with the idea of heading back to the motel where I'd stayed before, but it's on the other side of town. If I waste any more time, I'll be far later than I already am. They take tardiness very seriously in high schools, I've noticed, as if it's some odd measure of teenage responsibility.

Although I have a healthy respect for punctuality, being late has saved my life more than a few times. In Neospes, predictability is something that can get you killed. After a few more minutes of hemming and hawing, I decide to head up to the farmhouse to see if I can get cleaned up and swipe a fresh shirt. On the porch, I'm torn between breaking and entering, or just asking for help, which is another utterly foreign concept to me.

I glance at the watch on my wrist—I can do it in five minutes. In and out. I try the handle of the door, and it opens inward with a loud creak. I sigh inwardly . . . looks like I'm going to have to play the damsel-in-distress role, and I almost laugh aloud. The thought of me being any kind of damsel is hysterical.

"Hello?" I call out.

No one answers. Not wasting any time, I check the doors along the front hallway, encountering a closet and a kitchen before I find a small bathroom. My reflection greets me like a still clip from a horror movie. It's worse than I've even imagined. Blood, blue-gray ichor, and dark brown and black smudges streak my face like an artist's palette. My hair is clumped into a tuft on one side of my head and plastered to my scalp on the other. My clothes are disgusting, and my pants are ripped all the way down one leg. I'm probably going to need some other clothes, but first things first.

I peel off my leather jacket, outer shirt, and ninjata harness, leaving on a thin tank, and dunk my entire head under the faucet, washing the grime from my face and shoulders with water as hot as I can manage. A couple minutes later, with a twinge of guilt, I'm toweling myself dry with one of the two pristine white embroidered towels from the towel rack, when I hear a sound behind me. Without thinking I swing around in fighting stance before I can blink, to see the face of a small boy. His blue eyes are merely curious, so I relax slightly.

"Hello," he says. "Are you one of my sister's friends?" I nod slowly and peer around his small frame to see if anyone else is there. The boy continues to chatter. "She already went to school. I'm sick today. Don't tell that I'm out of bed, okay? I only wanted to get a drink. Mommy's out checking on one of the horses. It's having a baby!" He starts coughing then until his eyes start to water. I follow him to the kitchen, where he helps himself to a cup of water. "You're really dirty," he remarks. "And you smell a little."

"What's your name?" I say in a soft voice, glancing nervously to the back porch. A seven-year-old I can handle, not a parent . . . especially one who would quickly recognize me as *not* one of her daughter's friends.

"Josh."

"You're right," I say. "I was on my way to school, and I fell off my bike. Do you think you could help me? I don't want to be late. I need to borrow a sweater from your sister. Could you show me her room, and we can get you back into bed?" My voice drops to a stage whisper. "Don't worry; I won't tell if you won't tell. I don't want anyone to know that I fell into horse poop. You promise?"

Josh giggles and wrinkles his nose at my confession, but his face warms with a conspiratorial smile. "Promise."

After grabbing my pack and dirty clothes, we head up the stairs. Josh points to his sister's room and heads into his own across the hall without a backward glance. Looks like I've lost his interest for the moment, so I move quickly to the room he'd pointed to.

It is painted completely in shades of pink with pristine white furniture, and is the most delicate room I have ever seen. A canopied bed dominates most of the room. Pink and white floral curtains flutter at the window. The carpet is plush, and also pink.

I'll be better off taking clothes from Josh!

The sound of a door closing from downstairs startles me into action and I open the owner's closet door. It smells like vanilla and roses, and everything inside it is also pink and white or pastel-colored.

I sigh, resisting the urge to gag, and methodically search through the racks . . . full of dresses, skirts, and sweaters, all color coordinated. Doesn't this girl own any *pants*? More noises from downstairs have me moving faster, but starting to panic. After a second, I see a pair of dark-wash jeans on a hanger, and I pull them on only to find that they can't button and are six inches too long. This girl is not only a princess, she's a tall skinny princess.

So that eliminates pants, I think to myself. Someone is moving around near the stairs, and I grab the only dress I can find that isn't vile and fling it over my head. It's a bottle-green color with a lighter green-and-yellow pattern of vines that comes to my knees, but at least it isn't pink. There's a floor-length mirror in the adjoining bathroom.

The soft cotton feels good against my skin. The dress doesn't look half bad, and I'm spared from looking too girly, especially as it's paired with my worn black combat boots. I pat down my wet hair and grimace. I look good but still edgy . . . a motorcy-cle-riding badass in a dress. It's not that I haven't worn dresses before; they're just impractical.

"You look pretty," Josh says standing in the doorway of the bathroom. "That's one of Sadie's favorites. It's from Grandma in New York."

A moment of pure mirth bubbles against my lip. "Sadie? Your sister is Sadie?" Josh frowns and nods as if I've asked the dumbest question, and I bite my lips. Sadie? As in Caden's girlfriend? I shake my head rolling my eyes skyward . . . someone has a sick sense of humor. I think briefly about changing, but a voice coming up the stairs stops me.

"You better be in bed, young man," a lilting voice warns.

"Pinkie swear, I won't tell if you won't," I whisper with a wink, kneeling and locking my finger with his before Josh bolts to his room. "See you around, Josh."

As Josh disappears across the hall, I swing my harness on, tuck in my blades, and pull on my jacket. I grab my backpack, stuffing my pants into it before stepping out of the window onto a narrow balcony. I'll get rid of them later. I shimmy down the apple tree leaning against the side. A few minutes later, I'm back on the bike and heading toward Horrow.

Breathless at my sneaky entrance to the school through the locker rooms, I slide into my seat long after the last bell chimed down the hallway, but it must be my lucky day because Mrs. Taylor is nowhere to be seen. A momentary panic grips me as I don't see Caden in his usual place in Physics. Shae had said that he'd be here. Then I notice that about half the class is missing.

"Where's Caden?" I ask.

"You're late. Nice dress, by the way," Philip says, and I glare him into silence.

"Where's everyone else?" I snap.

"They're in lab. Group lab experiment today, remember?" I can only stare dumbly at him. "We go in for the second half of the class when they come back. It was the homework from last week?"

"I was sick. What homework?" Philip doesn't answer, but Charisma looks over at me shyly and slides over her notebook to my side of the table.

"It's about refraction and diffraction. Don't worry; I've got you covered," she whispers. In an even softer voice, she says, "I never got to thank you properly. Thank you, Riven. I don't know what I would have done if you hadn't been there."

"It's okay," I say, stunned into momentary silence by her gratitude. "They had it coming."

"Where'd you learn to fight like that?"

Before I can answer, Mrs. Taylor walks into the room, her dark eyes piercing. They land on me immediately, and I feel myself shrinking down in my seat. The last thing I need is any kind of confrontation, to draw even more attention to myself. Her brows snap together as her eyes dart to the clock and back to me, but she doesn't say anything, just walks over to her desk for a folder and leaves the classroom. I'm grateful for the reprieve, as small as it is, and stare down at my textbook even though I feel her eyes flutter like a moth on me once more at the door.

"Did you hear about Caden?" Philip whispers, confirming that she'd left.

"What about Caden?" I say, suddenly alert.

"His house burned down. Electrical fire, they're saying. His aunt was in there. Everyone's talking about it. Where were you this weekend? Under a rock?"

"I was sick," I repeat. "Did they find his aunt?"

"No," Charisma says. "But she's missing. They're assuming the worst."

I say nothing. It's likely that June's body will never be found in the hidden basement room. My guess is that the Vectors who tracked us into the tunnels torched it completely once they figured out where we went. "How's Caden doing?" I say.

"He seems really out of it, but I guess that's to be expected. He was at a travel meet when it happened, I think. I don't even know where he's staying. Maybe at Sadie's."

I try to resist even thinking about Caden being in that frosting-colored room or lying on that pink ruffled bed covered in frivolous throw pillows, but it's useless as a sour feeling invades my stomach. I crush it with a hiss and make my mind blank. What Caden does with Sadie makes no difference whatsoever to me.

Mrs. Taylor walks back in and announces that the rest of us should make our way to the lab. In the hallway, I see Caden a split second before he sees me. His eyes widen as they glance from my face to my boots, and I can hardly hide the answering scowl overtaking my face.

"Nice dress," he says, echoing Philip's earlier words as we brush shoulders.

"Yeah, if you're homeless," Sadie says, standing next to him with narrowed eyes. She's dressed in a pair of white pants and a pink sweater. I'm actually breathless with anticipation to see if she will recognize the dress as hers, but of course, she doesn't. Still, I can see her brain ticking, considering the fact that somehow—as impossible as it seems—we own exactly the same dress. "It's hideous."

I can barely hold back the truth that stings my lips. Instead, I smile sweetly at her and say, "Like you would know anything about fashion. I think it's from New York. It's *designer.*"

She shoots me a look that would incinerate a building. "Well, you should stick to pants. Dresses don't really suit delinquents," she says nastily.

I bite back a grin and shrug. "Takes one to know one. And I'd rather be a delinquent any day than look like a frosted cupcake without any imagination."

I won't admit it to anyone, but it actually feels good to have a pissing contest with Sadie—if anything, to take the edge off everything that's happened during the last few days. In a weird way, it feels normal, and just the feeling of being able to flay Sadie with my tongue instead of my blade gives me great satisfaction.

Caden's eyes are burning through me, even though he's remained quiet during the entire exchange. I feel his arm brush against the sleeve of my jacket, and then their group is past us. As we walk into the lab, I pull a piece of paper from my pocket. Shae must have given him a heads-up that I'd be back.

*Meet me in the boys' bathroom in ten minutes*, it reads. I crumple it and tuck the paper back into my pocket.

I fumble my way through the experiment, but Charisma is as good as her word, picking up my considerable slack. Philip doesn't volunteer anything, but I can see from his expression that Mrs. Taylor will undoubtedly hear about it at some point. Although I'm familiar with the subject matter, I am too distracted to pay attention, which is probably for the best. I'd rather be noticed for being brainless than for knowing far more than I should. Refraction is something we learn as part of our weapons training, since some of our more advanced laser weapons harness refraction technology. Philip's eyes would likely bug out of his head if he knew that our technology could bend lasers around corners.

After eight minutes, I excuse myself and bolt to the bathroom. It's empty but I wait in the last stall until I hear the outer door open and close. Caden is dragging the trash can against the door as I step out of the stall. His eyes are clouded, and his face is tired. The last two days must have been a whirlwind for him.

"You okay?" I ask.

"Is Shae okay?" Our words merge into each other's at the same time.

I nod. "She's fine. She told me to meet her in the gym after school."

"Yeah, she texted me the same thing. Is she hurt? That thing almost got us. She told me to go, and the last thing I saw was her running toward it."

"She took care of it," I say.

Caden stares at me awkwardly. "Look, Riven, I'm sorry for what Shae did. I don't know why she did it. She didn't explain anything to me. But I wanted to say that I was sorry."

"It's okay. She did what I would have done." I tug with strangely clammy hands at the skirt of the dress. For some reason, being in it with Caden looking at me is making me feel edgy and uncomfortable. When I'm wearing my own clothing, it's like armor. I'm a soldier first and a girl second. Now the reverse feels true. I don't like it.

"I'm still sorry." Caden's voice is quiet and my heart is thumping like it's going to jump out of my chest as he steps closer until he is so near that I can see the downy fuzz on his cheekbones. I stop breathing as goose bumps break out along my arms. Thank the stars my jacket is covering them. "I was really worried that one of those things would have gotten you."

I clear my throat, the rough sound gritty in the brief silence between us, and swallow. "Don't you know? I can take care of myself," I say, desperately trying to sound nonchalant and only succeeding in sounding breathlessly weak.

"I know." Caden's fingers are soft as they trail down the side of my head, and it's all I can do to not lean into them. The soft caress is more than I've felt in a long time, and pressure builds behind my eyes and across my cheekbones.

*Get it together,* I tell myself angrily, and step backward, only there's a sink in the way and there's nowhere else I can go. My eyes slide to Caden's chest and focus on a button, as I force myself to toughen up. *Don't even think about crying!*

But it's like trying to stop a dam that has too many cracks, and my tears are no match for Caden's aching gentleness. And so they come, hot and earnest, as I lean my head against him and feel his arms wrap around me. For the first time, I forget what I am and give in to just being a girl . . . not a soldier, not a grown-up, just a girl.

I cry for myself, I cry for Shae, and I cry most of all for Caden. Deep down inside I know that no matter how much I love Cale and where my loyalty lies, there's no way that I could ever be the one to take Caden's life from him . . . even to save Cale. It's a realization that leaves a part of me numb. It's also one that terrifies me, because for the first time I'm confronted with some of the feelings I know I've been hiding. Shae's right—I do care about him.

And it will be a problem.

Caden's arms are tight, holding me so close it's as if we are one body. I hadn't realized that my arms are twisted around his, my fingers gripping his shirt. There's not even room for breath between us, and even though my tears stop, we still hold each other close. Truth is, I don't want to move, because I know that the moment I stir, things will be different. They have to be. There's no way I can let this *thing* blossoming between us get in the way of what I have to do . . . of who I am. But for one moment, I can pretend that we are somehow more than we are, that we are in a universe of our own making, that we are in love and the world is ours.

Caden's breath brushes against my skin, and I feel his lips press into the hollow of my temple. It feels as if my entire body is disappearing into the imprint of his touch against me. My body tenses automatically, rejecting the light caress.

"Just let go," he whispers against my hair. "You don't have to be strong every single second. Let go, Riv."

For one millisecond, it's the only thing I want to do, as I let my eyes find the deep green vulnerability of his. I can't even think around the knot in my chest at what I see there, and I know he's waiting . . . waiting for me to say something . . . to agree, to do something to make it all real. But I can't.

*Love is weakness*, my father's memory hisses in my head. *It infects your will.*

I close my eyes as the lessons of my childhood overwhelm me with barbed cruelty. We're taught early on to curb our emotions and to make decisions with sound logic. Love isn't something that's valued in Neospes. Families are engineered based on survival abilities and genetic compatibility, not love. It's a useless emotion that causes people to do stupid things in its name. Emotion is the seed of weakness, and making any more of this thing between Caden and I will lead to nothing but loss or pain.

"Riv?" His voice is gentle and so beautiful that every cell in me bends toward it. But I can feel the cold chill of reason battling within me. Nothing good can ever come of this.

"I can't," I whisper, and push myself away with all the strength I can muster, the cold edge of the sink grazing against the small of my back as I twist past it. It hurts more than I can imagine to even look at him. "I just can't . . . not with you. Not with anyone. I'm not built like that. You'll only get hurt, Caden. I don't know how . . ."

My words trail off and I press my hot palms to the cold porcelain of the neighboring sink, my eyes falling away from his. My face is unrecognizable in the mirror above it—puffy eyelids and flushed cheeks. My hair is mussed, and I fix it automatically, sweeping away any evidence of Caden's fingers. I splash cold water on my face and feel better, more like myself. But I still can't face him, so I dart a look at his reflection.

He's standing quiet, his face open and vulnerable. The fleeting thought that Cale would never be this way flits through my brain. He's always been unreadable, the master of all emotion. Some call him cold, but I see it as a gift. Hardly anyone ever knows what Cale is thinking. In the same breath, I understand that maybe this is what gets to me about Caden—he's so *different*, so unguarded.

Our eyes meet and he smiles, a deep gentle smile unhinges any resolve I have. "Don't shut down, Riven. Pleas I know what you've been taught to be, but there is something real between us. I know you feel it, too."

"You're wrong."

"Am I?" He's standing right behind me again, his gaze impaling mine in the mirror, daring me to lie. I don't answer. Instead, I swing around and shove my hands into his chest so hard that he crashes into the metal doors of the stalls behind us. I resort to the only response I know: combat.

"You're going to fight me, Riv?" he gasps, hugging his chest with one arm.

"If I have to," I say. "Just stop. Stop right there."

"What if I don't?" he says, advancing once more toward me, one step, then two.

"You won't like what you get, Caden. I don't want to hit you."

Another step. "That's a risk I'm willing to take."

"I'm not," I say, and drive a closed fist into his shoulder. But either I'm not committed to the blow or Caden's gotten faster than I'd given him credit for, because he deflects my strike with an easy dart to the right and grabs my arm, my own momentum spinning me with considerable force into the wall at the end of the bathroom. Caden's right there with me, his breath warm in my face. "Let me go," I seethe through clenched teeth. I twist my knee up, but he presses his body into mine so hard that my limbs are glued to the wall behind me.

Irritation courses through me in violent waves. But something else flows hotly, too, and I feel my breath falter. The truth is, I don't want to move. The only thing holding us in place is the length of his body against every inch of mine. Something unfamiliar stirs in my chest. I wrangle my free arm up under my jacket to pull out one of my weapons, but Caden grabs it with his hand. My breaths get shorter and shorter, and suddenly his mouth is crushed against my lips.

Every thought in my brain fizzles into shocked silence. And then I'm kissing him back, following his lead, with an intensity that has our teeth grinding together. I don't even know where he begins and I end—my lips are part of his mouth, and his part of mine. My hands, now free, are twining in his hair, and his arms are locked around me. Every living part of me is caught up in him.

The grating sound of the trash bin grinding across the floor pierces through the fog encasing us both, and I open languorous eyes to see Sadie, her body shaking with rage.

"What the *fuck* is going on?"

# 12

# SCARS

"WHAT THE HELL happened to you?" Shae blurts out as we meet her in the gym parking lot after school. Shae, for her part, is looking a lot better. She's clean and has on a pair of dark jeans and a green sweater. Most of the blood is gone from her face and she looks semi-normal.

I, on the other hand, am a completely different story. After a trip to the school nurse and principal, the rest of the day had passed in relative quiet, despite the occasional censuring look from students and teachers alike. I touch the three claw marks on my face and grin. Caden stares at the ground, but I can see that the corner of his lips is twitching.

"Sadie happened," I say.

Shae's eyes narrow, jumping from me to Caden and back again. "Caden's Sadie?"

Even though I bristle inside at the comment that Sadie was Caden's anything, I shrug. "She's a little high-strung, if you hadn't noticed. Anyway, she attacked me for no reason," I say. Caden launches a hot look in my direction, but I ignore it. "I took care of it; don't worry."

"What do you mean, you took care of it?" The suspicion and patronizing edge of Shae's voice irritate me. I know that this isn't Neospes, and apart from what she may think about me, I do have half a brain in my head. I throw my hands into the air in exasperation.

"I drowned her in a toilet," I say, and then after seeing Shae's expression, "Kidding! Look, Princess Pinkalicious is fine. She'll have to go to the salon to fix those curls, but a little toilet water never killed anyone."

"Don't look at me!" Caden says as Shae turns the force of her glare on him. "I got punched in the face. And I think she broke up with me."

The brief flutter of elation I feel at Caden's words disappears under the heavy weight of reality as Shae herds us toward a green car parked in the lot. Deep down, I know that Caden will probably be a hell of a lot better off with Sadie than with someone like me. Despite letting my guard down in the bathroom, I don't know the first thing about being anyone's girlfriend or letting someone get close to me.

"You're better off without her," Shae says, catching my attention. "There's something about her that rubs me the wrong way, like she's too perfect. I never got why you liked her. She just didn't seem like your type."

"And yet you let me date her for a year?"

Shae shrugs. "I only protect you. I don't smother. If Sadie was your idea of a girlfriend, then that was your choice. Out of curiosity, though, why'd you go out with her?"

Caden flushes, embarrassed at the direct question, but he answers Shae. "Because it was easy. I didn't have to think about anything. And you're right, she isn't my type. I didn't even know I had a type until recently."

"So what is it?" Shae asks. She sounds as if she's only making conversation, but I'm listening very carefully.

"Not her," Caden says. His glance slips to me, and then falls to my lips before looking away. An immediate response sears through me, but I refuse to think about the kiss and the way it'd made me feel like a live electrical wire. I'd never even kissed anyone before, and now I can't look at him without my ears flaming or my pulse racing. I hate it. I hate how unpredictable it makes me feel, like I can't depend on myself anymore, like a part of me is caught up in someone else. It's unfamiliar and unwelcome territory.

"Where are we going?" I snap gruffly to Shae.

"Somewhere safe."

I nod to the dirt bike I left parked on the right side of the green car. "I'll follow you guys."

Not that I don't want to go with Shae, but I like having my options open, especially if I need a getaway ride. I also don't want to be in such close proximity to Caden. He makes me agitated for obvious reasons, and I need to have all my wits about me going into this blind. Shae's expression remains calm, but she flicks a raised eyebrow in my direction.

After a couple of seconds, Shae jumps into the car and nods for Caden to get in. Instead, he walks over to me sitting on the bike. I tense immediately at his soft touch on my shoulder. "What's wrong?"

I can feel Shae's heavy stare through the car window. Sighing, I look Caden full in the face, steeling my voice and my heart. "It never happened, okay? This thing with you and me. It *can't* happen. Do you understand what I'm saying?"

"Why? What do you mean?" His voice is wounded, and my eyes fall away from his, unable to bear the pooling hurt there. "I thought—"

"No, you were wrong, Caden. I didn't feel anything. I was testing to see how far you would go," I say without inflection. I know the words are like daggers to him, but I don't care. I have to end it before it grows into something worse, something that could endanger the both of us. So instead, I deaden any emotion inside of me with practiced ease. "I'm sorry you thought it was something more. It wasn't. I just don't feel that way about you."

The pain in his voice is worse than I could imagine. "You were *testing* me? For what? To lead me on? To see me make a fool of myself?"

"Yes." The word is like a gunshot, but it fulfills its purpose. Caden backs away, his eyes wide and angry. I can feel my betrayal eating away at him. And even though my insides feel like a pulverized mess, I know what I'm doing is right. Maybe in a different time, we could have been more, but not now . . . not with everything at stake. Wearing Sadie's dress has made me weak. It has made me just as selfish and as self-indulgent as she is.

"Shae was right, wasn't she?" he whispers. "I thought she was out of her mind when she called you the ice queen. But you are, aren't you? You're heartless, Riven."

I flinch at his words, but I shrug, nonchalant. "I've been called far worse. You'd do best to keep your distance from me, Caden. I'm no good for anyone," I say quietly. My voice is barely a whisper now. "Shae knows me better than most. I don't know how to love. Just ask her. She'll tell you."

"How would she know anything about you? You just met."

I stare at him sadly. "Because she's my sister," I say, and gun the engine on the bike, pulling away as fast as I can from the shattered look on his face. At the end of the parking lot, I wait, watching as he gets into the car with Shae. He doesn't even look at me as they drive past, and I'm grateful for that even though it cuts through me like a hot blade.

As I follow Shae's car, my thoughts inexorably return to the kiss. It had been so unexpected and so fiery that even now my chest heats up just from thinking about it. I don't know what I feel about Caden and whether those feelings are indeed separate from Cale. The thing is that Cale is like a brother to me, but with Caden, there's something more. I was primed to love him just from knowing Cale, but I'm falling in love with him because he's Caden. I'm so confused that it's making me crazy, my thoughts whirling into a blurring jumble in my head. The only thing standing out from everything else is whether I'm being disloyal to Cale.

Because I can't help but feel like I am betraying him somehow.

Ahead of me, Shae slows down in front of a wide iron gate. I can't see the house from where we are, but I expect that there is one behind the imposing wall of metal. The gate is attached to a high stone wall, and for a second I wonder what whoever lives there wants to keep out. Or in.

A small camera is mounted on the right side of the gate, and I can feel its eye centered on me. After a couple seconds, the gate slides open. My pulse is racing, but I follow Shae inside onto a long and narrow driveway flanked by slender pine trees. The gates close noiselessly behind us, and the creepy silence of it is unnerving. The thought of an asylum drifts through my head and I shiver. Something isn't right. I don't know if it's nerves or adrenaline, but I'm on edge and my instincts are screaming.

Before I can accelerate to cut in front of Shae to voice my misgivings, we pull up in front of a looming stone house. It's as forbidding as the iron gate and stone wall surrounding it. Removing my helmet, I dismount and check to make sure all my weapons are in place, just in case. Even if they're Shae's friends, I still don't trust easily. Everyone is an enemy until they prove otherwise.

There's a person on the stairs in front of the giant double door, and Shae's shaking hands with him. I follow, intentionally tucking Caden behind me. His feelings toward me are obvious, but I ignore them. His safety is paramount. The person turns, and for a second, my breath halts in my chest as a pair of familiar obsidian eyes freeze my body in its tracks.

"Mrs. Taylor?" I say, dumbfounded. "*You're* the Guardian?"

A tight smile. "Riven," she says with a nod. "Welcome to my home. Any friend of Shae's is a friend of ours. Please call me Era."

Caden's eyes are as wide as my own, but he remains silent. I hide my own surprise with indifference as I walk past her through the door. Her home is dark on the inside with heavy shutters covering all the windows. My tension ratchets up a notch, and the hairs on the back of my neck are at stiff attention. It takes everything inside of me not to draw my weapons.

"Drinks? Food? Can I get you anything?" Era asks as we follow her down a few steps into a long hallway that has no windows.

"No, thanks," Shae says. Caden nods that he didn't want anything either, and I stay silent. There's no way I'm eating anything in this house.

Shae and Era are at the front with Caden behind them. I'm bringing up the rear. In the narrow hallway, I feel my instincts kicking in, and not in a good way. I catch up to Caden and squeeze his arm. His eyes meet mine. For a minute, it seems like he's going to ignore me, but then he falls back alongside me.

"What's up?"

"Look," I whisper. "If anything happens, get behind me, okay?"

"Why? What's wrong?"

I purse my lips and shake my head, any awkwardness between us forgotten for the moment. I pause, checking that Era and Shae are still far enough ahead of us. "Something doesn't feel right. If Mrs. Taylor knew about us, why didn't she say anything? It doesn't make sense."

"Maybe she didn't know," he says. I feel his eyes studying me. "I didn't even know you and Shae were related, remember?"

"Stop," I hiss at his potshot. "Even if she didn't know about me, she had to know about *you*. And if she is a Guardian, why wouldn't Shae have warned her about me?"

There's a long pause before Caden answers. "I see your point."

Up ahead, Shae and Era have stopped at a gray metal door at the end of the hallway. It reminds me of the door that June had in her house, the one leading to the secret room in the basement. Only on either side of this door, there are two recessed keypads with LED biometric pads. The lights in the corridor flicker and I frown. Era turns to me with a tight smile.

"It's nothing; don't worry. A power surge," she says, and nods to a white table in the corner. "Please leave any weapons you're carrying over there."

"What's behind that door?" I counter flatly, ignoring her reassurance that does nothing to reassure me one bit. Neither does the command to leave my weapons out here. The muscles in my neck remain as tight as coiled springs. A power surge? What's in that room that would affect all the power in the house? Some kind of electrical torture chamber? My frown deepens.

Era smiles a smile that goes nowhere near her eyes. But it doesn't surprise me—she's a Guardian, and an *active* Guardian at that. They're chosen for their complete lack of reaction. They make decisions based on logic and reason, and they don't deviate from the jobs they're supposed to do.

It's hard to reconcile the two Mrs. Taylors—the teacher at school and the uncompromising Guardian standing in front of me. Without a doubt, I know that she's a Guardian first and a teacher second. She isn't my friend—after all, I'd flaunted the Guardian's cardinal law by defecting to this universe. The only reason she's giving me the time of day is because she thinks I'm an ally of Shae's. I wonder just how much Shae has told her about me. Would she have told Era the truth? I take a deep breath to calm my panicked thoughts.

"I mean it. I'm not going in there," I repeat. "Especially without my weapons."

"It's okay, Riven," Shae says. Then she grasps my arm, and leans in. "You have to trust me. We'll be safe. Just do as she says."

I shoot her a scathing look but remove my jacket and harness, tossing my backpack into the corner. Caden does the same. Era nods with satisfaction before she and Shae punch in some kind of simultaneous code on either side of the door and lean in for a retina scan. My unease spirals.

What in hell is behind that door?

As the door swings open on noiseless hinges, I don't realize I'm gripping Caden's wrist so tightly that he winces and pulls away. But I can't even think to apologize. Instead, as pale blue fluorescent light and the nauseatingly familiar smell of formaldehyde rush out to greet me, I'm frozen into immobility.

The room is circular. The floor is metal. There are men in blue head-to-toe suits walking past us with steel trays and tablet computers. Computer flat-screens are everywhere full of trending data that I can't even begin to process, but I'm guessing that it's some kind of laboratory. My eyes take in the details, categorizing them in my head and assessing for danger. And there's a lot of it . . . that I know for certain.

Caden pushes past me to follow Shae and Era inside, and I do the same only to be assaulted by what awaits me. I forget the men in the blue suits immediately. A row of Vectors stand in circular man-sized specimen tubes strapped vertically to the wall, a handful of them to the right of where I'm standing. My jaw drops to the floor and stays there.

"What *is* this place?" I hear Caden say.

"It's a research facility," Shae responds. "Era's been studying them for years, trying to recreate the parameters to evert as they do."

"But you have to be dead," I say automatically.

Era impales me with an unnerving, piercing stare. I hold it this time and raise an uncowed eyebrow. "Not necessarily," she says. "We can reduce certain things to mimic the state of the Vectors, to put a body at rest if you will."

Skepticism threads my voice. "No, the bodies have to be dead to withstand eversion from anywhere. Anything less than a zero gravity point will pulverize us."

A slow smile. "Come now, Riven. Put that physics knowledge of yours to good use," she says in a patronizing voice that sets my teeth on edge. "Why do you think the Vectors generate so much electricity when they evert?" She waits, and I shrug. I never got into the technicalities with my father. All I knew was that they were dead things that could jump from anywhere and we could not.

Era smiles. "The electrical energy generated by the nano-plasm inside of them acts as a force field to protect the human tissue. Dead or alive, it doesn't matter. We can increase the electricity inside our neurons to jump as they do."

"How?"

"We've developed a serum," Era says, her hand gesturing to the men walking around us. "Come, let me show you."

We follow her past the Vectors, but I can't help staring at the darkly veined, translucent bodies on display. On close inspection, I can see the outline of their bones as well as the metal wires from the lithia core connecting the spine to the skull. I step closer. Numbers are inked into their skin. One reads 104. The one closest to me twitches, and I almost jump out of my skin.

"Are they active?" I blurt out.

"Of course not," Era says. "Don't worry, pet; you're safe. They can't hurt anyone."

Ignoring her supercilious tone, my gaze falls back to the Vectors. They're all still functioning, but somehow they've been neutralized. I wonder for a second how they'd been able to deactivate them. It isn't like they have a kill switch, and all of my father's programming is strongly encrypted. But then I remember. Shae would have provided some, if not all, of that information.

"How did you get them?" I ask, nodding at the five Vectors standing inside the glass half tubes against the wall. I can't help the edge to my voice. "And how did you deactivate them?"

"With great difficulty."

Shae turns toward me. "They were older, first generation. When we . . . left, I took any of Father's research I could get my hands on. I knew he'd send the Vectors after us, and I was hoping I could use it to avoid them. Era discovered that they were programmed with some kind of kill code."

"The Vectors all have self-destruct codes," I say slowly. "It's in their operating parameters. If their objectives are compromised, the nanoplasm shuts down."

"That's where I come in." I dimly recognize the voice but not the face behind the blue mask.

"Philip?" Caden asks, and his voice startles me. I'd forgotten that he was even there. But he's staring at the person removing the gaskets connecting a wide helmet to a blue safety suit.

"Wait, *Philip*?" I echo.

"Extra credit," he says in a bland voice. "And training. I'm next in line." He jerks his head toward Era. My brows snap together, eyes darting between Philip and Era. The resemblance had not been obvious before, but now I see the same long noses and the wide, angular cheekbones, even though Philip's hair is blond and not dark like Era's. I feel a flush redden my cheeks as I recall the strange look Era had given me when I'd lied saying that Philip seemed to like me. Cringing embarrassment hardens my voice.

"Wait, what? You're in training to be a Guardian?"

Philip nods briefly and gets back to business, consulting a tablet he's holding in his left hand. He types in a sequence. "I embedded a code to override the self-destruct programming. These three on the left," he says gesturing to the Vectors closest to us, "have been completely deprogrammed."

"And the other two?"

"They were the last ones we got. Still working on them. Their security has an additional layer that we haven't been able to get past, some kind of eleven-digit code. They're slightly more advanced. I've run different algorithms, and nothing."

My mind is racing. I still don't quite understand what they want to achieve by everting from any point like the Vectors, especially using first-generation Vectors from twelve years ago. My legion had been third-gen, and I'd bet anything that the Vector commander we had fought before was far more advanced than any I'd ever had under my command.

"I'm sorry. I don't get it. Why *would* you want to evert from anywhere? What's the point?"

Philip doesn't answer and Shae avoids my eyes. Of course; I see it now. It's an exit strategy if anyone pursing them—like me—somehow manages to get too close.

Shae nods, confirming my guess. "It was our way out if they sent anyone after us."

Her voice is quiet, and I notice she doesn't imply that I'm one of the people chasing them. It occurs to me right at that moment that she hasn't told Era the truth about me. It seems odd that Shae would protect me, even after everything. "I just didn't think it was going to take this long to get a workable serum."

"So how does the jump work?" Caden's voice is small. He's been quietly listening all along and trying to put together the pieces, from what Shae and I had told him earlier to what he was hearing now.

Philip brings up a controller on his tablet and keys in some numbers. A picture forms on the flat-screens in the center of the room. It looks like an hourglass broken up into small squares. "That is a two-dimensional drawing of a traversable wormhole. It's basically a bridge in space with two different end points. Think of the universe as made up of an infinite number of universes. Some of these universes are coupled by a gravitational field, which means that we can communicate between them. Okay so far?" Caden nods, and Philip continues, pointing to one side of the diagram. "In this case, this is our world, and that is Neospes, where Shae—and the Vectors—are from."

Philip pauses to bring up another image on the computers, this time a series of numbers and symbols on a graph with moving waves. "How it works is a whole other story. We're talking string theory and sub-quantum mechanics, basically the relationship between space-time, gravity, energy, and matter. Okay?"

"Not really. You lost me at string," Caden says, dazed. I bite back a smile.

"What Philip is trying to say," Shae explains, "is that our physicists figured out a way to manipulate electrons and gravity to jump between one universe to the other. Like through a kind of passage."

"You mean like a *stargate*?" Caden offers, remembering my earlier jibe. "You know, the movie?"

Philip sighs and rolls his eyes. "Sort of, only there's no gate, but the transference is similar."

"Okay, so why doesn't everyone know about this? I mean, it's amazing," Caden says. "Can you imagine if everyone could do that?"

"They can't." Era moves to the front screen and taps in some more commands that clear them all. Her voice is hard. "Though the universes exist in parallel, we're not meant to go between them. We were breaking the laws of evolution and nature. And nature has a tough way of evening things out. Where do you think the bubonic plague came from that wiped out millions of people in Europe? We couldn't control it, so we closed the wormholes and founded the Guardians on this side." She nods toward Shae. "They created the Vectors on theirs to police and deal with illegal jumpers."

"What about them?" My voice is harsh in the vacuum of silence following Era's words. "Why wasn't Leila or Shae dealt with for jumping illegally?" I'm more curious than anything—

the Guardians have such rigid laws that it doesn't make sense as to why they would allow Shae to remain here.

"Caden's mother was seeking asylum to return home with her son from the Lord King at the time," Era says. "The Faction could not deny it."

At her words, Caden is already backing away, his face confused and betrayed, staring from Shae to Era to me. His anger finds an easy mark.

"I'm the *target* you were talking about in my house that day?" he hisses in my direction. "I'm what you were looking for? The next in line to your stupid monarchy?"

"It's not what you think—" I begin, but he cuts me off.

"No. It's not what *you* think," he says. "I don't belong there. I belong here. I'm not going with you. Not now, not ever. I could care less if your idiot boyfriend is dying."

I'm flinching inside at the words he's throwing so carelessly at me, but the truth is, I *am* here to take him back. My voice is cold when I respond. My words are for everyone.

"That idiot boyfriend is your brother and the reason you're even alive. And you're going whether you like it or not." I turn to Philip, who's staring at me like I've grown a pair of horns on my forehead. "Try these numbers." I reel off a series of numbers and he hastily enters them onto his tablet.

"What are they?"

"My name and my birth date. Trust me, that's the code you're looking for."

Philip punches in the numbers and for a second, nothing happens. My father had been anything if predictable with the earlier versions of his pet project. Maybe I've got it wrong.

"I'm sorry—"

But the wailing of a loud siren—the sound of security being breached—cuts off my words. Philip's eyes are wide and horrified, focused on something behind me. Era is already diving for some kind of control pad on the computer desk, slamming her left hand down so that more alarms are shrieking. In her right hand, she's holding an electro-rod. In that millisecond, I notice that it's not set to stun.

It's set to kill.

Shae screams and pushes Caden to the floor as people in blue suits streak past us. Doors start closing, separating the room into smaller quarters. I turn in slow motion, only to meet the cold dead eyes of one of the Vectors that I had clearly just activated.

# 13

# TRACK OR TRAP

FATHER HAD BEEN predictable, all right.

Predictable enough to know that one day I'd be the one to initiate the Vector spies that had gone missing in this world. I curse myself again, reaching for my ninjatas, but there's nothing there but bare skin. This time, I curse Era for making me leave them outside of the room that is now sealed behind a giant metal door. Scanning the space, I see another white door on the other side of the room that has a small window in the center of it. Caden's face is peering at me from the other side. His eyes are terrified, jumping from the Vector to me. I nod reassuringly—at least he's safe for the moment.

"Open that door," I shout.

"We can't; standard security protocol," Era says from behind me. Her voice is controlled and calm. She's holding two electro-rods in each hand, and one of them is pointed right at me. "They'll stay closed until the situation is resolved. Who are you? How did you activate them?"

"I didn't—"

"What the hell did you do?" Philip says angrily. "And why is it just standing there?"

Philip is right. The Vector across from us is not moving, even though its eyes are open and staring at the three of us. Something's not right. Vectors don't hesitate—they follow a program, a very specific program. This one is waiting for a reason.

"Era," I say urgently. "There were two of them, right?" She nods, the electro-rod dropping slowly downward. "Two. Where's the other one?"

In slow motion, we both turn to the white door in the center of the wall at the same time that a bright swath of blood splashes across the window. My heart leaps into my throat, but neither of us can get to the door, as the one in our room darts to stand between us and the computer panel. I've never seen a Vector move that quickly. This one is different. For a second, I wonder if the other one in Caden's room is as quick. Shae will protect Caden, I tell myself. She has to. That thought is the only thing keeping me together.

The Vector moves again, this time delivering a blow to Philip's head and spinning behind Era. Her cry is loud even as she lunges toward it, but it's too fast, darting out of her way with incredible speed. I skid over to Philip. He's still breathing, and I shove him under the console in the middle of the room. "Stay here," I tell him, and he nods woozily.

Era has gotten in a couple good hits. I can see the charred skin from where she's shocked the Vector, but he's too quick for her to strike where it will disable him.

"Why isn't it fighting back?" Era shouts, edging back to where I'm standing next to Philip. "Do you see that? It's toying with us. What's it waiting for?"

Its movements seem vaguely familiar to me. I've seen one of these kinds of Vectors before. They're wiry and fast, and aren't programmed to fight. They're programmed for other things.

I think back to the moment when Murek had planned the coup and killed his brother. He'd been with a Vector like this one. I remember thinking at the time that it didn't seem like much protection, but Murek had insisted that the creature accompany them. Then they'd been flash-attacked. Murek had miraculously survived, but his brother and most of the group had been killed, including the strange Vector. Whatever had attacked them had known exactly where they would be, because the attack had been strategic and swift. By the time the royal guards had gotten there, the attackers were already gone. Murek had said it had been doomed timing, but I'd known better.

"It's a shadow," I breathe.

"A what?" Era's voice is suspicious. "What the hell is a shadow?"

"They're spies. They send out some kind of signal to call for more Vectors." Era doesn't answer but Philip does. He's holding his tablet in his hand and staring at it in horror.

"She's right," he whispers. "There's some kind of radio wave that wasn't here before."

"You can track signals?" I ask.

"We need to deactivate it right now," Era says, veering toward the thing before I can stop her. Just then an explosion rocks the wall in the back of the room, and I see chunks of colored plaster fly into the small window. But I can't even think about Caden and Shae. I have way worse things to worry about, staring from Era to the shadow Vector. She's going to make it worse.

"Era, no!" I tackle her from behind, and we both roll crashing into the unresponsive Vectors on the far side of the room. She punches me in the face and I feel my head snap backward from the blow. Stars spin in my vision, but I manage to block her second strike. "Stop!" I scream. "It's a trap; if you hurt it, it will explode. That's what just happened in the other room. I don't even know if the others are alive."

"But if we don't disarm it, we're dead either way," Philip yells.

But there is another way. That is . . . if the thing will listen to me as the other one in Caden's bedroom had. "Let me try." I approach the Vector slowly, my hands in the air. It watches me but doesn't move out of my way. I glance back at Era and then Philip, both staring at me with wary expressions. "Stand down, soldier," I say firmly. I can feel the hot lasers of Era's eyes on my back, but I have no other option. "That is a direct order from your commanding officer."

Its answer is to lurch forward and grab my neck in its cold hands, so fast that I can barely get my own hands up to block it. Black dots dance in my vision. And then everything goes eerily quiet. I don't know if I'm dead or dreaming when the big metal doors swing open, and Caden rushes in, sword in hand to cleave the Vector's head clean off its body.

Someone's screaming for us to get out, and I feel rough hands pulling me. Vaguely, I see Shae's face at the doorway holding it open with painted red arms. I have no voice. The metal door closes behind us and an explosion rocks the entire house, throwing us to the floor and plunging the entire hallway into darkness.

"Riven, get up. GET UP!"

Maybe I am dreaming. And we're all already dead. But Caden's voice in my ear is not a figment of my imagination. I feel his hands on my face, and then under my arms, lifting me. I stand on shaky feet—that thing had almost killed me. My breaths are labored pants, but I'm starting to feel like maybe I'm not actually dead.

"Caden?" I croak. "You're alive. How—"

"No time, Riv. They're already here." Shae's voice comes from the other side of me. "We have to move." She shoves something in my arms, and I realize that it's my backpack and my jacket. "Let's go."

"This way," Era says. We navigate the dark hallway, holding on to each other, until we're at a narrow staircase. "This will take us to the office on the third floor." Noiselessly, we make our way up, listening for sounds that we're being followed or that something's waiting for us at the other end.

But we're safe for the moment. The office is empty, but the electricity works. There are only six of us now: Shae and Caden, Era and Philip, one of the research guys who looks like he's in some kind of shock, and me.

"Everyone okay?" Shae whispers. She's once more covered in blood and gore, as is Caden.

"She's one of them," Era says glaring at me. "An officer."

"I know," Shae says, surprising them, and me most of all.

"And you brought her here?" Philip hisses. I throw a scowl in his direction and he scowls back just as fiercely. I am the enemy.

"She's with us now," Shae says firmly. "Right, Riven?" I notice Era says nothing, but I can feel her eyes on me, studying.

I nod—I need their help if we have any hope of escaping the Vectors. For now, "the enemy of my enemy is my friend" is truer than ever.

"How many?" I ask, glancing toward the office door.

"We got the one in the room," Caden whispers. "Jim overrode the system so we could get out through an emergency hatch, but we lost two of the other guys in the explosion. We had to circle around to get to the door to your room. Shae got one of the other Vectors, and I took one out, but there's more. Those things told them exactly where we were."

"You mean she did," Philip says with an accusing look in my direction.

"Shut up, Philip," Shae says, but I still feel an unwelcome stab of guilt, knowing that I'd been the one to reactivate them. "It's not your fault, Riv," Shae says softly in my ear. "I was going to suggest the same thing. He played us both."

I nod, silent. "What now, then?"

"We try to get out of here." She turns to Era. "The exit tunnels, are they still usable?"

Era shakes her head. "The explosion in the lab would have compromised them. We can't go back down there. The only way out is up to the third floor and then off the balcony to the back."

"We have to be very quiet, then," Shae says. "There's too many of them for us to take them head-on."

"Okay, let's go," Caden says, and I'm surprised at this side of him . . . a leader. In the last few hours, he looks older and harder. He said that he'd taken out one of the other Vectors—not bad for someone whose skill is based on sport fencing. My lip twitches, and then I remember that Shae had told me that she'd trained Caden, and that he was good enough to fight me. The beginnings of the smile fade away and I stare at him with a grudging respect.

I follow them on silent feet as we make our way to the staircase leading to the third floor. There are crashing noises on the lower level, and it won't be long before they come upstairs. But we have some time. They are nothing if not methodical and will strip each floor completely before moving on to the next. Their programming gives us a tiny sliver of opportunity to escape.

Caden's shoulder brushes mine. "You okay?" I whisper to him, and he nods. He looks uncomfortable for a second and then leans in.

"I'm sorry for what I said earlier," he whispers back. "You know, in the room. About Cale. I didn't know." The sound of Cale's name on his lips is like a painful dart in my chest. "Shae explained that he was sick and that I'm the only one who can help him."

"Yes." It's the only word I can manage. I can only imagine what kind of lies—or truths—Shae had told him about Cale or why I was there. But nothing prepares me for Caden's next words.

"She said it was up to me," he says quietly. "She told me that she's dying and can't protect me anymore. But that I would be safest with you no matter what." He pauses to stare at me searchingly. "So I'm in."

"Next door on the left." Era's voice drifts back to us, but we're both standing still staring at the other until we're alone in the hallway.

"Are you sure?" I grit out. "I can't promise you anything, Caden. And I don't even know that Cale is still alive. Maybe you're better off here with Shae and Era. Shae's going to be fine. Trust me, you don't know her like I do."

Another crash from downstairs makes us both jump. Caden links his hand into mine, and squeezes. "All I know is that those things want to kill me, and with you I have a shot of survival, whether that's here or there. So I'm in, whatever you decide. I just wanted you to know that."

"You guys, come on!"

Era's hiss has us both moving, and we follow the others silently into the room. Shae's already got a rope tied to the balcony. Her gaze flutters to our hands, and she nods just once before hopping over the side. Jim, the research guy, has already gone, and so has Philip.

"You go after Shae, Caden. Then her," Era says, nodding at me. Her glance slips to our fingers and something in it makes me pull away, self-conscious. "I'll bring up the rear in case any of them make it up here. Go!"

Caden leaps over and shimmies down the rope. It's three stories up but he slides down easily and gives me a thumbs-up once he's on the ground. I turn around to let Era know that I'm going, but am completely blindsided by the blunt metal that crunches into my face. Something snakes around my wrist and pulls it tight against a hard edge.

Dazed, I feel warm wet blood trickling down my face and blink through the blood to see Era jumping over the side. Her black lifeless eyes meet mine for a brief second and I see nothing there, not even regret for her betrayal.

I am still her enemy.

"Era, you're making a mistake," I gasp. "Shae can't make it without me."

"You're with them," she shoots back. "You were the one who brought them here."

"No," I say, desperate. "I didn't. I'm against them; you don't understand."

Era slides me a circumspect look. "So you're not their general?" I want to lie, to say anything that would make her release me, but I know that it would only backfire in my face. I had to take a chance that she would believe the truth.

"Yes; I mean I was but not anymore. I defected to find Caden. He's next in line for the monarchy." But it was the wrong thing to say. Her face hardens, and I gnash my teeth in frustration at my foolish mistake.

"Yes, for parts, correct?" Her voice is acidic. "You deserve to die with your kind," she spits toward me.

"No! You're wrong. I'll figure something out, please, Era!" Pulling against the plastic tie tethering my hand to the metal screen door, I try to reach for her, but she's already gone.

In the room, I can hear noises of movement on the stairs. They're coming to this level. I know that I only have a couple minutes, if that, before the Vectors swarm. I swing myself onto my stomach, pulling against the plastic tie so hard that I can feel its edges slicing into my skin. But I take the pain for the moment, twisting my free arm up and back to get one of my swords. My fingers touch the bottom hilt and peel their way upward, but they're slick with sweat.

I tilt my body and my fingers find a grip. The sword is in my hand just as the first Vector enters the room. The curtains to the balcony billow with the wind, but I know that it will search routinely unless I attract its attention. As quietly as possible, I slide my blade's edge toward the plastic shackling my wrist, wincing at the pain, and with a quiet snap, I'm free.

But I'm afraid to even take a breath as another Vector joins the first, and then a third. The smell of them is gagging. The rope is still tied to the top of the stone balustrade, but it's on the other side of the balcony from where I am. There's no way I could be quick enough to get to it and get safely down without drawing their attention, especially with the only cover being the sheer curtains and two double glass doors.

Sliding my blade soundlessly into its sheath, I step quietly to the edge and without hesitation fling myself over the side just as one of them comes through the doors. Without daring to breathe, I hang by the tips of my fingers on the lip of the stone's edge, hoping beyond hope that the Vector doesn't do any kind of heat scan. Luckily, it doesn't, and after a grunt, I hear its footsteps recede into the room.

My fingers feel like they're going to break off even though it's only been about thirty seconds, and I dig the points of my boots into the wall behind me to get some leverage. But it's no use; I feel my fingers start to slip from their precarious hold. And then I'm sliding down, panicked, until my feet slam into a three-inch decorative ledge of stone running around the side of the house. I hang on for dear life even though the skin on the pads of my fingers is red-raw from the sharp rock.

The scrabbling noises of my fall have two of the Vectors back out on the balcony. If they look over the side, they'll see me dangling like some kind of weird spider in plain sight, but fortunately for me they're distracted by the rope. One of their suits emits a series of loud, short beeps, and they all march back inside.

I'll have to find another way down, and fast. I start inching toward the right corner of the house. I cling to the shadows along the wall and keep moving, hoping for a miracle. I squint in the darkness—there's something long and dark in front of me. A gutter pipe! I almost lose my hold in my haste to reach it, and then I'm moving downward without hesitation like a monkey, hand over fist.

Floodlights illuminate the lawn just as I reach the bottom, and I flatten myself against the wall behind some shrubs. They're prickly and scratch my face and legs, but I don't feel any of it. My attention is riveted on the couple dozen Vectors flowing out of the house. Where had they all come from? The others wouldn't stand a chance against so many!

"Find them," I hear a guttural voice command, and my blood turns to ice. It's the same commander, the one that had been tracking us, my father's number one. "Bio sensors on."

One of the Vectors makes its way toward me, and I crawl backward, mindless of the sharp branches. Against the wall, I slide my swords out without a sound. I stop breathing as it comes within inches of me, and leap up to silently sever its spinal cord. Its body slumps backward, and I shove it under the bushes before swiping its bio sensor and communicator, and then I'm running into the cover of the trees as fast as my feet can take me.

I have to find the others before they do.

The biometric readings on the device show Caden about half a mile away from my present location. I run hard, knowing that the horde of Vectors is right behind me, until my lungs are burning and my breath is coming in shallow, desperate pants. And then I hear them, crashing through the underbrush all around me. I'm too late.

"Riv! In here." I look around but all I can see are three big rocks and some bushes. "Up here."

They're in some kind of cave on the top of the rock ledge. Without a second thought, I hoist myself up and climb into the brush, not looking back. I can hear the sounds of movement on my heels, but it only makes me climb faster. After a couple of minutes, I see an arm and then Caden's face. Shae is leaning against him and her eyes are closed. My relief is tangible, even though Shae looks like she's on her last legs.

"Where are the others? Era and Philip?" I whisper.

Caden shakes his head. "Philip lost it and took off. And then Era went after him, and that was the last we saw of either of them."

"How's she doing?" I whisper with a nod at Shae.

"I'm fine, little sister." Her voice is barely a wheeze, but her grip is strong as she grabs my hand. "It's time."

"Time for what?"

"You know what: to go," Shae says. "We can't last in here. They're already out there. There's too many, and the only way is to evert. Now."

"But we can't. We need an eversion point."

Shae wheezes again. "Hand me my bag." She pulls out the silver case I'd given her. There's one injector dose left. She stabs it into her leg, wincing, and places the empty cartridge next to her on the ground. She pulls out a white bag and removes two more injectors. The liquid is a deep jewel blue color. "It's the serum we've been working on."

"What if it doesn't work?"

"It does. I've used it," Shae says with a smile. "To get away from you. We were trying to refine it. The aftereffects were bad on the nervous system." Her smile turns sad, and something inside of me crumples. "As you can clearly see. Someone had to be the guinea pig. I'm just glad it was me."

"Shae—"

"Riv, you promised, remember?" A thin dribble of blood leaks from the corner of her mouth. Her voice is urgent. "When you inject it, evert right away. Run as fast as you can on the other side, because you'll be in the Outers. You have thirty minutes to evert back before the serum becomes compromised. That should be enough time to get you away from them in any direction. After thirty minutes, you'll need to find an eversion point to get back here. Whatever you decide, keep Caden safe." Her fingers clutch mine, and I feel her knuckles slide against my face. "I believed in you, you know. I never stopped."

And then before I can say anything, she shoves her backpack and an eversion device into my hands and pushes past us, jumping down to the clearing below. I'm already twisting to leap after her when Caden's hands haul me back. I can feel the tears on my face, hot and violent. I want to hurt them, the Vectors—*him*—for ripping us apart again. My rage is all-consuming until I'm nothing but fury.

"Riven, no," Caden says, grasping my shoulders. "Don't make her sacrifice be in vain. We have to go."

"She's my family," I growl.

"She's mine, too. It's what she wanted. Please, I can't do this without you. There's nothing for me here anymore. My life is in your hands now."

His words are like a bucket of cold water. Inside I know he's right, but still, the agony is scalding my insides like acid. Going out there would be suicide, just as she'd known it would be. But she'd done it for him . . . and for me. Caden is the priority. He'd always been the priority, even if the rules had shifted and the playing fields flipped. I nod once and pick up the syringes.

"For Shae," Caden says.

"For Shae," I agree, swallowing past the grapefruit-sized knot in my throat. "On the count of three," I say. "One, two, three."

We stick the injectors into our legs at the same time. Caden's eyes are wide, and I smile reassuringly at him, even though I'm falling apart inside.

"I'm scared," he whispers. "Will it hurt?"

"Just hold on to me," I say dully, my voice breaking. Truth is, I don't know if it will hurt. But at the moment, it feels like nothing could hurt as much as the gaping hole inside of me. "It'll be okay. Shae said we'll be okay. And she's never steered us wrong before."

And then I pull Caden close, and we're both crying against each other for the sister we're leaving behind . . . the one who had surrendered herself to save us. I hit ENTER on the eversion device.

Hot white light glows around us in the small cave, and within seconds, we are gone.

# PART TWO

# NEOSPES

# 14

# OVER THERE

WE'RE ON A training ground, running back-to-back, the wind in our hair and glee on our faces. Our enemies fall gracefully to our weapons, because together we are invincible. I turn to Shae, the wind lifting her braids off her face, and laugh out loud. We are breathless with victory. But suddenly, something in her face shifts, and she backs away, her hands outstretched, warding off something horrible.

I call her name over and over, but my feet are leaden and stuck to the ground, and she doesn't stop moving. In a few seconds, I am alone and the orange sunshine has disappeared behind a dark, ominous cloud. The ground crumbles beneath my feet, and I'm lying in a desert with a mouth full of sand. Something crawls into my eye and I can feel it moving inside me, feeding off me. I can't stop screaming, but no one hears me.

My mouth tastes like metal—dirty, sour metal. I spit and it's an odd blue color, dead Vector blood. The caked, parched ground sucks it up greedily, like it's something precious. Some kind of creature is crawling toward me. It looks like a black scorpion, only it's shiny and metallic, and its eyes are glowing white orbs. It crawls up onto my arm and then digs its sharp forward claws deep into my flesh and starts to feed on me. I am disappearing into this thing's mouth until it's gigantic and sated on my flesh, and I am nothing but a speck.

It has eaten me, absorbed me. I have become the monster. And I feel drunk with it, exhilarated. Alive.

And that's when I see Shae, running toward me and throwing herself into my arms as if she hadn't seen me in weeks. She smells so good that I can't help myself. She is sunlight in a world of darkness. My mouth opens and I take her into me without a second thought. She must die to feed the monstrosity I have become.

I can't stop screaming.

"Shae, no. I'm sorry." The words feel like knives, tearing into the roof of my mouth, and I gag reflexively. Everything hurts. I don't know if I'm awake or asleep, or if I'm dead or alive. Wetness soaks my cheeks.

"Riven, wake up." A hand is shaking me. "It's okay, it's okay. We're okay."

I pry open my sticky eyelids, and Caden's worried face swims into focus. I'm shivering so hard I can almost feel my bones rattling. "Whererewe?" I mumble unintelligently.

"Neospes, I think," Caden says. "But it's so desolate. I can't see a city. There's nothing for miles."

"How long have we been here?" I try to sit up. I've never blacked out during eversion before. I don't even want to think about what that means. My blood feels hot, like it's on fire, but when I touch my skin it's icy cold. I rub my hands up and down my arms. The movement hurts.

"I don't know. A half hour, maybe more. I tried to wake you, but you weren't even blinking. Your eyelids were moving, so I knew you were alive, but your heartbeat was so slow. I wasn't sure whether you'd had some kind of reaction to the serum. But I felt fine," Caden rushes out. "Then you started murmuring, and a couple minutes after, you woke up. Where are we?"

I look around quickly. We're in a barren stretch of land. There's not a tree in sight, but I know it's all an illusion. The scavengers would smell us. "We're in the Outers."

"That doesn't sound good."

"It's not."

"So should we run a bit and then evert back?" Caden asks. I shake my head and check my watch.

"We couldn't do it and be safe. If I've been out as long as you say, we're way past the thirty-minute mark that Shae was talking about. It'd be too risky. Plus, my blood feels like it's on fire; I don't think I'd survive another jump." I pause, staring at my skin. "Maybe you're right and I did have some weird reaction to the serum."

"So what do we do?"

"We make our way back to the city, but first I need to figure out exactly where we are." I open my backpack and pull out two of the Vectors' uniforms I'd stuffed in there. I toss one to Caden. "Get undressed and put this on." I glance up at the sky that's still covered in a reddish haze. "It gets really hot here during the day. We're going to have to find a spot to rest, quickly."

Caden looks confused as he shrugs out of his clothes and into the Vector's uniform. "Wouldn't it be safer to travel by day?" His face reddens as he notices me stripping out of my clothes at the same time, and he turns away. I shrug. There's no room for propriety.

My reply is short. "Not here."

I zip up the second uniform, thankful that it doesn't smell, and throw Sadie's dress into my pack—cotton is rare here, and it would be unwise to leave it. I slip my ninjata harness on over the uniform, tightening the straps across my chest. I roll the leather jacket and tuck it in the top. The red power button on the suit's computer is blinking, indicating that it's already charging. Nearly all of the suit's power comes from solar energy. I tap the keypad on the forearm of the suit and type in a sequence of numbers, wincing at the pinch at the back of my neck. I repeat the same on Caden's. "What are you doing?"

"Resetting the suit to calibrate to our bodies. Hang on a sec; this may hurt a bit." His eyes widen at the sting.

"What was that?" Caden hisses, jerking away.

"It's okay. It won't hurt anymore. It's a wire that the suit connects to your nervous system. Works in tune with your biometrics."

"Oh."

"It may look like a piece of nylon, but it's really pretty advanced technology. This computer controls the whole suit; it records your heart rate, the amount of fluid in your body, and basically makes sure you stay alive. It's thermo-responsive, too."

"Oh." I smile this time at Caden's dazed response. "What's thermo-responsive?"

"Our daytime temperatures are very different from yours. It's boiling hot during the day, upward of a hundred and fifty degrees, and very cold at night, like negative sixty. The suit adjusts to each, keeping your body at a constant temp."

"It can do that?" Caden's voice is still full of amazement. "Wow, no wonder you wanted to take them off the Vectors."

I raise my eyebrows. "That's just the beginning of what they can do, but let's get moving. I'll fill you in later. The Outers isn't exactly the most friendly place, and we need to find somewhere safe to rest for the day before we fry," I say.

Off to the right, there's nothing but more flat land, but on my left I can see the vague outline of some mountains. I type in a command on the suit keypad, and a hologram of a compass hovers in the air. Beneath the 3-D rendition is a map. Neospes is to the north. The map says that it's over sixty miles away. That's three days of hard hiking in very unfriendly terrain. . . . *extremely* unfriendly terrain.

I glance at Caden. He's poking through all the pockets on his suit.

"Here, take this," I tell him, handing over one of the two handheld crossbows from Shae's bag. I strap the other to a special hitch on my suit that has a retractable lead. "Your saber isn't any good against flying things. And they come from all sides here."

I haven't gone through everything she has in there yet. I'm a little terrified of what I may find or not find. I have never been this unprepared for an eversion—no food, no supplies, no medical gear . . . nothing. All I have are the weapons—*better than nothing!*—and half-used supplies in the bottom of my backpack. But Shae was always prepared for any eventuality, and I can't help hoping that she somehow planned for this. I'll wait until I've found us somewhere safe to hide before doing a full tally of what we had, and pray that it will be enough.

"If anything moves, shoot it. Don't think, just shoot," I say to Caden. "Okay?"

Caden's eyes are dark, but there's no fear in them. It lifts me up a tiny bit. "Are there Vectors out here?"

"No, they don't come out this far, unless it's a raid or a search party. Out here"—I gesture to the barren landscape around us—"there are worse things than Vectors." I glance upward. "And the worst thing of all is that sun, so let's move."

We jog in silence for a while, tracking north on the compass. Our pace is hard and it's already sweltering. The ground is covered in an oily red haze that makes it look as if it's shimmering, and I can feel the sweat slicking across my forehead. Glancing at Caden, I see his face is determined. I check the computer on the suit. The temperature gauge reads one hundred and ten degrees. The worst part is that it's not even seven in the morning.

I quicken my pace, and Caden follows without complaint. By my calculation we have about two hours before we get to the base of the hills on the map, and hopefully some cover.

If we make it. . . .

A noise overhead has me twisting around with my crossbow in hand. It looks like some kind of bird, but I know instinctively that it's not a bird. Sunlight glints off its wings as it drops lower, making a beeline in our direction. I wonder if it's some kind of tracking spy, and I toy between killing it midflight or figuring out exactly what it is. The things that exist out here live by no rules—they live to survive any which way they can.

"Caden, drop!" I shout and Caden rolls to the ground just as the thing dives past his head, talons outstretched. It's far bigger than it looked at first, smaller now as it climbs into the sky. It's not going to attack again, I notice, but there's no way I can let it attract any more attention to us. I place the bolt and shoot. My aim is true and the thing drops like lead to the ground.

My crossbow remains at the ready, although blue sparks from my first arrow ripple across the bird's body, rendering it powerless. Up close, the bird's wingspan is about three feet across, and it reeks of rotten flesh. Metal wires crisscrossing and woven into bands of tissue make up the bird-thing's body. I can see the faint outline of a skeleton between the gaping holes. Where the eyes should be are only two glowing white orbs. I feel the bile rising.

"Stay back," I warn Caden, but he ignores my words of caution.

"I want to see what I'm up against out here," he says pushing past me, and then freezes, his body like rock. "What the *hell* is that?"

"It's a hybrid. Half-android, half-something alive." I shrug. "It's just one of the many things out here."

"Android?" Caden repeats. "Like a robot?"

I shoot him a glare. "You know, like the Vectors? Only, they take whatever parts they can get out here. It's slim pickings in the Outers, and we are like Mecca, so let's go. I have no idea if there are any more of these floating around."

I grind the heel of my boot into the thing's head, and it makes a sizzling sound. The eyes dull, but I'm not taking any chance. Sliding the short knife from my boot, I sever the wires connecting the head, cringing from the rot of decay.

"Come on," I tell Caden. "We wasted ten minutes on this. Here, this will be better." I click a button on the neck of his suit and a hood with a thin transparent mesh unravels. I tuck it over his head, and the suit seals the closure. I do the same on mine, and at his look, I say, "It's so your skin doesn't burn off. Let's run."

By the time we get to the base of the hill—which is more like a rock cliff than a hill—the sun has climbed high into the sky and is beating down on top of us with the force of a hammer. The edge of the hill is shrouded in pale shadow, but with every passing second, the line of sun moves inexorably toward it. If the sun catches us climbing that face, it will be a struggle.

I'm wheezing, and I can hear Caden's labored breath behind me. My legs are burning and my heart is pounding. My mouth is so dry that every time I swallow, my tongue sticks to the roof of my mouth and I have to peel them apart. One of the side pockets on my pack holds a thin root, and I break it in half, offering part to Caden.

"What is it?" he asks.

"A root; chew it."

The root provides some reprieve, filling my mouth with spit. The more you chew it, the more saliva it releases. I look upward along the cliff face, shielding my eyes from the unrelenting sun, searching. And then I spot what I'm looking for, a dark dot under a ledge. "Up there. You see it?" Caden nods, and then we are climbing faster than we've ever climbed. We're racing against the line of sun burning a fiery path up the rock beneath us.

"Won't the suits protect us?" Caden grunts.

I don't answer because I'm not really sure. I haven't been back to Neospes in three years, and these suits are newer than the ones I'm used to. The earlier prototypes used to become unstable in really hot temperatures. I glance at the heat reading on my forearm, which reads: one hundred and nineteen degrees and mounting. I can't take the chance of any malfunctions, especially when the suit is directly connected to our bodies.

As we get nearer to the small cave mouth, I pause, signaling Caden to wait before grabbing a flare from my pack and throwing it inside. Other things would be looking for shelter, too. The flare hits the back wall and flames brightly for a second. Nothing happens at first, and then some kind of huge lizard-like creature shuffles out. My long blade is embedded in its head before it could even spit venom in our direction.

"Is that a hybroid?" Caden whispers.

"No, it's like a Komodo dragon," I say, kicking the carcass to the edge of the ledge. "Only—"

Caden interrupts me with a wry look. "I know, worse."

I grin. "You're getting it. This one's pure. No metal. They're survivors through and through. And they're carnivores, so keep your eyes open for any others." I nudge its mouth, shuddering at the jagged shark-like, rust-colored teeth. "They're poisonous and can spit their venom to paralyze their prey."

"Sick!" We share a laugh that quickly evaporates to silence. Levity is a luxury right now. I squeeze his shoulder and shine a flashlight into the shallow cave. It's not bad for shelter, with the top ledge dipping down like a lip. The Komodo must have just been resting there, because there's no sign of a nest or excrement. We should be safe enough from the sun or other predators.

The dead Komodo is already starting to stink. Leaving it visible would be like putting up a "free buffet dinner" sign. I don't say anything to Caden, but if we run into a bind on the food front, it would be foolish to waste such a windfall, especially if Shae hasn't been as prepared as I hope. But I can't even look at it and think about eating it without gagging.

In Neospes, most of our food is powdered or in gel form and engineered. We don't grow crops or have farms. Our food is processed in factories underground in one of the sectors responsible for food production. Half the time, we don't even know what we're eating; all we know is that it has exactly the right combination of calories and nutrition to keep our bodies at top functioning capacity. The only time I've ever had the luxury of organic food was during the Solstice Games.

Occasionally when we were younger, on raids to the Outers, Shae and I would trap some of the animals. For some of the poorer people on the outskirts of the city, that's all they had to eat. I remember one old Artok woman telling Shae and me that some of the Outers Komodos used to be delicacies in the old days. She'd offered us some, and while Shae had gamely eaten the roasted beast, I hadn't been able to even stomach the abnormal, charred flesh. I'd thrown up immediately afterward.

A smile twists my lips. My revulsion for cooked animals had shifted pretty quickly when I everted to the Otherworld. It was either eat or starve, or become what they called a vegetarian. In Neospes, food was not a pleasure; it was a means of survival. But that didn't mean anything in Caden's world. Food was celebrated and revered to the point of excess. It shocked me.

I stare at the carcass and kick it with all the force I can manage off the ledge. It makes a wet thud near the bottom, and from where I am, I can see a thin line of black ant-like creatures mobbing it in seconds. Only thing is . . . they're not ants, and they're not small. I duck back into the cave and almost crash into Caden standing beside me.

"Was it poisonous?" Caden asks me. "You know, to eat? I mean, we have to eat, right?"

"No. I just couldn't . . ." But I have no explanation other than my own stupid disgust. I sigh. Caden's right.

"It's just meat, Riven." I stare at him, and after a couple seconds, Caden makes to leave the cave. "I'll go get it. We don't know how long we're going to be out here."

But I stop him. "You can't go down there. It's already gone."

Sure enough, the carcass has all but disappeared, picked clean to the bones, and even half of those, too, are gone.

"What the . . ." Caden's voice is small.

"They're carrion eaters, scavengers. Those"—I jerk my head to the ground below—"are hand-sized burying beetles. They'll scavenge anything. Dead or alive. They can smell dead things from miles away." I turn to him. "Which is why we're probably better off with the Komodo down there."

It's boiling now. The temperature reading is a one hundred and thirty-two, and the sun's arms are about halfway down the rock face. Soon, nothing will be out in the noon sun, not even the metals. The shade of the rock doesn't provide much relief from the heat, but it's a lot cooler and the suits do the rest. I unroll a flat black shade from my pack and run it along the cave's mouth. The powerful magnetic edges curve and seal to the rock.

"What's that? More fancy cloth?"

"Yep, a holo-tube," I agree. "Sort of. It's like a body tent. If I couldn't find any shelter, as an emergency, I could roll up in this, but it can't hold two people." For some reason, I'm blushing. The tube could hold two people but they'd be literally sandwiched together. Shae and I had done it once, and we'd been much smaller than Caden and I would be. I shake the unnerving image out of my head. "It blocks out all UV light and heat. And it's holographic." I point to a tiny control pad on one of the edges. "The outer side mimics the surrounding area. Like camouflage. So anything out there would just see rock face."

"Cool." Caden inspects the edges of the material and rubs it carefully between his fingers, frowning at the evenly spaced bars beneath it. "What are these? Magnets?"

"Yes. They stick to the lodestone." I raise an eyebrow. "How's your geology?"

"Naturally occurring magnetite in igneous rock," Caden says primly. "Supposedly magnetized by lightning."

I grin, impressed. "Well, here it's from all the electrical fields during the War."

"Wait, what about our gear?" Caden asks. "Wouldn't the fields affect them, too?"

"Nope, shielded." I say, leaving Caden to ponder the geological and technological wonders of my world, and head to the back of the cave where I empty out both Shae's pack and mine.

I sort everything into three piles: food, medicine, and gear. Shae was prepared. There's a lot of food from the Otherworld, including dried strips of some kind of meat and packets of dried fruit and grain, but Shae must have stockpiled a ton of our powdered food whenever she'd everted back here. There are a few dozen thin tubes, more of the water-root, and both water bladders on the inside of each of the packs are full.

The water we'll have to use sparingly, more so than the food. The suits will keep us from losing too much of our body water, but we will die faster without water than food. My guess is that the Komodo would have had a water source not too far away. If we're lucky, maybe it will be on the way to the city.

Most of Shae's bag contains more food than anything, but I still have my med-kit from before, so that will have to do. I remove all of the various weapons I stole from each of the Vectors and line them up in a row. Three night-vision goggles, two coiled electro-whips, one rod, my ninjata swords, the two crossbows with bolts, Caden's saber, and a handful of throwing stars and knives. On top of that, I also have two communications headsets and the eversion device that brought us here.

All in all, we aren't in terrible shape. My fingers catch against something in the front pocket, and I pull out a tiny device that looks like an electronic thumb drive. I frown. There's a piece of paper on it that reads "For Riven." I shove it back into the pack. I'm not ready to process whatever it is that Shae has prerecorded on there. I'm also not ready to admit to myself that she's really gone or to hear her voice and see her face.

"You okay?" Caden says, watching me from where he's still sitting near the front of the cave. "Need any help with anything?"

"No, I'm okay. Just doing inventory."

"Then we should add my stuff in there, too." Caden crawls over and tosses the contents of his backpack into the mix, and I frown.

"What's that?" I ask, pointing to a slim leather-bound case the size of a watch box that had fallen out next to June's gun, and a pile of miscellaneous junk looking vaguely like random Eagle Scout supplies. I don't say anything about the gun, because it could come in handy, but the box looks elegant and out of place.

"Something my mother left me."

"Your mother?" I ask, startled. "May I?"

Caden smiles sadly. "Go ahead. It's some kind of chip. We couldn't read it, no matter what we did. I put it in there just in case."

I open the box carefully. Inside, there's a silver ring with a dark blue circular stone. The Neospes royal crest is emblazoned on it. The chip Caden's talking about is a pill-sized silver cylinder. I stare at Caden. "Shae didn't tell you what's on it?" I ask.

"No, she said she didn't know."

But Shae did know. We all did. She must have had some reason for not wanting to tell Caden what the chip meant. I slide it and his ring into an inside pocket on my vest. Caden doesn't object, and together we repack everything, including Caden's thermal blankets, fire-sticks, water packets, emergency food bars, flashlights, and snare wire.

"Where'd you get all this stuff?" I ask, fingering an odd-looking multi-tool that will undoubtedly come in handy. I'm unwillingly impressed by his foresight.

"Online," Caden says with a grin. "All I had to look up was survival gear for the zombie apocalypse."

"The *zombie* apocalypse?"

"What can I say? We like to be prepared. Hurricanes, tornados, and zombies."

I can't help the laugh that rolls its way out of my stomach, and I'm laughing until my sides feel like they're about to split. Go figure for a world that has instructions on how to survive a zombie apocalypse. Thinking about it sets me off again. I don't stop laughing, not even when Caden throws a water packet at my head.

We eat a couple strips of meat and dried fruit, saving the longer-life food items for later, and lie alongside each other on the rocky floor of our little cave. I haven't forgotten about the chip sitting inside my vest pocket. It's almost burning a hole into my skin.

It's time for Caden to tell me everything he knows.

# 15

# IN THE OUTERS

WHEN I AWAKE, my throat feels gritty like I've chewed on sandpaper. Despite the hard ground, we've managed to both get some sleep. Caden is curled up on his side, something on a silver chain curled in his fist. He showed me the locket last night when he recounted everything he knew from his childhood. It was tarnished platinum with a photo of his mother inside wearing one of the flowing dresses that she'd loved. On the other side was a photo of Caden as a baby. Caden said that he never took the locket off.

It's boiling in the cave, but the temperature is already changing, lowering. Sometime during the day, I shrugged out of the suit and just slept under one of the thermal blankets. I stretch as quietly as I can, soothing the aches out of my muscles, and get dressed after taking care of minor bodily functions in a back corner of the cave. I smile, remembering that Caden asked whether the suit also took care of those kinds of needs.

"The human ones can inhibit waste," I told him, "but these are designed for the Vectors. They don't need to use the bathroom," I explained. He stared at me like I'd grown two heads.

"They can *do* that?" His eyes were wide. "Do they process your pee so it's drinkable, you know, like in *Dune*?"

Then it was my turn to stare at him. I shook my head. "That's gross. No, our suits are designed to inhibit those needs, at least until we take the suits off." I pointed to the neuron connector at the back of the neck. "Remember? They're not designed for long-term use, although I'm sure they've probably figured that out by now. As you can probably guess."

"How do you know all this stuff? Like how it works?"

My answer was a toss-up, but I chose the least complicated answer. "My father designed them."

I glance over at Caden as he turns in his sleep. He, for his part, had told me everything that he could remember, but it still wasn't a lot. His memories were sporadic, mostly centered around his life in the other world. His mother rarely smiled, Caden said, and when she did, it was always short-lived. It was as if a part of her had been missing, like she was living lost in a daydream somewhere else half the time.

Caden hadn't known about Cale. Neither his mother nor Shae had told him anything of Neospes or where he was truly from. And yet, he faced the Vectors that had come in search of him with innate courage and bravery. He accepted the near-impossible that I was from a parallel universe, just as Shae was. And I know he has more questions, but it seems like he is waiting . . . waiting for me to tell him the truth of who he is.

My mouth twists. I wouldn't even know where to start.

Hey, Caden, you're the son of a king in this world. Your father was murdered by his brother, your uncle, by the way, who now wants to kill the brother you never knew you had, and kill you before you can somehow save him so that he can assume the throne. Oh, and we live in a giant glass dome of a city, because everywhere else is contaminated because of an android war that pretty much killed off everything in the process.

And by the way, I'm somehow falling for you.

Maybe I'll leave out that last part. Love is the seed of weakness, as my father had always said. I'd be better off burying any feelings I have for Caden, and he'd be wise to do the same. I touch my fingers to my suddenly warm lips, thinking of our unexpected kiss in the bathroom at Horrow. It seems like eons ago instead of mere days. For a brief second, I allow myself to savor the feelings blooming inside my chest, if just for that moment.

"Why are you staring at me?" Caden murmurs sleepily. An embarrassed flush invades my face and neck.

"I wasn't. I mean, I was but I was looking through you," I mumble.

"You were smiling."

"Yeah, well, I was thinking of ice cream and donuts," I snap, irritated. "Come on, we have to get moving. The sun's just setting and I want to get a head start."

We gather up what we've used and tuck them into the packs. Caden has Shae's pack, since it's more lightweight and durable like mine. His saber is in its sheath lying along his back underneath the pack. Caden stares at me and grins.

"We look like ninjas."

My mouth twitches. The description is appropriate. "We'll need to fight like ninjas to get through the next two days."

"What about the wrappers and garbage?" Caden asks looking around. "Shouldn't we . . ."

"Forget it. It's extra weight. Just leave it," I say over my shoulder as I'm repacking the holo-tube at the entrance. "Don't worry; it'll get used by something out here. The things that live here use everything they can get their hands on. Think of it as natural recycling."

The landscape is still red, but a different kind of red with tinges of gray along its edges. It's seventy-nine on the temperature monitor. Here and there, we spot movement. I try not to let my tension show, but it's a guarantee that we'll run into some kind of trouble. Predators in the Outers are vicious. I wasn't kidding when I told Caden earlier that the creatures out here use everything they could get their hands on. I meant it— they'd slaughter each other for hair, teeth, and bone. They'd rip us apart for less. A shiver races across my back.

"Here, let's put these to work," I say, grabbing Caden's wrist and pressing one of the buttons on the keypad. "It's a security protocol that identifies any metal, I mean, hybroids. You'll feel a vibration and this console will flash."

"How does that work?"

"Sound waves."

We climb down the mountain quickly, moving across the terrain at a good pace. We keep our hoods off, as the warmth of the open air is comfortable for the moment. The sky is an odd mixture of crimson and gray and black. There's no blue in the

Neospes sky, but it has its own unique beauty. I realize that I've missed it, but a part of me misses the blue, too.

Our pace is grueling, but I'm relishing the chance to push my muscles hard, to run so that my heart is pumping like a piston in my chest. Caden keeps pace with me easily, and the realization that he's fitter and stronger than I thought is a delayed one. He's not as lean as Cale, even with their identical build, but I misjudged him. I wonder if he fights as easily as he runs, just as Shae boasted. She said that he could take me. I doubt that, but it doesn't mean I'm not curious. Cale was good, but he could never take me in a one-on-one fight, not even with all his years of training.

I've always had a good sense of where people are going to be before they strike, like a fighting sixth sense. It gave me that extra edge that I put to good use in my unprecedented rise to the rank of general. No, Caden wouldn't be able to best me, especially not having been trained in our ways from the beginning.

The landscape starts to change as the sun disappears and the moon rises into the night sky, covering everything in an oily silver veil. Normally, moonlight is beautiful, but out here it has different implications. Moonlight is ominous, insidious. It means hunters are on the prowl and predators out for prey. And so we have to be extra vigilant.

"What *is* that?" Caden huffs, his gaze drawn by something off to our right. I don't want to stop, but I look over and my breath hitches just as the console of my wrist-pad vibrates and the light flashes red.

"Stop," I hiss, and drop to the ground. Caden follows unbidden. Removing the infrared goggles from my pack, I stare silently at the group of six or seven raptor-sized creatures pawing and shoving into each other. They're about a mile away from where we are.

"What are they? More hybroids or real things?" Caden whispers.

"Definitely hybroids. They're pack hunters. Reptiles." I'm hoping that they haven't seen us . . . or smelled us. They're machines that have taken on the most savage aspects of territorial beasts, and have fused themselves with horns and tusks, teeth and scales. Reptiles are notoriously hard to kill and even harder to outrun.

I turn the goggles to the left of where we are crouched. There's a dip where the landscape shifts, a gorge of some sort. I hadn't planned on going in that direction—as much as the inhabitants of the Outers live aboveground, the worst of them prefer the underground. Or so it's rumored.

In the city, scary tales of the Outers filled our ears from birth. They were the stories that people whispered into children's ears: "the monsters from the Outers will get you!" or "break the law and risk exile to the Outers." That one had been the worst one—to be banished from the city and forced to survive was a fate worse than death. Many traitors had killed themselves to avoid the outcome of the Outers. No one exiled there had ever returned.

"Follow me," I say to Caden, making a decision. "We're going to crawl over there to where that drop is, got it?" Caden nods. "Just try to move slowly, without any jerky movements."

Commando-style, we inch our way across the dusty ground. I can feel the dirt like grit against my teeth, clogging my windpipe. The fine dust is everywhere. I cough softly and spit to the side, and my saliva is rust-colored. My elbows and knees are burning from scraping against the hard earth, but we're almost there. I can see that the cracks along the ground are starting to widen. Soon they'll be big enough for us to drop into and at least be safe if the hybroids do see us. Once we're out of sight, we'll be out of mind.

I look back triumphantly to Caden, and he's a few feet away, his face screwed up and frozen. He looks as if he's just stuffed an entire lemon into his mouth.

"Don't—" I warn. But it's too late. The sneeze echoes across the open ground like thunder. In the next second, all we hear is the rumbling of distant hooves and screeching that could rival an oncoming hover-train. "Run, Caden, run! To the chasm! Run!"

And we are sprinting for our lives as the thunderous rumbling draws closer. I don't want to look back, but I do. I have to see how close they are . . . whether we have a shot in hell of getting away from them. One we can probably take, maybe two, but definitely not six. With their breath hot on our backs, now I understand why anyone exiled to the Outers would prefer death. They'll capture us and take us back to whoever their tribal leader is, and then we'll be stripped for parts—skin, bones, organs, blood.

"Don't look back," I gasp to Caden, but his face is already a mix of pain and terror. Ignoring my own advice, I glance back again. One of them is faster than the others and gaining on us with every leap. It's the runner. All the pack Reptiles have a runner—the quick one that snares the prey, and then the others follow to immobilize it. They're all fast, but the runners are faster.

I run out in a wide arc veering away from Caden. "Keep running to that gap, okay," I scream. "No matter what."

"What are you doing?"

"Trying to keep us alive."

And then I can't think as I'm running into the Reptile runner head-on, ninjatas in both hands. I have thirty seconds before the others close the space between them and the runner. It's smaller than the ones I've seen before, about horse-sized, but I know it's no less lethal with its heavily muscled and metaled body. Its eyes glow white as its pointy snout gapes open, full of sharp, cracked teeth. Angled plates curve down its back and tail into some kind of pike.

We are seconds from head-on impact, and in full sprint I roll head over heels, slashing out with my blades at the same time, snapping through the intertwined wires and tissue at the base of its hooves. I don't stop. Momentum keeps me going, and I'm on my feet and running back toward Caden, but I hear the thump and screech of agony as it bowls forward onto its face. A triumphant smile graces my face for a second. It won't be running for a while, that one.

I've earned us a sliver of time; the rules of existence in the Outers mean that the others will fight to pick the fallen apart. It's survival of the fittest and strongest. Sparing a look behind me, I see they're already converging on their fallen pack-mate. I dash harder, pumping my legs like pistons until I'm almost flying. I have no idea where my extra strength comes from; I just go, taking advantage of my second wind. The pounding of hooves behind me echoes the pounding in my chest.

Ahead of me, Caden barely squeezes into a tight gap, and I throw myself down behind him, crashing into his back and sending us both spiraling into the rocky walls of the narrow grotto. We're both hauling stale air into our lungs and clutching each other with numb fingers, even as dirt, rocks, and sour saliva fall on us from the creatures already snapping their mouths above us, trying to get in. We crouch farther down into the shaft but we're safe. They're too big to follow.

"You okay?" I gasp.

"What is wrong with you? You could have killed yourself!" I'm startled at the reprimand and his snarky tone, but I give him a tired smile.

"Better me than you. Come on."

Caden doesn't return my smile. He stands in front of me, staring at me with fiery eyes. "Riv, you can't do that anymore, okay? I know you're way better than I am navigating this terrain, but moving forward, it's both of us or neither of us. Got it? We do it together."

I nod, an involuntary smile curving my lips again. Something in his voice makes me feel funny deep down inside, like he wants to protect me. People don't tend to question my orders, especially here in Neospes. I lead and they follow. The smile grows into a full-on grin as I imagine what Caden will do once he finds out that I've been a general, commanding an entire legion here, or even worse that I'm now some kind of marked-for-death, dangerous renegade.

"It's not funny, Riven," Caden hisses, misunderstanding my expression. "I already lost Shae. I can't lose you, too."

"I know," I agree, his quiet comment slapping the grin from my face. "Together, from here on out."

Above us, the Reptiles are still scrabbling—they'll do anything to get in here as long as we remain this visible, including digging out a bigger hole, which they've already started to do. The foul steam of their breath swirls around us. I stare at Caden, and we both nod at the same time. We need to move. They'll give up eventually and move on to some other target once we're out of sight.

The gap opens out to a deep gorge, above which the Reptiles are furiously digging, but underneath the crack to our right, the tunnel burrows downward, disappearing into darkness. We don't have much choice but to follow it.

"Let's go. Be vigilant," I whisper to him, switching on the halogen lights on our suits. I'm torn between taking the lead and having to worry about him behind me every step of the way, or letting him go ahead and having to face any dangers head-on. In the end, I decide to take the lead. "Stay close, and don't stop for anything. Got it?" Caden agrees and then we are off, moving as quickly as we can deeper into the gritty tunnel.

I sigh inaudibly, feeling the weight of the dark earth on all sides of me. Why does it always have to be tunnels? They're everywhere—in Neospes, in the Otherworld. I'm no longer claustrophobic, but tunnels still irk me. I was locked in a box underground for hours at a time to learn to face and harness my fear of enclosed spaces. It sounds cruel, but it worked. A key part of our mental training means I had to face and understand all of my fears.

Shae had had a fear of heights, so she'd had to jump off the tallest point in Neospes every day for four weeks. The day she did it without crying was the day she overcame that fear. She was still wary of heights, but it no longer weakened her. One of the trainees in my group had a fear of snakes. He ended up dropping out, unable to take the counter-fear measures.

The system is brutal, but it's effective. An initiate can always lie about their fears, but it's counterproductive. Facing fear in a controlled environment and trying to overcome it without any preparation in a hostile environment are two vastly different things. In Neospes, fear is the paper-thin difference between life and death.

The tunnel widens a bit and I drag my gloved hand along the oddly-hewn edges of the rock. It's curiously smooth in areas and roughly chopped in others. I frown. My instincts warn that it's probably because some combination of living tissue and metal had grated against it, but a part of me wonders whether I'm being overly paranoid after the run-in with the Reptiles aboveground.

"Cade, you okay?" I whisper back. He's tucked his hood around his neck, and even though the temperature is dropping consistently, there's a thin sheen of sweat on his forehead. His eyes are dark in the stark halogen lighting of our suits.

"Yeah. Where are we now?"

I consult the holographic compass and map, which works just as well underground. We're still making good time and heading in the direction of the city, about a quarter of the way there, but it's far slower now that we're not running. I squint at the map, noticing that it has now placed us belowground.

The technology of the suit has dynamic virtual properties that allow its various operations to self-adjust, depending on external stimuli.

Curious, I touch a spot on the base of the hologram that is highlighted with an *S*. The map is interactive and immediately shifts to show the entire network of the subterranean tunnels around us. Caden's gasp is soft beside me, but I'm still staring at the intricate web of tunnels that connect nearly to the edges of the city so many miles away.

Have those always been there?

"Wow," Caden breathes. "So I guess this means we can pretty much stay down here and not have to deal with those things up there."

"We don't know that things *exactly* like that aren't down here," I say flatly. "Or worse."

"You're right," Caden agrees. "But we haven't seen anything even close to any kind of life for the last couple hours."

"Doesn't mean they aren't there."

I move the map with a swish of my thumb and forefinger, opening a wider subsection of the part nearest the city. It's not connected, but it's definitely close enough to get us to the east side—the least-policed side of the city. I trail my finger back toward the dot that indicates my current position, noticing several other tunnels below us that go deeper underground, but there's no way I'm going to risk heading down one of those.

"See here," I tell Caden. "Here's what we're going to do. See this path, nearest the surface?" He nods. "We'll take that. It may take longer, but it could be safer. And that way, if we do run into trouble, we can always get out." I point to a few thin white lines marked at the surface by some odd red dots. "I think these are cracks like the one we came in. It looks like this runs along the base of the Peaks."

"The Peaks?" Caden repeats.

I flip the map back to an over ground view, and show him the ridge of cliff-like mountains. "We're running along the base of that." I frown. "Actually, I think our path may even go under in parts. The inside of that mountain is literally pure volcanic glass. No metals can live there for some reason. Some kind of electromagnetic pulse."

Caden echoes my frown. "Volcanic glass."

"Ever see a mountain that has no caves, that looks like a sheath of sheer black glass? Well, get a good look, because that's one." I tap the map, switching the view to what the cliff mountains would look like at that moment on the hologram. "Used to be an active volcano thousands of years ago that the metals pulverized. Now it's dead and impenetrable."

I close the map and pull a food bar out of my pack, handing it to Caden. "Now's as good a time as any. Let's rest for a second." We eat in silence and drink a water packet each.

"Can my suit do all that, too?" Caden asks, and I flinch at the sudden sound of his voice in the quiet between us. I nod and show him the control panels on his wrist. The overview is brief, but Caden picks it up rapidly and is soon flicking through all the versions of the map. Just in case, I also quickly run through the security parameters of the suit that I initiated for both of us earlier.

"The suit is intuitive and attuned to you. It stores your data. Technically, we're not really supposed to interchange the suits—they're designed for each person—but Shae and I used to steal the Vectors' suits because they had way cooler tech. I developed an algorithm to erase the programmed data so we could use them."

I blush and trail off, realizing that I'm showing just how much of a geek I am, but as Shae used to say, the apple doesn't fall far from the tree. My father knew what I was capable of at an early age and fed my brain a steady diet of bioengineering, physics, and advanced robotics.

It was a conscious act of rebellion on my part when I opted to train with the soldiers and become a part of Cale's personal guard. My father ranted and raved for days that I belonged in his lab with him. It incensed me to the point that I requested living quarters in the castle under the guise of protecting Cale, when it was only to escape my father's manic rages. In the end, he twisted it to suit him, because I ended up leading his greatest creations—the Vectors. I'd never understood why he was so pleased about that, but it got him off my back, and that was reward enough for me.

Caden's voice makes me jump again. "I think it's cool that you know all that."

"We learn different things than you do," I say, shrugging. "But it doesn't make what you know any less important. We just evolve differently based on where we live."

An indistinct sound brushes gently across my ears, and for a second I think that I've imagined it. But then I hear it again, like a single note of something. It's some kind of bell-like sound. "Did you hear that?" I whisper to Caden.

"No, what?"

"It's a chime or something. Listen."

We both sit in silence, our ears straining, waiting until the sound comes again. "There it is! It sounds like music," Caden says, his eyes wide. "Count it; it'll come back in six beats, I think. Listen."

Caden's right. The sound repeats, nearly inaudible as if it's coming from a long distance away. It's barely an echo of an echo, but we're both standing and staring at each other, our eyes shifting around us. I glance down at the security pad on my suit and check Caden's for good measure.

Nothing.

It doesn't beep, not even when the shadows materialize from the walls before us, with weapons pointing directly at our hearts.

# 16

# THE OTHERS

"WHAT THE—"

"Shut up, Caden," I hiss, staring at the five men in dirty brown tunics. Despite the weapons pointed toward me, I shift slightly to the right so that Caden is standing behind me. My eyes slide down to the keypad at my wrist—the alarm is still silent, confirming that none of them are hybroids. One of the men steps forward, and I tense automatically, wishing that the empty water packet in my hand was one of my blades.

He holds a wand-like device in his hand, which he waves up and down our bodies. I realize quickly what it is—some kind of metal detection tool. But unlike our suits, it makes a harsh static sound, as if it's malfunctioning. The man bangs it against his side, staring at it and then our uniforms as if confused.

Does he think we're Vectors?

"Come," he says, and I frown. His voice is nonthreatening but firm. I have no idea who these people are, but it's clear that they want us to go with them. The fact is, I could take them all out easily without endangering Caden, but I'm curious. I've never heard of people living in the Outers. I stare at the men. They all look physically fit, if a little thin.

"Where?" I ask.

"No questions," he says, and then jerks his head to two of the men behind him. They remove our packs and our weapons, and I let them. Nodding for Caden to do the same, I study the leader carefully. There are no marks on his face or any other distinctive characteristics giving any clue as to who he is, but it is clear that he's in charge. His body is lean with muscle, his eyes clear and bright. I need to know who these people are and what they're doing out here.

The men bind our wrists behind our backs, and we walk in single file down a tunnel offshoot that is completely concealed behind a bit of rock face right in front of where we had been sitting. I kick myself mentally, knowing that I should have investigated the tunnel maps in more detail when I found them earlier.

They don't blindfold us to conceal where they are going, and I understand the reason for that relatively quickly. I try to keep track of where we're heading, but it's difficult with all the twists and turns, and after a while, I realize that I have no idea where we are. Everything looks the same. Rock and more rock. Dirt floor. Dirt ceiling. The floor tilts slightly, and I wonder for a second how long we'd been walking downward. I hadn't even noticed.

After a while, the tunnel widens into a large cave that's lit with some kind of sconces. A guard at the end of the space eyes us ferociously. Caden tenses beside me, but I throw my shoulder into his and force a reassuring smile on to my face. When I pass the guard, I glare so hard that I see the shock in his face. He's barely a boy, I notice with a grin. Good to see that my general mojo still works.

In the cave beyond the one we're in, the walls are black and shiny. The air feels cooler, as if some kind of draft is coming in from outside, but I know that that's impossible if we're as far down underground as I'm guessing we are.

There are a few more people now, dressed in the same brown garb. They stare at us with anxious, scared expressions as if we are somehow the enemy, and some of them even scurry away. A small face peeps from behind one of the adults, and I feel my heart lurch. A child, barely three years old, stares curiously at me.

"What is this place?" I ask, but the only answer I get is a burlap sack over my head. I struggle against the ties at my wrists and fling my head back so hard that it crunches wetly into bone.

"Stop!" a voice yells, and then lowers to my ear. "No one's going to hurt you, but we do not know who you are, and so we cannot trust you. If you are judged to be a friend, then we will remove the bag, but until then you must keep it on. Please do not struggle. There are ways for us to restrain you, or worse, sedate you."

"Where's the boy?" I grit out, knowing I'm indeed at the voice's mercy. I don't know what kind of sedation techniques they use here, but I don't want either Caden or me to find out the hard way. "I need to know he's with me, and you have my word that I will not struggle."

Something heavy and warm is thrust into my left side. "Caden? Is that you?" I ask urgently through the bag. "You okay?"

"Yeah. I'm good. Caught a hook to my chin, but can't say I blame them. I kicked out when I felt the bag on my head." He pauses and leans closer, led only by instinct. We're standing back-to-back at that point, and I can feel his head pressing into my shoulder. "Where are we?"

"I don't know," I answer honestly. "I've never even heard of people, as in real live people, living out here."

A prod, and we're walking again. I stay close to Caden, making sure that our arms are always touching at every step. His voice is nearly silent. "Are they going to kill us?"

"I don't think so," I whisper back. "At least not right now."

Engaging my other senses, I can feel the air change against my body. The space feels far more open than any of the others before. If I didn't know better, I would guess that we were once more outside. It even smells different, but my sense of smell is a little undermined by the musty odor of the bag over my head. Once in a while, I'll also hear a gasp or a voice. More people? It baffles me that there's a whole community of humans living in the Outers, obviously by choice. The Outers is a place devoid of life, devoid of anything but metals left over from the war, and hybroids that scavenge to survive.

A few minutes later, we stop walking and the bags are removed. I blink against the sudden light. Only three of the initial men are with us. We're standing in some kind of hold-ing room, with a roughly hewn door barred with metal on one end and two thin cots on the other. They thrust us into it and swing the door shut behind them. Our packs are placed along the wall near the outer passageway. Our weapons are nowhere in sight.

"Wait!" I shout, but they've faded into the darkness before I can take a breath.

"What do we do now?" Caden asks. He looks concerned but no worse for wear, other than a reddening bruise on his chin.

"That looks like it hurts," I say.

He grins wryly. "The one who hit me was my age, I think. I saw it coming, but my brain said freeze instead of duck. Don't worry; I have my eye on him for a little payback when we get out of here."

"Cade," I begin. "I don't know who these people are or what they're doing here, but you need to know that they may not want us here." I don't say that they wouldn't want *me* there, especially if they know anything about who I used to be. But if they are from Neospes, sooner or later one of them will recognize me. "And if they don't, we need to do anything we can to get out, okay, even if they look like kids your age."

"I get it."

"No, you don't. In this world, we are taught how to kill before we even learn how to talk. They are not kids like you are. If they see you as the enemy, they will take you out without blinking."

"Riv, I said I got it," he snaps.

I stare at him but he looks away. I can tell that it's bothering him. That kid had probably hit him out of pure gut instinct, and he maybe hadn't expected it to hurt quite as much as it did. I, for my part, was happy that it had only been a fist and not something worse.

My head feels fuzzy, and I'm not sure it's because we're underground. Something feels off but I can't quite put my finger on it. I lean against one side of the room and close my eyes for a second before taking stock of the cell we're trapped in.

The walls of our prison are the same dark, shiny rock from the first cave, and it's oddly warm and smooth to the touch. There are no openings, but I can feel airflow coming from somewhere against my legs. I push off the wall to follow the changes in the air to an inch-long vent carved into the floor. The air is cool and smells fresh, as if it's being piped in from the outside. I find that odd and am intrigued, because it seems like this whole place has somehow been *constructed*. Such an elaborate venting system hasn't happened by accident.

Someone enters the hallway beyond our door with a tray. It's a young girl. Her face is covered with a veil, but she doesn't look at us. She's been instructed to deliver whatever is on that tray and leave without any eye contact.

"What's your name?" Caden asks, his hands wrapped around the bars of the door as she slides the tray underneath along the floor.

Startled, she answers automatically. "Sela, sir."

"Thank you, Sela, for the food."

She smiles despite herself at his gentle words, and then without warning, her eyes grow wide and terrified as she glances up into the far corner of the room. Realizing that I'm following her gaze, her eyes drop hastily to the floor. Sela shuffles out far more quickly than she'd entered and is gone without another word.

"You scared her," Caden says reproachfully to me.

He pulls the tray to the middle of the room, and I squat next to him. There are two wooden cups of water and some kind of ground meal in a bowl. He stares at me.

"You think it's safe?" he asks. I frown. "You said if they wanted us dead, they would have killed us by now, right?"

"Yes, but killing by poisoning is far less messy than an arrow in the stomach."

Caden rolls his eyes at me and stares greedily at the food. "I'm starving. It feels like hours since I ate that food bar. And I'm so thirsty." He looks away from the tray with effort. "The smell of it is killing me."

For a second, I stare at him mutely, wanting to answer but unable to. The outline of his body shimmers into two people as my vision flickers. Forming the words in my head takes energy. "You can eat if you want to, Cade."

"Are you going to?"

I shake my head thickly. "No, not until I find out where we are and who these people are. Force of habit."

"Are you okay?" Caden asks me, frowning. "You look a little woozy."

"I feel really tired. You?" I ask. Caden shakes his head. "Must just be me then."

I stretch, circling and pumping my arms to get the blood flowing in my body. It helps a little. I study the tiny black spot on the corner of the wall. If Sela hadn't looked directly there, the spot would have been unnoticeable, as had obviously been intended, but now it bothers me. What exactly had she been so afraid of when she'd looked up there? The way her eyes had dropped to the floor right afterward makes me think twice about it.

Squinting out of the corner of my eye, I study the dot. Something flashes—it's the barest hint of a reflection in a lens—and I belatedly realize that I am looking at a minuscule camera. Someone is looking at us right at that moment, and has been looking at us all along.

"Caden," I hiss. "Don't even think about touching that food."

"But you just said—"

"I know what I said," I say exasperated. "But I didn't know two minutes ago that we were being watched like rats in a cage."

Caden's hand drops so quickly I almost laugh, but the shaken look on his face makes my humor fade instantly. He shoves the tray under the door.

His voice is a worried rasp. "Where?"

"Upper left corner of the room. Don't look now," I warn, grimacing as his eyes flick toward it.

"I see it." After several moments, he mouths. "What's the plan?"

"No plan. We wait."

Caden frowns but I shake my head imperceptibly. If they can see us, I'm pretty sure that they can hear us. My guess is that they're waiting for the direction of some leader, some person who will decide what to do with us.

I want—*no*—I need to know who that person is and what they're doing here outside the boundaries of the city, and building some kind of secret sector in the Outers. And most of all, how do they stay safe from the Reptiles and the metals? It's baffling. Neospes, like other city pods around the rest of the world, was built on the knowledge that the Outers were uninhabitable. And yet, real *people* are living here.

Have things changed that much in the three years I've been gone?

There's no doubt in my mind that the tiny camera has a full view of the entire room, and while they've taken our weapons, we still have the suits. I can at least try to understand the layout of where we are being held and where we are on the map.

I hold my arm up and press the map command. Nothing happens. I press it again but there's no response. Frowning, I tap in the security sequences to power up the suit but the entire thing remains unresponsive. I swear under my breath and try again. But it's no use. The suit has somehow been deactivated.

"What's wrong?" Caden asks.

"It's not working."

"What do you mean, it's not working? I thought you said the suits were automatic?" Caden whispers. He averts his eyes hastily as I unzip and roll down my suit, separating the connection from my body and studying the microchips around the neural connector. But there's no light whatsoever.

"They've definitely been deactivated," I say quietly. "Let me see yours."

Heedless of the camera or the fact that I'm clad in just a sports bra, I detach Caden's suit and roll it down to his waist, but it's the same as mine—completely unresponsive. He moves to shrug it back on, but I put a hand on his arm.

"Don't," I say. "I don't know if the neural connectors are safe if the suit's been disabled." My fingers are still resting on his arm and I'm startled at the unexpected warmth of his skin. My eyes flutter to his leanly muscled chest, and my hand falls away along with my eyes. I step back, irritated at myself for being distracted. I've seen Cale shirtless countless times, but seeing Caden without a shirt bothers me far more than it should.

The buzzing in my head grows louder and my vision distorts once more, so much so that the floor starts to undulate beneath my feet. I shake my head roughly, trying to clear the static that seems to be crackling and coming from the inside my skull.

I don't realize that I've slumped to the floor until I feel Caden's hands on my shoulders, shaking gently. "Riven? Are you okay? You're freezing."

"Get off me," I say, shrugging him off. "I'm fine."

But Caden is right. My body is cold, as if it can no longer regulate my internal temperature. My teeth are chattering so hard that it feels like they'll break at any second. And claustrophobia overtakes me—a feeling I'd conquered years ago. As if on cue, my heartbeat elevates rapidly and suddenly; I can't breathe.

Caden whips one of the scratchy wool blankets off one of the cots at the end of the room and throws it around my shoulders. The fuzziness in my head gets worse, like some kind of high-pitched drill. The walls seem like they're closing in, amplifying the sound tenfold. I clap my hands against my ears, but if anything, the sound grows louder. Caden's shouting something but I can't hear him over the noise in my brain.

*Focus*, I tell myself. *Focus. Breathe. Focus. Breathe.*

It's an old mantra that Shae had taught me when I'd been held underground during fear training. It calms the noise as my breathing evens out. My skin feels warmer to the touch already. I have no idea what caused the episode, but I'm sure it has to do with some kind of post-traumatic eversion stress or some weird extended reaction to the serum.

"Something's wrong," Caden is saying to the dot in the wall. "Can't you see that? We need help!"

I'm about to tell him that his cries for help are useless when I see movement out of the corner of my eye coming down the passageway.

"It's about goddamn time," Caden says, and then stands back as one of the same men from before opens the metal-barred gate. He walks to stand next to me, his arms folded against his chest. "I don't know what you guys did to her, but you better fix her fast."

Caden's expression is stony like his voice, the realization that I could be in real danger hard-hitting. All traces of the boy Caden are now gone.

"I'm fine, Cade," I say weakly. "I feel better." I try to smile reassuringly at him, but it fades as one of the men steps forward. As before, they are all dressed in the same brown clothing, their faces stoic and expressionless. Caden's hand comes to rest on my shoulder, squeezing gently. His fingers knead the muscles, releasing some of the built-up tension, and I let my eyes drift close, despite the risk.

"Who are you?" The voice is soft and musical . . . a woman, then. My eyes snap open. "Who sent you?"

"No one sent us," I say, keeping my voice modulated and my hands flat against my sides. But the woman squints at Caden and steps closer. I see recognition dawn in her eyes, and my heart sinks. She stares from Caden to me, and again, there's an odd familiarity in her expression. Does she think he's Cale, as I'd done at first?

Still, she's not too sure about me and steps close enough to touch the faded blue braid wound into my hair. My rank. Her fingers drift down to touch the inked seal on the side of my neck— the one that marks me as a general of Neospes—and lingers against the black lines beneath it.

"You're the general," she says. "The one who defected three years ago." Her eyes narrow, but something in her voice tugs at me . . . a familiar tone, perhaps. Maybe I'm still fuzzy. I've never seen—or heard—this woman before in my life. "Have you been here all this time?"

"No," I say. I don't confirm or deny that I am whom she guesses. Caden is staring at me with wide eyes, but the understanding swirling in them is indisputable. Cat's out of the bag now, and there's no use pretending I'm not who I am.

"Who are you?" I toss my own question in response back to the woman, who's studying me with an odd expression that makes me feel open and uncomfortable. Naked. I tug the blanket across my shoulders and stand. All the men behind the woman rest their hands on the hilts of their weapons, but I ignore them. "Who are you?" I repeat, my tone sharper.

She laughs at my posturing. It is a sound devoid of any humor. "We're nobody. Exiles. Traitors. Enemies of Neospes. *Defectors.*" She says the last word with the hint of a smile, but I am growing tired of this game. They're toying with us. I can take the five of them out blindfolded, even in my unfamiliar state. Without looking at Caden, I tighten my body into a state of readiness but freeze at her next words. "You really don't know me, do you, Riven?"

As before, I'm certain I've never seen this woman before, but then again, her hair is covered in a brown wrap. Her face is the same color as her clothing. Her eyes look dark in the light. She could be anyone.

I shrug, arrogant, raising my palms upward in expectation.

She lifts a hand and removes the wrap, and her hair falls loose, so long that the silken waves reach past her back. It is so blond that it's nearly white, and I know without even seeing them that her eyes in the daylight are light gray. Silver.

Like mine.

The only thing I inherited from her.

# 17

# A WEB OF LIES

"YOU'RE NOT HER. You can't be her," I say in an emotionless voice. "She's dead. My mother died years ago, strapped down to a bed in a lab. I saw her with my own eyes."

The words sting like poison barbs against my lips, scorching my insides on the way out, and I can't even look at this woman who makes my heart pound and my eyes burn. No one in Neospes has hair that color, but where she came from—one of the cities on the other side of the burned oceans—that hair color is common.

It's not her.

My heart argues otherwise, but my brain sees it for what it must be . . . a trick, some kind of lie to disable me. I cross my arms over my chest. My eyes narrow. "Don't push me. Who are you?"

"I did die that day," the woman says. Her voice is soft so only I can hear it. "Just not in the way that you think."

"I don't know what game you're playing, and I don't care. You know who I am, and you know that if I choose, none of you will be left standing." The men once more bristle at my words, but I ignore them. All I can feel is the hot emotion welling up inside me like a tide, uncontrollable and violent. It's at odds with the coldness of my words. "My mother is *dead*."

"Look again, Riven. Trust yourself, not what you've been told."

"I know what I saw," I say flatly.

"Look again."

At her gentle insistence, I struggle to keep myself in check, but it's too late. There isn't a shred of doubt on her face, no sign of untruth in her eyes, but I refuse to give in. I can't . . . because if what she says is true, then my whole life has been a lie. She has to be lying.

How dare this woman presume to be my mother?

My rage erupts like a volcano, burning my mind with lost memories and thoughts I want forgotten. Without thinking, I drop to my knees in a crouch and spin behind her. I clip one of the men with my boot and take another out with a jab to the jaw before anyone can blink. The other two lurch toward me with their weapons, but I'm spinning again, my feet and hands darting out with swift, lethal purpose. And they, too, join their brothers on the floor.

The woman hasn't moved or drawn any weapons, but I still let my fury pin her up against the wall, my forearm under her slim neck.

"Riv, no," Caden says from behind me. "What are you doing?"

"Shut up," I growl to him. "She's an imposter. An *exile*." I turn back to her. The compassion in her clear eyes irritates me even more. "Otherwise, why would she and all her followers be hiding out here instead of in the city? And she's a liar. A fucking liar!"

My voice breaks on the last word, but still the woman doesn't move, staring at me with those brilliant eyes and daring me to believe the impossible. I flinch against the light palm pressing along the base of my spine. "Riven," Caden says again, his voice soft, "Stop. You're not a soldier anymore. Calm down. What these people are doing here is anyone's guess, but it's not our place to judge. We need their help. Remember why we're here?"

His words are tentative, but I can't see past the emotion storming inside of me. The fact that some stranger could elicit such a frightening response out of me because of the mere color of her hair or her eyes makes me furious . . . furious at myself, and furious at her for claiming to be someone that she isn't. Caden's foolishly timed words nudge me over the edge of my tenuous control on my anger.

My voice is calm. Deadly calm. "It became my place to judge when they imprisoned us here." I turn to face him, my expression echoing my voice, releasing my hold on the woman so that she slumps back against the wall, clutching her neck but still silent. "And don't you ever talk about me not being a soldier, ever again. You know nothing of it. I will be a soldier until the day that I die. So don't presume to think that you know me or what I am, ever. Understand?" I jab at the seal on my neck. "You asked me once what this was. It's a seal, a brand. It marks me as theirs and I can *never* escape it as long as I'm alive. And the black lines"—I'm spitting now, advancing on him, my words merging together—"mark the lives I've taken, those I've *killed.*

Still think I'm not so tough?" I say, mocking his words from his bedroom, a lifetime ago.

Caden is up against the other wall and I'm so close that I can feel his shallow breaths on my skin. But there's no real fear on his face; instead his eyes are wide and worried, focused on me. His hands are flat against my shoulders but nonthreatening.

"I may not know who you were, Riven," he says quietly. "But I know who you are now."

"Lady Aurela!"

I jerk and spin around at the shouts behind me, but it's the name that knocks the wind out of me. My mother's name. This *has* to be some kind of intricate plot. They're all in on it, trying to weave some convoluted web around me, but for the life of me I can't seem to figure out all the pieces. Why does my head feel so clouded, as if I can't think properly, like there's something blocking me, confusing my thoughts, and weakening my resolve?

"Get off, Caden," I mutter, my anger at him draining away, and shoving his hands off my shoulders. "You don't know anything about Neospes and you don't know anything about me."

My eyes are drawn to the blur of movement in the outer passageway, but the woman holds up a silent palm, and the men milling there stop. "You're not angry with him. You're angry with me," she says, walking forward. "Riven, it *is* me. I didn't die that day."

"I saw her die," I insist. "On that table."

Aurela shook her head, her eyes darkening with pain and regret. "You shouldn't have been there. He knew you were there, too. He wanted you to see it so you'd know what challenging him would cost."

"It's common knowledge that I was in that room, and what my father was capable of," I say softly, but my words have less conviction. "It still doesn't make you her."

"Riven, please," she says. "I know you've changed. You've had to, but I know that you know it's me. Listen to what your heart is telling you and not your reason. You and Shae—"

"Don't you talk about her," I hiss, pain seething through my voice, but Aurela continues despite my interruption.

"—were everything to me. She asked you to come with her, but you didn't. She couldn't tell you about me, because he would have found out, and as you said, you know what he was capable of."

Despite my mistrust, my mind is reeling. "Shae never asked me . . ." But my voice trails off as the memory snaps into my brain, followed by Shae's answer to why I had chosen not to go with her: *He owned you then, and he owns you now.* I stare at Aurela. "She never said anything about you."

"She couldn't. The quarters were monitored. He would have killed her."

I push past the growing knot in the pit of my stomach. My voice is cold and hard. "So you left, and she left. You left me with *him*."

Aurela is in front of me now, her face constricted. "If I could change that night, I would. I would go back to get you whatever the cost; you have to believe that, Riven. No matter what."

Everything inside me wants to argue, to scream, to rail against this woman who had always told me she loved me in the dead of night when only my nightmares kept me company, but suddenly I am tired of fighting. I am tired of pushing away everyone around me. I am tired of loss. I'm wary of letting logic rule my every action when it's obvious that my heart knows it's her. The emotion of it is overwhelming . . . splintering all of my carefully constructed walls.

Caden is watching me, and as I meet his eyes, he nods just once. He will support whichever path I decide. I shake my head tiredly and sit on the edge of one of the cots. The woman is quiet, waiting and knowing that my next words will decide how we leave this room. Truth and anguish and regret are written all over her face. I close my eyes for a long time.

"No, it would have been a suicide mission for anyone to come back," I say eventually. "That was the night he activated the Vector program . . . because of Shae. There were kill orders on sight for all defectors of the realm." I pause, the bitter question burning a hole in my mouth. "How did you survive?"

Aurela's face is wet with silent tears but she answers. "Annis."

Annis was my mother's research assistant. Like my father, my mother was a brilliant advanced genetics scientist. They were paired to lead the bioengineering and robotics programs, but when my father grew interested in reanimating the dead, my mother disagreed. She fought him tooth and nail on it, saying that it was a gateway mistake heading straight back to what they were just rebuilding as a society—from the Tech War. But my father was headstrong and arrogant.

Their intellectual arguments were epic, their fights shattering. Shae used to take me into our sleeping cell with her fingers covering my ears. Then one day, it went too far. In a fit of rage, our father had shoved her and she'd hit her head. Hard. Everyone at the hospital had said that Aurela's odds of survival were excellent, but somehow, she'd still died the next day.

They'd never been able to prove anything, but I knew. I'd seen the security footage that he'd stolen and hidden—saw him screaming at her in the dead of night alone in that hospital room, trying to force her to stay with him. She'd wanted to leave him and take us with her. In the end, he'd poisoned her. I saw him inject the poison himself into her intravenous tubing. If he couldn't have her, then no one else would. That was the day that I lost both my parents.

"Annis?" I say weakly. "But he poisoned you. I saw."

A soft smile. "She was there, hiding. She bled the poison out and then she helped me to flee Neospes before she returned to fake my death."

"Yes. I remember. She handled your organ reassignment and cremation."

"Someone else's, but there had to be a record."

"So where did you go?" I ask. "Here?"

"Not immediately. I was too weak to survive the Outers, despite what little we'd heard about others surviving. So I went to Sector Seven where my great-aunt still lived. She concealed us, and then when I was well enough, we made our way out here."

I nod slowly, shaken by the onslaught of memories. "It never made sense to me after you died why Father still branded you as an enemy of Neospes. You were dead. Why sully your memory and what you had contributed?" The realization is numbing like icy water. "So he knows you're not dead?"

"Maybe," Aurela concedes. "He never believed Annis, even though the data was all there. He sent waves of soldiers out to all the sectors, saying that I had been named a traitor and had stolen valuable crown research. He offered wealth and food and weapons, but the Artok are a proud tribe. They protect their own. I was never found. So for all intents and purposes, I *am* dead."

"But does *he* think you're dead?"

"I honestly don't know," Aurela says.

"And Shae?"

"Unlike your father, Shae never stopped looking for me." Her words unlock another memory, one of Shae telling me at night that our mother would always care for us no matter what, and that I'd see her again one day. But I never believed her. I cried and nodded but never believed. Once more, Shae was right. Aurela smiles again; this time, it's a proud smile. "She's so tenacious. She made Annis tell her, and two days later, we found her wandering out here on her own, nearly half-dead." Aurela stares at me expectantly, and I feel the dread unfurl in my stomach. "She's not with you?"

I try to speak but I can't. The words are lodged in my throat like sharp stones, choking me with their broken edges. I open and shut my mouth like a flailing fish, gasping. Caden answers from behind me.

"She didn't make it," he says. "Shae's dead."

Without warning, Aurela falls back like a rock, and I find myself lurching forward to catch her. Her skin is warm and she smells the same as she did ten years before, of vanilla and earth. If I wasn't convinced before, I am now. Her silvery eyes find mine and then I'm hugging her so tightly, I can't even breathe. I'm sobbing and breathless, and I pull even tighter.

"I'm sorry, I'm sorry, I'm sorry. She . . . died to save us. So stupid and so bullheaded."

My face is wet against hers. "Shhh," she whispers, comforting me as if I'm still two years old, crying from a skinned knee. "It's okay. Shae knew what she'd gotten into. Like you, she had a soldier's heart. I just . . . Nothing really prepares you to lose a child, does it? Don't worry; we'll get through this together."

It seems like forever that we've been lying on the ground, until I hear a sniff behind me and glance up to see Caden hastily wiping his face. I do the same and roll my eyes at him. Already, I can feel the cold numbness seeping through my body—my usual self-defense mechanism against emotion. Showing vulnerability is still not something I'm entirely comfortable with, despite my deepest tiny desire to stay in my mother's arms forever.

I stand, pulling Aurela up with me, and step away as if it will erase the last few minutes. But this time, the deadening numbness is slower than usual. My regret cripples me, as do whatever feelings I have for this woman I haven't seen in a decade. My mother.

"This is Caden," I rasp.

"I know who he is," Aurela responds, pulling Caden into a long hug. She looks at me over his shoulder. "Thank you for keeping him safe."

I want to agree that that's exactly what I've done, but for some reason I can't hold her gaze. My eyes drop to the floor and I mumble something unintelligible. The truth is, I went to the Otherworld to find Caden at Cale's request. Not to keep him safe at all. I haven't even been sure of what I'm going to do with Caden once we get to the city, but that's what has been driving me. Complete the mission. Worry about everything else like feelings and casualties later.

Only now, we were stuck in some underground secret village in the Outers on the outskirts of the city—a flourishing city that *isn't* under the thumb of Neospes.

"How do you know who I am?" Caden asks, quietly interrupting my thoughts, staring from Aurela and back to me.

"I've known you a very long time. Come," Aurela says, "Let's go to my quarters, and we'll talk more."

The men in the passageway clear a path as we walk past in Aurela's wake. I grab our packs on the way out despite some hard stares from the men standing there. A quick search through the contents confirms that nothing of value has been removed, other than the missing weapons.

"Where are my blades?" I ask.

"They're safe," Aurela responds. "Come."

As we move away from the room, I notice that the rock composition of the wall shifts into something less glassy and more earthy, although still marbled with the black rock from the cave before. At the same moment, I feel something vibrate at my waist, where the shirtsleeves of my suit are wrapped beneath the blanket I still have slung over my shoulders. The lights on the keypad are blinking as if the suit's trying to reactivate.

I frown, shrugging off the blanket and pulling the top half of the suit back over my shoulders, wincing at the slight sting of the neck connector plugging into my central nervous system. It's trying desperately to reboot, but something's still running interference.

Aurela glances at me out of the corner of her eye. "It's not going to work," she says quietly.

"What?"

"The suits. Do you know why they didn't work? Especially in that room?" Aurela waves a hand at the black-veined walls of the tunnel. Her voice is still careful and quiet. "It's electromagnetically charged volcanic glass. It disables all computers, all robotics." I frown at her words. Volcanic? Are we near the Peaks? I'm still frowning as she continues. "It's how we're safe from the metals and the hybroids. Even in here, where the pulse is less strong, it still interferes with any computer signals. We're virtually undetectable."

I power down the suit and remove the neural connector to ask the question heavy in my mouth. "Are we near the Peaks?"

A laugh. "Honey, we're *in* the Peaks."

"But how is that even possible. . . ." I gasp. "The Peaks are impenetrable."

"To androids, yes," Aurela agrees. "But not to us."

She ushers us into another room, this one veined with light blue quartz-like glass. Oddly, I feel like a huge weight is lifted off me. I don't know if it's the color of the walls—it reminds me of the sky in Caden's world—but I take a long, deep breath and feel less muddled. The remaining cobwebs in my head clear as if by magic, just as my suit boots up. Aurela is watching me closely, a slight frown marring her forehead, but she looks away when I make eye contact.

I turn to look around. A huge table surrounded by chairs dominates the room. In one corner, there's a long desk with several flat-screen computers, data flashing across all their screens. I turn to Aurela but Caden beats me to the punch.

"I thought you said no computers worked here," Caden says. He, too, had been listening quietly and paying attention.

"They do in this room. We have to have some means of communication with people outside and to keep up to date on what's going on in Neospes." She nods at my clothes. "Those will work now."

But I'm already powering up the suit. I can see that the three men who have accompanied us all have their hands on their weapons. Obviously, the technology of the Vectors' suits is something they are wary of.

And rightly so.

The suit just doesn't just control temperature or create awesome topological holographs. It's an advanced bio-weapon itself. At the touch of a button, bladed spikes rise from the fabric of the suit. It can harden like armor in less than a second or change color to fade into a background. The suit is designed for espionage, insinuation, and attack, and its defensive and offensive properties are legendary. But as I'd showed Caden, the best thing about them is the neural connector that taps into the brain's signals to the body. Regardless of programmed or natural human impetus, the suit responds to flight or fight signals in a millisecond. In some of the later models, the suit calibrates to your very thoughts.

I've never been a fan of the automatic-pilot mode. It's too unpredictable when tapped into humans. That technique works best with the Vectors because they're emotionless and run by computers. Humans are too subject to emotional decisions, especially under stress. If the suit receives mixed messages, it will opt for the first directive, even if there's a later counter-command. It'll then have to be manually overridden, which in many cases means it's already too late.

Still, limitations aside, short of flying, it's a super-suit, unmatched in design or abilities.

*Defense,* I command silently, and feel the programming engage as the suit tightens against my body. The movement is barely noticeable to human eyes, but the slight smile twitching along the corners of my mother's mouth irks me. It's no surprise—she knows the suits better than anyone. After all, before she defected, she invented bioprogramming of the early prototypes.

I stare at her with narrowed eyes.

"You still don't trust easily, do you?" Aurela remarks.

I'm hard-pressed to wipe my standard frown off my face. "Not really. Where are my weapons?"

"Why do you need them? Surely you're protected enough already." Her meaningful glance dips to my uniform, but in the same breath, she gestures to a cot against the far wall, and with relief I notice my harness and scabbard on top of it along with our two crossbows. I walk over to inspect them, but they seem the same as before. If anything, my swords look like they've been cleaned and oiled. I frown and sling the harness over my arm.

Aurela sits at the table and inclines her head for Caden and me to do the same. I place the ninjatas carefully on the table and take a seat. At a glance from their leader, the men who had accompanied us leave the room. The last one—a boy near my own age—shoots a glare at me that could melt rock, but I just grin, baring my teeth at him in a mockery of a smile. It's a look that has scattered crowds. His glare fades quickly.

"Haven't lost your touch, I see," Aurela says, noticing the exchange. At my stare, she continues, her voice soft. "There are many stories of you, even ones that as a mother I wish I'd never heard. But you did what you were commanded to do, and you did it extraordinarily well." I remain silent. "At fourteen, your reputation preceded you. Even grown men were terrified to face you. What made you leave? Defect?"

I knew the question would come. I spare a brief look to Caden but his face is carefully expressionless. He wants to know the answer, too. "Cale ordered me to find Caden." I pause, searching for the right words. "I was to bring him back alive."

"Why?"

"You know why," I snap, evasive.

Aurela's return stare is measured. "We need to trust each other, Riven. I know you feel you can't trust me, and that I will have to earn that from you. Even though I don't fully know your motives, you're here and he"—she says with a searching glance at Caden—"is safe." She reaches her fingers across the table where my hand is resting, but I pull it away at the last second. She lets hers rest where mine had been. "I know that my daughter is in there somewhere. I felt it before. I don't know what happened with Shae, but she would have moved heaven and earth to keep Caden away from you if she thought you were a danger."

"She did," I grit out. "She failed. She didn't trust me, either."

"She didn't at first."

"How do you know that? Did she tell you?"

Aurela nods, folding her hands in her lap. "Whenever she everted back here to evade the Vectors or you, she apprised me on what was happening in the Otherworld."

I slam to my feet, anger coloring the inside of my skin with dull red flame. "And you let her? You let her evert over and over again, knowing what it would do to her? How could you do that? Knowing it would kill her?" The words are rushing out of me like a river of pain from between clenched teeth. "What kind of mother are you?"

"A fighter, like you."

"You sent her to die!" I scream, fists curling at my sides.

"She was there to protect him from *you*."

All I could see is my mother's face behind the fire burning in my brain, inflaming me. And then I'm lurching toward her. Out of the corner of my eye, Caden jerks out of his chair, but I don't let it distract me. For an older woman, my mother is fast, darting out of my way and spinning across the top of the table like a gymnast. I leap over it. I don't know whether my rage is blinding me, but I don't see her strike until it's too late. Her arm catches me across my side, knocking the wind out of me. In her other hand, I see the glinting blade of my ninjata that had been on the table. Its point is pressed against my neck.

Caden flings himself on top of me before I can move. "Riven, stop," he growls. "Shae was there for me. You know that. She told you that. Stop blaming yourself or anyone else for her death. It was what *she* wanted."

All the fury seeps out of me like the air in a balloon, and I close my eyes. My voice is strangled and bitter. "She died for nothing."

"That's not true," Caden says. "She died for us."

"Then she died for nothing." I open my eyes to meet his and then Aurela's. The pity in hers is suffocating. "It is true. My mission"—I spit the words—"was to bring you to Cale. He's the king here. And he's sick. He needed me to find you"—my heart twists, but Caden has to know all of it—"for parts."

"For parts?" he echoes vacantly. Caden's eyes are horrified but I have to finish. I have to tell him what he is. He'll find out sooner or later, and either way, he'll hate me for it.

"Body parts. You're a clone, Caden. You're not real."

# 18

# CONFESSIONS

AURELA'S INCREDULOUS LAUGH is long and hollow and cold at my bombshell. I push Caden off and stand slowly, dragging him up beside me. Aurela is wiping tears from her eyes, waving away the people who had rushed into the room at the crashing sound of Caden's chair.

Caden jerks away from me, shrugging off my arm. "What do you mean, I'm a *clone*?"

But I don't answer, my eyes still resting on Aurela, who is shaking her head with an expression of complete disbelief on her face. Caden is a clone, I'm sure of it. I'd heard it from Cale's own mouth.

"You're no clone," Aurela chokes and then looks at me, her stare discerning. "Is that what Cale told you?"

I flinch inwardly at her words but I nod, wary, studying her face for deception. But her eyes are clear and her voice even more so. "He's not. Caden is the real prince of Neospes."

"That's impossible." Though I think them, I don't voice the words. Caden does. He sinks into the chair behind us with a stupefied expression. "I'm *not* . . . not a . . . prince."

"You're wrong," I say to Aurela. "He's not. Cale is."

"Am I? Think back, Riven. You know I'm telling the truth."

Had Cale lied to me? Or is Aurela the one lying? But as quickly as I ask myself the second question, I'm replaying the events in my head, searching for anything that could have told me Cale was lying. Why should I doubt him now, if I hadn't then?

Unless I hadn't seen it. I hadn't wanted to see it.

Cloning is an old technology, used only by the royals, and forbidden everywhere else. It has undesirable side effects—we learned the hard way that clones had odd frailties—like weakened immune systems or psychosomatic disorders. In a world rebuilt on utopian principles, genetic purity was critical to survival, and cloning was outlawed shortly after the Tech War. But clones were still commissioned as safeguards for the monarchy, an extra layer to protect the royal line from insurgents. When Cale confided that his clone had been taken, I was suitably outraged on his behalf. He said that he was sick and would die if I weren't able to locate and bring the clone back to Neospes. I was the only one he could trust.

After his father was murdered, I was so eager to do Cale's bidding, so eager to save him that I agreed without a second thought. But in hindsight, I still don't see any deception. Had I been so gullible? Am I still?

"I'd rather be a clone," Caden says dully to no one in particular. "I always knew I was different, but this just takes the cake."

"So there's no clone?" I ask slowly, Caden's inane words piercing the sudden fog in my brain.

"No," Aurela says. "There is. It's just not Caden."

The realization hits me through the fog like a ton of bricks to the face. I feel my feet stagger backward, and my hip braces against the side of the table. Grasping the edges with numb fingers, I hold myself from sliding down.

"Cale's the clone." My voice is a monotone. Aurela nods, her expression compassionate. The realizations come more quickly after the first. I quickly put two and two together. Cale's mother had left when he'd been four. "Their mother left to protect the prince," I muse quietly, sparing a glance at Caden, who still looks like he's in some kind of waking dream. I don't blame him. My mind is spinning like an unstoppable top. I can't imagine the confusion he's feeling.

Aurela nods. "She suspected Murek long before. She knew he was collaborating with your father to assassinate the king. It was only a matter of time before they came for her son." Aurela stops, lowering her voice. "They wanted to use him. Leila knew she was in danger when she realized she was in the way. When she took him, she went to the Artok. They brought her to us, but the only real safe place for her and the prince was her world."

June wasn't lying after all. Leila had always been from over there, and she took her son to the only refuge she knew. And that's why June and Era broke all the oaths they'd taken as Guardians to protect her. The puzzle is far more intricate than I've ever imagined. I shake my head. "Even if she did switch them before she—"

"She didn't switch them," Aurela interrupts. "That was your father's idea after she everted. They needed a puppet, so they made up this story that Cale's mother had died. But Cale—"

"—told me the truth. That she'd everted with the clone. I mean, that's what he thought. Or what he'd been told." I pause and half stand. "By Murek and my father."

It all made sense. My father knew that Cale was the only person who I ever had any loyalty to, so when Cale got sick, he took the opportunity to tell him about the clone, and it was natural that Cale asked me—his most trusted confidant—to track down the clone, even if by obeying his orders in secret, it made me appear to be a defector in the eyes of everyone else.

"I see you now understand."

"Why would they send me?"

"Because you were the best," Aurela says gently. "You *are* the best. The Vectors reported that Caden was with Shae in the Otherworld, and Cale knew you were the only one who could fight or beat her."

"So is Cale really sick, or is that all a lie, too?"

Aurela pours something black that looks like coffee into three mugs, and sets a steaming cup in front of Caden and then in front of me. I take a gulp, and although the bitter taste overwhelms me at first, the aftertaste is thick and mellow like butterscotch.

"No, our reports confirm that he is sick." Her words cause the cracks inside of me to widen into furious chasms that I can feel splitting me apart. Relief seeps in to flood the fractures as I realize that Cale didn't lie to me. He didn't send me on some fool's mission. He didn't betray me to my father. He sent me to help him live, even if it were part of some misguided plot of Murek's. I'm sure Cale would never betray me. He is as much a victim of Murek and my father as we are.

Sighing heavily, I glance over at Caden, who hasn't moved, sitting with his head in his hands, staring into the mug as if it holds answers only he can see. I can't even imagine what this must be like for him.

"You okay, Caden?" I ask.

"What do you care?" he rasps without looking up. "You brought me here to die, didn't you?"

"No!" I say, pounding my fist on the table so hard that the shock runs up my arm and through my back. "I didn't. I mean, at first you were a target, but now . . ." My voice trails off, caught in the turmoil of what exactly Caden has come to mean to me.

"Now, what?" he says, turning around with eyes so green, they're like the grass in his world. It's like they're seeing right into me, past all the flesh and bone, deep down where there's nothing else but truth. "Now what, Riv?" he whispers.

I stare at Aurela, but she can't say the words for me. Instead, her face is compassionate, as if somehow she already knows. She knows what I feel . . . everything I've kept buried under my orders. I owe Caden the truth, don't I?

"But now . . ." My throat is clogged and my eyes are smarting. "Now, it's different. You're my friend." I can see that those words are not enough. Caden's gaze drops from mine to stare once more into the coffee mug.

I'm struck dumb. My mouth won't move. Nothing is moving. A single tear weeps from the corner of my left eye. I leave it, feeling its hot path meandering down my cheek. My tears are the words I cannot say.

"Come," Aurela says gently, interrupting the heavy tension between Caden and me. "Let's get you two settled for the night. We'll talk more tomorrow, once you've had some rest."

The minute we leave the room, I feel disoriented again, as if I'm suffering vertigo. I take deep breaths as Aurela escorts us down some more dark passageways. It helps. I notice that the men fall into silent step behind us, guarding their leader at every moment. Even though I know how important she is in this small community, for the first time I start to question just *how* important she is. She holds herself with a quiet confidence—the same self-assurance I remember as a child. But there's no arrogance in her words or her manner. She is one of them even as she leads them.

Caden has a room all to himself with an armed guard. Now that I know who he is, I'm not surprised. Aurela is taking no chances that word has already gotten out about Caden's identity or that some zealous defector will try to get back into Murek's good graces by offering up the runaway prince.

"Cade," I say at the entrance. "I'll see you tomorrow. Okay?"

"Yeah." But he doesn't look at me at all, not even when he lies back on the cot at the far end of the room and lays his head on his palms, staring up at the ceiling. I stand there for a moment, uncomfortable, before I hear Aurela gently calling my name. "Night, Cade."

He doesn't answer as I turn to follow Aurela. She stares at me with a knowing expression. "Don't worry; we're not far away. And he'll be different in the morning. It's a lot for him to have to take in; just give him some time." I know that she's right, but Caden's aloofness hurts more than I ever thought it would.

The thought of Cale pops into my brain, and I shove him away. I can't choose. I won't. I'll have to find some other way around all of this . . . some way to save them both. I'll give myself up to my father if I have to, if there's anything he can do to save Cale.

"This is where you are," Aurela says. She points to an adjoining room. "My quarters are just over there." Glancing around, I see that people are taking notice of where I've been placed—a room adjoining hers. Aurela reads my expression easily. "It's because you're the bigger threat," she says smoothly.

But inside, I know there's more to it than that. She could have left me in the cell we'd been detained in, surrounded by armed guards. Instead, I'm like some guest in her private quarters. It's a message.

A message that I am important.

For some reason, I don't like it. I'm not sure that I've forgiven her for everything between us, for everything that Shae knew . . . that I did not. For leaving me behind with *him*. My voice is bitter. "I'd rather stay in the first room."

"Riven, that is a holding cell. None of them trust you as I do."

I narrow my eyes at her. "Why? Why do you trust me? You know who I am. What I do. What I've done."

"Yes, I know all of that. But I also know that you are my daughter, and there's some of me still in there, no matter how much he's tried to weed it out of you all those years."

"What do you mean?" I snap.

Her voice is quiet. "Nothing." Aurela stares at me for a second, her white-blonde hair curling around her shoulders. "Get some rest. Things will look better in the morning," she says, and then, "Riven?"

"What?"

"I lo—"

"Don't say it," I snap back, cutting her off midsentence. "You don't even know me." I stare with dead calm into her silver eyes. "And you're right. He did cut every last part of you out of me. Everything human, everything that should feel something. He made me emotionless just like him. And you know what? I like it."

I am so proud of the strength and conviction in my voice, but her simple smile is my undoing. She steps forward and I hold my ground. I don't even blink when she takes a strand of hair that is stuck to my cheek and tucks it behind my ear, nor when her fingers trail over the tattoos on my neck to rest on my shoulder with a reassuring squeeze. "And yet you wouldn't tell me this if you weren't fighting it within you this very moment, would you? Sleep well, my little blackbird."

And with that, she was gone.

I stare at the wooden door between our rooms for a long moment. She called me little blackbird. The words draw me backward, and I'm sitting in my room, crying my eyes out.

"Why'd you name me Riven? It's so horrible," I was wailing. "It's not even pretty. It's ugly, like me."

"You're not ugly, darling," my mother soothed. "Your name was supposed to be Raven, which is the name of a tiny blackbird that visits me from the gorge behind the house. It has the prettiest whistle. When you were born, you made that sound."

"Really?" I asked, still sobbing but now curious.

"Yes, but well, mistakes happen. And your name was recorded as Riven." She kissed me on the nose then. "I have an idea. How about if I call you little blackbird, just you and me? It could be our little secret."

And I nodded, thrilled with having a secret name that remained a secret between us until the day she died . . . I mean, until now. Even Shae didn't know. If I had any doubt that she was who she said she was—my mother—I didn't anymore. No one would have known about that name but the two of us. It was ours alone.

I glance around at my quarters. From force of habit, I'd already taken inventory of the small, square-shaped room the minute we'd walked in, but it looks the same as all the others— spartan, with the exception of a small table and chair on one side, next to a cot. Nothing, except its position next to Aurela's, marks it as superior.

The flame of a small candle dances against the wall, illuminating the white quartz and onyx colors in the rock. I stare at the rock and tilt my head to one side. I don't feel as claustrophobic or as unbalanced in this room. It's odd how I feel more uncomfortable in some areas of the Outer underground than I do in others, almost as if the rock composition is tied to my ability to function, like the computers. I laugh—I must be more worn out than I think.

I glance at the cot, but I can't sleep. Too much nervous energy is swirling inside of me. My mind still feels muddled, so I strip down to my underclothes, taking care to fold the suit over the chair. I sit cross-legged on the floor and pull energy into my center for a long period until my heartbeat is steady and my breathing full. I extend each arm forward, and then ease my legs out into a side-split, stretching my tight muscles. The sequence of calisthenics falls into place as I twist my torso over my left leg, and my mind goes blank, muscle memory kicking in.

Nearly an hour later, my body is dripping with sweat, but I haven't felt so alive since being underground. I'm wired, energy coursing through me and filling my cells with vibrant life. Without missing a beat, I grab my ninjata blades and start swinging them in a graceful arc, my legs extending outward at the same pace.

The exercise starts out slow and then gradually builds in speed until I'm gasping for breath and whirling the blades with incredible swiftness. I'm moving so quickly that the glossy blades are a blur in the room, the flicker of candlelight reflecting off them almost making them look like liquid flame between my fingers.

The swords are moving faster than I am, and my body strives to keep up, moving faster and faster and faster, until something hot nicks the back of my leg. I jerk to a halt, staring at the watery crimson trail that is welling against my skin. The voice at the corner of the room takes me by surprise.

"Getting a little rusty?"

"What are you doing here?" I pant, wiping the sweat off my face with my forearm. "You should be sleeping."

"Like you are?" Caden saunters into the room and pulls out one of the chairs at the table, straddling it with his legs on either side and his arms across the top. His dark hair is unruly as if he's been running his hands through it one too many times. He rests his chin across his crossed forearms staring at me through squinty eyes.

"I need the exercise," I say.

"And I couldn't sleep," he tosses back. "You know, a boy doesn't find out he's a prince from the magical land of Far Far Away every day." The sarcasm is heavy in his voice, and I bite back a smile at the reference to *Shrek*.

"At least you're not an ogre, and it's probably a lot less magical than the one you were in."

His stare is assessing, a lock of hair curling into one eye. "So, tell me something. When you thought I was a clone, you were coming to get me to bring me back here, and Shae was protecting me from you?" I nod, uncertain of the direction of his questions, but continue my movements, albeit more carefully now. "So I was your target?"

"Yes." I slow my pace further with the swords, lunging and stretching both my arms in an arc over my head before pulling them around to the front and twisting away from him.

"So am I still your target?" His voice is louder than it was, and I whirl around. But his voice isn't louder, and Caden is no longer sitting. He's right in front of me. His hands grasp my wrists, halting them mid-motion.

He's so close that I can feel his warm breath feathering against my cheek. In a smooth motion, he removes the ninjata from my left hand, stepping back and swinging it in a slow circle. I take a slow breath.

"Don't hold a weapon—"

"—that you're not prepared to use," Caden finishes. "Shae told me."

"Cade . . ." I begin.

"What? Are you so afraid to fight me?" he asks softly. There's something in his voice that I can't identify, something painful and aching.

"I don't want to hurt you," I say. "These are real swords, you know. Not fencing foils."

"I know."

And before I can think, all I see is the flash of a blade curving toward me. The clash of steel in the small room is like thunder as my blade meets his in a shower of sparks, but Caden is already sidestepping and striking from the underside.

In a few seconds, I'm aware that Caden is more than good. He's *really* good.

Shae wasn't joking about how easily he holds a sword. I sense that most of it is instinct, but he has the basics of what we are all taught in Neospes. He's taken that a step further with his own fencing training. Despite the fact that I've spent the better part of two hours practicing, Caden has me on my toes. Even though my body wants to go into full attack mode, I restrain myself.

"Why are you holding back?" he taunts, reading my slowed movements accurately.

"I don't want to hurt you."

"We'll see about that."

I drop to a crouch and jerk upward, only to find the top end of my sword crashing into the bottom of his on its way down. His ability to read responses is uncanny, almost as uncanny as my own, and I grin widely at the unexpected challenge.

Caden's bare foot catches my heel and I fall backward, only to catapult to my feet in a crouch, my sword at his back. He fends me off capably, and then we are spinning to the discordant tune of crashing metal until I am against the wall with his sword upon my neck. Caden's eyes are triumphant.

But so are mine.

I tap the point of my sword against the inside of his hip, and as he looks down, I grin. And then I'm laughing, and Caden is laughing, until his fingers slide against my cheek, and the laughter slips from my lips. His eyes are so green, it feels like I'm drowning in them. I want to move, but my body won't listen. My arms drop to my sides, and my tongue slips out to moisten suddenly dry lips. I pull my lower lip between my teeth.

"Don't do that." The harsh whisper is Caden's.

"Don't do what?" I say chewing unconsciously on the corner of my bottom lip.

His eyes darken. A storm-tossed meadow. "That thing with your mouth."

"I didn't—" But his lips silence mine in mid-sentence, the soft warm pressure of them hugging the curves of mine like they'd known them forever. Our breaths mingle as we draw apart, and Caden is staring at me with those impossibly green eyes. I can't help myself. I lean into him, parting my lips and slanting my mouth against his. His hands are at the back of my neck and around my back, drawing me against him so tightly I can barely breathe. But I clutch him tighter—lost.

The second kiss of my life.

Kissing is an anomaly in Neospes. Couples are paired by genetic compatibility, not by what or how they feel about each other. But humans are social creatures, and sometimes love blooms after the pairing, although that is incredibly rare.

I remember one boy in my training group who developed an affinity for another trainee. It'd affected his performance so clearly that within a day, the girl had been transferred to another sector.

Love made us vulnerable, made us weak. Those were our rules.

But Caden's kiss makes me weaker and stronger all at the same time. And the way it makes me feel—like I am flame on the outside and liquid on the inside. It makes me feel alive, as if I can take on anything. And the only time I ever feel like that is when I'm fighting, when the adrenaline takes over and I'm only fire and fight.

Now I'm fire and entirely something else entirely.

My hands tangle in his hair, into the soft mess of it, and I draw him closer. Not even the clatter of the swords on the floor tears us apart. Eventually, we come up for air, and as we pull apart, my mind drifts to our first kiss in the bathroom at Horrow, so similar to this one but so intoxicatingly different. My fingers slide against the square line of his jaw and across the sharp rise of his cheekbone.

Caden presses his lips into my hair and stays there for what seems like an eternity. I can't move, not even when he leans into me and rests his head on my shoulder, turning his face into my damp neck. In fact, every part of me is motionless as his lips find the curve of my collarbone, winding their way up to my ear, fanning the fire once more unfurling in my chest. My legs are unsteady.

"I love you."

"I love . . ."

For a second, I imagine that's what I started to say. And then I'm splintering into an abyss of darkness and cold and pain.

# 19

# DECEPTION'S DAUGHTER

"IS SHE GOING to be okay?"

White, bright lights are flashing everywhere. They hurt my eyes, even closed. I try to move, but my arms are restrained. So are my legs. I'm lying on a cold, white surface in what appears to be an emergency medical bay. I crack open an eyelid, squinting at the wave of agony that threatens to send me back into an unconscious stupor.

A hologram of a human body is suspended in the middle of the room and surrounded by all kinds of shifting miscellaneous data. I blink. Everything is so white. Even the medical garments barely covering my torso are white. My lips are cracked and sore. My tongue is glued to the roof of my mouth, and when I try to talk, my voice crumbles like dust. I blink again, opening both eyes and try to focus. Pain stabs through my head.

"Water," I manage to gasp.

A shadow looms and the rim of a cold cup is held gently to my lips. The water is like ice, soothing the dryness inside my mouth. I want more, but the cup is gently taken away.

"WhereamI?" The words merge into one. I try to sit up, but forget that I am restrained. The panic is immediate. "Where am I?" I scream, my throat seared raw.

"Sector Seven," a voice says. "You're safe."

My brain registers only two things. I'm back in the city, in a Sector on the outskirts of Neospes. And there are no bioengineering facilities in Sector Seven. Where am I being held?

Flashes of Cale and Shae and my mother wind their way through my mind, and then I see another face. It's Cale's but not Cale's. And he's looking at me with gentle eyes full of something that terrifies me. It terrifies me because my heart understands what his eyes are saying, and my heart feels the same. Who was the boy? A dream? A figment?

My mind is angry, squelching the tiny spark of emotion. I am two separate things. Memory and present. Frailty and strength. I have to be strong. The boy is nothing to me.

But he's not a dream. The shadow forms into focus, and I see him. His name is Caden, my brain whispers. He's the target. You brought him here. You have to take him to Cale, the Lord King. But not yet.

Why not yet?

The questions are overwhelming, dueling inside of me.

"Hey," the boy says with a crooked smile. "You okay?" I nod, and close my eyes, turning away from him.

"Caden," another voice says, a woman's voice. "You need to get some rest. We're through the worst, and she's awake now. You'll be able to talk to her soon."

"What happened back there?" I hear Caden ask. "No one told me anything."

"Get some rest. I promise I will explain later."

I hear the sound of the door closing as Caden leaves. The woman checks my arms and the neural leads that run from my chest and temple to the base of the metal table. It connects below to the row of computers monitoring my vitals. I realize then that the suspended holo body is mine.

Her fingers are gentle. I stare at her through my lashes, surreptitious. She has long silvery blond hair that has been tied into a row of braids across the top of her head, and hangs thickly over one shoulder. Her eyes are clear, her face youthful.

*She is your mother,* my mind tells me. Aurela. But it is a piece of information, nothing more. I don't feel anything overwhelming, not like the rush I'd had with the boy earlier. I open my eyes to meet hers.

"How long have I been here?" I ask hoarsely.

"Three days." Her hand brushes across my forehead. Her touch feels odd against my skin, tingly and tender. I shy away automatically. "Do you remember anything?" she asks, but I only stare at her silently. "What's your name?"

"Riven. Legion General." I watch her face slide from relaxed to anxious to pained.

"Do you remember the Otherworld? The Outers? Anything?"

"Yes, of course."

Aurela studies me, her eyes narrowed as she comes to some understanding in her head. It worries me, and I feel my brow furrow, uncannily matching hers ridge for ridge. "What is your mission?" she says slowly.

"To secure the target." I blink. The response is automatic, programmed in my brain, but something doesn't feel right.

The feelings in my head don't match the words in my mouth. They're coming from somewhere else . . . some alternate source of information feeding answers to my lips. The thoughts are there but something tells me that they are not my own.

They're orders. Someone else's orders.

"No . . . I don't know," I say, pulling my arms against the steel manacles. "Someone is in my head. It's not me!"

"Riven, calm down," Aurela says. "Let me get the doctors. Everything will be okay."

But my panic is swift, and I'm wrenching my arms on the table until the metal starts to cut through my flesh. Oddly, I don't feel a thing. The veins in my arms and neck are corded so tightly that they are raised and navy against my skin, and I'm mesmerized by the intertwined deep red and pale blue fluid oozing from the lacerations at my wrists.

Red. And blue.

The machines are beeping so loudly that they sound like some kind of terrible security breach. One hand breaks free, the twisted wrist bracelet still attached to the table, and I'm clawing at my other hand. I don't know where I'm finding the strength, but I rip off the leads stuck to my chest without even blinking. More machines bleat in immediate succession, but they've dulled to a low hum in the back of my mind as everything becomes strangely calm. My only objective is to escape. It has ahold of me like a starving dog defending a bone, relentless.

A team of people rushes into the room, and Aurela's face is hovering over mine. Something cold slides into the back of my neck and spreads through the rest of my body. Aurela's eyes are clear, holding my own. I can see the answers in them. The last thing I think before sedation grabs hold of me is that she knows. She *knows*.

She's always known.

When I awake once more, I'm no longer in the operating analysis room. I'm in a small four-walled gray cube, lying on a thin bed. There are cameras in the ceiling and a metal stool and table in the corner of the space. Someone has dressed me in soft flannel clothing.

I try to sit up and surprisingly do so with little pain. It feels weird, like I am somehow back to normal. I stretch my neck in slow circles, but everything feels fluid and strong. It almost seems that everything I remember must be some sort of bad dream, but of course, I know that it is not. I run through my mental checklist in my head, confirming all of the factual information I know about myself and who I am.

My name is Riven. I am a legion general. My target is Caden. I have acquired the target. Caden is my friend.

The last thought shoots into my head like an errant arrow, and I analyze it carefully like a piece of forensic evidence. I feel nothing for the thought itself, but it's an oddity that intrigues me. In Neospes, friends are a luxury and oftentimes, in my opinion, more of a hindrance. Unlike family, they complicate things. Lines become blurred, and I like being able to make decisions objectively. As a result, I have no friends, so it's odd that I would have a memory that a *target* had become my friend. My only "friends" have been Cale, and Shae once upon a time.

Shae.

The name is a bullet exploding inside of my consciousness . . . a part of my brain that I know is wholly mine. A wave of agony ripples through me, and my body folds in on itself, the memories flooding my head like boiling lava. My arms grip around my torso so hard that I can barely breathe. I can hear someone screaming—*keening*—and it takes a second before I realize that the sound is coming from me.

Shae is dead. She died to save me. My sister is dead. She died to protect Caden.

Caden is my friend.

The waterfall of memories assaults me anew, and it all comes back in a rush—Cale, the Otherworld, the Vectors, Shae, Caden, the Outers, Aurela.

All of it.

The keening sound continues, and I'm rocking back and forth, curled over. I feel like I am being torn down the middle, between an overly rational part of my brain that doesn't even feel like me and the tiny insistent part that barely does. Neither feels like who I am. Because I don't know who I am.

"Who am I?" The words spit themselves from my lips like acid. I stand in front of the camera in the corner of the room and scream the words again.

The door opens and a man clothed in a black uniform walks in, his hand on the butt of an electro-rod sitting at his hip. He is a legion commander; I can see the seal on his neck clearly. I feel my eyes narrow, and I unconsciously sink my weight back into my haunches. His hand hovers over the weapon, correctly interpreting my movements. But he has no chance.

My reaction is instantaneous, despite my lack of practice. I run at the side of the wall, kicking off of it and somersaulting to land directly behind him, my elbow around his neck and his left arm up against the middle of his back before he can even breathe. I jam the heel of my foot into the back of his leg, and he sinks to his knees.

"Move and you die," I say. "Where am I?"

"You're in Sector Seven," the man gasps. "Please . . ."

So I'm still in Sector Seven. That surprises me. Are we still in the bio-research facility?

"Where in Sector Seven?"

"Underground research lab," he answers. "Off the grid. Look, I can explain if you just let me up." I can feel myself wavering between wanting to eliminate the threat and getting answers. A fully stocked bio-research plant that's off the grid? In all my years in Neospes I've never heard of one of those. My arms tighten involuntarily. "I'm . . . I'm Aurela's first-in-command," the man gasps. "She left me to watch you."

Releasing my hold a fraction, I remove the electro-rod from its harness and toss it away. Against my better judgment, I let him go, and he falls back to his haunches, his hands to his neck.

"Aurela's first-in-command," I repeat slowly. "What do you mean, she left you to watch me? Where is she? Who are you? Why do you have a commander rank seal on your neck?" My questions are fired in immediate succession. The man smiles and removes his black beanie to run his hands through his white-blond hair.

"I'm Commander Sauer, an active soldier in Sector Seven," he begins. "But I'm also Artok and your mother's guard," he adds.

"She never mentioned you," I snap, unmoved.

"It was part of our agreement," he says quietly, his stare meaningful. I understand where he's coming from. He's her agent on the inside. If he'd been connected to Aurela in any way, especially after her defection, he would have been targeted and executed as an example.

"So you're a spy."

"Yes," he says.

I study the seal on his neck and the colors that mark him as Sector Seven. He is a sector commander, which would give him—and Aurela—unrestricted access to valuable information. Still, being an inside spy in a place like Neospes is incredibly risky, as in face-the-Vectors risky. I eye Sauer with a little more respect.

As the legion general of the elite Vector task force, I never heard of him, but Neospes is a big place, with allotted sectors policed by different branches of the monarchy, so it isn't far-fetched that we never met. Unless, of course, I had been the one to catch him being a traitorous spy. The old me would have fed him to the Vectors myself.

"How old are you?"

"Twenty."

"Did you grow up here?"

"I came here with my grandmother." Sauer is unfazed by my rapid-fire questions. "Any more questions?"

His cool attitude annoys me. "Why is this place off the grid?"

"Aurela started to build it before she left. She needed a base with the appropriate technology to face whatever your father was planning. We finished it. It's not a registered facility." Sauer smiles again. "If Murek knew this existed, he'd probably torch the whole sector."

I frown. "So everyone in Sector Seven is a part of this?"

I think back to what I know of the area. Sector Seven has always been a peripheral colony and classified as non-confrontational. Their citizens have always lived on the outskirts, keeping to themselves. They'd been deemed artisans—despite some of their Artok roots—and weren't considered a threat to the monarchy. How wrong we'd been, I slowly realize. From the little I knew of the Artok, they'd been far from a placid tribe of people. There are obviously more of them than anyone had guessed living in Sector Seven, and my mother now leads them all.

Sauer nods. "Not all but most of us. We're the liaison to the Outers, to Aurela. We keep tabs on Murek and the Lord King." He says the last words quietly, and I can feel his eyes on me. I keep my face expressionless. The doubt in his voice is easy to read. He doesn't trust me. And why should he? I don't even trust myself. I don't even *know* myself.

Sauer stands slowly and stretches his arms across his head. My body tenses, but I don't move. He hasn't made any offensive moves toward me, and even if he'd been lying, we would have been surrounded in seconds by scores of Vectors desperate to get their hands on their absconding general.

I turn on my heel, giving him my back. It doesn't really mean anything, but I've learned that it implies a level of trust and vulnerability. It's a misconception, though—I've been trained to detect shifts of movement in the air by fighting blindfolded with steel weapons. If he pulls any kind of weapon to attack me, the outcome will be the same.

I walk over to the cot and sit on it. Sauer, to his credit, hasn't moved an inch. "Let's assume you've been telling me the truth all along," I begin. "Why are we in Sector Seven now?"

"That's for Aurela to explain."

"Okay. So where is Aurela?"

"She's . . . engaged at the moment." His evasive answer irritates me.

"Okay. So where is Caden?" My tone is patronizing, my anger under tight control yet simmering just below the surface. I cock my head to one side and lean back on my arms, waiting. I am deliberately trying to provoke him, goading him into an answer. He is obviously under orders.

Sauer smiles tightly. "In a room just like this one. Resting." His emphasis on the last word is clear, and I almost grin at his blatant suggestion that I should be doing the same.

"I want to see him."

"That's not possible."

My eyes narrow. "You do know that I can leave this room at any point with or without your consent? And I can find Caden myself if I have to."

Sauer shrugs and nods. He knows exactly what I'm capable of. I clearly showed him when he'd entered. He walks over to the chair on the side of the room and slides it out.

"May I?" he asks politely, and then sits, crossing his ankle over the opposite knee. His eyes are penetrating, staring right through me. I don't say anything caustic at his expression because I'm a little intrigued by him. The more I stare at him, the more I see the resemblance to Aurela's people and the marks of the Artok tribe. Apart from his hair, which is the same distinctive silvery white, they have a similar angularity in their faces. Despite my caution, I'm fascinated by any connections to Aurela's past . . . to *my* past.

Sauer's voice is soft, interrupting my thoughts. "I've always wanted to meet you, you know. My entire division recounted accounts of your fearlessness, of soldiers who cowered at the sight of you. A girl, far younger than I was, leading the Vectors. The Lord King's private guard." I hold Sauer's gaze without responding. "Impressive record for one so young."

"If you say so," I return in an inflectionless voice.

"But of course, your father engineered you to be that way," Sauer muses. I frown, but remain silent. "He built you to be the perfect soldier. What made you defect?"

"I don't know that I have," I say carefully, my brain firing at his provocative words. I am no one's puppet, far less my father's. "I was following orders from my king. My loyalty lies and will always lie with him." Sauer looks like he has something more to say, but doesn't. A sour expression crosses his face for an instant as he leans back in his chair. It fades after a moment, replaced by his former thoughtful expression.

"I knew Shae," he says. The mere mention of her name sends my stomach into a tailspin. I feel the tide of emotion surge inside of me. It's all still there, simmering. I shove the thoughts away, but my fingers clench into fists at my sides. "She often told me that I would like you."

"Well, she was wrong. And she's dead."

I'm unprepared for the naked ache that slashes across his eyes. My normally acute ability to read people has taken a beating over the last few weeks, but even Sauer can't conceal his feelings for my sister from me. Sauer has just gotten a lot more interesting.

"You were the reason she kept everting back here," I say slowly. Sauer doesn't answer, but his clear eyes are so pain-ridden that it's obvious. "I knew it wasn't just to provide updates to Aurela or throw the Vectors off Caden's trail. He was safe. The Vectors tracked *me* there, not them. So she was coming back here for you?"

"Yes. We were . . . in love."

I laugh, and the sound in the room is ugly, echoing emptily against the stark walls. I can barely get my mind around it. My mother had been paired with my father because of their combined brilliance and what they could contribute together to the monarchy. People didn't fall in love. They didn't get to choose who they wanted to be with. Partnerships were *allocated* based on what was best for Neospes. I laugh again. In the end, love had killed Shae.

"Love?" I spit in his direction, launching to my feet. "Do you know what you did to her? Did you see what you were doing to her? She was dead on her feet, but she still came back here for you!" I'm in Sauer's face now, not even bothering to control the violence of my rage. "You. Killed. Her." My finger jabs into his chest with each word. "You made her weak."

Sauer doesn't even respond to my vitriolic words. Instead, he watches me with those same heavy eyes. I can see the regret—and his love for Shae—in them, but I don't want to see either. I don't want to see anything that reflects the feelings inside my own heart. I don't want to admit that somehow, somewhere, I'd let compassion or love weaken me, too. So I let my anger take over. I let my fury fuel me. They are the things I know, the mind-sets I understand.

"Get up," I rage at him. I slap him across the face, and then a second time. "Get up and face me like a man. She deserved that much, don't you think?"

"I'm not going to fight you, Riven," Sauer says. His face is bright red from where I've struck him, but his voice is even. "You're right. I failed her. I let her die. I deserve everything and more that you say, but she wouldn't want this. She loved you, too."

Something hot and responsive rushes inside of me at his soft words, and then something cold immediately floods my veins, suppressing it in seconds. I step back and then back again, until I feel the bed against the backs of my legs. My mind is clear one minute, and then fogged the next. Once more, the feeling of being two different people threatens to tear me apart.

"What's wrong with me?" I say, clutching my head in my hands. "What's happening? Every time I think about her, it hurts. I'm splitting in two."

"It's the programming," Sauer says gently, walking forward to fold me into his arms. I let him, shivering so hard that my teeth are rattling. Sauer's words sink in slowly.

"The *what*?" I whisper.

"The programming," Aurela says from the doorway. I hadn't even noticed her there. "I see you've meet Sauer. I'm sorry I wasn't here when you woke up, but I had to take care of something. How are you feeling?" She tips my head back gently to peer at my face.

My brain is spinning, but somehow I already know. A hazy memory of the pale blue fluid combined with the blood on my wrist in the operating room fills my eyes. "What programming?"

"There's no easy way to—"

"Just say it," I whisper. "Say it."

Aurela's face is tormented, her hands fluttering against my head like protective mother birds trying to safeguard their young. But she can't protect me anymore. The damage has already been done. She didn't protect me then . . . and she can't protect me now. Sauer's words fill my head: *he built you to be the perfect soldier. . . .*

"I want to hear you say it," I repeat doggedly.

She nods, just once. "Your programming. To control the nanoplasm inside of you."

# 20

# ON THE BRINK

"SO I'M A Vector?"

I'm amazed at how calm my voice is, but the truth is, somewhere deep down, I've always known that I was like them. There were too many inconsistencies, things that made me better than everyone else . . . things that made me less human—or maybe better than human. I could run faster, react more quickly, heal miraculously when injured. There's no way I could have been normal. I don't even feel any sense of violation that my own father experimented on me without my knowledge. Yet.

"I'm an android," I say.

"No," Aurela says. "You're . . . a hybrid. Your father experimented with nanoplasm before the early success of the Vectors. He experimented on himself and then you when you were little." Aurela holds my face in her hands, but my eyes are unseeing. "I never knew, but when I found out, that's when I knew I had to leave. I had to find a way to stop him."

What kind of man experiments with an unproven technology on his own child? I feel the hate inside of me boil and metamorphose into something large and ugly. I'm not even human. No wonder he'd loved that I'd chosen to lead the Vectors. I'm one of them. Controlled, just as they are. Built. Engineered. A thing, like them.

Dead, just like them.

The self-disgust must be evident on my face, because Sauer's arms tighten around me. I've forgotten that I'm still caught in his grip. "Let go of me," I tell him. "I'm fine."

But he doesn't, so I shove him away easily. So easily, like his arms are nothing but string. I stare at my clenched fists, for the first time aware of the tensile power in them . . . power that isn't mine. It's fake, engineered strength, driven by the robots in my blood. My hands drop to my sides in revulsion.

"Riven," Aurela says, and I jerk at the sound of my name. So apt, I think. My name means broken . . . it's a perfect name, after all. I raise burning eyes to hers. "You're nothing like them," she says, correctly reading the thoughts rising to suffocate me with their poisonous intensity. "You're different."

I shake my head, struggling to reconcile everything I know about the Vectors and everything I know about myself. I'm not just different . . . what my father has done is impossible. I'm a live person made of flesh and blood and bone.

"I'm missing something," I say to Aurela. "How is this even possible? I thought you couldn't combine nanoplasm with human DNA?"

"I believe your father experimented on himself before you were conceived." Aurela pauses, as if thinking to herself. "He planned it all a very long time ago. His body eventually rejected the nanobes, but yours didn't, because your DNA had already transmutated as a result of his earlier testing. When you were conceived, the law of natural selection allowed your cells to adapt. He'd hoped all along that they would have some sort of genetomorphic effect."

"Did you know?"

"Not at first," she says tiredly, running a hand through her hair and sitting in the seat that Sauer vacated. "But he would take you to the lab with him, even when I insisted that you didn't have to go. After a while, I started to suspect something untoward, but he denied it." Aurela stops, her face wet. "Then I found contaminated blood samples he'd hidden. Yours. And I knew for sure. That was when I told him I was leaving with you and Shae. My mistake, of course, was to tell him at all."

"I thought you were fighting about the Vector tech?"

"No, my darling, it was always about you. Then you had your first training op, and he was so proud that you, the youngest of all your peers, had finished way ahead of everyone else. *Way* ahead. You were a prodigy. His prodigy. After that, he never let you out of his sight."

Aurela is talking about the placement trials. At four, we are put through a rigorous series of mental and physical exercises to determine when we're to start our training and instructor assignments. I was placed in the elite section with children far older than me. My father was so proud. I bite my lip so hard that it bleeds, a metallic sourness filling my mouth.

Of course he was proud—his creation, his abomination was a smashing success.

But even in his jubilation, he had to keep it all a secret, because what he'd done went against all our laws. After the

War, any combination of human genetics and android technology had been forbidden. But my father had flaunted the laws, driven by his own pride.

"And the Vectors? Was it his plan that they'd be his own private army? Loyal to him because they were loyal to me? Was that in my *programming*?" My sarcasm is acidic.

Aurela sighs. "Only your father knows what he intended to create. Even now, we don't know where his loyalties truly lie." She glances at Sauer and then me, as if working out something in her head, something more that she has to tell me. "So many things have changed since you left, Riven. The monarchy is unstable. Murek and your father have spies everywhere. The Vectors are stationed in every sector, even here."

The thought of the Vectors leaves a sour taste in my mouth. My stomach heaves. I don't want to be anything like them. The big Commander from the Otherworld fills my visions, and I remember the sound of my father's voice coming from its mouth.

"They're thinking now," I say, remembering the chilling words of the Vector that it was more alive than the others but less alive than me. Even it had known what I was . . . what I am. "The Vectors. There was one in the Otherworld that spoke with his voice. He wants me back. Badly. I don't know for what but he does."

Aurela's face blanches at my words. Understanding is in her eyes as she nods. "He wants to replicate your genetic code."

I feel a hot tear slide down my cheek, and I swipe it away viciously, furious at myself for even shedding a single tear for the monster that was my father. "I'm just a thing to him. An experiment. A Vector."

"No," Aurela insists. "You're not."

"Barely. I'm half-alive, and they're dead. But I'm the same . . . a *thing*." My voice is as lifeless as the words coming from my mouth.

"No, Riven, you're alive. *You* control the nanobes, not the other way around."

But a troubling thought occurs to me as Aurela says those words. If I do control them, why is everything within me suddenly shutting down? Has something set them off within the parameters of their code? I frown, confused. "So, what happened before? You know, with Caden, before Sector Seven, when I blacked out? What caused it?"

"My guess is that it was some kind of fail-safe in your father's programming, a phrase or something," Aurela says, and I feel myself flush, knowing instantly the phrase that had caused it all—Caden said he loved me and I returned the sentiment. It makes sense. My father despised weakness and anything that caused it, especially love. "Whatever it was caused the nanoplasm to reboot, restoring a set of baseline defaults, which is why you were so confused about who you were and couldn't remember everything."

"Will it happen again?" My question flies through gritted teeth. The last thing I need is anyone using some programming catchphrase that will prevent me from doing what every bone in my body wants to do—make my father pay for what he did to me.

"I don't think so," Aurela says. "I worked with my engineers to erase and rewrite the default programming. We backdoored all the code. It's clear."

"Thank you." It's the least I can offer. "Did Shae know?" I ask after several minutes of silence. So many things are falling into place . . . all of Shae's sidelong glances, her pointed questions about my healing ability, other things she wanted to say to me in the Otherworld and couldn't. She wanted to tell me; I see that now. But the sad truth was that I never would have believed her and she probably knew that, which was why she always stopped herself.

Aurela nods. "That's why she tried so hard to get you to leave with her, but she knew that a part of you would want to stay with him. She was so afraid that you would tell him about her . . . about me, in spite of yourself. You were a risk, and one we didn't fully understand." She pauses, her face earnest. "We didn't know how deep the programming went or whether it undermined your own thoughts."

"Does it?" I blurt out.

"No, it's built to obey your commands."

The knowledge is overwhelming, but things are starting to come together in my head, like migrant puzzle pieces. "So that's why I felt so sick in the Peaks. Because I have machines inside of me," I say. "I should have known." I gesture at my body. "You know why I used to feel so comfortable leading the Vectors? It was because deep down, I felt just like them. And I followed orders just like a good soldier, just like a good little Reptile." I swing around to stare at Sauer who is standing near the far side of the room. "Now you know why I was so good, because I was one of them."

Sauer shakes his head, a small smile darting around the corners of his mouth. "No, Riven," he says in that soft drawl of his. "You're better than they are. You're super strong, you heal quicker than any of us could ever hope to heal, you can think more quickly. And you're alive. You're still you. That has to count for something."

His words strike a chord inside of me, and realization dawns slowly but surely. As brilliant as my father is, he isn't a genetic scientist. I stare at Aurela. "It was your genetic coding that made this possible, wasn't it?" I say to her. "You were the only one who could have found a way to string nanoplasm with live human DNA."

"Yes, you're right. I developed the bio-gen coding," she confesses sadly. "He was working on a project to test the nanoplasm on live creatures and convinced me that he needed to test to see if it could operate within a live host." Aurela grabs my shoulders. "I never would have helped him had I known that he was going to use it on himself or you; you have to believe that!"

I nod, because I can't speak. My tongue is bonded to the roof of my mouth. I swallow painfully. "So can you take them out? The nanobes?"

"No," she says, "they're part of you. Unlike the nanoplasm for the Vectors, which fire off a lithia core, yours are linked to your body. They fuel from food just like your blood does because they're tied in to your DNA. If we even tried to separate the strands, you would die. Your body has already adapted to coexist with them. You're unique, Riven. That's probably why he wants you so badly. You're the experiment that went viral. His biggest triumph."

I'm at a loss. I don't even know what to think, far less say. I have live microscopic robots inside of me that can never be taken out. I can never be fully human, never be normal. Everything inside funnels into a tornado of fury against the man responsible for making me into a freak. The man who thought himself some sort of god. His arrogance would be his destruction.

I would be his destruction.

"Hey, guys," a voice says, and I whirl around, only to collide with Caden. His hair is rumpled around his face and pillow lines are creasing his skin as if he's only just awakened. He smells like soap and outdoors. I've never wanted more to fling myself into his arms and close my eyes, but I control myself. "Glad you're awake," he says to me, his eyes gentle. "You scared me for a while."

"I'm fine," I snap more harshly than I intended. Hurt flashes in his expression as if I've slapped him, and his eyes pan slowly from me to Sauer to Aurela.

"What's going on?" he asks.

"Nothing. We're talking logistics," I say dismissively, and turn to Aurela. "Can we get out of here? This place is making me sick."

The rest of the bio-facility is the same as any I've been in with my father, a veritable maze of white walls and white doors. Once in a while, people dressed in white walk past us. They all nod or bow respectfully in Aurela's direction. She's more than a leader, I realize. She's their unofficial queen. Even Sauer walks a step behind her, I notice, in some kind of dutiful deference.

We enter an elevator at the far end of one of the corridors and make our way to the top. The elevator opens into a simple, nondescript two-story house. I look backward as the wall

slides shut behind us, completely concealing the hidden elevator behind it. Aurela was right; there's so much I don't know
about what has happened over the last three years.

"Make yourself comfortable. I'll be back," Aurela says, and
walks downstairs.

The room we're in is simple, with a long dining table surrounded by wooden chairs. It's sparse but comfortable, and
unlike the clinical austerity of the bio-facility beneath us, it's
painted a peaceful yellow. Silvery moonlight filters through
one side of the house, and the cool air and smell of civilization hits my face through the open windows. It's never smelled
so good. Even in the outlying sectors, Neospes had a unique
odor. It's not offensive or foul, just achingly familiar, like an
odd combination of well-oiled machinery and bread. I breathe
deeply, walking to one of the half-opened windows.

It's nighttime, but I can see the tip of the citadel rising in
the distance. It has been my home for so long that a part of
me twinges. I squash the feeling quickly—it's been a cage, not
a home, and all part of my father's plan. I push the shutters
open and lean out slightly, watching the people bustle on the
street below as the cool air rushes in. Even though it's night, it's
nowhere near as cold as it was in the Outers. I look up at the
giant glass perimeter of the dome spanning as far as the eye
can see. It performs a double function. It protects us from any
predators from the Outers, and it regulates the unpredictable
temperatures of our atmosphere. So right now, the night air is
crisp rather than freeze-blood-to-ice cold.

But any way I look at it, we are all still prisoners in a giant
fishbowl, and a small part of me would rather be out there than

in here. Sirens go off in the distance, and Sauer's voice from behind me jerks me from my thoughts.

"Be careful," Sauer warns. "The Vectors are on high alert."

My eyes narrow. "Why?"

He shoots me a wry grin, putting some tableware and a pitcher of some liquid on the long table. "Mostly rumors that you're back. Of course, since you removed your tracking chip, you're off the grid, too. But as much as the Artok are our allies, we can't stop people from talking, especially those loyal to the monarchy." He grabs my pack from a corner of the room and tosses it to me. "Don't worry; I'm sure you're more than familiar with their search techniques. And if worse comes to worse, you can take care of yourself just fine."

"Thanks," I say drily, but I shut the window carefully behind me. The contents of my backpack look the same, but I know that Aurela's guards would have been meticulous and careful in their search. "What about you? Are you off the grid?"

"No, they know where I am. But I'm off duty, and technically this is my house, so we're good." Sauer adds three differently shaped bottles to the table and pours himself a glass from one of them. After a pointed glance from Caden, Sauer slides him a glass across the table. Caden knocks it back in one swift shot as if he's done this a hundred times before. I can smell the alcohol from where I am standing. Sauer nods at an empty glass and then in my direction.

"No, thanks," I say. I've never mixed well with spirits of any kind, even though it feels like I probably should have a glass like Caden to calm the storm still simmering inside of me. I look away and haul two deep breaths into my lungs. I'm pretty sure that giving in to the temptation would only have a worse outcome . . . like me running off to confront my father in a blind rage or something equally stupid.

"Where are my jacket and blades?" I ask sifting through my bag.

"They're still in the Peaks," Sauer says. "Caden grabbed your pack when you passed out. Don't worry; Aurela sent some men to retrieve them."

Most of the other, smaller weapons are in the bag. I notice that Shae's thumb drive is resting on the top of everything else. I still haven't been able to bring myself to see whatever she has recorded. In hindsight, I probably should have listened to it the minute we left the Otherworld—no doubt she would have mentioned Aurela or even the thing that I am. A shudder rips through me at the thought, and I slap the flap closed.

Sauer stares at me over the rim of his glass as I stretch the corded muscles in my neck. He bangs the glass on the table, making both Caden and I jump. "Come on, I have an idea."

"What about Aurela?" Caden says.

"She'll be a while, and we're not leaving the house," Sauer throws over his shoulder. "We're just going to get some tension out."

Caden and I follow him down the stairs to the main floor and then down another set of stairs into a wide room that's lit with overhead recessed lighting. I recognize the layout immediately—it's a training room. The floor is padded and two opposite walls are lined from top to bottom with mirrors. There are a few combat dummies on either end of the room, all of them battered, with chunks torn out of their torsos and faces. A vast array of weapons, from knives to spears to lances to pikes, lines one of the other two opposite-facing walls, but what takes my breath away is the antique collection of intricately carved Artok bows lining the near wall.

"Wow," I hear myself say.

"Shae's," Sauer says softly. "She used to say that it inspired her."

"It's beautiful," Caden agrees.

I agree wholeheartedly but I can't speak. The thought that my sister fought—*trained*—in this room fills me with an odd choking sensation that leaves me lacking for words. There was so much of her life that I missed, so much that I didn't understand. If only I'd made the choice to go with her all those years ago, how different everything could have been. I'd have had a sister *and* a mother, instead of an egomaniacal father who cared more for his zombie robots than he did his real flesh and blood.

But "what if" never did anyone any good, far less me. I made my choice. I didn't go with them, and now my sister is dead. I feel the unspent anger swelling within me again like a monstrous tide, and I understand why Sauer has brought us down here.

Training is what he knows. It's what I know. I throw off my outerwear and join Sauer where he and Caden are standing in the middle of the room.

"Standard warm-up drill?" Sauer asks as I windmill my arms.

I nod and glance at Caden, who like Sauer is only wearing black fatigues. He isn't half as chiseled as Sauer, but the sight of his lean chest makes my stomach waver. A faint flush fills my cheeks, and I cover it up with gruffness. "You want to watch first and then join in?"

"Shae taught me," he says.

"It's not like fencing practice," I toss back.

"You just try to keep up." I almost snort out loud at his over-confidence, and then I remember his skill when we sparred back in the Peaks. Bowing mockingly in his direction, I take a deep breath and focus, centering my energy.

In a line, we bend and twist through a complicated series of rhythmic calisthenics, moving and breathing in silent unison. The movements are slow and long, extending to the edges of my center of gravity, strengthening my core. In the mirror, I can see that Caden is keeping up easily, his body as flexible as ours, as if he's been doing the exercises for years. Obviously, Shae taught him well.

Completing the first stage, we move sinuously into the second phase, which incorporates more jumping, kicking, and thrusting. Our training is built on a dynamic combination of hard and soft martial arts that focuses on energy and core strength as well as defensive and offensive strategies. I'm covered in a sheen of sweat, but it feels so good—every jab and shove helping to dissipate the raw tension in my body.

Nearly two hours later, Sauer retrieves three long, slender black staffs from the side and hands them to Caden and me. We're moving into the soft-weapon stage of the training, which comprises delicate and quick sparring movements against each other, the staffs acting as extensions of our bodies. We spin and lunge in unison, and in the mirror we are a blur of graceful but lethal movement. The staffs click against each other in a precise, dangerous staccato as we meet in various steps of the exercise.

The final phase of the training is actual sparring. We pair off for a sequence of moves and then spin back to the third opponent. Sauer is strong but occasionally leaves his flanks unprotected. If we were in actual combat, he would be a worthy opponent, but I know that I would eventually beat him.

Caden is another matter altogether. His movements are graceful and catlike. He reads my strikes almost in advance, like a mind-fighter, nor does he expose many weaknesses. He doesn't falter in his offensive strikes, and his defensive moves flow like yin and yang. He knows when to attack and when to withdraw, which is something only learned after years of experience.

I'm slowly realizing that Caden has mastered most, if not all, of our elite training techniques. With a grin, I understand now that Shae wasn't kidding when she said he could probably take me. Caden had been her final and best trainee. I spin out of the way of his staff at the last minute, but it still catches me on the back of the shoulder.

Wincing, I see that Caden is grinning. "Almost had you that time."

"I was distracted, and almost doesn't get you any points," I shoot back, and then incline my head. Credit should always be given where it's due. "But yeah, you were good."

"Feel better?" Sauer asks.

I nod. "That was exactly what I needed. I forgot how good it felt to work the routine from beginning to end. In the Otherworld, I only got to practice it in pieces, and finding an adequate sparring partner was difficult." I squeeze Caden on the back, ignoring the spark of electricity that shoots up my fingers at the damp touch of his skin. "Shae taught you well."

"Thank you. She made me practice every day before school, rain or shine," Caden says. "She was relentless."

Sauer hands us each a cup of drinking water. "You were both good." He glances at me knowingly. "But you, you were holding back. Why?"

"I wasn't," I begin, but realize that Sauer is right. Despite my fatigue, my body still feels like it could go for several more hours. I shrug. Before knowing the truth, going all out was the only thing I knew. Now, it feels weird. It feels fake because of what I know I am . . . as if I'm cheating somehow. I stare at the ground, tension hovering against my shoulders, eager to weigh me down once more.

"Try this." Sauer walks to the wall and removes a thin longsword. The scabbard is blood-red with black markings, and the sword's handle is black interlaced with silver. Sauer's face is solemn as he stands in front of me, slowly removing the elegant silver blade, and only then do I see the inscription of my name near the hilt. I gasp.

"Shae had this made for you in the Artok way," Sauer tells me. "The sword's name, like yours, is Riven. It means 'to cleave asunder.'"

"I know what it means," I say for lack of anything else, taking the sword reverently in my hands. The craftsmanship is extraordinary, the weight of it perfect.

"So," Sauer says. "Let's see you try it out." I frown at him, but he is staring at me expectantly. I glance at Caden, who agrees and moves to sit with Sauer at the far end of the room, giving me enough space with the deadly weapon.

Holding the blade vertically between my palms in front of my face, I take a deep breath and then lay the sword flat out in front of me on both palms, as I sink into sideways lunge and bow. I close my eyes, letting my breathing and the movement of my body guide me.

The training studio fades away and I am alone. Flicking the hilt of the sword up, I grab it easily and spin into a complicated series of thrusts, jumps, and parries. This time I don't hold back as the sword flows in and out of my movements like a binding thread, a fluid extension of me.

I'm spinning faster and faster, letting the power heating up within me take over, letting the part of me that isn't human lend me strength, until I am nothing but shadow and flashes of light. And still I go faster. I can feel my heart burning, a vortex of flame and liquid exhilaration. Perhaps Sauer is right—maybe I am better than the Vectors. My chest pounding, I finish with a final slash and bend into a forward lunge with the blade held over my head in perfect symmetry.

I open my eyes. There is dead silence in the room. Self-conscious, I stand, only to find that it's no longer just Caden and Sauer standing there. Aurela is there too, accompanied by six people in hooded cloaks. I hadn't even heard them come in.

I recognize four of them immediately as the sector leaders of Sectors Three, Four, Six, and Eight. The other two I don't know, but they're all staring at me with identical expressions of astonishment, awe, and something else I'm not quick to identify, despite seeing it thousands of times before.

Fear.

# 21

# REVOLUTION

I WIPE THE grime off my skin with a washcloth, using a special cleansing oil. What I wouldn't give for one of the decadent showers of Caden's world. That's one of the things I treasured—that and the beauty of a world that hasn't been ravaged by war. For a second, I think of the lake in the mountains that I saw with Shae, and my heart aches. I won't see either of them again. They have become synonymous with beauty and loss.

Despite the unexpected audience at the end, the training exercise was exactly what I needed to feel normal . . . to feel like myself again. Throwing on an undershirt and a pair of leggings, I drag a brush through my hair. It's gotten longer, but I haven't bothered to cut it. Staring at myself in the mirror over the water basin, I hardly recognize myself. Faded chunks of green intertwine with darker strands. I've lost weight, and my cheekbones ridge prominently on the sides of my face, but my eyes are bright and cheeks rosy.

My thin blue-weaved braid hangs over my left ear to my shoulder. Carefully, I unravel the braid, using my knife to hack off the strands to match the length of the rest of my hair. I don't know why I left it—but it's been a part of me for so long, a status of my rank. Of course, all that has changed. I am no longer a legion general. I am no one.

No, I am worse. I'm a fugitive.

Like my mother. Like Shae.

Thinking of her, I glance at the long blade resting in its scabbard on my bed and feel a tear slide down my cheek. I was on her mind even though I barely spent a second thought on her. She was always the more compassionate of the two of us, and no wonder; I'm half a real person with little empathy for anyone. A flash of bitter self-loathing surges through me . . . for the thing that I am.

Grabbing my backpack roughly, I rifle through it to take my mind off that train of thought. My hand is drawn to a slim rectangular object. Shae's drive. It's the last remaining piece of the puzzle. Swallowing hard, I plug it into a holograph port resting on the small table on one side of the room. Shae's face swims into focus. My stomach swan dives to my feet but I force myself to double-tap the play button.

*Hello, Riven.* My entire body flinches at the sound of her voice and the soft expression on her face. She could be sitting across the table from me. My fingers curl into my sides, bloodless, as her words continue. *If you're seeing this, then I'm gone. And hopefully you and Cade are still alive and you found your way back to Neospes. There's so much I have to say to you, so much I need to explain, but finding the right words is a challenge in itself. First of all, I love you. I'm pretty sure you don't think I ever did, but it's true. I've always loved you and I always believed in you. The real you.*

I want to throw the drive and the hologram against the wall. I can't even bear to look at her beautiful face. Every cell in me is shaking with regret and grief. It's nearly more than I can take, but I force myself to listen despite the gut-wrenching anguish spiraling through me.

*You're probably going to find out a lot about yourself if you're back in Neospes, things about your father and our mother. She's alive, Riven! I wanted to tell you that day when I came back for you, but it would have been too risky for her safety. She's been here all along. She's the one who got Caden and his mother out. She's the one who sent me to protect him. If you haven't found her already, find her. Go to Sector Seven and ask for Commander Sauer. He will take you to her. If you do see Sauer, tell him I'll see him again and he's always with me.*

*I know you're being extra careful about staying off the grid, but trust no one.*

TRUST NO ONE. Shae's face and words are emphatic.

*One last thing, my sister. Thank you for looking out for Caden. He's the real deal. Cale's the clone. I'm sure you already know this by now, but if you don't, I'm sorry about him and that you had to find out the truth this way. I know you were—are—close. But there are things underway in Neospes that make it hard to see where the real betrayal lies . . . with Murek, your father, or even Cale himself.*

*Please be careful, and watch out for Caden. I tried to train him in our ways as best as I could without having to reveal everything. I think he will be ready for whatever comes your way, whether that's in the Otherworld or in Neospes. How I wish I could have been there with you, to protect and fight with both of you, but everything happens for a reason, doesn't it? You're meant to be Caden's protector now. He's the future of everything. Don't fail him; don't fail us.*

*I know you won't, because you don't know how to fail.*

*One other last thing.* I smile at the tone in her voice, watching her eyes rolling and the sideways smile that was unique to her. *You're probably going to learn some troubling truths about yourself. But you know who you are, Riven. You've always known who you are. Don't let that change you. You're strong. Stronger than I could ever be. So don't fight it; instead, accept it and take it for all the good things that make you so incredibly unique.*

*Love you, Riv; don't ever forget that. Wind at your back, my sister.*

The voice spins into silence, and the hologram grows fuzzy and then disappears. But I don't need it to hear her words that are replaying over and over in my head. What did she mean that Caden was the future of everything? It sounded so ominous. There's so much I don't understand, and it's not that I don't trust Cale. I trust him with my life. He hasn't lied to me—he has been sick. I've seen it with my own eyes. He sent for Caden because he thought he needed replacement organs, and my mission had been of the utmost secrecy because of Cale's mistrust of Murek and my father.

A soft knock on the door jerks me out of my chaotic thoughts.

"Who is it?"

"It's Aurela." I eject and throw the drive into the pack, sweeping a hand through my hair and tucking the freshly shorn strands behind my ear self-consciously. Maybe she won't notice.

"Come in," I say. "I'll be done in a sec."

She has changed into a gilded blue tunic and wide skirt. She looks feminine and delicate, two things that I can never seem to master. I'm no spring flower, that's for sure, but then looks have never mattered to me. Survival has. Sighing, I smooth my plain tunic and leggings, and sit to pull on a worn pair of combat boots before standing to face my mother.

She smiles gently, her eyes landing with the touch of a butterfly on the side of my head where the braid had been, but doesn't say anything. Instead, she just nods. I can feel her approval, and for some reason, it warms me.

"I'm sure you have questions," she says. "Ones that Sauer or I didn't answer earlier. I want you to be prepared before you go into that room."

She's talking about the room where all the other sector heads—the ones who had been watching my performance earlier—are waiting.

"She told me to find you, you know," I say softly. "Shae."

"Yes, I know."

"She knew about me." It's not a question, but Aurela nods, her eyes compassionate. For a long second, we stare at each other. Shae would have looked just like her when she got older, with the same features . . . the same eyes. There is grace in Aurela's shoulders, but there's hard strength, too. I swallow. She's at the head of this whole revolution, this whole coup against the Neospes monarchy. She's more than strong. I realize the core of steel I'm seeing in her is the very same core in myself that men have grown to fear here in Neospes. I'm more like her than I care to admit.

Distracting my thoughts, I grab ahold of the black and gold wrap lying on a chest and tug it over my shoulders. Dress golds. It's a plain shift with a high collar and shiny black buttons, one of the more formal items of clothing usually reserved for award ceremonies or funerals. I smile at the irony. We aren't exactly going to either.

"Are you going to war against the monarchy?" I ask, deftly fastening the over-garment's ties around my waist. The soft material drapes nearly to mid-thigh.

Aurela shoots a glacial smile in my direction. "It's complicated, Riven. War isn't the answer for anyone. But what Murek is planning will undermine everything we have built, not just in Neospes, but also in the Otherworld."

"What exactly is he planning?"

"If my intelligence is correct, he's building an army," she says. "An army of Vectors to take to the Otherworld. Guardians have been assassinated. We believe that he means to make the people there into slaves and to control their vast resources. Water, to name one of the most important."

"He who controls water controls the world," I murmur. It's an old Neospes saying. Water here is traded like gold. If Murek somehow manages to control the Otherworld's resources, he would become more than a king; he'd be a god. "But even if he were able to create a bridge, we can't survive in their world," I blurt. "I mean, you and the others. Your immune systems are too different. You'd die."

I flush, knowing that it was only because of my unique nature that I'd been able to survive, thrive even. Aurela stares at me, and for a second I see something like a flash of sympathy in her eyes.

"That's where you come in," she says softly. "The next phase. It's why your father wants you so badly. You're the only living person who has ever adapted to the nanobes."

My words come out in a rush as I collapse back onto the bed. "He wants to clone me?"

"More specifically, replicate your DNA."

My breath is coming in short bursts, but her words are no surprise to me. As much as I hate what I am, I know that she is right. I am the blueprint to universe domination, because the laws of natural selection do not apply to me. No wonder I stopped having any side effects in the Otherworld. My body—my nanoplasm—was forced to adapt once I stopped taking the pills.

"Aurela, I know Cale's not involved in any of this. Shae"—I nearly gag on her name—"said that I shouldn't trust him, but I do. I'd been at his side every day before I left to find Caden. He is dying. Murek killed his father, and his mother left to protect her other son."

Aurela nods. "We will protect him if we can." She pauses. "But Caden comes first. He is the true crown prince; do you understand that?"

"Yes."

"Good, then let's go, unless you have any more questions." She stands and stares pointedly at me.

"Just one more question," I say, but my eyes drop to the ground as a rush of warmth races across and down my back. "When you and father were paired together . . . did you ever feel anything for him?"

Aurela's stare morphs into something pained. "Your father was very different when he was younger. He was smart and vibrant, and I admired him very much." Her voice is at odds with the painful emotion in her eyes. "We were friends as children and often played together. Our partnership was a natural progression of that."

"But did you love him?" I blurt out, and feel the heat of a thousand suns on my neck.

"I loved you," Aurela says gently. "And Shae."

I understand her restraint. How can one ever love someone who is a monster? And inside, I'm just like him. He's made sure of that.

Aurela moves to stand in front of me as if reading my thoughts and grasps my arms. "Your father was driven by a desire to prove himself. He had no room in his life for love. You have me in you, too, and we are Artok. Our choices, our lives are based on love."

"I'm not Artok," I say automatically.

"But you are."

I ignore the tender look on her face and the gentle fingers that slide against my cheek. I've never felt connected to my Artok roots. The Artok do things differently than most other people in Neospes. Although they believe in the inherent value of genetic preselection, they also believe that emotions like love are important in relationships. Maybe I felt the disconnect because my mother had left, and the only *love* I'd ever known was from a father whose sole goal was to make me a monster.

"Did you love Shae's dad?"

Aurela's eyes grow even sadder. "Yes."

Shae's father—also Artok—was killed in the Outers when Shae was barely a year old. Shae told me the story when we were children. Her father was an atmospheric field technician who never returned from an Outer mission. His entire group was attacked by Reptiles, and everyone had survived but him. Shortly after, Aurela had been reassigned to my father.

"Did he do it?"

"Did who do what, Riven?" Aurela's voice is thick, and I know that she is lost in her own memories of the love she has lost . . . and the daughter she's lost.

"My father," I spit in disgust. "Sounds just like him, so convenient. Did he arrange to have him accidentally left alone? Did the guards do it and blame it on Reptiles?"

"It was an accident, Riven. The transport sensors were faulty, and there was nothing anyone could do." Her voice is calm but her words are monotone as if she's already thought through some other explanation herself and come to the same conclusion that I'd had. "Your father would never—"

I interrupt her. "Never what? Destroy people to get what he wants? Right." Walking toward the door, I glance over my shoulder. Aurela is watching me carefully. "The next time we meet face-to-face, I'm going to be the one to destroy him; that I promise you. He will pay for what he did to you, to me, and to Shae. Now let's go plan a war."

The room is deathly quiet, even though it's full of people. I stand like a shadow in the back, watching, listening, and waiting. The hood of my jacket obscures my face so that I look like half a dozen of the other soldiers dressed in similar uniforms in the room. Caden, too, is clad the same, with his hood covering much of his face.

I stare at my mother, who has become this dynamic, tough-jawed person at the front of the room. She looks regal but stone cold, with eyes like slivers of ice. In a few minutes, I can see why they all defer to her. She's incredible.

They've already been over the plans and strategy, and the best way into the castle. Caden is standing to my left, half hidden in the darkness, and Sauer is on his left. We're all near the doors just in case things get disruptive—Caden has to be protected at all costs. But since he insisted on being present, Aurela wanted to keep him as inconspicuous as possible. I peep around the edge of my hood and Caden catches my eye.

"You look good in dress golds," he whispers.

I roll my eyes at him. "Too flashy for me." I glance at him, wearing similar colors to mine. "You look good, too. Now shut up and pay attention. You asked to be here, remember?"

"What do you think about what they want to do?" Caden asks under his breath, but Sauer gives us both the eye of death and we fall silent.

Truth is, I don't know that what they're suggesting will work. The Winter Solstice is around the corner, and it's one of the two times in Neospes that there are any festivities. The other is during the Summer Solstice. We celebrate Winter and Summer with Games—a combination of exhibition combat, dancing, and trading—when all the Sectors come together, even the Royals.

For the most part, each Sector operates independently, focused on its particular role. The scientists stick with scientists, the farmers with farmers, the builders with builders. The only common threads are the soldiers who are ensconced in every single Sector. It pains me to think it, but after experiencing the freedom of the Otherworld, Neospes is little more than a police state. Soldiers are everywhere, enforcing the rules—and the will—of the monarchy.

But despite the fact that armed guards surround the celebrations—and more recently armed Vectors—people still love them. It gives all of the people from the different Sectors a reason to come together. They compete in friendly exhibition games like sword fighting and archery. They trade animals and goods. Parades of dancers and acrobats make their way to the castle for an all-night ball in the grand courtyard. But in spite of the revelry and the communal spirit of the Games, security is always tighter than normal.

Which makes what Aurela is suggesting so dangerous.

She is planning to stage simultaneous attacks—one to destroy my father's robotics facility and engage the kill switch for all the Vectors, and the second to infiltrate the castle during the ball and reveal the corruption that has corroded the once-revered monarchy. I've added a third step—to save Cale from any fallout.

Caden nudges me in the side, as if reading my thoughts. "I don't get it," he whispers. "Why would there be an actual kill code in the facility? That's like having a computer password written in a diary next to your bed."

"It's part of robotics security. During the Tech War, we couldn't shut them down, and the rogue droids executed the programmers who had all the kill codes. When we started developing the Vector technology, the king mandated a fail-safe in case the unexpected happened again." My mouth twists in a rueful grin. "So yes, dumb but necessary." My grin turns wider. "Plus, it's not like it's going to be in a bedside diary . . . more like in a locked triple titanium-enforced room surrounded by around a hundred Vector guards."

"Oh."

"Shhh!" Sauer's hiss is loud, drawing the censorious stares of two people at the end of the long table. Caden and I shut up.

One of Aurela's commanders is showing something on a hologram that's projecting in the middle of the room. He's making things move and appear with his fingers, shifting diagrams and plans to either side of the screen. His fingertips hold and drag an image from the center that explodes into a hologram of the castle blueprints across the middle of the table. I hear Caden's audible gasp and bite back a smile. Our technology, despite the ravaged world we live in, is remarkable.

"Pretty cool, huh?" I say to Caden under my breath with an anxious glance at Sauer.

"It's the same tech as the suits, just way more advanced, right?" I nod and stifle a snort at Caden's slack-jawed expression. Luckily, Sauer doesn't hear me and instead moves to the front of the room, where he takes charge of the presentation. As Sauer launches into an advanced schematic of the castle's security, I find my gaze wandering again, this time around the room.

I recognize a few soldiers, although I am unable to put names to any of the faces. I'm not surprised. Soldiers don't have a long life expectancy in Neospes. They don't comfortably retire. The strong survive, and the weak do not. It's that simple. Most of the others are high-ranking officials, and they, with the exception of the four Sector heads I recognized earlier, likely came into power after I left in search of Caden.

My eyes collide with a pair of steely black ones. A willowy girl at the far end of the room is watching me and making no attempt to hide that she is. At first glance, she is pretty, but then I see the scars . . . three long, ugly scratch marks marring her face. They are nearly white against her dark skin, and not even her thick curly hair can conceal them. The girl's face tugs at my memory. She is dressed in camouflage gray, the color of Neospes dust, and wears the stripes of a commander. I frown, trying to place her face but the memory evades me.

As if sensing my stare, Caden nudges me in the ribs again. "Who's that?"

"What?"

"The girl over there who looks like she wants to grind you into teeny tiny pieces with her eyes."

"I don't know," I answer automatically before glaring at him to stay quiet.

I'm bored by the sudden political turn of the conversation, and I'm agitated by the offensive stare of the girl I can't quite recognize. I know I've seen her before, but I can't place where. Her face with her violent scars is making me edgy. And the fact that she's a commander makes me crazy. I'm longing to ask Sauer, but he's still up near where Aurela is now sitting. Instead, I sink farther into the shadow of the wall and try to ignore the girl.

What seems like hours later, Aurela finally announces the results of the vote. It is unanimous. Her plan will proceed as indicated. I'm still not convinced that they'll be able to infiltrate the labs and the castle, but I'm a spectator . . . a hired gun at this point, with no say in their martial strategy. I'm going along because any distraction they create will help me with my objective—to locate and kill my father.

I turn to leave with Caden in tow, but Aurela's voice halts me in my tracks.

"General Riven will require some volunteers," she says, waving her arm in my direction. "She's taking point on a side assault."

As all eyes converge upon me, the silence in the room is even worse than in the beginning. It is heavy with a dark undercurrent. They don't trust me, not because of what I am—no one really knows the truth other than a few—but because of *who* I am . . . my reputation.

"General Riven?" someone hisses. "We can't trust her."

"Where has she been all this time? How convenient that she's back."

The noise in the room escalates as pandemonium erupts. The dark-eyed girl is watching me with a smirk. My mouth curls down, and it's all I can do to tear my eyes away.

"Silence, please." Aurela's voice is quiet, but the voices recede. "Our plans do not stop at removing Murek or exposing his endgame to the people of Neospes. It also extends to reinstating the true crown prince alongside his brother." The murmurs in the room rise again and once more regress at Aurela's hand. "That is where General Riven has been, protecting said prince in the Otherworld."

"The *Otherworld*!" someone else gasps.

"Still, she's the general," a voice argues. "Loyal to the false prince. We know who she is."

"Yes, she is the general," Aurela agrees mildly. "And no, she is bound to us and to Prince Caden. I trust her, and that should be enough."

I feel Caden squirm next to me, at odds with all the sudden attention. But my mind is whirling at the fact that my mother and leader of the rebels has openly supported me—stating that anyone who doesn't accept me does not accept her. I'm at a loss for words, breath even, at her complete and utter trust.

For a brief second, I wonder whether that trust in me is misplaced.

And in that same moment, I realize who the dark-eyed girl is. She's been someone *I* trusted. Once upon a time, I would have considered her a loyal teammate. But when she went against orders with a group of insurgents led by her brother, the king called for swift justice.

I know exactly who she is. She's a commander I exiled to the Outers four years ago; she is the single broken line tattooed on my neck.

And now she is one of us.

# 22

# FATHER DEAREST

DESPITE THE FACT that Loren, the soldier I'd exiled, was one of the volunteers to be on my team, things were on track with Aurela's wishes. I was suspicious the minute Loren voiced her desire to come with me—she obviously had a bone to pick. After all, I executed her brother and exiled her.

But at the end of the day, I know that it doesn't matter. I don't trust anyone, and no one here trusts me either, for good reason. I'd been the worst of the worst, and a part of me is still that person. I was programmed to be emotionless, to obey orders, to kill without question. And because of the nanoplasm, I'm faster and fiercer than anyone else. I'm death in a girl's body.

It stands to reason that people will hate me.

But I have a job to do, and I can't let some soldier with a vendetta get in the way, even if she has every reason to want to stick an electro-rod through my guts the first chance she gets. We all have our demons.

And the old saying about keeping your enemies close is true enough.

"Why are we breaking into your old house again?" Caden asks, bringing me back to the present.

We are crouched behind a building, dressed in identical gray fatigues, the same as the soldiers on the streets wear. I stole them the day before once I realized what I needed to do as part of my plan to infiltrate the palace. I debated against bringing Caden, but leaving him behind wasn't an option. And it isn't exactly the most dangerous situation—my father will be at the lab—and we'll be in and out before anyone realizes that we've gone. We'll be safe as kittens. I hoped.

"I need something. Something important."

"Won't Aurela be pissed that we snuck out?"

Exasperated, I turn to face him. "Well, she's not going to find out, is she? If we hurry up, that is. Come on; we don't have all day. In and out, okay?"

My father's home, the place where I grew up, is in Sector One. Naturally it's the closest sector to the castle, but, oddly enough, doesn't have that much security. People from other sectors don't voluntarily go to Sector One. Shae and I always joked that we needed guards to keep people in instead of keeping undesirables out. Sector One citizens didn't mingle with people from other sectors—they were the cream of the crop, the brains of Neospes.

I borrowed Sauer's transport hover without his permission but I figured that's what they were for . . . emergencies. Caden and I had lugged the hoverbike near the side of a warehouse behind some crates and covered it with a tarp.

"Get changed," I snap to him, and toss him a silver oversuit.

"Why?"

I wave a hand around us and shrug into my own jump-suit over my clothes. "Notice that everything in Sector One is silver? It's a sign of privilege. And we need to blend in. The fatigues were only to get us here."

There aren't many people walking around. Most of them are at work, and the younger ones are training in their chosen vocation or in the fields. The elite training fields are between Sector One and Sector Two, and most of the soldiers' families are housed in Sector Three. So Sector One is quiet.

"Stay close," I warn Caden. "And be vigilant. There are cameras everywhere. If they scan us without a chip, we're toast."

It's a fine line between appearing casual to any onlookers and staying out of sight of the many electronic eyes in each Sector. In Neospes, peace isn't a result of freedom. It's a result of swift military action. Break the law and face the punishment. Those electronic eyes watch everything all the time—and freedom is the price we have to pay for the security of life in the dome.

"I thought you said this was going to be easy."

"This *is* easy. Come on."

We make our way along the side of a row of identical white and light gray-patterned housing cubes, staying out of sight of the main street and weaving in and out of smaller alleys, until we come to a house with tiny purple flowers planted along the edges. My heart trembles in my chest. Shae and I planted the flowers when we were little—in defiance of all the gray and white. Surely my father would have destroyed them. Why has he kept them? As a memory of what? How much we hated Sector One? How much we both hated *him*?

"This is it. There shouldn't be anyone here, but be alert," I say. "Quick, around the back."

I don't want to draw any attention by going to the front, street side, especially for a wanted fugitive. Located on the far side of Sector One, my father's house backs onto a deep, rocky gorge.

The gorge appears bottomless and beautiful in a raw-nature kind of way, with a sheer, reflective rock face on one side and broken rubble on the other. The sun glints off the different colored minerals in the rock so brightly that it's like being inside a prism. Free of security cameras and prying eyes, the gorge was one of my favorite places to hide.

"Wow, so this is where you lived?" Caden says. "It's amazing."

I allow myself a smile. "See that ledge over there? Across the gorge? That's actually a cave; it used to be my hideout. My secret place to get away."

The mouth of the cave is barely noticeable. I can see him squinting, so I move closer to show him, lining my face up against his and pointing. Caden turns into me, and it brings back memories I don't want to think about. Not now, especially given what happened the last time. Despite the electric zing in my belly and my sudden breathlessness, I step away. A wounded look slashes across Caden's expression, but he hides it quickly.

"So it was like your tree house. What'd you keep in there, dolls and stuff?"

I snort. "More like a stash of knives and electro-grenades."

Caden's green eyes flash with humor. "Come on, every little girl has to have dolls somewhere."

"So then," I toss back, "where was your stash of dolls?"

A wide grin. "Are you calling me a girl?"

"Hey, if the shoe fits . . ."

"I'll admit I played with dolls, only they were called GI Joes, so technically they were *action figures*. But if you still think I'm a girl, I'd be happy to prove otherwise." Caden's grin turns wicked and makes a hundred butterflies go aloft in my belly. A flash of his sweaty, defined abs in the training room at Sauer's jumps into my head, and this time I can't control the crazy blush that invades my entire body. He is definitely all boy.

"No thanks, I'm good." I manage to sound normal, even though my heartbeat is on a rampage following the shameless turn of my thoughts.

*Get a grip, Riven,* I hiss to myself. *This isn't the time or place to be lusting after a boy like a slutty Sadie clone.* But now that that door is open, it's kind of hard to get the images out of my head.

"Well, if you change your mind," Caden says, wiggling his eyebrows suggestively and sashaying his hips.

"You are such a freak," I retort, blushing. "Come on, let's go. And keep it together, will you? We could get arrested or die any second."

"So you keep saying."

Pulling a small laser device from my pocket, I hold it up to the keypad sensor on the back door. A whine, and the locks click back. Inside, the house is exactly the same as I remembered. Not just a little, but exactly the same. My father, as brilliant as he is, has never been one for any kind of change. The small but efficient kitchen is spotless—so is the high table with its benches. Off the kitchen and dining area is a larger living space, but it looks unused. The sleeping quarters are on either side of the main area.

Caden is behind, silent. His eyes are wide and he's taking it all in. I know he has to be curious about where Shae and I used to live. After all, he'd been with her for years in the Otherworld, only to find out that he didn't know the truth about who she actually was all along.

Or me either, for that matter.

"Try not to touch anything, okay? He can't know that we— or anyone—has been here."

"Aren't security cameras in here, too?" Caden asks nervously.

I shake my head. "No, my father is exempt from many of Neospes' laws."

My fingers curl into knots at my side, knowing exactly why my father hadn't wanted to be seen. I don't bother to go to my parents' old room. I don't even want to think about him more than I already have. Instead, I push open the door to the room that Shae and I shared, my gloved fingers cold on the thin metal door.

Caden's gasp behind me is audible. "What the . . ."

"Now you understand what we're dealing with?" I ask quietly. "A psychopath."

The room is a shambles, littered with broken furniture. The top bunk, soldered into the wall, is now chopped into white and black remnants with bits of mattress strewn all over the floor. The bottom bunk hangs drunkenly off its remaining hinge. It looks like he'd gone after the room with a blowtorch. Huge black gashes discolor the walls.

It's the work of a madman . . . one consumed by unimaginable rage.

He'd torn holes in the thick carpet and ripped our remaining clothing to shreds. Not much of Shae's was there after she left, but he shredded my old uniforms until they were nothing but tatters. The only thing left intact in the room is the glass case with all my trophies won during the different Games. They meant more to him than they ever did to me.

"Wow," Caden breathes, staring at the garish display. "You won . . . like everything."

"Robot blood. What can I say?" I reply drily. "Technically, I cheated, so I don't deserve any of those."

"He cheated," Caden reminds me. "Not you. You were innocent."

A deep guttural laugh that I recognize as my own crawls from my mouth. "Don't make me into some kind of martyr, Caden. I was never an innocent, not for a second. Not after all I've done. *I* did all those things." I thump my chest emphatically. "Me. Not him, not anyone else. Me."

"Riv," Caden says slowly. "I understand you did all those things, but you did them because you were following orders, and you didn't question them, because you were compromised by your father." Caden grasps my shoulders, tugging me around to face him. I don't want to look at him but I do. I meet his eyes and it's like I'm standing at the edge of the gorge outside, on the brink of free falling. "You have to stop punishing yourself for something that was out of your control. Can't you see that? You have to see that."

It isn't his voice that convinces me. It's the complete faith in his eyes . . . those green eyes that I've somehow known my whole life. And for the first time, I don't think of Cale.

It's only Caden . . . this boy who believes in me more than I believe in myself. And I'm terrified. I've never been more afraid of anything in my life. I shift backward but his arms tighten, drawing me against his chest. His chin rests on top of my head, his breath warm against my hair.

"Let it go, Riv," he whispers, so close that I can see the soft pulse beneath his skin. "Let go of the past. It can't hurt you anymore."

And then I'm weeping, long silent tears that soak my face and his shirt . . . tears for all the years of pain and anger and loss. I cry until there's nothing but dry sobs racking my body, and still I can't stop. I cry for myself and my inability to love a boy who's clearly in love with me. I'll only hurt him. I'll destroy him, just like everyone else in my life.

"I'm scared. I can't lose anyone else." My voice is so soft, it's more of a rasp than words against his shirt. But Caden raises his head. His hands move on either side to hold my face on either side.

"I know. But fear is just fear. It can only hurt you if you let it." His thumbs rub gently against my cheekbones. "And I won't let you let it." His voice is hypnotic, weaving through all the broken parts of me and somehow bringing them back together. "Look at me, Riven," he says, his eyes capturing mine easily. "You think I don't know anything about fear? I know that if you let it, it can consume you." His voice is so soft I can barely hear it. "You can't be afraid all the time, afraid to lose everything. Shae told me how you did it in your training. Faced it, confronted it head-on. This is the same thing."

"I didn't save her," I say, my words distraught.

"You *couldn't* save her." His voice is gentle. "Stop beating yourself up for something that was out of your control. You only control what *you* do. Not the actions of others."

Caden is right—he's seen right through me, right into the core of me. And he loves me. Just as I love him. I started to say it before my internal programming went berserk. I've never allowed myself to feel anything for anyone, not when everything I've been taught is the opposite; love precedes weakness. Then why do I like knowing that Caden feels something for me?

I like it. I like *him*.

His eyes widen as if he's reading my thoughts, the internal battle I'm waging with myself . . . the war between want and reason, between girl and soldier. And I'm losing. I'm losing myself to him. My eyes speak the words that my mouth cannot.

Yes, they say. Yes.

Caden leans in as his right hand slides into my hair to the nape of my neck and brings my face toward his, his eyes never letting mine go. At the last minute before our lips touch, I close my eyes. The kiss is soft and featherlight, but I still slide my hands up his arms, gripping tightly, pressing myself against his body and demanding more.

He smiles against my mouth, and our kiss deepens into something fierce and frantic. Suddenly, I can't even think, standing there in my father's house as the pain and fear fall away. All I can do is feel . . . the soft contours of his lips against mine, the taste of his mouth, the strength of his body. My fingers clutch his clothing and I am overwhelmed, breathless. Weightless.

Caden trails kisses against my temple, my eyes, my nose. His eyes are a stormy jade, dark with passion. He kisses me again, and this time everything around us disappears—my father's house, my destroyed life, my broken self. All that remains is Caden.

Fingers tangle in clothing and zippers as we fall to the floor together. My palms are flat against the taut planes of Caden's chest, and my breath is unsteady at the sheer beauty of him above me. His body is not bulky with muscle; instead, he's sleekly toned, his stomach and sides hard against my wandering fingertips.

He is kissing me again, and we stop only to pull my tunic over my head. A sudden shyness envelops me and I feel my face flush. No one has ever seen me this unclothed. No one. Not ever. My embarrassment must be obvious because Caden grins and grasps my chin.

"You're perfect, Riven," he whispers.

"No. I'm not," I say, my thoughts burning, my hands fluttering to hide the scars peppering my rib cage and stomach. "But you make me feel that way."

His smile transforms his entire face and he bends toward me again, pushing away my embarrassed hands. His kisses grace my ear, and then my neck, and wander lower, kissing each raised welt, each ugly wound that I tried to hide with aching gentleness. My fingers thread their way into his hair and down his neck. Caden growls low in his chest as my hands slide down his shoulders and his muscled back, and lower still.

We are combustible, electric.

I'd never kissed anyone before Caden, far less gotten half-naked with anyone, but this feels more right than anything I've ever done. He's the one who makes me feel less splintered, less shattered. I feel whole when I'm with him. That has to count for something, doesn't it? I have to tell him the truth about how I feel.

"Caden," I begin.

"Mmm," he says, trailing more kisses up my arm. But before I can continue, the sound of a door slamming jerks me into action. I shove Caden to one side and press my fingers urgently against his lips, my eyes wide. Someone is outside.

How could I have been so reckless?

Shrugging my arms into the white overalls, I crawl along the floor to the thin window of glass against the far wall and slide up to the right of it. A quick glimpse confirms that there's a vehicle outside. It's black and sleek and official looking.

"We have to hide," I mouth to Caden who has already dressed. His hair is tousled and his eyes are still glazed from what we'd shared seconds before. I'm sure I must look the same.

"Where?" he mouths back.

My father ripped the room apart in rage, but he still didn't find the secret space that Shae and I painstakingly built. Half of me wants to leap toward it to get what I came for and make a run for it, but the other half warns that getting caught would be foolish. I glance at Caden. I can't risk putting him in danger, not with my father.

So instead, I jerk my head toward the twisted bottom bunk bed. "Under," I say. "Now."

I slide in behind him until we are both jammed up against the wall. Every inch of Caden's body is glued to every inch of mine, but there's no fire between us now . . . only cold dread.

"Don't breathe," I warn.

Sounds reach us from the other room. A door clicking, a staccato of footsteps on the floor, voices. He's not alone.

"Sir," a voice says. "Reports came in of trespassers in the back."

"Any confirmation of what they looked like?" My father's voice is mellifluous and just as loathsome as the last time I'd heard it. My stomach curdles like spoiled milk and lurches unsteadily. A cold sweat pinpricks its way along my back.

"No, sir. There's no sign of them. And no sign of forced entry on the perimeter. It's clear."

The footsteps draw closer, and I press myself even harder against Caden. I'm not even breathing by the time the door to the room slides open and a shiny pair of black boots come into view. His smell assaults me . . . still the same: a dark, musky scent of spice.

It spins me back into a whirlwind of memories—my father and I playing chess in his laboratory, my father glowing with pride at my first-place trophies for archery and swordplay, my father pinning my rank of general to my vest. It's hard to reconcile the man I'd known as a child to the monster I now realize he is.

The seconds drag by and still the black boots don't move, but I can sense heavy eyes roving slowly over every inch of the space. I scan the floor in a panic, but nothing appears noticeably different from the overall chaos of the room. My eyes swivel back to the black boots. The room is so silent you could hear an eyelash fall. Neither Caden nor I are breathing.

I'm so sure that he's going to peer beneath the bunk that my pulse thrums and my blood rushes madly in my ears. My body tenses, and then I feel Caden's fingers, quiet against the small of my back, stroking, soothing. They slide over and intertwine with mine. My pulse slows and calms.

"All clear, sir," the other voice says. "There's no one here, now."

After a minute, the boots retreat and the door slides closed.

Still, I don't breathe properly until I hear the hum of the engine outside. Tense, I crawl silently out from under the bed and press my ear to the door. There's no sound in the rest of the house, and the car is gone.

We're safe for now.

I cross the room swiftly and pull the trophy case gently from the wall, sliding my hands along the floor. I pull back a portion of the carpet, and press the bare tiles gently in a certain sequence. A soft click, and one of the tiles glides back to reveal a hidden compartment.

Inside, there's a box. I don't have time to sift through all the contents, even though my heart stings at some of the treasures Shae and I had hidden there. Bits of ribbon, silver stars, letters written to our future selves.

"What's in there?" Caden asks.

"Stuff we didn't want anyone to find." I pull out the thing I'd risked our lives to come here to get.

A Vector's uniform.

Only this one is different. This one, my father recalibrated to work with my own DNA. A wry smirk twists my mouth. We were so shocked and proud that the suit responded to me—thinking my father brilliant—and little knowing that the suit responded to the nanoplasm inside of me instead of pure human DNA. The suit was *designed* for me.

*He* knew. And he created the perfect defense for his perfect weapon. The suit is unmatched in its capabilities, offensive and defensive. No wonder he tore the room apart trying to find it, and then assumed that I'd somehow hidden it or taken it with me.

"Let's go," I say to Caden. "We're done here."

We sneak out the back after checking carefully to make sure we aren't being watched, and make our way to where we'd hidden the hoverbike. The journey back to Sector Seven is far quicker than the time it took to leave, and my stomach sinks as we pull into Sauer's garage.

Aurela's face is blacker than a thundercloud.

# 23

# THE WINTER SOLSTICE

AURELA IS STILL furious, even though I've assured her a hundred times that we hadn't encountered any danger. Of course, I hadn't mentioned our near discovery by my father himself. She would have flipped her lid and put both Caden and me on lockdown. To his credit, Caden had followed my lead like a pro, and after only an hour of intense interrogation Aurela had relented.

We're back in the meeting room, going over the plans one last time. I toss a casual glance at Caden, who's sitting next to Loren. Caden's eyes meet mine meaningfully over the table, and I'm glad I'm sitting, because my knees suddenly feel like water. Earlier, he had told me that he'd have given anything for a few more minutes before my father showed up.

Even though I feel far older at times, Caden has more experience in the relationship area than I do. I have exactly zero skill when it comes to boys, the not-beating-them-to-a-pulp kind, I mean. Caden's been with Sadie, and she's not exactly the unadventurous type. Sadie is a girl who calls the shots, especially in the relationship department.

Dragging my eyes away, I focus instead on Loren's piercing glare. We haven't spoken since she volunteered to be on my team, and it's clear that she doesn't trust me. Then again, I don't trust her, either. I agreed for her to join us because before I exiled her, she'd been one of the best. And now, with her skills honed in the Outers, she's only become more so. I'm not about to begrudge someone a chance to change, not after everything I've learned about myself.

I turn my attention to Sauer's computer tablet in front of me, showing a schematic of the castle. Security is near impenetrable. There are four layers of guards, two sets outside on the perimeter and two sets inside. They are only the human line of defense. There are also Vectors at each entry point. I sigh, steepling my fingers in front of me, and meet Sauer's eyes. Getting in undetected will be a challenge for one person, far less four.

"What are you thinking?" I ask him.

"The Winter Games are two days away, but we still have a lot to do," he says. "To even get past the castle guards, we'd have to register by identity chip, and technically, you're already off the grid. So is Caden."

I removed my implanted birth chip the minute I decided to leave Neospes—it was incredibly painful but a necessity. At the time, I hadn't known if the Vectors could track an implant even in another dimension, but I didn't want to take any chances. Given that all citizens of Neospes have to be accounted for at all times, Sauer explained that both Caden and I would require new identity chips, which means fake ones, and they aren't that easy to get. It's tricky, because if someone dies, the system automatically records it. You have to use the chip of someone who is still alive. If someone's chip is forcibly removed, it releases an alarm that goes straight to the Vectors. After Leila disappeared with Caden, those precautions were deemed necessary.

Caden is frowning with a confused look. "I don't get it," he says, staring at me. "You took your chip out three years ago. How come they didn't get you?"

"They did, but I killed the Vector who'd caught me. Then I everted."

"So basically, I need a chip, and you need a chip?"

"Yes," Sauer says. "And Aurela, but she already has a fake one she's been using for years."

Caden's frown deepens. "So what do we have to do, exactly?"

Loren answers. "You get fitted with a new one. Aurela's people have been growing fake people for years. So technically, you'll get the chip of someone who's only alive electronically."

"Wow, fake people," Caden breathes. "That's extreme."

"Extreme times call for extreme measures," Sauer says matter-of-factly.

Loren leans forward. "Aurela has been planning this for a long time—very, very carefully. She knew identity chips would be needed one day for those of us who'd been exiled, so she made sure we could be accounted for." Her voice is monotone, but I avoid her stare like it's the plague.

"So who do I get?" Caden asks.

"They're all soldiers," Sauer says, and then looks at me with a weird expression, his face reddening. "Well, most of them anyway."

I don't hesitate. "What do you mean?"

"Your identity is a . . . um . . . danseuse." His face dulls to a dark red. "Loren was assigned the last female soldier chip."

My chair flies back crashing into the wall. "A *what*?" I scream.

Danseuses are nothing more than paid female escorts, paid to entertain wealthy citizens of Neospes. Aurela's calm voice breaks through my fury as she walks into the room. "It's the best disguise for you, Riven, to infiltrate the palace. If you look like a soldier, people will recognize you. Don't forget who you were . . . who you still are here."

But the thought of it fills me with disgust. "I'm not using the identity of a freaking floozy! Pick something else. I'll be a cleaner, a goat trader, anything."

"We don't have any other female identity chips, Riven, and this is the best for you. Trust me," Aurela says. She walks to stand in front of me and turns me toward her. My chest feels like it's going to explode. I've never been asked to do anything more ludicrous. I'm a *general*, not some dancer dressed in a handkerchief! I don't even know how to dance.

"Aurela, I can't."

Aurela's voice is harsh, harsher than I've ever heard it. "You have no choice. If you don't, we abort. It's that simple. You want to save Cale. Well, you are the only person who can ensure his safety if we get you into the castle." Aurela pauses with a long stare at me. "You decide."

I know she's right, but I can't reconcile wearing some kind of revealing costume with any of it. It's a huge strike against me—*Riven*—the name that strikes fear into the hearts of all men will now cause ridicule. But I know that's only my pride talking. I should do whatever I have to do to save Cale and Caden without being selfish. Being a danseuse for ten minutes is only a means to an end. A crappy, ridiculous means, but it will get the job done. I'll get into the castle unnoticed.

"Fine," I snap, stalking to the far end of the room, where I pour myself a shot of spirits. I drink it quickly, ignoring its hot path searing my stomach. Loren is laughing at me, her dark eyes mocking.

Hours later, three of Aurela's lackeys are in my chamber, fussing over my hair and my face and my clothes. I have never felt more conspicuous or more ridiculous. Strange dark-gold extensions have been applied and braided intricately with sweet-smelling blossoms into my hair. My skin has been oiled to a gilded sheen and colored shimmery dust applied to my eyes and cheeks. The women gesture for me to step into my costume—a filmy white and silver getup that looks like some kind of confection instead of a dress.

There's a knock at the door, and one of the women answers it.

"I'd hardly recognize you, Riven," Aurela says. She's dressed head-to-toe in black stealth gear, pretty much what I want to be wearing.

Instead, I'm a porcelain doll. An ugly, scowling porcelain doll. I turn to glare at her. "That was the point, wasn't it?" I gesture down at myself. "I couldn't attack a fly and win in this dress. In fact, the fly would probably try to eat me, since I look like a giant frosted cupcake."

"A what?"

Belatedly realizing I've mentioned a food from the Other-world that doesn't exist here, I shrug. "Never mind. It means a

delicious but totally useless food . . . which is what I look like."
One of the women draws me to the mirror, and my half-joking,
self-deprecating words desert me completely. I don't recognize
myself.

The girl staring at me in the mirror has glossy dark braids
piled in rows along her head and draped artfully to one side.
Her eyes are lined with kohl, making their normally dull gray
depths vibrant and jewel-toned. Her cheeks are glittery and
flushed with color, her lips glistening. The dress is impractical
but undeniably lovely, falling in triangular swathes of chiffon
to the ground.

I am an imposter.

It can't possibly be me, but I blink and the girl does the same.
I resist the urge to pick a fight with the first soldier I can find.

"You look beautiful." Caden's voice is hushed and awed, and
I spin around only to find my swift retort cut off from my own
mouth. He is resplendent in a silk moss-green shirt and black
dress pants, complete with an official-looking scabbard.

"So do you," I blurt out, and then immediately look to
Aurela, who is busy addressing one of the women who had
helped get me ready. Thank the stars she didn't notice my
schoolgirl response to his appearance. I flush and Caden grins,
reading me easily.

"Thank you, my lady. I'm supposed to be your . . . er . . .
partner."

"My what?" I splutter. "But you were supposed to be a soldier." In a rush, I notice the lines of gold stars and royal stripes
decorating his upper left breast pocket, marking his status as a
lord of Neospes.

Aurela walks over with an approving smile at Caden's garb. "Too obvious a disguise. This way, you can be near each other without too many questions. Caden's a wealthy lord and you're his entertainment escort for the ball." I can't help the blush that heats my face at the thought of being anyone's escort, far less Caden's.

"You know," Caden begins laughing at my obvious embarrassment, "there's a name for that where I'm from—"

"Shut up," I say, swearing under my breath. "Or you'll see exactly how entertaining I can be with two sets of blades."

"Oh, feisty. I like that in my women."

"Aurela!" I protest weakly. "Really? Can't he just be a soldier and go with Sauer? That way, I don't end up killing him by accident or something."

But Aurela rolls her eyes and throws me a sling pack for my gear. It's a form-fitting pack that I can wear around my waist under the dress. There isn't much room under there, but I'll be damned if I go anywhere without weapons. She also hands me some kind of frilly fan that I just stare at, dumbfounded.

"It's a fan," she says helpfully. My scowl deepens as I grasp the offending object as if it's a snake. "Ready to go in ten," she reminds us with a quickly concealed smile. I swear that she's laughing under her breath.

Smoothing the ruffled skirt of the dress, I turn to Caden once Aurela is a few feet away and engaged in conversation with one of her maids. "Joking aside, you don't think I look ridiculous?"

"I hardly recognize you," Caden says honestly. "I mean, I've never seen you out of cargo pants, unless you count the time when you wore Sadie's dress." He winks and I choke out a startled laugh.

"You *knew* about that?"

Caden smiles drily. "I think Sadie knew about that, too, but she wasn't going to admit it in a million years." He shakes his head. "You have no idea how pissed off she was."

"Sorry, but she deserved way worse, and you know it."

"Well, I wasn't too upset. The last time you wore a dress, epic things happened, so win-win for me," Caden says with a meaningful look, clearly referring to our last day at Horrow. He leans in so only I can hear him. "Can't wait to see what happens this time." At his whispered words, I can't control the tingle that weaves its way through my body, but I fight it just the same.

"Keep talking, *my lord*," I snap with a glare, "and the only thing that's going to happen is your ass meeting the ground, dress or no dress. Now, go away."

Caden backs away, hands in the air, grinning, and I stare at myself in the mirror again, blinking just to make sure it's still me. The top of the dress is lower than anything I've ever worn, and I tug at the bodice uncomfortably. "Seriously Cade, I look like a stranger. This isn't me. And how the hell am I going to fight in this?"

"Just because you're wearing a dress doesn't make you a different person, Riv. Plus, Sauer's got your suit and your sword for when we get inside. It's just clothes . . . wear a tunic underneath if it'll make you feel better. And you don't look like a stranger; your eyes are the same, and those I'd know anywhere."

"I *am* wearing a tunic and I still feel naked," I flash back. "And these don't even look like my eyes. Mine are more dirt-colored than silver."

Caden's glance is like velvet. "Well, they always look like this to me."

It's all I can do not to melt inside, but I keep my face expressionless, then scowl slightly for good measure. I sneak one last look at the mirror and sigh.

I have a job to do.

Sauer and Loren are ready and waiting by the time we get downstairs. Outside, the streets are already crowded with people heading to the training fields between Sectors Two and One for the Games. When evening starts to fall, everyone will eventually find their way to the castle, the final event and celebration of the Winter Solstice.

It's a tradition dating back to the beginning of Neospes, one of the first decrees of the then newly crowned king. It used to be a celebration of our survival after the War. Now, its meaning has become far more mundane—merely a way for the monarchy to fawn over itself and its power. We've lost sight of what's important, as has our leadership.

Aurela is right—I see that now. And I understand why it has to change.

I glance at Sauer, who nods curtly in my direction as we merge into the throng of people on the street. He's all business, a commander first and a friend second. His role as a double agent is about to end, once we wage our combined attack on the monarchy. Until today, I hadn't realized how deep the unrest reaches . . . and how many followers Aurela has, not just in Sector Seven but *all* the sectors. She has thousands of reserve soldiers on hand if things get ugly.

But that isn't Aurela's plan. She prefers a quiet, stealthy infiltration. She doesn't want hundreds of innocent people to die, especially at the hands of the Vectors. Our population is devastated enough without diminishing it even further. Which is why we split into three groups—me, Sauer, Caden, and Loren to safeguard Cale; Aurela's team to infiltrate the lab and locate the kill code for the Vectors; and finally, the third team to depose Murek.

My father will have to wait until Cale is safe. Then I have my own plans for him.

"You okay?" Caden asks, jerking me out of my murderous thoughts.

"What?"

"I said, are you okay?"

"Of course," I snap. "Why wouldn't I be? It's just a mission. Stay as close to me as possible. I don't want to draw undue attention."

"I'm pretty sure that's the point of how we're dressed, but don't worry, I won't embarrass you. I'll just think of it like going to prom."

I half-choke, half-snort on my retort. "*Prom?*"

Caden grins at me. "Yeah, you know . . . the whole life-or-death school dance thing in my world when girls murder each other with their eyes, and guys are expected to fall in line or face certain death. Don't worry; got it down pat."

Which is why I am grinning from ear to ear when Sauer announces that we are splitting from the other groups. Just before we jump into Sauer's hovercraft, I feel Aurela's hand on my arm.

"Riven, be careful," she says quietly. "And please don't do anything rash. I'm trusting you."

"I know," I say. "Cale and Caden will be safe, I promise you." She frowns at my evasive response, but I climb into the hover.

There's nothing that will stop me, once Cale is with Sauer, from doing what I have to do where my father is concerned. And if the opportunity presents itself during the raid, I'll take it. But I know what Aurela is worried about. I turn around. "Don't worry; I won't jeopardize the mission," I say. "The code in his lab is my birth date. At least, it was until I defected. And Mom, you be careful, too." The hover accelerates, but not before I see the startled look on her face that I'd called her something other than Aurela.

Driving is slow going, especially around all the people, but after a while Sauer pulls off onto a less major road where there's far less pedestrian traffic. The Games are well underway, and the training fields are packed with huge colored tents full of participants and street vendors selling wares and trinkets. People are laughing and dancing, and cheering on the various combatants.

We ditch the hover and make our way to the main tent in the middle. It's where the exhibition fighting is and where anyone important will be. Falling into my role, Caden and I separate from Loren and Sauer, pretending to be interested in a couple battling it out with swords in the middle of the tent. It's an exhibition match, so the opponents are clothed in protective padding. Still, it is amazing to watch. Their technique is faultless and perfect in its form.

Out of the corner of my eye, I see Loren taking up her position near the entrance of the tent and Sauer making his way to the far end, where there is a raised dais, likely for any royal attendees and their court. Although I'm straining my neck to tell who's there, I can't quite see over the heads of everyone, so my attention swings back to the exhibition fight. Four Vectors are stationed around the ring like silent, dead pillars. There seem to be a lot more of them than usual, I notice, frowning. Has someone tipped them off about Aurela's plans? Or maybe I've just been gone too long from Neospes. Shaking my head, I let go of my heightened paranoia—this stupid dress is making me edgy.

A fat man in a gaudy gold outfit jostles me, and my fingers curl into fists at his lascivious leer. He's staring at my chest like it's a giant pile of precious stones. My fists tighten. I've never wanted to smash in someone's face more.

"Not here," Caden warns in my ear, moving to stand between me and the man who's just been spared having my fist in his face. He turns to the offending man. "The lady is with me," he says quietly. His words aren't threatening, but the low growl underscoring his words is.

"I wasn't going to do anything," I grit out as the man moves away with a lingering glance at me. "I'm fine."

Ignoring the low burn that Caden's possessive tone had ignited in my belly, I turn my attention back to the exhibition match and notice that the combatants have switched to double-edged Artok weapons similar to mine. The one on the right is half a step slower than the one on the left, but they are evenly matched. Again, their combat technique is brilliant.

I wish I could see who they are, but they're both wearing antique decorative face masks. The truth is, I probably wouldn't know them, anyway. Our mortality rates aren't that great, and they're probably up-and-comers in the ranks. The fighter on the left drops into a low crouch, spinning to the left to catch the other unawares, and wins the point.

"He's good," Caden comments. "The one on the left."

"Not that good," I say snarkily, still semi-peeved to be in a dress. To tell the truth, a part of me wants nothing more than to be in that ring, showing off and strutting my skills. Winning meant everything to my father, so I won everything I could, including all of my exhibition matches, which didn't technically have winners. His approval used to mean so much.

I turn away, unable to watch, and catch Sauer's eye. He's gesturing to someone on the dais. Caden gasps, his eyes connecting with the four Vectors standing on either side of it. But I knew they'd be there. I want to see who they're protecting so vigilantly.

We inch our way forward, the throng of people thinning the closer we get, and I recognize the gaunt face and the bulbous, fish-like eyes immediately. Instinctively, my fan opens in front of my face, concealing my own features from view as a hollow feeling spreads in my stomach. My disguise may fool most people, but there's one person who could see right through it . . . a master manipulator and schemer himself.

Murek.

Usurper. Traitor. *Murderer.*

# 24

# THE WINNER TAKES IT

TWILIGHT IS FALLING as the last of the Games wrap up, and people are already starting to take the revelry to the castle courtyard for the Midnight Ball. The streets are lit with multi-colored halogen lights with shiny decorations draped over storefronts and houses. Everyone is laughing and dancing . . . well, everyone except us.

I want to leave but am at the mercy of Sauer's lead. I still haven't seen Cale. He's nowhere to be found in the main tent or the surroundings, and Murek did the presentation of the Games' trophies in his stead as if he were already acting in the position of king. I wonder for a moment whether Cale is already dead and hidden away somewhere deep in the castle where no one would ever find him. Murek is twisted like that.

My father is also mysteriously absent. Not that I expected that he would attend the Games, but he'd been present at every single match I'd ever won. His pride would keep him away, I realize. My only hope is that he isn't in the lab—he is my prize, not Aurela's. I have to be the one to make him pay for what he'd done to all of us.

"Riven," a voice rasps in my ear. It's Sauer, standing with his back against mine. "Remember the strategy. We separate after entry and regroup thirty minutes later. You take point to extract Cale, and Loren and I watch for Vectors. Here's your comms." He palms two tiny skin-colored devices into my hands. "Stick to the plan, and remember your cover. Code word for help is *Reptile*." There's a clear warning in his voice. "Clear?"

"Clear." My own voice is terse, ready.

The wireless comms device is a tiny bean-shaped pod that tucks snugly into my ear. I hand the second one to Caden, who does the same. Together, we join the crowd walking toward the first security checkpoint. Loren and Sauer fall in a little way behind us.

"Scan, please."

Caden goes through first without any problem. I hold out my wrist underneath the scanner, and for a second my stomach lurches as the screen flickers before validating my identity as Tania, a danseuse. The electronic words are tiny, but they may as well have been on a neon banner over my head. Inside, I'm cringing at the knowing look the soldier tosses my way, but instead of punching him in the face, I smile coquettishly, thinking of Sadie, and play the part I'm supposed to play.

"Bravo," Caden says. I purposefully stomp on his toe as I walk past him. "Ow! What was that for? I was paying you a compliment."

"You know what for," I hiss back. "And I was only channeling Sadie; so glad to see her ridiculously simpering ways still work on you."

"What—?"

"Come on," I snap, inexplicably angry. I'm a soldier, not a seductress. The pretense does not come easily.

The next security checkpoint is at the entrance of the courtyard beyond the tall and forbidding gilded gates. Cale and I used to scale them as children—a fair feat, given that they are over eight feet tall and spiked, but we were inventive and determined. I glance up at the parapets overlooking the grand courtyard that are decorated with brightly colored banners and flags, hoping to see a glimpse of Cale's face, but he's not there.

My body freezes at the sight of the two Vectors stationed with the guards at the checkpoint. Just seeing them standing there, their milky blue eyes staring at nothing, sends a chill deep into my bones. To think I used to command them without a second thought! Now I'm the enemy.

Following in Caden's footsteps, I flick my wrist through the scanner, and the screen flickers and then fades to snow. The guard frowns and taps the scanner lightly. One of the Vectors swivels his eyes toward me, his gaze heavy. Feigning a bored look, I hold my wrist out even though my heart is racing. The guard scans my chip again. This time, it goes through.

I feel the Vector's eyes on me all the way to the middle of the courtyard.

"What happened?" Sauer's voice is tinny inside my ear. I can barely hear him over the loud music.

"I don't know," I reply, touching my ear gently. "I think the nanobes are attacking the chip. They must think it's something foreign. There was a lot of electronic interference on the scanners. I'm not sure that it will work again."

"Okay," Sauer says. "Be careful. Those two were the main checkpoints Aurela knew about so we'll figure out any others. And Riven?" His voice is quiet, raising the hairs on the back of my neck. "You have a Vector on your tail. He's been with you since the checkpoint."

Sauer's right. I can still feel the Vector's oily, wet gaze on me. So I do the only thing I can do. Half-dragging a bewildered Caden to the platform in the center, I throw my arms on his shoulders. I giggle loudly, a flirtatious sound that sounds grating and false to my own ears, and wave my fan teasingly in front of my face. Caden's eyes widen.

"Put your arms around my waist," I hiss urgently from behind the fan. "Don't you know how to dance?"

"I thought you didn't do dancing."

"I don't, but we have company, and I need it to not consider us a threat."

"Happy to oblige." Caden's hands slip around my waist to the small of my back, pulling me close. He has that smile on his lips again . . . the one that makes me breathless. He raises an eyebrow.

"Oh, get over it," I snap, watching as his smile turns into a full-fledged knowing grin. "Really, Cade? We're on a mission, remember?"

"I know, but we're dancing, so let's at least try to enjoy it."

"Why do you do that?" I ask. "Play around when you're supposed to be serious?"

"Because life's too short. Even if one of those guys"—he gestures to the Vector watching us— "wants to kill me, I'd rather die with a smile in my heart. Life is for the living, and death is for the dead."

That shuts me up.

We make a few showy turns, not realizing that others on the dance floor have given us a wide berth. Apparently, hard-core martial arts and weapons training give a person an edge in the dancing arena. I feel as if there's wind beneath my soles, and although I know that most of it is probably due to Caden's expert partnering, I have no trouble keeping up.

"You're a good dancer," I tell him.

"Fencing," he says. "Half dancing, half fighting. Oh, and Shae made me take ballroom. Don't laugh," he says at my incredulous expression, twirling me around him. "It was either ballroom or singing, and since I can't hold a tune, well, I didn't have much choice."

"Did she say why?" I ask, mirth in my eyes.

He shrugs. "Something to do with being well-rounded. Honestly, I was seven at the time, so it was just something interesting to do. All old-school, too, like waltzes and the fox-trot." As if to demonstrate his point, Caden twirls us into several complicated loops, my toes barely grazing the floor.

"You do it very well," I say.

Caden's grin is wicked as he spins me outward and pulls me back toward him so quickly that my body snaps into his like a rubber band. "Constantly surprising you, aren't I?"

I am breathless.

Being this close to him in front of so many people is sweet torture, flashes of two days prior tormenting me. His dancing is as masterful as his . . . kissing. I realize that I'm staring at his finely shaped lips and drop my eyes hastily.

"I want to, too," he whispers in my ear, lowering me into a graceful dip.

"Want to what?"

"Kiss you right now."

I almost lose my grasp on his shoulders, but Caden slips his free hand around my back and brings me back up. My cheeks are flaming and my heart is bursting. The music stops and Caden bows with a flourish to the loud sound of cheering. I sink into a dazed half curtsy, and we move off the dance floor.

"The Vector's gone," Caden says, handing me a thin, fluted glass of something misty.

"What?" Again, he has caught me unawares. I flush dully. I'm still thinking of him kissing me. "Oh, right."

The ice-cold vapor in the glass helps to slow the burn in my chest, bringing me back to reality and some semblance of self-control. If I don't get it together, this is going to be an extraction gone horribly wrong. I shove any thoughts of Caden and kissing out of my head.

Moving along the edge of the crowd, we walk to the stone terrace that branches off into the castle's lush rose garden. I don't know why I never noticed it before: so many people without water in Neospes, and here it's indulgently wasted on roses. My time in the Otherworld has changed me, made me appreciate the little that we do have. We walk casually into the garden.

"Anyone see us?" I ask.

"No," Caden says. "And even if they did, they'll just think we came in here to finish what we started out there on the dance floor."

"You're disgusting," I say, but my cells are firing at the very thought.

Gritting my teeth and ignoring Caden, I locate the duffel bag that Sauer has managed to stash under a bench in a shadowed corner of the gardens. The sky is a deep bluish purple, and the faded moonlight barely illuminates the small square.

"Turn the other way," I say primly to Caden, who of course grins even more widely but complies. Stripping off the offending white gown, I pull on the black Vector suit I retrieved from my house. I don't link the neck connector to my nervous system just yet. Instead, I clip some weapons onto the suit's belt and throw my star-shaped sheath over my shoulder to fasten it over my suit, flush against my back. My ninjata blades scissor into the bottom of it, and the long sword Shae gave me slides in down the middle from the top. Finally, my pack goes over everything.

"Okay, your turn," I say to Caden. "I'll keep watch."

"You can watch."

"You're so annoying. I said *keep* watch. Just hurry up!"

But Caden is already slipping off his shirt just as I'm finishing my last words, and my breath slams against my lips. Every curve is as chiseled as I remembered and looks even better in the moonlight. I drag my eyes away and stare at a point on the castle wall so hard that my eyes ache. He's a distraction . . . and one that could get us killed—get me killed.

I slow my mind and focus on the task at hand, each breath hardening my resolve. Caden fades into the background as my body readies itself for action, my brain sharp and thoughts fluid. An icy sensation slips through my veins, and for the first time I recognize it for what it is—the android side of me, readying itself for battle, too.

"Time to go," I say, my voice rigid. "You good?"

"Yes."

It's as if Caden, too, has flicked a switch inside of him. Now the teasing smile is gone. In its place is a look of grim determination. He's also dressed in black gear similar to Aurela's and has stuffed the duffel out of sight. I pinch the collar of the suit against my skin and feel a small jolt as the suit powers up.

"Radio silence," I say to Sauer, pressing my earpiece. "On my mark."

"Clear."

And Sauer is gone.

Guards are patrolling, but security doesn't seem any tighter than usual. Like shadows, we cross the rest of the garden, keeping ourselves pressed against the bushes until we reach the far wall. There's a seldom-used passage in the back. All of the servants will be on full duty tonight, so we shouldn't encounter anyone.

Caden and I split up, approaching the entrance from opposite sides. There's a guard to the right of Caden. He takes the guard out effortlessly with two jabs to the temple. We've all agreed to minimal casualties, so the guard is only unconscious.

The crumbling stone staircase is narrow and smells musty with disuse, but we're still careful not to step on anything that could draw unwanted attention to us. Noises and voices filter through as we pass a part of the kitchen, continuing upward until I've counted four floors and stopping at the back of a heavy wooden slab.

"Where exactly are we?" Caden asks softly.

"East wing, fourth floor. It's the library."

"How do you know for sure that no one's on the other side of this door?"

"Cale and I used to sneak out without anyone knowing using this passage," I whisper to him. "I don't think anyone knows that it exists anymore. Come on."

The slab cracks open, and as expected, there's no one in the room. We slip out and the other side of the door—an actual bookcase—slides back into place with a low click.

"This way," I say.

Aurela was right that everyone would be outside during the ball. We haven't encountered a single person, not even a guard. As soon as the thought crosses my mind, a shiver flutters across my neck. *Why* aren't there any guards? Where is everyone?

Signaling to Caden to stop, I creep around a tall pillar and peer down into a section of the hall on the floor below. Not a body in sight.

"Something's wrong," I whisper. "Something's not right. We have to find Cale now."

Moving with urgent purpose toward the west wing with Caden close behind, I slip into Cale's old room. I'm unprepared for the onslaught of memories, especially of the last day I saw Cale . . . sick and weak. He begged me to find Caden so that I could save him.

"Cale?"

"Riven, no," Caden warns in a low voice behind me, but I'm already moving toward the canopied bed. Someone is sitting behind the curtains—I can just see his outline.

"Cale? Is that you?"

The figure turns and moves into the light. "No, but it is good to see you again, General." It's the Vector commander, the one with the terrible voice. "Your father said you had returned."

"My father?" I blurt out.

"Of course," the Vector said. "Your mother told him."

"You lie!" I spit, but then compose myself in the next breath. "My mother is dead. If you had your facts correct, you'd know that." The Vector stands, and I hear Caden's short hiss of indrawn breath behind me. I forgot how big the giant was, but I ignore the thrum of panic in my abdomen. "Where's Cale? Where's the *Lord King*?"

"Indisposed."

"What did Murek do with him?" But even as I ask the question, I know I'm not going to get any answers. That thing is there solely for one purpose—for me. I shift into a battle stance, but the creature just watches me, its milky gaze fluttering to land on something just beyond my shoulder. In the next instant, I realize that I'm dead wrong.

That thing is there for Caden.

"Looks like they fixed you up good after the last time we met," I taunt, knowing it won't elicit any kind of response. It's what makes them the perfect killing machines—they don't feel; they just obey. "There won't be much left of you this time; that I can promise you."

My ninjatas are in my hand and I'm springing toward the Vector with lethal precision before the last word leaves my lips. It meets me with a swift sidestep and an elbow to the back of the head that has me reeling. It moves fast, faster than the last time I'd seen it. I'm operating on old data—this thing has been recalibrated.

Caden circles around the back to jab with his sword, but the Vector deflects the strike easily with its armored forearm. We attack it full-on from either side, slashing and weaving between offensive and defensive moves, but despite the double attack, we don't land any lethal blows. Frowning, I see that the Vector has been programmed to protect its vulnerable spots . . . or maybe it had somehow *learned* our tactics from our last fight.

As if reading my mind, the thing speaks. "Let me have the boy."

"The boy's right here if you want him," Caden says defiantly, and I shoot him a glare. This is no time to be flippant. We could be stuck here in a never-ending fight with this thing preempting our every move while Cale inches closer to dying. The insidious way the Vector said "indisposed" makes my skin crawl.

We need backup.

"Reptile," I say urgently touching my ear. "Reptile!"

But there's no response. We're on our own.

Without wasting time, I tuck my body into a spin crouch, slashing at the Vector's sides. I connect, but the damage once more is just minor. The giant dances away, light on its feet. Its face slashes open in a grimace, baring broken, stained teeth. I can only imagine it's some kind of macabre grin. It's toying with us.

"Don't make this harder than you have to, General. You don't have a choice."

"What's it doing?" Caden mouths, as confused as I am by the Vector's cavalier attitude toward us. "Why isn't it attacking?"

"I don't know. Orders. I think it's waiting."

I don't bother to hide what I'm saying. We're probably already surrounded. Pressing a button on my arm, I engage the suit's internal armor. Time to piss the big brute off while we still have a fighting chance. Caden and I attack simultaneously, slamming into the Vector from both sides. It only has two arms and we have four between us. Caden bears the brunt of the defense—slamming into the side of a bedpost like he's fluff—but it gives me the opening I need.

Propelling my body toward the creature, I leap, my foot pressing off of the Vector's thigh, and I twist my torso in midair, slamming my blades forward. A row of spikes on the outside of my leg rips into its arms just as my ninjata blade sinks itself hilt-deep into the back of the Vector's thick neck. I wrench with all my might, ripping upward through the corded muscle. It grunts loudly, trying to shrug me off, but I'm hanging on to the hilt protruding from its neck with everything I have left.

My second blade, as sharp as it is, won't penetrate the Vector's uniform in armor mode. Instead, I swipe at its arms as they claw at me, trying to get me off its back. My strike is true as three of the creature's fingers fall like stones to the floor. Blue fluid sprays me in the face.

I spare a glance to Caden, who is still lying on the floor. He's alive but dazed from the blow. He won't survive another hit like that, even if the Vector wants to keep him alive. Time to end this. Swinging my legs up, I literally crawl up the Vector's back and throw myself around and over its neck so that my thighs are straddling its head.

And then I twist, throwing us both to the ground and hearing the sick crunch of bone as its neck dislocates. My attack won't kill it. It will only disorient it for a minute, if that. I land hard on my shoulder and the pain rockets through my bones, but I lurch to my knees, conscious not to waste the precious little advantage I have. The nanobes do what they're supposed to, assuaging the painful areas immediately and repairing any internal damage, so only seconds pass before I grab Shae's sword and swing it with both hands . . . right at its head.

Our eyes meet in the nanosecond it takes for its android brain to recognize its imminent destruction. The Vector's hands still crunch into my sides and grasp at my neck. But it's already over—the blade slides through tendons and wiring like they're nothing but paper. Its body crashes to the ground.

"Try fixing that, asshole," I growl.

Very carefully, I remove the ninjata that was spiked into its neck and jam it into the base of its cerebral cortex, where any thought processing function would likely be. Cutting open a flap of skin and ignoring the blue foul-smelling fluid oozing out, I dig my fingers in until I find the small square.

"Riven . . ." Caden's voice is thready but I don't turn around until I've destroyed the chip. "Riven!" His voice is more insistent.

"What?" I snap in irritation, spinning around and freezing.

A dozen or more Vectors line the far perimeter of the room. They stand—unmoving—in a silent, deadly line. I glance back at the open balcony doors. Even if I grab Caden and escape, it's a four-story drop to the bottom, and there's no way I can take them all on my own, even if I am a super advanced hybrid humanoid.

The devil we do and the devil we don't—we're dead if we don't do *something.*

I inch my way slowly toward Caden, who's only a couple of feet away. The Vectors watch me carefully but don't take any action. Unlike the commander I just pulverized, as soldiers, they're operating on direct orders only. I hope.

"You okay?"

"Yeah, feel like I got hit with a sledgehammer," Caden whispers back, rubbing his head. The side of his face is covered in blood, but it looks like it's only from a long cut at his temple instead of a cracked skull.

"You did," I say with a grimace. "Look, we have no chance against all of them, and it looks like they want to keep us here, not attack us. So we're going to make a run for those doors. We need to find Sauer."

"Riv, it's a long way down."

"Do you trust me?"

His eyes are wide. "Yes."

"Good. Now hold on to me and don't let go!"

And then we run like hell for the doors. The noise behind us is sudden and thunderous, but I don't look back. As I'm running, I unwind a length of black cord that's hooked to my belt. The end of the cord opens into a metal three-pronged device, and I throw it just before flinging myself over the balustrade and grabbing Caden with one hand.

We're free falling in space for an eternity before the rope snaps tight and we swing to the parapet that's just below us. Releasing the rope, we roll to the ground, unhurt. My blood feels hot, but I'm energized with adrenaline, my heart pounding in my ears.

"Move," I yell to Caden. "There's an entrance on the far side."

Outside, the noise is deafening with music and shouting and singing below us. We run the length of the parapet, the same one I looked up to when we went through the security checkpoint. The courtyard is packed with people, but no one's looking up at us. Half of it is shrouded in shadow, and the other is brightly lit from the castle floodlights.

I still can't shake the feeling that I've missed something . . . that despite our escape, we're somehow being *herded*.

The Vectors, including the commander, were prepared for us in advance, which explains why we aren't being treated as trespassers and why they aren't attacking us. Someone in control wants us alive. Murek? My father?

"Hey!" a voice shouts from behind us. It's Loren, running as if her life depended on it. She doesn't slow down until she reaches Caden, who's a couple feet behind me, closest to her.

"Where's Sauer?" I yell.

The smile that breaks across her face is full of malice as she slams an electro-rod into Caden's side. His eyes widen and I lurch forward instinctively, but I'm too late as her thumb hovers over a button on the rod.

"Yes, you know what that is, and it's not set to stun. Weapons down, *General*." My hands lower, releasing the ninjatas to the ground.

"Loren, what're you doing? We're on the same side," Caden gasps weakly.

"I was never on your side," Loren laughs, spit flying from her mouth. "The minute I found out who Aurela's daughter was, I knew I'd do anything to take her down. It was fate that you returned." Her eyes are manic, staring at me. "You destroyed my family, as I will destroy yours."

"Caden has nothing to do with that," I say softly. "That's between you and me."

Her laugh is hollow, but something in it makes the hairs on the back of my neck stand at nervous attention. "He has everything to do with it."

I whip around at the sound of another familiar voice behind me. "All in good time, Loren, all in good time."

Murek.

He isn't alone. A squadron of Vectors and armed guards is fanned out behind him. We are hosed. I swing back to Loren. My instincts were correct about her, but it went far deeper than I ever thought. I thought she'd want to get even and it would come to blows at some point, but I never suspected that she was some kind of spy for Murek.

"Aurela *trusted* you."

Another satisfied smile. "She did. I wanted her to. I was going to bring her down . . . all of it, her plans to infiltrate the palace. She deserves to die just as my brother died. And then you came back, and things couldn't get any sweeter. Two for the price of one."

I need to antagonize her, to get her to drop Caden. "What do you get out of this? Vengeance? Your brother's still dead." Her eyes flash with anger, but I continue to push forward, sick inside at the vitriol spilling from my lips. "You couldn't save him then, and you can't save him now, because you're weak."

With a cry of fury, Loren dives toward me, but I'm ready for her attack, sidestepping swiftly and swinging my elbow up and outward into the back of her head. She stumbles to the ground, and I'm already moving toward Caden. Together, we back away from Murek.

"Thank you," he says nastily. "She was a loose end that needed tying up."

"But she's still alive!" Caden blurts out.

"She isn't now," Murek says, watching as one of the Vectors electrocutes her with the butt of his weapon, the smell of singed flesh hot in the air. Loren's body arches upward twice and collapses. Caden's eyes are wide with horror. "There isn't a way out, General. You know that. Surrender, and you'll live." Murek's voice is low and compelling and as slick as I remembered. "We have Commander Sauer. We have your mother. It's over. Hand over the boy."

"I can't do that," I say.

"Then we have no choice."

"Enough," a soft voice says from behind us. Caden stiffens as I turn around in slow motion, disbelieving. My heart beats with the impossible hope that he is somehow still alive and that my mind isn't playing tricks on me. He was sick and near death when I'd left.

But it is he, and he looks better than before. Emotion clogs every part of me. Strong, healthy . . . and dressed in exhibition clothing.

Cale, the Lord King of Neospes.

# 25

# SIBLING OF FLESH AND BONE

"THAT WAS YOU in the ring?" I demand through clenched teeth, recalling the Vectors who stood at stiff attention during the exhibition fight. I'm kicking myself—I should have recognized Cale's fluid style immediately. But in the grand scheme of things, it doesn't matter. There's nothing I could have done differently.

"I'm surprised you couldn't tell," Cale says.

"Are you better? Why didn't you send word? I would have come back."

I'm ranting now, with Cale watching me from the corner of his private salon. Caden stands in silence by the window, his glance flitting from us to the two guards standing on either side of the door. For all intents and purposes we haven't been restrained or disarmed, and I still have my weapons. If push comes to shove, I can get both Caden and Cale out of there without breaking a sweat. But I'm too angry to consider alternatives. I continue my tirade.

"Do you have any idea what I've been through? I thought you were dead and Murek was in control."

"Riven," Cale begins gently. "He is. It's the only reason I'm not dead yet."

"What? I don't get it." I'm stunned. "But you're alive, Cale. You're strong again. How could you let someone like him take control?" Cale remains quiet, his eyes more distant than I've ever seen them. He hasn't even given Caden more than a cursory look after we were ushered into his private room. In fact, he's doing his damnedest not to pay him any attention at all, which is odd, considering that they are mirror images of each other. Wouldn't he be curious? Frowning, I remember what Loren was saying.

"Did you know about Aurela? That my *mother* was alive?"

"And that she was planning some kind of coup?" I flinch at the acerbity in his voice. "Of course I did. It's my job to know about those who want to usurp me."

"Usurp?"

He ignores my outburst and leans back in his chair. His manner is indolent, scratching against my rattled senses like nettles. "That's why I sent Loren in. When she first approached our soldiers in the Outers, I realized it was my chance to find out exactly what your mother was planning. And then when you came back with *him,* no less, it was perfect."

A cold feeling makes its way through me. "So did you know she was alive before you sent me to the Otherworld?"

He doesn't answer, but I see the truth in his eyes. "You were the only one, Riven. The only one who could find him and bring him back." Only then do Cale's eyes drift to Caden—his exact likeness—and remain there, cold and unflinching. "He has something of mine. Something that my mother stole, and I need it back."

"What?" Caden bursts out from behind us. "I don't have anything of yours. I didn't even know about you or any of this"—he says gesturing into the air with his hands—"until a few weeks ago!"

I'm shaking my head slowly as understanding filters through my brain. "You lied to me?" Cale shrugs, opening his hands wide, palms upward. "You're not really dying, are you?"

"Not exactly. Your father fixed me, gave me electronic lungs. But I needed you to believe that I was dying so you'd go." He cocks his head to one side like a bird, his gaze speculating, switching between Caden and myself. Calculating. "Did they tell you what you are?" Cale says slyly to Caden.

Caden looks to me, confused. "But Aurela said . . ."

"Let me guess," Cale says, ridicule tainting his words, "They said that you're the heir, and I'm the by-product? Well, you're wrong. I'm the only heir. Give me the chip, *brother*."

"Chip? What chip?" Caden says, but I can hardly hear him. I completely forgot about the chip I pocketed from Caden in the Outers. That and the blue signet ring.

"Come now, don't play dumb. She would have given it to you—it's the only way for you to prove who either of you are. By the way, my condolences; I heard that she died, quite painfully as it were. It would have been something to see, I'm sure."

"Cale!" I've never seen this cruel side of him, and every instinct in me is reacting to it. Caden's eyes are stormy, his fingers clenching into fists at his sides at Cale's ugly, provoking taunts.

Aurela was right. Cale *isn't* who I thought he was. He's changed. How could I have not seen the malevolence eating away at him earlier? Have I been so blind to Murek's evil influence? Or have I changed after my time in the Otherworld . . . after my time with Shae and Caden?

"I don't have it," Caden grits out. "I lost it in the Outers."

"He doesn't have it, Cale," I say, stepping forward. Out of the corner of my eyes, I see the guards' hands drop to their weapons. I raise an eyebrow to Cale, who shoots me a look in return that clearly says his security comes first. "I have it," I say. I feel Caden's panicked glance, but I can't even look at him. I need to be the general, not the girlfriend. "What's so important about it?" I toss back at Cale.

I can see the wheels in Cale's head turning, as if he's trying to figure out how much he can tell me. For my part, I've never underestimated anyone more. "Like hell you don't know, Riven. That chip is a record of my birth. It does not belong to him," he says, jerking his head toward Caden.

"And you need it to prove that you're the rightful king." And now I have something he wants desperately. "Or the people will always question your right, especially if they know Caden has returned."

"Yes, your mother took care of that when she and her rebels sowed the seeds of dissent in Neospes." Cale is scowling now, but the dark expression vanishes from his face in seconds, replaced instead by something more conciliatory. "Riv," he says, placating. "You *know* me. You know who I am, don't you? Don't you trust me anymore? Can't you see they're lying?"

"I don't know who to trust, Cale," I answer honestly. "Everyone has lied, even you. The only one who hasn't lied to me is Caden. I don't know what's truth or not."

"I knew you'd take his side," Cale sneers, his face twisted in an ugly grimace. "He told me, you know, your father. About what you were doing in his house. With *him*." I feel myself color, heat blooming in my cheeks, followed by horror that my father knew I was there, somehow saw what Caden and I did. I should have known that he'd have cameras in the house. He is far more paranoid than he used to be. I kick myself mentally for the tenth time for being so foolish and reckless.

My eyes narrow. "Where is he?"

"Taking care of some personal business at the lab," Cale responds in a sly tone. "I am sure it will be a very sweet family reunion, don't you think? Now give me what I want, Riven, or I will take away what you want." He jerks his head in Caden's direction, nodding to the guards, who step forward obediently to restrain him.

My heart slides downhill at the betrayal. I've been such a fool.

"So Murek isn't after the throne?" I ask in a soft voice. Cale smiles widely, shaking his head. "He's your tool," I breathe. "You use him just like you used me."

"Well," Cale murmurs conversationally so only I can hear him. "Father and I had different ideas about the monarchy. I thought he was far too soft with the people. When my lungs started failing, he started asking questions. Pointed questions. I think in the end, he knew that I wasn't his real son." He spreads his hands wide. "So I took care of him."

"You murdered your own father?"

"Technically, my uncle did it, but yes, it was at my behest." His eyes are cold and dead like the monster he had become. "Don't worry, the Reptiles took care of him quickly, I heard."

"You're insane," I whisper.

"Ah, the dreaded insanity," Cale mocks. "That's another thing I need your friend for. As brilliant as your father is, it's not like he can create a whole new perfect brain for me."

Appalled, I can only stare at him. "What does he get out of helping you?"

"Why, you, of course." Cale rolls his eyes skyward. "Must be some skewed father-daughter thing."

Despite his sordid insinuation, I breathe a sigh of relief. Cale doesn't know about me . . . about what my father had created. And of course my father didn't say anything, because he had something to hide . . . something he knew that others—like Cale or Murek—would desperately want.

Me.

A part of me prays that Aurela circumvented whatever confrontation awaited them, but I know it's a hope beyond hope. If he knew she was coming, he would have been prepared with a thousand Vectors. She's probably already dead. The only tangible thing left to negotiate is Caden's safety.

"Cale, if I give you the chip," I begin, "will you promise to let Caden return unharmed to the Otherworld?"

"No!" Caden hisses, wrenching against the unbreakable grip of the Vectors.

"Yes," I say. "You belong there. You never belonged here."

"Riven, I have nothing to go back to. I belong with y—" He falters. "Here."

Loud clapping interrupts our exchange. "Isn't that so touching? The captive fell in love with the captor." Cale turns to me. "You've done your job well, General. So yes, you have my word that he will be allowed to leave unharmed as soon as I have the chip."

Saccharine treachery drenches his words. If he can murder his own father without a second thought, he will never let Caden go once he gets his hands on the only proof of any claim to the throne. We're at an impasse—Cale staring at me with persuasive eyes and Caden staring at me with fury in his.

"I'll tell you where the chip is right now if you let him go."

"No, Riven!" Caden shouts, but I ignore him. "Don't do this. Don't let him do this." My heart feels like it's splintering inside my body but I know it's the only way. It's the only way for me to keep Caden safe from Cale's insanity.

*I'm so sorry, Cade.*

"So where is it?" Cale snaps, waving his arm impatiently.

I deflect his question with one of my own. There's no way I can give him the chip here in the castle with us under Vector arrest. Neither Caden nor I would have a chance. "What happened to you, Cale? Things used to be different. You believed in Neospes and rebuilding what your ancestors started."

A hollow laugh. "Didn't you get the memo? They aren't really *my* ancestors. I'm merely a by-product of *him*." Cale's hands are shaking with rage as he points to Caden. "That doesn't mean that I'm any less than he is, but the sad truth is, everyone will think that way. As soon as I understood what I was, I knew that I had to get rid of him for good." His face is tortured, and my chest fills with an unfamiliar ache. He is my best friend—one for whom I'd sworn a blood oath to protect. "Do you know," he continues bitterly, "my father tried to banish me? Murek was the one who told me, who *saved* me. So my father had to die. It was him or me."

"Cale, you can't trust Murek. He's a snake. He's always been a snake. You know that. You know what he's planning with the Vectors and the Otherworld?"

A slow, cunning smile rolls over Cale's face. "Of course I do. It was my idea."

"What?"

"I will be greater than any king of Neospes, and when we take the resources from the Otherworld, I will rule them, too."

"Listen to yourself, Cale. This is madness. The Guardians will never stand for it. You know what happened before, when people jumped back and forth centuries ago. We were decimated by disease. Our very existence was nearly derailed." I'm almost screaming now. "There's a reason the anti-eversion laws are in place . . . a reason the *Guardians* exist."

"The Guardians?" he mocks me, laughing cruelly. "What Guardians? What do you think the Vectors have been doing all this time? Surely you didn't think they were only looking for either of you?"

"What have you done, Cale?" I say. I can't keep the horror from my voice as I remember what Aurela said about Guardians randomly dying. "The Guardians are neutral. Untouchable."

"By whose authority? The Faction?" Cale scoffs venomously. "Some obscure group of *universe* overseers from a thousand years ago?" His face is contorted with malice. "They're just humans whom the Vectors have killed with no penalty whatsoever. The Faction or whatever they're called is a made-up entity. *I'm* the king. I call the shots."

His face is manic, and it's clear Cale has completely lost his mind. His thirst for power has consumed him. But even though I know it will be of no use, I still try one more time. "Cale, what you are doesn't define you. It's *who* you are inside, who you make of yourself. Trust me, I know." I want to tell him the truth about me, but I know that I can't. "Being the master of two universes won't make you happy. It won't make you whole or feel any less broken. You are what you are. The choices you make are the things that define you, and this *isn't* you. I know you."

"You know a ghost." Cale's jaw clenches and his eyes darken to a stormy green. "We're done here. Where's the chip?"

"I can't give it to you," I say. "I know you'll never keep your word. I could always tell when you were lying, and you are now."

"So be it," Cale says, his face hardening even more. He nods to the guards, who escort Caden through the door into the main hall. "They kill him if you so much as twitch toward me, Riven," he warns. He glares at me to follow, a twisted smile curving his lips in warning. He knows that I'm itching to take him out now that we're alone. But there's too much at stake, and with Caden's life hanging in the balance, I can't risk it. I grit my teeth and follow Caden through the doors.

The great hall is full of Vectors, and the chemical smell of them all is almost suffocating. Murek is standing next to a bloodied but alive Sauer, and staring at me with a self-satisfied smirk on his bulbous face. I send him a clear message of my own—if I get within an inch of him, his life will be mine. This time, I smile.

"You see," Cale whispers in my ear. "I know you just as well, Riven. I knew you would say no to me, so I have something very special planned for you." Cale walks to the throne at the end of the hall, where the two Vectors are waiting with the restrained Caden. I don't meet his eyes. I can't meet them, because I need to be strong for whatever is coming next. Murek bows respectfully as Cale takes his place on the throne.

"Lord Murek, please bring out our special guest."

I am prepared to see Aurela bound and gagged, because there's no one more important to me than Caden other than her, and for the moment, he's safe. It would be amusing if they had somehow put back together the commander I'd destroyed earlier. Folding my arms across my chest, I paste a bored expression on my face.

But nothing prepares me for what comes through those doors.

Murek walks back into the hall with a malicious, triumphant smile. At his side is a Vector, but it's not just any Vector. This Vector is slim in stature and has the face of someone I love.

Someone I loved.

Shae, my heart breathes her name. *What have they done to you?*

My stomach plummets and the world spins out from beneath my feet. I'm backing away with an outstretched arm, my other hand clapped to my mouth. My eyes are burning. As if from a dense fog, I hear Sauer's pained shriek. I feel wetness on my cheeks—everything hurts, and I'm choking.

"No," I gasp.

"Yes," Cale shouts, clapping.

My sister is a Vector.

"Come on, Riven; let's see those infamous skills of yours," Cale crows.

"You are a monster. You'll never rule Neospes. I will kill you first. I'll kill you all." I'm screaming as I'm keening, my rage and pain making me berserk. Now I understand why he'd let me keep my weapons. I can hardly see through the cloud of fury that's flaying me, but somehow my eyes meet Caden's. Although his pain is as great as mine, maybe even greater, there's something else there . . . a silent glance that slices through the haze in my brain.

Do what you must.

And everything disappears—all the anger, the hurt, the aching sadness—all of it, and it's just Caden anchoring me to him. Caden is my past, my present, and my future. He is my world. He's the only whole thing in all of this broken madness, reminding me of everything that's true . . . everything that is real.

My sister died in the Otherworld. I grieved. I mourned her. This is not my sister.

Cale and my father have made a mockery of what she was. They'll pay for that, too. They all will. I leave the war paint of tears on my face—they're for her.

Grimly, I turn to face my opponent, ignoring the long dark-blonde braids and the curve of her cheekbones. Instead, I focus on the milky eyes that are nothing like her vibrant full-of-life ones. Her arms are long and slender, no longer full of protection and caring. They wield a deadly staff with double-edged blades at both ends.

"Hello, Riven," it says in Shae's voice.

Reeling, I don't see the first blow coming until the last second, and I duck, but the edge of the blade clips my temple and forehead, just missing my eye. Blood splatters along the floor following the arc of the staff flying upward, and drips down my neck.

She's a talking Vector, like the commander earlier, nothing more.

"Miss me?"

This is not my sister.

Gritting my teeth, I pull out the sword—the Artok sword my real sister had made for me—from its sheath, swinging it upward just in time to meet the blow of the staff coming toward me. The force of it ricochets up my arms. She's strong . . . stronger now. I have to tell myself again that this is not Shae. It's a Vector . . . a tough Vector that has her face and her voice, but one that will never fight with her heart, or her skill.

So we dance.

Most of my moves are defensive. I'm watching her movements, learning what's been programmed. We circle each other, the violent sound of steel clashing echoing in the huge hall. We could be exhibition sparring in the training field. I need to change the game, to get her to slip up. I step in, ducking under one of her strikes, my foot colliding with her chest so hard that she staggers backward, but it doesn't stop her. Advancing, I whip the sword up to catch her across the chest, but her Vector suit is in armor mode and deflects the strike harmlessly. She lunges toward me as I spin and crouch, throwing my leg out to catch her in the back of her knee. She stumbles but rights herself with the inhuman grace only a Vector has. She smiles, cocking her head to one side.

"You left me to die," she says. "You didn't even try to fight. You wanted me to die."

Her words are worse than her blows. Guilt chokes me.

I left my sister to die.

Grinning, she comes at me again, swinging that staff of hers in a circular motion like a fan. I weave and bob, but I can feel the wind of the blades whipping far too close to my face. I'm disoriented, disabled by her barbed taunts. At the last second, she stops, the weapon in one hand, her dead eyes holding mine.

"You killed me," she whispers, and then twists to kick me in the ribs. Payback. The sick crunch of bone snaps wetly and I double over, only to feel the flat of her weapon crashing against the back of my head.

I drop like a sack of stones, pain rocketing through my body. The sword skids across the room. Everything is swimming through my blurred vision as I crawl to my knees. It feels like I'm moving through quicksand, and the booted foot comes far too quickly, smashing me in the side of the face. Color explodes like fireworks inside my eyelids, and blood fills my mouth as my entire body flips up and over from the force of her kick.

I cough, spluttering blood through loose teeth.

Cacophonic laughter echoes around me. It's Murek, his face lit up with glee. Cale is sitting on the edge of his throne, something hungry in his expression—his desire to punish me is more than personal. All eyes are on us, even the rest of the dead Vectors standing silently around the hall's perimeter, but the only ones I care about are fixed on me. I can feel Caden's strength, willing me to get up.

I can't.

*You can*, his eyes say.

I shake my head. She's too fast, faster than any Vector I've ever fought. She's invulnerable.

You're faster than any human.

It feels like the words are Caden's words, but I know the conversation is entirely in my head. Still, he's right or I'm right. I'm faster than any human. I'm like them, only better, a reverse-engineered *Reptile*.

I turn over, spitting a mouthful of blood to the floor and pulling my arm underneath me. The suit's armor is already on, but I enter a sequence on the wrist-pad engaging synchronous mode. The suit will attune to me, and I with it.

I'll fight fire with fire.

Somersaulting to my feet, I feel myself powering up, the nanobes inside of me responding to the energy from the suit. I am human. The smile that opens across my face is the Vector's only warning before I launch myself toward her, running at full speed and drawing my ninjatas from the harness.

One I toss in Cale's direction, and I see the momentary shock on his face. But it's not meant for him. I don't even turn around in response to the satisfied thud of steel into flesh or the thump of Murek's dead body on the ground. Instead, I'm leaping, launching myself like a missile to the abomination in front of me.

Her staff goes flying and we both fall to the ground, rolling. The smell of her and formaldehyde fill my nose as I straddle her chest. This time I stare into the milky blue eyes.

"You are *not* my sister," I hiss, and slam the remaining ninjata up through her chin into her head. Blue fluid spurts out.

Her leg swings up and over my neck, thrusting me forward, but I jump easily to my feet. So does she, her staff back in hand. The blade is still stuck in her neck, the hilt of it protruding outward. She starts the spinning trick again, but this time I stand my ground. The blade whips so close to my hair that I see wisps of it falling to the ground. I bare my teeth in a grin.

"No," I say, grasping the staff in the middle and stopping it mid-motion, my gloved fingers closing on hers. The armored suit is a fluid extension of me, unbendable and unyielding. The Vector tries to pull it away, but now I am as strong—or stronger even—than she is. I move closer, looking deep into the Vector's eyes that once belonged to my sister, because I know he's watching remotely.

"I'm coming for you, Father."

And then I lean back and kick the hilt of the ninjata sideways so that it rips across the Vector's spinal column and clatters to the floor in a spray of blue. There's dead silence in the hall for an instant as the Vector falls to the ground. Out of the corner of my eye, I see Caden flip up and over, twisting the arms of his captors. He slams their heads together, and they crumple to the ground. Grabbing the wounded Sauer and tossing him over his shoulder, he darts toward me in the center of the room.

"Restrain the prisoners!" Cale screams to the Vectors surrounding us, and suddenly pandemonium erupts as we're rushed on all sides.

There's no way in hell we can win. But we won't go down without a fight. I'm going to take as many of them as I can with me. I feel Caden's fingers slip into mine, and I squeeze. We lock eyes, and I know that we're in this together. Sauer stands weakly next to us, the crossbow in his hand already firing into the oncoming horde. With a deep breath, I raise the staff I took off Vector Shae and prepare to do battle.

But then the unexpected happens.

Every single one of the Vectors stops in its tracks, their arms and weapons falling to their sides, eyes going blank and dull. The remaining human guards back away in confusion. There's no way they will take us on without the Vectors.

"What happened?" Caden asks, his voice loud in the unnatural silence. Even Cale is staring at us in the middle of an unmoving mob with his jaw on the floor.

"Aurela," I breathe. "She's done it. She's deactivated them."

Only then do I notice the row of red-clad masked fighters surrounding Cale's throne. Where did they come from? Who are they? As if in response, the doors to the great hall open, and a woman walks in, followed by more of the same ominously garbed warriors. I recognize her immediately, and this time, my jaw drops to the floor.

Era Taylor.

# 26

# LONG LIVE THE KING

"WHY IS MY physics teacher from the Otherworld in Neospes? What is she doing here?" Caden's eyes are as wide as I'm sure mine must be, so I know I'm not seeing ghosts. Era Taylor— a *Guardian*—is here in Neospes.

"Era?" I say warily. "What are you doing here?"

Her dark eyes are as piercing as I remembered. "We are the Faction."

"What?" I repeat dumbly. The Faction is here? And Mrs. Taylor is a part of it? Which means that the scarlet-clad warriors are the Faction's infamous Red Guard. "But you're a Guardian."

Era smiles a humorless smile. "A Guardian and also the leader of the Faction, an order far older than your young king standing over there."

"How dare you!" Cale shouts back. "I am the king of Neospes! What have you done with my guards?"

"He's not my king." I glance at him dispassionately and turn my attention back to Era, who is still assessing a murderous Cale with her eyes.

"You will be tried and judged for your crimes," Era says calmly to him. "Your guards must obey the Faction first and the Neospes monarchy second. At least they, if not you, still understand the chain of rule." Cale falls silent.

"Era, how did you get here?" Caden asks quietly. "We thought you were dead. Did Philip refine the serum you were working on?"

"Yes, he did," Era answers. "And I'm not dead, as you can clearly see. We tried to find you after we got separated but only discovered dead-end tracks. We found the cave later, but there was no trace of you."

"We everted," Caden gulps. "Shae died."

"I gather that, and I'm sorry for her loss. She was a great asset."

Of their own volition, my eyes fall on the nearly decapitated body of my dead sister. It wasn't her before, but it's her now. It's her body. My rage resurfaces. My father has gone too far this time, defiling her for his and Cale's own nefarious ends. How he must have loved punishing her and pretending it was me.

I walk over to where Cale is still sitting. The red ninja-clad warriors restraining him are silent, only their glittering eyes visible through their masked hoods. "You are despicable," I say. "I trusted you. How could you let him do that to Shae? You made her a monster just so that you could hurt me?"

Cale's eyes are as dead as the metal lungs in his chest. "You betrayed me."

"I did what you asked. You're the one who lied."

Cale's eyes flick to Caden. "You were mine. You betrayed me with *him*."

"I was never yours," I say. "As flawed as you are, I believed in you, and there was a time that I did love you. I would have done anything for you, and I did. I went to another universe for you . . . just so that you could find someone you wanted to kill. *You* betrayed *me*. You want to know the truth?" I lean in so that my lips are nearly touching his ear and only Cale can hear my words. "Caden is everything you are, and more. He's more of a king than you will ever be."

Rage reddens Cale's face. "Shae got what—"

"Don't!" My open palm collides with his face. "That's for my sister. I hope you get everything you deserve for what you've done. Either way, you are dead to me."

I walk back without a backward glance to Era, who nods to her guards to take Cale away. He'll be held until Era decides what his punishment will be. Caden's arm drops across my trembling shoulders, and he gathers me close. We both ignore Era's raised eyebrows.

"What happens now?" he asks her.

This time Era's smile is real. "Now the rightful Lord King of Neospes takes his place."

"What? No, I couldn't—"

"Yes, Cade," I say, pulling out of his hug. "She's right. You have to. This is what you were meant to be, why your mother risked everything for you. Why—" my voice breaks, and I glance over to where my sister's corpse is lying, "Shae protected you with her life. You were always the rightful heir."

"Why didn't my mother ever tell me who I was?" Caden's voice is small.

Era flicks her hand to two of her guards, signaling them to take Shae's body to the mortuary, and folds her arms across her chest. "I'm sure she meant to someday, but she didn't get the chance; her immune system was too weak. You survived because you were young and strong." Her gaze flits to Murek's dead body still lying near the throne with my ninjata buried in his chest. "She was right to take you away." Era's eyes have a faraway look in them. "I was young then, newly part of the Faction. When she came to me, desperate for help, I agreed to let her evert. You would both be safe there, and when the time was right, you would return. But things changed. Murek grew more cunning—he knew what Cale was, and he was the one who told the king that your mother had taken his real son, not the clone, and that you were both dead. Your father was consumed by grief and refused to recognize Cale as anything but an imposter. It began to eat away at Cale, and he turned to the only person who seemed sympathetic: Murek."

"So Murek was playing both sides?" I say, and Era nods.

"But he was still his son," Caden whispers. "I mean, he was me, wasn't he? He couldn't help what he was."

"The king didn't see it that way," Era says gently. "Royal clones are meant as a fail-safe to the line, not meant to be recognized as part of it."

"But I saw him. He was still real. He's still a person."

"One who ordered the murder of your father after I left," I remind him quietly. "He was my friend, remember? But Cale is twisted. He's not the same person I once knew. His bitterness killed him from the inside out. Clone or not, he's still broken inside."

"And Murek couldn't have planned it more perfectly—he had what he wanted nearly in his grasp. His own kingdom," Era says, walking out of the hall and indicating that we should follow her.

Caden looks to me, and I nod. It's her show now. A few of the Red Guard fall in line with us, the majority remaining behind to sequester the Vectors. Before we leave, I retrieve Shae's sword and my ninjatas, wiping them clean and re-sheathing them.

In the hallway, Era continues speaking, her voice low. "Even Cale didn't understand the complexity of Murek's cunning. He told Cale about the chip that would disprove his place as heir, and that Caden was indeed still alive. Cale's plan was to kill Caden and destroy the chip, but Murek had other plans. He wanted the chip to dethrone Cale, and he knew that Cale would send Riven." Her black eyes meet mine. "You were the only one who could hinder his plans."

"And me? Why did you leave me for the Vectors?"

Era's glance turns into a thoughtful frown. "I didn't know then that you'd turned. But Aurela vouched for you . . . her life for yours. I found it curious. I found it even more curious to learn that your father almost killed Murek for using you to find Caden."

"What do you mean?" I am careful to hold Era's stare. I don't know if she knows the truth about me, but it wouldn't surprise me. The Faction seems to have eyes and ears everywhere, based on what she's telling us about the whole Murek mastermind show.

"Murek and Cale needed your father to build an army of Vectors, so they gave him free rein to experiment and play around with unsanctioned robotics."

"So the Faction knew?" I toss back. "Why didn't you stop him?"

"It's not our duty to interfere in the politics of each universe. We protect the Guardians and maintain the separation of the two worlds," Era returns calmly. "But once we learned about their plot to bridge the worlds, then we were oath-bound to act."

"So my father basically got carte blanche to do whatever he wanted?" My voice is bitter. "Hurt whomever he wanted, take whatever he wanted, destroy whole lives."

"Your father was driven by his creations . . . by his ego." The voice comes from behind us, and I jerk around to see Aurela entering through a door.

I can't help myself; my feet are already racing toward her. She's dirty and weary and limping slightly, but her face is victorious. We embrace, her fingers grazing the oozing cut on my temple, and I search her eyes.

"Did you see him?" She nods silently. "Is he dead?" She shakes her head. For a second, I wonder why she's avoiding my questions, and then I realize that all eyes are on us, including Era's and the Red Guard. Sighing, I say, "I'm glad you found the kill switch for the Vectors. It got a little hairy in there."

Aurela squeezes my hand as we walk back toward the others, and gives Era a brief recap of what happened at the lab. Era nods in satisfaction and walks to a pair of heavy wooden doors. It's Cale's old bedchamber. We enter the room, where servants are already waiting to attend Caden.

"Time to look the part," Era says to him.

"I'll be waiting right outside, okay?" I smile reassuringly, wishing we'd gotten the chance to speak privately. His green eyes meet and hold mine. This time, he's the one reassuring me. I smile and walk outside.

Two guards station themselves inside the door, and two outside of it. Era stops to give them instructions, and I use the opportunity to speak to Aurela.

"So he's not dead?" I ask urgently.

"No," she says. "He everted at the last minute."

*"Everted?"* I gasp. "To the Otherworld?"

"I don't know."

"Did you talk to him?" I ask.

She stops to squeeze my shoulder, her eyes pained. "He's not going to let you go, Riven. He's never going to let you go." Her voice fades to a barely audible whisper. "He's lost it; he's so consumed by what you are. In his eyes, you belong to him, and he'll kill you if he can't have you." Tears are streaming down her face. "I tried to reach him, to see if some part of the man I knew was still in there, but he's gone. There's nothing in there now. He's as dead inside as the Vectors he creates."

"Then there's only one thing I can do; I have to find him first, before he finds me."

"Riven, there's something else. We need to let the Faction know about you," Aurela says. "About what you are and why he wants you so badly. They can protect you. If he gets his hands on you, who knows what he's capable of? We can't risk it."

I know that she's right, even though a part of me wants to hunt him down in silence on my own terms, but I also know that that's my ego talking. I still want to be the one to punish him, but I also know now more than ever that I cannot underestimate him. He is devious and brilliant . . . and utterly insane.

Era joins us, and I excuse myself, nodding to my mother to do what she has to do. Outside, the revelry is loud. I can't imagine that they have any clue as to what has happened inside the castle—that a false king has been replaced by the true heir, that people have died, that Neospes is finally about to enter a new phase . . . one not undermined by a king with his own selfish interests.

I hope that Caden will be a good king and that he'll be a true leader to our people. I have no doubt that he will be. After all, he is forgiving to a fault. He is smart and will take the time to listen and learn. Although he has been shaped in the Other-world, his heart is here. He is everything that is the best of both worlds. I find myself smiling, watching all of the joyful faces below me. His mother would have been proud of what her son had become.

"Hey," Caden's voice is soft.

I turn slowly, my eyes widening, butterflies causing havoc in the pit of my stomach. It's still not a feeling that I'm comfortable with . . . that any one person could make me feel so shattered and whole at the same time. Caden looks magnificent in monarch purple and black, his long overcoat trimmed in sable. His hair has been combed back off his face, and his eyes are a sparkling green. He looks beautiful, perfect.

I find my voice. "You clean up good."

"Thanks."

"You look like a prince."

"I feel like a weirdo," Caden says with a grin. "I mean, have you *seen* this cape?"

I grin back. "Sadie would definitely approve." The look in Caden's eyes drives any other words about Sadie from my mouth.

"Do *you* approve?"

"Yes," I say. "I definitely approve. You belong here, Cade. This is where you were meant to be; this is who you are."

"I thought you wanted me to go back to my world," Caden says, stepping forward to brush a strand of hair out of my face.

His light touch makes the butterflies take flight, and unconsciously, I lean into his caress. "At the time, it was the only place where you would have been safe from Cale. But everything worked out, didn't it?"

"Riven," Caden says, moving to stand directly in front of me, both his hands pressed to the sides of my face. "None of this could have happened without you, you know that, right? I mean, you're the reason I'm here and alive. You're the reason I even know who I am and what I'm meant to do." Caden pauses, staring out at the throng of people below us. "The only reason I don't feel like I don't belong here is because of you. You made me fall in love with Neospes just like I've fallen—"

"Cade," I interrupt him, blushing furiously. "You always had Neospes in your heart. It's in your blood."

"Will you let me finish?" he says, bending his head to graze my lips so softly that it's barely a touch, but it silences me effectively.

"You know what happened the last time," I breathe, my eyes fluttering closed, and tilt my face up to his, pressing my lips against his mouth. His hands slide into the hair at the nape of my neck, and he deepens the kiss, opening his mouth against mine. My fingers curl into the fur of his collar, pulling him closer. I never want to let him go.

That kiss says everything that Caden wants to say and more, and I kiss him back, leaving him with no doubt of my own feelings. Because now, more than ever, he needs to know how much I do love him, especially with what I know I have to do.

The loud sound of cheering breaks us apart, and we glance down to see the crowd below staring up at the parapet with their hands in the air.

"Go do your thing, Cade," I say, drawing away from the edge of the stone balustrade. "I believe in you. And I will always be here." I clutch my fist to my heart, the tears burning a pathway behind my eyelids and down my cheeks.

"Wait, why are you crying?" he says.

"Because I love you, and I'm so proud of you. Now go, address your people," I say with a laugh, swiping my face with the back of my hand. "And stop making me say such reckless *feeling* things."

Watching Caden address the crowd, I have no doubt that he will be a great leader, and with people like Aurela and Sauer at his side, he will unite the people of Neospes. I walk back to where Era and Aurela are standing. Era stares at me and I shift uncomfortably, but her stare is curious instead of anxious.

Even if she is Faction, I still don't quite trust her. Maybe it's the way her eyes seem to pierce right through me, or the fact that she is one of the most powerful women in our combined universes. No one person should have that much power. That said, it's not like she ever abused her power. She stepped in where she had to.

And I know I'm going to need her help if I am to track down my father.

I feel Aurela's arms encircle me from the side, and I lean into her, inhaling the scent of my childhood. My arms cross over my mother's arms and I squeeze.

"Take care of him," I tell her.

I punch in a sequence on the arm of my suit and pull out an eversion device from the pack at my side. Time is of the essence, and every second I delay here means my father will get further away. I meet Era's eyes with a wry grin. I don't need her serum—I can evert from anywhere just as the Vectors do.

Just another one of the perks of being a half-human, half-robot hybrid.

"Guess I'll see you in physics class," I say to her with a forced grin, even though it feels like my very bones are splintering inside of me.

My eyes flit from Aurela to Sauer to Caden . . . my family is no longer broken. It's beautiful and it's more real than anything I can imagine. I never thought it would be so hard to leave anyone, because I never had anyone to leave before.

No wonder people say that love begets weakness. It hurts like a beast. But I know that it isn't weakness; it's might. It takes far more strength to care. It makes you want to fight harder . . . to live for something worth believing in.

It makes you more.

As if he can sense what I'm about to do, Caden turns around, his eyes widening in delayed understanding. I smile to reassure him, but my lip quivers. I can't even lie to not hurt him . . . all I can see is the pain in his eyes, those intense green eyes asking me why, pleading for me to stay.

But there's no time for answers, no time for reasons. I can only smile and weep.

Everything fades to black, the fabric of time and space shimmering around me, but I hold on to Caden's face. I hold on to his green eyes. I hold on to him and the weightless way he makes me feel. I hold on to the touch of his lips upon mine and the salt of his tears in our kiss. I hold on to love.

I know I will see him again.

# ACKNOWLEDGMENTS

TO JULIE MATYSIK, who is a rockstar, thank you so much for taking a chance on *The Almost Girl* and *The Fallen Prince*, and finding them such a perfect home at Sky Pony Press. Huge thanks to Amanda Rutter, *The Almost Girl*'s first editor at Strange Chemistry—this book will always be part yours. Equally huge thanks to Alison Weiss, my wonderful editor at Sky Pony, for taking on the orphans and making them more awesome than ever—you deserve all the cookies. To my superstar agent, Liza Fleissig, I am so grateful to have you in my corner. Thank you for everything.

To my extended family, friends, and fans, a heartfelt thank you for being such amazing champions. There are too many of you to list, but you know who you are. I'm so thankful for each one of you. To all the bloggers, booksellers, conference leaders, librarians, educators, and readers who spread the word about my books and humble me with their unwavering support, I wouldn't be here without you. Thanks for doing all that you do. Much gratitude to my parents, who always encouraged me to fuel my voracious imagination and to push the boundaries of possibility. Thank you for never holding me back. To my brothers, thanks for always looking out, no matter what. Lastly, to the loves of my life—Cameron, Connor, Noah, and Olivia— thank you for making no other universe equal this one.

# THE RIVEN CHRONICLES

# THE
# FALLEN
# PRINCE

"Non-stop action
& smart science.
I couldn't put it down!"
—Page Morgan,
author of *The Beautiful
and the Cursed*

# AMALIE HOWARD

# PROLOGUE

THE FLARE OF blue fire is blinding. Then again, it's gone so quickly that even if you were staring right at me, you'd blink and it'd vanish. The emissions from the process of eversion—shifting between universes—are unavoidable. However, I try to be careful, everting in concealed areas away from people, and away from the eyes of the Faction and the Guardians. They're always watching for those who break the law—those who don't remain where they belong.

Me, more so than ever.

I belong in Neospes, a domed city in a parallel dimension to the Otherworld. But I'm here in pursuit of a man who everted over a year ago. A man who nearly destroyed my world in his quest for power. A man so consumed with retaliation that to let him loose in either world would be a colossal mistake.

And so I hunt him. I've *been* hunting him—across thirty states and always a step or two behind. He's clever, brilliant, and a master strategist.

After all, he's my father. And he's my *creator*.

I may look like an ordinary girl, but I'm far from one. It's something I'm still coming to terms with, ever since I learned the truth. I am a product of genetic experimentation and advanced robotics. I am the girl with nanoplasm for blood—the perfect combination of human and machine, an aberration of nature—and yet, its greatest creation. I am the only one of my kind.

My name is Riven.

And I am a killer.

# 1

# DEEP IN THE OTHERWORLD

STOOPING TO LACE the untied shoelace of my combat boot, I meld into the crowd at Grand Central Station in New York City. It's strange to think that once upon a time in my world, infrastructure like this could have existed. Pre-Tech War, that is. Not that I would know—I was born in a dome where the tallest building is a castle three stories tall.

But my people often recount tales of grand mirrored spires that rose to defy the skyline, and thriving metropolises with skyscrapers that'd dwarf the ones in this world. Our historical records talk of buildings that were twelve times the size of the Empire State building I've just seen, and of hovercraft that flew between the towering structures on aerodynamic super-highways.

Everything was computerized, automated.

The offshoot of civilization on my version of Earth saw the human race building machines that superseded the rules of our own programming. We invented metal monsters, reveling in our superior brilliance, so much so that we didn't see it coming. In the end, when the artificial intelligence we'd built became self-aware and turned on us, *we* became theirs—vast cities of human slaves, caught in a nightmare of our own making and bound by the very electronic shackles we had created.

Our citizens rebelled—and eventually won—but only at enormous human and environmental cost. Ten long years of devastation in a war against our android captors saw our oceans gone and entire populations decimated. Surviving cities are covered by huge glass domes; ones built to protect the people within them from the unpredictable elements and volatile temperatures beyond.

While extant pockets of humanity claim the unburned plains of my world, the rest of it is ruled by the Reptiles—half-organic, half-android hybrid scavengers. They're the worst things surviving in the Outers beyond the city walls—amalgamations of animal and human parts in various states of decay, coupled with robotic operating systems. Some of them live in packs, others are more solitary, but they are all intelligent . . . and they're lethal.

Feeling the rush of bodies passing beside me, I glance upward at the artistically etched ceiling of the station, admiring it for a brief second. There is nothing like this in Neospes. Not anymore. But even though my world is a shadow of what it once was, we are rebuilding beneath a new king with new hope.

My pulse thrums at the thought of Caden. The boy—now king—who had stolen my heart without my knowledge, and the one I'd had to leave to make sure he and the people of Neospes would be safe. It's been so long since I've seen him, almost a year. I wonder if he looks the same with his too-long hair and his intense green eyes—eyes that I vividly remember, even now. Eyes that could always see right through me.

Awareness prickles along the back of my neck, and I tuck my head below my arm, scanning the area behind me. The Guardians had closed in before I'd shaken them off in Boston, jumping on a bus outside the city. I'd considered everting, but the electrical displacement leaves too much of a trace. And the Guardians are nothing if not vigilant, particularly after the influx of Vectors under the last King of Neospes's rule.

The Vectors were a soldier army created by my father— reanimated corpses fueled by nanoplasm—the very same nanoplasm coursing through my veins. And because of the microscopic nanobes in my body, I run hot—way hotter than any normal human. Suffice it to say, I'm as easy to track as the Vectors are. I set off the Guardians' eversion detectors like clockwork.

Standing cautiously, I duck around the circular information booth and peer over my shoulder. It's clear. I flatten myself against the window, trying to get a look around the other side, and catch a glimpse of a green jacket that seems vaguely familiar. I shake my head. I'm overreacting. Green is a popular color.

"Ma'am?" a voice says. "May I help you?"

I meet the impatient stare of the clerk sitting on the other side of the window. "What? No."

"Then, kindly make room for those who are waiting."

"Um, sorry," I reply.

Stepping away, I feel the prickly sensation again at the edge of my consciousness, and I crouch to fiddle with my boot. Precious seconds fly by before I see them—two men and a woman scanning the area. Looking for someone. Looking for me. I narrow my eyes, the nanobes in my retinas running a brief threat analysis. To anyone else, the three people seem ordinary, dressed in dark pants and dark shirts, but the advanced weaponry holstered out of sight on their belts suggests otherwise. So does the careful, methodical way they're casing the area. My jaw clenches. There's no mistaking it—they're Guardians. How did the Faction catch up to me so quickly?

I take a breath and make a run for it, skittering among bodies and ducking beneath a couple holding hands.

"Stop her!" the woman shouts. "She took my purse!"

A thousand eyes pivot in my direction as I dodge the two NYPD officers rushing grim faced toward me, and dart down a long poster-plastered hallway. The policemen are hot on my heels. Glancing over my shoulder, I count the two officers and the three people I'd seen before. Two more guys in army fatigues and really big guns join them. I curse under my breath and pick up the pace. Now's no time to play it safe. If they catch me, my father will disappear for good.

Gritting my teeth, I let the nanobes in my blood take over. Within seconds, my body receives a jolt of adrenaline so powerful that it makes my back arch with the force of it. Everything inside of me electrifies as my internal programming responds to my commands, my legs pumping like well-oiled pistons. I throw another look backward to my pursuers, hearing the broken static of two-way radios and shouted directives. The distance between us is now considerable.

Shoving the jacket cuff off my wrist, I engage the nano-suit beneath it, tapping manual commands into the console. *Defense.*

The suit's armor solidifies against my skin, just as I slide across a railing leading to an underground staircase, taking the stairs six at a time. I weave in between columns and double back up another staircase to the previous level with the giant posters on the walls. A sign above my head indicates I'm near Forty-Seventh Street, but that's too obvious an exit. They'll expect me to go aboveground.

Instead, I swing right in the wide passageway near the escalator, darting up yet another narrow staircase a few tracks down. A loud beeping announces that the waiting commuter train is about to leave. Without a second thought, I slip through the doors as they close. While the tinny voice of the conductor announces the stops, I take an empty seat, hunching down near the window, and pulling my hood over my head. Connecticut is as good a place to crash as any.

I calm my labored breathing. That was too close. Although, I'm not entirely sure what would happen if the Guardians *do* get their hands on me. Era Taylor, the leader of the Faction, knew that I'd be coming after my father. I'd made no secret of it once we found out that he'd everted to this world. There's no way I can let him get away, not after everything he's done, and knowing everything he is capable of. My father is a scientist at heart, one driven by the demands of his ego. There's no telling what he'll do with any technology at his disposal, and I can't afford to take the chance that he won't attempt to re-create another monster like me.

I consider my options. I could evert, but who knows where I'd end up—in the Outers, or somewhere way worse. The only safe eversion spot that leads directly back to Neospes is in

Fort Collins, Colorado, and I'm two thousand miles away. I'd everted once out of desperation with the Guardians hot on my heels in Nevada, and had ended up in the midst of a Reptile nest back in my universe. I'd escaped by the skin of my teeth. With my luck, I'd evert from this train and end up in the deep end of an acid swamp. No, I'll take my chances here.

I slouch down in my seat as the woman and the two men from earlier burst through the staircase entrance to the platform, steely glances combing the windows of the departing train. For a second, the light falls on one of the men, and I blink. A face shimmers into my memory of a boy I haven't seen in months—Philip, Era Taylor's son. But it can't possibly be him. The facial structure is similar, but that's where the resemblance ends. This boy is taller, broader, and bearded. I'm imagining things. There's no way Philip would be in New York. For all I know, he died that day we faced the Vectors *en masse* . . . right before Shae did.

My heart skips a beat at the memory of my sister. She'd died to save Caden and me, and everything she'd ever done had been to protect us. My jaw aches from clenching it so tightly. That's another thing my father will have to pay for—because he'd made her into a monster, too.

The train picks up speed on its way out of the station, entering the darkness of the tunnels, and I heave a sigh of relief. I'm sick of running from the Faction when all I want to do is find my father. Every time I get close, he manages to slip away. It's frustrating. If I didn't have to keep an eye on the Guardians every infernal second, maybe I'd have caught him by now.

I pull a thin tablet from my backpack and punch in a sequence. The facial recognition software that's been my breadcrumb trail runs in the background. This world may not have the advanced technology of mine, but some of the software is remarkably useful. I've patched in to the FBI database, bypassing their security with a mimic program of my own design. To them, I'm just another field agent accessing their internal database.

I tap on the screen and a pattern of red dots shows up. My father has been busy. The trail has no rhyme or reason—a handful of dots along the east and west coasts, with the majority of them located in central Colorado. My best guess is he's looking at zero-gravity eversion points because whatever he's planning has to be connected to Neospes. His last known position was here in New York City but, as always, I'd been a hair too late. It's almost as if he's toying with me, leading me on a wild goose chase just to prove that he can.

Six months ago in Los Angeles, we'd come face-to-face in a nightclub with only a six-inch-thick glass partition between us. It had spanned the room, separating the diners from the bar, and in the precious seconds it would take to get around it, I knew he'd be gone. Without the stupid barrier, it would've been so easy to reach out and lodge my ninjata through his traitorous heart. Instead, I'd stood there powerless, in furious silence.

"Riven," he'd said coolly as he leaned back in his chair and placed his tumbler on the white table. "You've been following me. Why?"

"To take you back to Neospes to answer for your crimes."

He cocked his head. "You and I both know that's not true."

"To kill you, then."

"Why?"

"*Why?*" I choked out. "You murdered Shae. And after what you did to me . . ."

He took a sip of the amber liquid in his glass, his insouciance making me feel like snapping those slender fingers, cupping the tumbler, one by one. "I made you stronger. I made you better. You're untouchable, invincible."

"You put tech in me when I was an embryo. You could have killed me. You could have killed Aurela."

"But I didn't," he said. "And your mother knew what she signed up for. You are the future, Riven. *We* are the future."

My fists clenched against my sides. "Don't you get it? There *is* no we. You have no future, Danton. I will hunt you to the ends of any universe, and I will kill you. Next time, there won't be a wall between us."

"So fierce, and yet, so foolish," he said, smiling as he indicated the seat on my side of the glass wall. "Sit. Chat a while."

A part of me knew that I should have walked away. Engaging with him was dangerous. He knew how to press every one of my buttons. But I couldn't bring myself to do it, not when he was right there.

I sat, rigid. Paralyzed. "Let's talk, then. What are you doing here?"

He shrugged, waving a careless hand—his gesture simultaneously elegant and ugly. "I should think that would be obvious. I'm saving our dying world."

"How? By destroying this one? We aren't meant to be here. We had our chance, and we blew it. You can't just take something from one universe and put it in another. The Faction won't stand for it."

"How is darling Era?" he said with a laugh. "The Faction is useless and obsolete. The only way for Neospes to survive is to take what we can from this world. Help ourselves to its vast resources. The people here have more than enough, after all, and they don't care for half of it. They are on the same path of destruction that we were."

My tone was laced with sarcasm. "So, you're trying to save them?"

"I am simply offering our people an alternative, and they will thank me for it."

"You're wrong."

"You never could see the big picture, could you, Riven?" He finished his drink in one swallow, and we both stood. "You'll come to heel soon enough."

"I'm not a dog."

"Aren't you?"

I shoved my chair back, punching into the transparent wall and watching tiny cracks branch outward in the tempered glass. "And still so predictable." He nodded to the two burly bouncers behind me. "That will be your downfall."

I'd shoved past the two men who were double my size, sending them skidding across the floor, then rounded the wall to the now-empty table where my father had been sitting. The only thing left was an empty tumbler with the imprint of his lips on it. I'd hurled it at the wall in frustration, and made a hasty exit.

Ever since then, I've been chasing a ghost . . . always several steps behind. And now the Guardians have upped the ante, closer on my trail than they have ever been.

Suddenly, the train lurches to a stop, the last carriage still touching the platform. The conductor's voice filters through the train car. "Please be patient. We will be on our way shortly."

*Maybe it's a coincidence*, I think. Mechanical trouble happens all the time with these commuter trains. But deep down, I know there's no way that I'm going to be that lucky—the Guardians will be on the train, searching it car by car. Pocketing my tablet and keeping my head low, I stand and make my way forward until I'm in the front car. Now there's nowhere to go but out— or stay and fight, risking the lives of innocent commuters in the process. I've never been a fan of collateral damage.

I unsheathe my ninjatas from their holster. The swords shimmer with incandescent blue lights as their microchip technology connects to the nanobes in my body. Several passengers hightail it out of their seats to the far end of the train car, eyeing the weapons with terrified expressions. I rap on the door of the conductor's box.

"Open up," I tell the man inside.

"I can't do that."

I eye him through the narrow window. "I don't want to hurt you, but I will rip open this door if I have to."

"You're just a kid. The police are already on their way." He glances at my blades, and then at my face as the nanobes rush there, flushing my cheeks with bluish fire. His eyes widen, but before he can move I crash the hilt of my blade into the handle and jerk the door open so hard that the metal tents outward. The conductor is trembling as I reach past him to grab the keys latched to his belt.

"Thank you."

"What are you?" he whispers with round eyes.

Ignoring him, I stoop down near the doorway to unlock the emergency release. One of the door panels slides back and I toss the conductor his keys before hopping onto the dark track. I have minutes at most to make my way out of there, a split second to decide whether I head into the darkness or back the way we'd come and risk running right into them. Then again, I'm never one to shy away from a challenge.

Re-sheathing my ninjatas, I backtrack through the narrow space between the train and the grime-covered tunnel walls. I'm careful not to step on the rails. With my luck, I'll electrocute myself and everyone within a five-mile radius. Voices filter from the third car, shadows moving past the windows as the search continues. I shimmy by silently, hoping the train won't start moving. I'm almost to the platform, home free, when I hear heavy feet thudding on the tracks behind me.

Time to run.

With a burst of strength, I leap onto the steel railing and haul my body over the lip of the platform, scanning the area. There are twenty-odd armed officers milling around. No civilians in sight. Smart. They've evacuated the area. I smile grimly. Works for me.

"That's the perp!" one of them shouts. In half a heartbeat as eyes and guns converge on me, I slam in the commands on the wrist panel of my suit—*offense*—feeling it shimmer responsively against my skin. I calculate the odds of getting out of this jam with minimum casualties.

"Stop, or I will shoot," a nearby officer barks. I note the stripes on his uniform and nod. A captain. He's the one in charge. "Hands up."

"If you say so." In slow motion, I raise my hands, crossing them behind my head.

"On your knees."

I offer an apologetic smile. "Now that, I can't do." With a swift movement, I grasp the hilts of my ninjatas and, again, pull them from their sheaths. The captain's eyes widen in disbelief—confusion, even. My grin widens. "What? You've never seen a sword before?"

"Nonlethal force!" I hear a muffled voice shout from the depths of the tunnels behind me. A female voice that sounds familiar, but I can't turn to see who it is as five of the men rush me at once.

"You'd be better off with the guns," I tell them, dropping to my knees and striking out on both sides. Two of the officers go down with identical incisions through the fatty flesh of their thighs. I don't want to kill them. My objective is to incapacitate. I dispatch two others—one with a jab to the temple with the hilt of one of my blades, the other with a reverse kick to the jaw. The nanobes are doing their job, rushing to the surface of my skin and flickering a hazy blue as they provide a dizzying jolt of speed and adrenaline.

The captain watches me with narrowed eyes before raising his automatic rifle and pointing it directly at my chest. I can see him considering not following the nonlethal force orders. "What *are* you?" he snaps through his teeth.

"Is 'your worst nightmare' too cliché?" I answer. My wisecrack falls flat, so I shrug and point to the gun. "That's not going to help you. Your best bet is to let me through. I don't want to hurt anyone."

"Like them?" He jerks his head at the four uniformed soldiers on the ground, clutching their injuries. "You think you're going to just walk out of here after assaulting four police officers?"

"They attacked me. I defended myself."

The man's mouth tightens. "Drop the swords." The remaining officers move to surround him in a semicircle, watching me and waiting for their orders. "I *will* shoot."

"So shoot," I say. "It isn't going to change the outcome."

"Of what?"

"Of you putting more of your men in danger, and of me leaving this platform. You're only delaying the inevitable."

"She's just a kid," one of the policemen mutters.

"No," the captain says, not taking his eyes off me for an instant. "She's not."

I grin and heft my swords, anticipating the furious volley of bullets. With inhuman speed, I bend sideways and feel them whizz past my head and torso, swinging into a crouch at the last moment before somersaulting toward the captain. The bullets lodge into the cement walls behind me, the sound like thunder in the eerie silence of the evacuated platform, but I barely notice. My blade is at his throat before he can squeeze off another round. Kicking the backs of his knees, I force him to the ground.

"Back off," I warn the rest of his men. "I don't want to kill anyone, but I will if I have to. Your CO's blood will be on your hands."

The remaining officers are watching me with varying degrees of shock and surprise, their guns locked and loaded.

"Stand down," an authoritative voice says from behind me. "I'm Special Agent Fields. We'll take it from here." The officers don't move, watching their leader for confirmation. He nods against my forearm, his pulse racing on my skin. He's nearly twice my size, but no match for my strength. With obvious reluctance, the officers back away, but three hooded soldiers dressed in distinct red uniforms are quick to replace them.

The Faction's muscle.

The Faction has their own special brand of brawn. They've been highly trained in martial arts, and I know from experience that these guys mean business. Divesting the captain of his gun, I release him and shove him out of the way. I sigh and brace myself, my ninjatas at the ready, but the Faction warriors remain immobile, watching me . . . waiting.

"Riven," the same female voice from earlier says. "We just want to talk."

I freeze at the sound of my name, and slowly turn. "Charisma?"

It's the quiet girl from Horrow, whom I'd saved from a group of drunken boys nearly a year before. She doesn't quite look the same as I remember. Her brown hair is in a businesslike knot and she's dressed in black trousers with an armored vest over her shirt. Her face is unsmiling and rigid. Charisma looks all grown up and in charge. My eyes flick to the tall bearded man at her side, the ever-present tablet in his hands. I hadn't been wrong earlier. It *is* Philip—he must have sprouted five inches in the last year.

"I thought you were dead," I say to him.

"Obviously not," he replies.

"How's mommy?" I ask. His jaw tightens. "She know you're here?"

"Yes."

"What do you want?" I say rudely.

"We want you to come back with us," Charisma says. "To Colorado."

"I'm afraid I can't do that." I'm starting to sound like a broken record. "Things to do, places to see." My eyes narrow at the thought of her working for the secret group of world leaders who police inter-universe activity. "So, are you with the Faction now?"

"No, not exactly," Charisma hedges.

Keeping a cautious eye on the red-clad ninjas, my hands slide to my sides, still gripping my blades. "You either are or you aren't."

"I'm not. Philip's a Guardian."

"Wow, *officially*? No way. Congrats." I fight an all-too-teenage eye roll. "None of that has anything to do with me."

"That's where you're wrong," Charisma says. "I volunteered to come with Philip to find you because I knew—I *hoped*— you'd listen to me. We used to be friends, remember? I'm begging you to come back with us. Please, Riven, just hear me out."

Something in her voice tugs at me. Besides Caden, she was the closest thing to a friend I had during my stint at Horrow High School. I sigh. Being in this world has softened me more than I care to admit. "Fine. Out of respect for our two minutes of friendship, you have two minutes to convince me."

"I only need two seconds," she says. "Caden's there."

All my breath and bravado peels away. "What did you say?"

"Caden's there. And he needs you."